Ashok Kumar Banker is reg... writers. He has been credited... first Indian crime novels in English, the first Indian tele... series in English, and now, to quote his own description, the first 'epic Indian' fiction. His work has received worldwide critical acclaim and tops bestseller lists in India. His Ramayana series is part of a lifetime endeavour to retell all the great tales of Indian myth, history and legend. His next project is a retelling of the world's longest epic, The Mahabharata.

To find out more about Ashok and his work, visit his official website at www.epicindia.com

Please register at www.orbitbooks.co.uk for the free monthly newsletter and to find out more about other Orbit authors.

Praise for the Ramayana

'Its epic scale is as globally relevant as Gilgamesh, Cuchullain and Beowulf' HISTORICAL NOVELS REVIEW

'A milestone. Banker brings a magnificent sense of predestination to his task' INDIA TODAY

'Banker spins a good yarn, full of colour and atmosphere and authentic touches' STARBURST

'I'm deeply impressed! . . . Spectacular in scope and vision' ENIGMA

'Sophisticated and absorbing' DREAMWATCH

'Banker creates a marvellous landscape of princes, demons, mages, and lovers' Kate Elliott

By Ashok K. Banker

The Ramayana

Prince of Ayodhya
Siege of Mithila
Demons of Chitrakut
Armies of Hanuman
Bridge of Rama
King of Ayodhya

Ashok K. Banker

KING OF AYODHYA

BOOK SIX OF THE RAMAYANA

www.orbitbooks.co.uk

ORBIT

First published in Great Britain in 2006 by Orbit

Copyright © 2006 by Ashok K. Banker

The moral right of the author has been asserted.

A CIP catalogue record for this book
is available from the British Library.

ISBN-13: 978-1-84149-331-2
ISBN-10: 1-84149-331-7

Typeset in Sabon by Palimpsest Book Production Limited,
Polmont, Stirlingshire

Printed and bound in Great Britain by
Mackays of Chatham plc, Chatham, Kent

Orbit
An imprint of
Little, Brown Book Group
Brettenham House
Lancaster Place
London WC2E 7EN

A member of the Hachette Livre Group of Companies

www.littlebrown.co.uk

PITRAPAKSH: IN MEMORIAM

To those who crossed the river before us:

Ramchandra Banker, 1913–1975, dadaji,
Polycarp Joseph D'Souza, 1898–1983, nanaji,
Indra Kumar Jain, 1931–1987, sasur,
Kamala Diwan, 1906–1996, wife's nani,
Sheila Margaret Ray D'Souza, 1946–1990, maa,
Agnes May D'Souza, 1916–1999, nani,
Brian Xavier D'Souza, 1952–2004, mama,
and
Anil Ramchandra Banker, 1933–2005, pitaji.

ACKNOWLEDGEMENTS

It took an army to complete this epic task:

Tim Holman, truly a Hanuman among editors, who championed this curious hybrid of imagination and mythology, and stuck by it to the very end. Thank you, Tim.

Gabriella Nemeth, Andrew Edwards, Bella Pagan, and all of you at Orbit and Time Warner Book Group, UK. Thank you, one and all.

Betsy Mitchell, the first to understand that this story was no relation to Tolkien, nor a typical 'epic fantasy'. If only she could have been there to steer it through the murky waters of post-9/11 America. Someday, Betsy. Someday soon.

The readers in the UK, USA, and across the world who dared to enter a world that predated Middle Earth by a few thousand years, and enjoyed it so much that they stayed on through six volumes. Those of you who are fellow desis, you know as well as I do that Rama called to you, just as he called to me, and now you are one with him. Those of you who are not desi, you are blessed now as well.

The critics, few though they were, who were able to take off their genre-blinkers and see through to the truth of a tale that has sustained an entire nation and billions of believers for well over three thousand years. You make literature possible.

Sabarish R. and Pavithra Srinivasan supported me long before anyone else even knew I existed. Readers like you are the reason writers like me write.

'Gypsyman' Richard Marcus came late to the party but made up for it by giving it new life. Live long and be well.

Yutaka Ohshima built a bridge from India to Japan to carry this tale home to his great nation. *Arigato*, my friend.

A big warm thank you to Epic Indians Ananth Padmanabhan (Paddy), Banwari Lal Sharma, Tapas Sadasivan Nair, Pushpak Karnick, Poorna Shashank Koppachari, Vineet Budhiraja, Vivek Sharma, Meenakshi Srinivasan, Meenakshi Sarup, Neeti Reddy, Angad Talwar, Saikat Chatterjee, Sapna Sundar, Atharva Dandekar, Rohit Dhawan, Nina Paley, Anita Ratnam, Tarun Rao, Akila Maheshwari, Sujeet Singh Bindra, Sushant Bhalerao, Richard Marcus, Richard Pierce, Mark, Amit Das, Mallika Chatterjee, Amandeep Singh Sapra, Swaroop C. H., Ankit, Saravana Kumar, Srividya Venugopalan, Suja Sivanand, Aparna Subhash, Unnati J. D., Stefano Notarbartolo, Balakrishnan Ranganathan, Kent Cave, Aravanda Rajkumar, Haimanti Nag Weld, Amit Chaubey, Durga Panda, Kim Chew, Shami Raj, Deepa Radhakrishnan, and all the other members of the Epic India group.

My dear friend Sanjeev Shankar. May you find your own way home as well.

My beloved wife, Bithika. My son, Ayush. My daughter, Yashka. I love you more than these words can say.

All of you who wrote in to me through the epicindia.com website, my erstwhile blog Indian English, and otherwise supported me and this series in various ways. You were the true vanar sena to this unworthy Valmiki. Stay in touch at www.epicindia.com

As for you, faithful reader, here's good news: Next stop, Hastinapura. Ride with me!

Jai Siyaram.
Jai Bajrangbali.
Jai Hind.

KAAND I

THE LEFT HAND OF DARKNESS

I

Rama.

From a thousand yards above ground, the Lord of Lanka surveyed his kingdom. Lanka, beautiful Lanka, lay in a shambles. The great sprawling city-state, so recently recast in a pristine white avatar, was a morass of smoke and ash and the smouldering embers of a thousand fires. Seen from this high vantage point, the city's aspect appeared as the face of a once-beautiful courtesan, besmirched and soot-blackened, scarred and dishevelled. Long lines of dark scorched ground marked the trail of the vanar's burning, like mascara left in the tracks of dried tears. Lanka's beauty was marred beyond recognition.

Rama is responsible for all this.

Smoke curled skywards from still-seething hotspots that only yesterday had been palatial mansions and fabulous estates. Virtually every one of the city's finer structures, being clustered close by the innermost ring of the city, near the tower palace of the king, were either destroyed, rendered uninhabitable, or hideously scarred. The unusual nature of the source of the fire meant that even miles out from the centre, entire neighbourhoods had been ravaged, as if whipped by an uncaring lash applied by a blind scourge-master.

Oddly enough, the farther out he looked, the less evidence of fire damage he saw. The most modest residential tenements, entire colonies comprised of the closely clustered cave-like rock-and-mud houses that rakshasas traditionally favoured, had escaped unscathed. This was probably because these poorer localities were on the outskirts of the city, some as much as a full yojana from the heart of the metropolis, and separated by ponds, lakes, and tributaries of the rivulets that snaked their way down from the mountain ranges to the south.

And farther out still, where the few farming tribes lived, using hybrids and half-breeds for farm labour – for rakshasas did not herd or cultivate – the rich plantations of savouries and spices were completely untouched by the vanar's antics.

No, not the vanar.

Rama.

The vanar only acted as his emissary, carrying out his orders. This was Rama's hand at work.

He finally deigned to lower his point of view to the place directly below the hovering craft which bore him aloft. To the spot where the great white tower had stood.

His self-control was tested to the limit. The site of the greatest edifice ever raised in this world, the soaring white and gold tower constructed through the power of his Asura maya and the ingenuity of Pushpak, the celestial device, was nothing more than a blemish now. He had scarcely believed his eyes when the vanar had expanded himself and leaped upon the tower's peak, pounding it down, down, until it was crushed into its very foundations. How could the monkey being have escaped the sorcerous spell he had wound around him? The chains with which the vanar had been secured were ensorcerelled as well, and yet when it pleased him, the creature had simply shrugged them to pieces, as if they were nothing more than paper fetters. But it was the power and size of the vanar that had taken him by surprise. Even the vanar's antics in the realms of the tower, the great slaughter he had wrought on those sorcerous levels, had not prepared him for something of this magnitude. To grow himself so large that he could pound the tower into the ground thus, that was beyond Ravana's expectations.

Hanuman.

He had underestimated the vanar from the very beginning, he admitted now with chagrin – but he admitted it only
to himself.

The vanar was a tool of Rama. But a dangerous tool. It
would take some scheming to eliminate him. And before he was
eliminated, he must be made to pay for what he had done here.
Pay with blood and agony. When the time came to face him
again, Ravana would not make the mistake of sending out
ordinary rakshasas to deal with him; he would call on someone
who was more than Hanuman's equal in size as well as strength.
Someone who could pound him down into the earth as he had
pounded the tower.

Time then. Time to awaken the killing machine. And prepare
to let loose the hounds of hell.

'Rakshasa.'

Her voice was small and soft. Weak. For she continued to
fast despite all his entreaties and admonitions. Yet she retained
the ability to command his attention.

He turned. She stood in the cupola of the flying vehicle, wan
and pale, a sallow shadow of the woman he had carried away
from the wilds of Panchvati. Her eyes were clear and met his
own without hesitation. He corrected himself: weak, yes, but
in body only. In spirit she was as strong as ever.

'Do you yield now?' she asked. As quietly, as proudly, as
would a warrior queen on a battlefield, with her armies around
her, her spear point at his throat and near-mortal wounds on
his person.

He admired her pride. Respected her strength of will. And
there was that stirring in his breast he had begun to feel every
time he set eyes upon her. Could it be that despite everything,
he had come to feel a smidgen, a smattering, just a smear or a
swab of some deeper emotion? Why else did he find the sight
of her heart-shaped face, those sallow cheeks and dusky eyes,
undimmed and unafraid even after all her travails, so hypnotic?
Why did he find himself unwilling to use force to ravish her

even though that was his right by sheer fact of possession, by rakshasa law? Why did he instead feel so desperately inclined to prove himself to her, to show her somehow that he was every bit the king that Rama would never be? To earn her respect and hope to win her over peaceably instead? And why was it that after each encounter with her, he always felt himself lacking in some immeasurable way, as if his best efforts to turn her feelings in his favour were futile? Why should what she felt even matter?

'Yield?' he repeated. 'You expect me to yield? Why? Because your husband's monkey messenger danced a fire-jig through my city? Tore through a few legions and, yes, slew a few good warriors and even my youngest son? So you think I should therefore yield and surrender all?'

She kept her chin high, painfully thin though it was. 'I meant only that you yield this particular round. Surrender me to be returned to Rama. Perhaps then I may appeal to his clemency on your behalf.'

He almost laughed. But she was so earnest, so bright-eyed and proud of her champion's exploits. He had seen her looking too. Gazing round-eyed at the destruction wrought by a single vanar in one night. And he knew of the conversation she had had with Hanuman the night before, wherein the vanar had pleaded with her to go back with him and she had refused, had insisted that Rama come himself to fight for her release, to restore his honour. 'This is a tired argument, princess. Rest it. If you wish to discuss clemency, then it is my clemency towards your husband and his people that you should demand. I do not deny that the vanar committed more havoc than I expected. I think you will find it was more than even your precious Rama expected. But such surprises are part of the game of war. The vanar was an un-expected hand your husband played. It was also the last hand he played. There will be no more war games now. Only a massacre. Of Rama and his forces.'

She looked upon him, unperturbed by his words. He observed

the way her eyes flitted from one face of his to another in quick succession. She was a clever one too. She had begun to understand his secret. 'Once Rama and his forces arrive on the shores of Lanka, you will be done for. This burning was only a prelude to the final devastation that will be unleashed. But you will not understand. I see that even with this evidence you still do not comprehend the full extent of his powers. So be it. Let Rama come to Lanka. And then suffer the consequences. Just remember that I warned you and gave you every chance to relent and repent. And you refused.'

And incredibly, she turned her back upon him. On him! Who was the captor here and who the captive? Her courage was admirable, her audacity marvellous to behold. He chuckled despite himself. Her back stiffened at the sound but she did not turn back to face him even after he began speaking.

'Princess Sita. You delude yourself. Or perhaps you assume that because you have been in Lanka a while and seen a few of its sights you know all there is to be known about this kingdom and about me. You would be in grave error to think thus. The truth is, you do not realise the full extent of *my* powers! Perhaps it is time you were given a glimpse that you may better understand what your husband and his monkeys and bears are up against.'

He willed Pushpak to take them down, down to the wrecked tower. He had the satisfaction of hearing her gasp as the vehicle fell out of the sky like a stone falling to earth. Even though Pushpak protected those that rode within it, it could not influence the way the sudden loss of height affected them; and he felt the loss in height cause a buzzing even in his ears. In her depleted state and delicate condition, it would probably cause vertigo, nausea. It gave him malicious pleasure to let Pushpak fall faster instead of slowing down as they reached the ground. From the head on the extreme left side of his rack, he watched her discreetly. She turned deathly pale and held on to a golden pole to support herself, but she did not utter another sound of protest, nor appeal to him. Ah, what a woman. She was wasted on Rama.

As they fell to earth, he continued to watch her. She could see now that they were heading straight for the ruins of the tower. Hurtling. Yet she did not flinch or turn away. Merely gazed steadily at the rapidly approaching ground. In that instant he almost hated her. Hated the calm, serene steadfastness she displayed in the face of certain danger, the stoic resolve, the unwavering assurance. Rama! Huh! How could she even think for a minute that the mortal would stand a ghost of a chance against him, Ravana? Did she not know Ravana's history of triumphs? The long roll-call of foes he had slain and defeated? The—

He snarled softly to himself. He would show her. He would make her tremble at his might and power. Before this game was played out, she would beg for mercy. Plead to be given another chance. To grace his bed, if only for a night. She would bow and cower and—

The ruins parted like the petals of a giant flower, opening a space just wide enough for the sky chariot to fit through, and Pushpak slipped in snugly. Darkness overwhelmed them as they moved beneath the surface, and even he felt the thrill of travelling at such speed without being able to see where they were going, or what lay ahead. Pushpak was infallible, of course, but that still did not keep the hackles on the back of his necks from rising. The darkness was absolute, inpenetrable. He probed with his other senses and smelled her fear, fear not just for her own person, but for the unborn life within her. That was something she cared intensely about, the child in her womb. It was her only weakness. Perhaps if he threatened to kill the child . . . or to harm it, maim it, endanger it . . . ?

They emerged into a brightly lit place. After several moments of darkness, the light seemed blinding. Ravana grinned with one of his faces when he saw Sita throw her hand over her face, shielding her eyes. It was good to see her respond in some way other than haughty posturing and misplaced pride. As Pushpak slowed, hovering in mid-air, she sensed the change and uncovered her face. He watched as she blinked several times, unable at first to accept what she was seeing.

One of his heads looked down at the view that greeted her stunned eyes, attempting to see things from her perspective. They were floating near the ceiling of a great subterranean cavern, so vast that the bottom lay almost a mile below, and the walls as far apart. It was roughly hewn, jagged spurs of mineral rock and blackstone giving the walls a shadowy texture that held the light in pockets and crevices. It made the whole cavern seem eerie, as if anything could be lurking in any one of the million shadows. At the bottom, the floor was covered with a great number of what seemed to be little egg-shaped rocks standing on end. He knew of course that they were not rocks at all. He gave her time to absorb what she was seeing. She peered down at the floor, frowned, unable to quite make out what the objects below were, then looked up at him. Already she had regained her queen-like composure. She waited with supreme patience, clearly expecting an explanation. He decided to provide one.

'Watch now, princess. See for yourself why Lanka is the most perfect breeding ground for the rakshasa race in all this mortal realm.'

She stared dispassionately at him, coldly, as if unimpressed by his words, but he saw her eyes flicker from one to another of his many aspects, and in that flicker he sensed uncertainty. Fear of the unknown. Mortalkind's oldest phobia. It was gone almost at once. Outwardly, she seemed never to have lost her composure. She glanced down carelessly as if unimpressed by anything she saw or might see, as if nothing he did or showed her could possibly matter.

He allowed himself a smile of bemusement, admiring her resilience. What impudence. What spirit. What a woman.

He raised his arms, all six of them, for the mantras were

complex and required a great deal of his energies, physical as well as spiritual. He began the complex four-by-four chant, one of his faces watching her react with pleasing shock to the familiar Sanskrit slokas. No doubt she had heard the mantras recited before, or had heard of them. She was a well-educated one, his Sita. It was yet another of the many qualities that endeared her to him. She respected the Vedic arts and the shastras. The sacred Vedic tradition of *upa-ni-sad*, which few of the women he bedded even knew meant literally 'learning at the feet of the guru'. Once all this was over, he would be her guru, and he would teach her all he knew. Well, perhaps not all. But a great deal. Enough to make her a sufficiently potent sorceress that she might keep pace with him. What marvellous magicks they could weave together. She would not even have to sit at his feet.

It had long been his bane that Mandodhari strongly dis-approved of Asura maya and went so far as to attempt to ban his use of it in her presence when they were alone together. Not that he actually heeded her words – he merely concealed the fact that he was using sorcery, and went on using it never-theless. But with Sita, he felt hopeful that she might learn to love the wielding of power, the unleashing of shakti, and that he might finally have a partner in magick. He watched her with one of his faces as she fought to blank her expression once more, trying not to respond to the sound of the Sanskrit mantras flowing from his many tongues, which must seem an act verging on blasphemy to her mortal ears. He relished her discomfiture, and his mastery of the slokas. Perhaps now she would begin to understand: things were not always black and white as most foolishly believed. He was no less adept in the arts of brahmancraft than any brahmarishi of her race. The only difference was that he used the power to meet very different ends. He saw the confusion reflected on her wan, pale, but still beautiful features, and loved her more than ever for her exquisitely mortal weaknesses.

Then he lost himself in the chanting, in the sheer beauty and throbbing power of the slokas. He surrendered himself to the flow of brahman, black and viscous like a river of oil that came from beyond and passed through his being, roaring through his veins, rushing out of his mouths and eyes and nostrils, igniting and forming a flaming torrent that he released into the cavern. The river of brahman fire fell like a waterfall from Pushpak, its intensity dispelling all shadows, illuminating the cavern in a searing light more bright than noon sunlight. It fell to the bottom of the cavern, and spread like a raging river breaking its banks, washing through the countless lines of oval stones, rising to engulf them, flowing over them.

In moments, the entire floor of the subterranean cavern was flooded with the shakti he had conjured. It washed up at the walls, splashing against them like waves against a rocky cliff. He increased the pace of the chanting, attenuating the power flow. The liquid brahman in the cavern below seethed and boiled, erupting in gouts and splashes. The rock-like objects embedded in the ground began to tremble, then shiver, then shake violently. One by one, they began to explode.

2

Despite her determination to give her captor no satisfaction, Sita felt compelled to watch the scene unfolding in the cavern. What were those rock-like things? What power was he unleashing? She had recognised some of the slokas he was chanting as part of a great and powerful maha-mantra; only the most elevated of brahmins could acquire knowledge of such verses. How could a king of demons come by such sacred learning? Just when she thought she had seen and learned all there was to know about Ravana, he surprised her once more. As his chanting increased in intensity, she made out several different voices speaking separate mantras at once. No wonder he was such a powerful sorcerer. He could work ten different spells at once – in perfect coordination – something that even ten independently potent brahmarishis might not be able to accomplish with such precision. It was strange and troubling to hear a being as evil as this reveal such great depth of knowledge and prowess in the craft of wielding brahman shakti. What was this Ravana truly? He was not just the black-hearted demon lord that everyone assumed he was. There were so many levels to him, so many faces, that it was hard to tell which was the real Ravana. Perhaps they all were Ravana.

Now she watched spellbound as the brahman fluid he had released into the cavern flooded the entire floor of the enormous chamber. The viscous smoking blue liquid gouted and boiled like molten lava freshly erupted, precipitating some reaction in the egg-shaped rocks. She watched as entire rows of the rocks burst open, spewing out sticky strings of amber-hued ichor. The top of each rock ripped open like a flower bud violently blossoming. And as she watched with growing horror, from each exploded aperture a creature emerged.

She saw one such creature appear from the blasted top of a rock, writhing and twisting, forcing its way out into the open. It was sheathed in a honeyed webbing that dripped thick strands of amber ichor. It tore open the webbing, ripping off strands and clumps to fling them aside, and gained its full stature, standing on two nether limbs. Its yellow lizard-like eyes blinked open, recording its first sights. Looking around with an expression of snarling hostility, it raised its head and roared out a cry of terrible anguish. If this was a birthing, then the creature that had been born seemed to resent its very existence.

The cavern filled with the roars of the newly birthed creatures.

As Ravana finished the chanting that had completed the birthing process, she saw his ten pairs of eyes open again, witnessing what he had wrought. She could see them flicking this way, then that, rising to the horizon of the vast sculpted chamber, then scanning the other way to the far end. The rows of rocks extended from end to end, hundreds of thousands of them. All hatching explosively in successive rows, as the brahman waves washed over them, birthing the Lord of Lanka's horrific creations. As the first ones trampled the remains of the egg-like things from which they had hatched, they looked around at their surroundings. Instinctively, drawn by the flow of brahman that still bound him to them, the shakti that had been responsible for birthing them all, they began to raise their eyes to the celestial sky chariot floating high above them, sensing that their creator and master was there. They raised their dripping snouts and growled, showing their gratitude and pledging their allegiance.

One of Ravana's heads muttered an incoherent command, and at once Pushpak began descending. This time Sita was ready for just such a move and did not give him the satisfaction of hearing her gasp as she had done before. Still, she felt the vertigo that had plagued her earlier torment her again, making her feel as if she were plunging down an endless spiral. She gripped the golden pillar of the vaahan and kept up a stoic front. Dignity and self-worth were her last bastion.

Ravana slowed Pushpak several hundred yards above the floor of the cavern. High enough to afford a view of all his newborn creations, yet low enough that they might see him and know their master.

And their father. For each and every one of these beings was created from his own seed. The seed of Ravana. Sita knew this without being told, because each of the rakshasa creations below resembled one face or another of Ravana himself.

As if to confirm this very fact, Ravana spoke softly. 'Behold my children,' he said.

She said nothing in response. But her eyes were riveted to the sight of the hordes below. Even at this distance she could tell that each of those rakshasas below was larger, stronger and more powerful than any of the other rakshasas in Lanka.

'This is the new army of Lanka,' Ravana added. 'They are the children of my mind, and will do my bidding, whatever it may be. They know neither fear, nor pain, nor retreat. These are the forces your husband would have to face . . .' He paused and added deliberately, 'If he were able to come to Lanka.'

At those last words, she responded at last. Turning her head slowly so as not to upset the delicate balance of her depleted senses, she said in a soft but clear voice, 'Rama will come. Do not doubt that. Even if you assemble all the rakshasas that have existed since the beginning of time, Rama will come and face them all. No force you create can stop him now.'

He chuckled. 'Your audacity is impressive, and your naive fealty is touching. But both are sadly misplaced. These are no ordinary rakshasas. They are touched by the power of the gods themselves.'

She could not help her expression. 'The gods?'

'Yes, my lady Sita. The gods themselves are arrayed on the side of Lanka in this conflict. This new breed of rakshasas you see before you is only one of the many ways in which we are empowered by celestial forces.'

She stared at him, shifting her gaze from face to face, trying to tell if he was lying. She could not be sure by his facial expressions alone, so diverse and unrelated were they all, but there was something in his words that was compelling. And she had seen ample evidence of how even rakshasas could be devout and suffer austerities. Could he be telling the truth? It made her heart sink. Surely the devas could not be aligned against Rama and his forces.

He smiled at her discomfiture. 'Do not tax yourself, princess. I will show you more evidence of how the devas assist us.'

He willed Pushpak to fly. The vehicle zoomed across the cavern at a speed so great the rock walls blurred past. She sucked in a silent breath, feeling the pit of her belly, so painfully deprived of nourishment, pressing back – against her very spine, it seemed. She said a silent prayer to the goddess for her unborn offspring, and exerted all her willpower to remain standing upright. Even so, she could feel the blood draining from her face and her head grew dizzy again. She almost blacked out as they sped at an enormous velocity towards the far wall of the cavern where, she now spied, a tunnel existed, hitherto hidden by the long shadows cast by the unnatural light.

A great roar rose from behind them as they reached the far end of the cavern, a host of rakshasas cheering their lord and creator. And then they had left the roaring hordes in the cavern behind and were flying at nauseating speed through a tunnel almost half as vast as the chamber they had left. She had a moment or two to wonder what it would feel like to simply let herself fall over the railing of the vaahan, to plunge down those several hundred feet to land on bone-shattering bedrock. It almost seemed tempting. But she suspected that Ravana would be able to catch her easily before she fell, and would derive great satisfaction from her weakness – and her despair.

So she gritted her teeth and held on. She had meant what she had said. Rama would come. Hanuman's visit had made her certain of that now. The vanar's incredible adventures in Lanka had filled her with hope that was food itself to her battered soul. Rama would come. And whatever Ravana threw at him, he would face it and defeat it, and teach this arrogant, malevolent, sloka-spouting monstrosity a lesson such as he had never been taught before. He Who Made The Universe Scream would himself be made to scream. She held on to the pillar with all her strength, buoyed by the conviction that the day of her release was approaching fast. Rama would come.

Her vision began to dim. She blinked, worried that she was losing consciousness. Then she realised that it was not her vision but the surroundings that were darkening. She looked back and saw the illumination from the cavern far behind, receded now to a tiny thumb-sized aperture. From the sharp upward position of the light behind them, she could also tell that they were plunging deep down into the earth, perhaps miles deeper. Turning back to look ahead, she saw they were approaching an area of utter darkness, a cavern that was not illuminated by Ravana's sorcerous light. She sensed a subtle shift in the air as Pushpak emerged from the tunnel into this new cavern, and then they were swallowed by the darkness.

'I will arrange for illumination in a moment,' Ravana's voice said out of the abyss. 'Do not be alarmed.'

She did not dignify that with a response. But the truth was, her skin was creeping. A peculiar smell had assailed her senses. It was sickeningly familiar. The smell of rakshasa but somehow subtly different. An odour of decayed flesh and mulch like no other odour on earth. Like deep Southwoods boar's offal and blood. Like stag musk on the bark of a pine trunk. Like river fish guts left in the sun for days. It reminded her, oddly, of the lingering odour in the stables in the princess palace of Mithila, except that whatever creature was stabled here was neither horse nor elephant.

She heard Ravana's voice uttering new slokas.

At first she thought it was another cavern filled with rock eggs, and that he would repeat the same awakening ritual he had used earlier.

Suddenly the cavern was filled with light, forcing her to blink and coronas to fill her hunger-dazed pupils.

And she saw that she had been both right as well as wrong.

The cavern was indeed filled with rakshasa. But not a whole horde of them. Just one.

'Devi protect us,' she whispered despite herself.

Ravana chuckled. 'You will excuse my brother's inability to greet you, princess. He tends to sleep a great deal. It is the natural consequence of an old curse, but the up side of that curse is his enormous size, which, as you might well imagine, can be quite a formidable advantage in a battle.'

He paused and gestured in the air. 'And now, I think, it is time to initiate the process of awakening him. Something that can take anywhere from hours to days, depending on the urgency of the matter. It is now almost five months into his usual sleep-cycle, only a month or so short of his full sleep period, but that does not make it any easier. I think you would not like to be present when he awakens. It often proves to be fatal.'

Sita saw that the floor of the cavern was now covered with several hundred kumbha-rakshasas running to and fro, pointing up at the flying chariot and shouting orders. A horde of them formed up into companies before a towering object at least a hundred feet high; that object was the sleeping rakshasa's outflung hand.

She could not begin to comprehend the sheer size of a being that large. The very cavern itself was so enormous, it seemed that if she were to look up she would see the sky itself, and the far end of it was like the horizon seen from an open shore. As for the being lying prone in the cavern, its proportions were beyond comprehension. She had thought Hanuman's amazing expansion incredible. This creature's size belittled even that miraculous feat.

'I give you Kumbhakarna,' Ravana said. 'My brother. Once

he is fully awake, I will introduce you properly to him. He will be pleased to meet his new sister-in-law.'

Before Sita could respond or react to that last comment, the vaahan was moving again, hurtling forward at fantastic speed. It was all she could do to hold on and keep her balance.

As they entered yet another tunnel and were embraced by pitch darkness, she used the opportunity to shut her eyes and try to regain her calm. Why was Ravana showing her all these things? To demonstrate his great military strength, of course, and to boast of his superiority in battle over Rama's forces. But also because he truly believed he would triumph in the coming war. His tone was one less of condescending superiority than of supreme complacency. He believed he would win. That he would defeat Rama and outlive him. And because he believed it, he was wooing her, Sita. For that was the part of his aspect that had puzzled her until now, and which she now understood. This was not a king displaying his military might; it was a paramour showing his betrothed the power of the man who was wooing her. She didn't know which made her more frightened, the fact that Ravana believed he would defeat Rama in battle, or the fact that he believed he could win her heart.

She sensed intense bright light upon her closed eyelids, and opened her eyes.

They were emerging from a cave-mouth overlooking the ocean. The bright sky and sea were blinding at first, causing her to blink, but the openness was a comfort after those subterranean caverns. She had feared he would take her still deeper and deeper, to the very depths of hell itself. For it was rumoured that Lanka had once been, and perhaps was still, a conduit to the nether realms. She had seen no hard evidence of that since coming here, and if she understood correctly what little she had heard, then the portal to the underworld had closed some fourteen years ago, when Lanka had been destroyed in the Asura race riots and Vibhisena had resurrected Ravana in the volcano. But the very knowledge that she was in a place where there had once existed a pathway to the hellish realms was frightening.

But this was no hell mouth, only a seashore. Filled with sunlight and the tangy smell of ocean and nature's rich, refreshing goodness. The rumours were true then; whatever had once been here had been closed years ago.

She breathed in the fresh, cool sea air, relishing the warmth of the sunlight upon her face and arms. It was autumn now, and the wind was bracing despite the fact that the sun was high in the morning sky, but she did not mind the cold at all. It made her feel alive and free. If she looked upward and outward, ignoring Pushpak's lines and the ten-headed being who controlled the vaahan, she could almost believe she *was* free.

Ravana began chanting again. This time, she neither recognised the slokas nor understood them. It was a mantra foreign to her education. She was not even sure if it was Sanskrit or some more ancient tongue.

Almost at once, the sky began to darken, the sun was shrouded by clouds, and the ocean began churning and seething. She swallowed drily. Ravana's powers were far greater than anything she had imagined. She stole a glance and saw that all ten of the demon lord's pairs of eyes were tightly shut. A jet-black onyx-like stone embedded in the bone of his grotesquely muscled chest glowed brightly with power.

The chanting went on for a long time, and all the while the ocean grew wilder and more furious, like a typhoon brewing. Then Ravana opened his eyes and lightning flashed in the stormy sky, thunder gnashed its teeth mightily, and the ocean itself rose in a great torrent to stand in a body several hundreds of feet high. Sita had thought she had seen impossible sights already. But this was beyond the limits of her expectations. Even without having witnessed such a thing with her own eyes before, she knew what she was seeing. That great anthropomorphically shaped body of sea water standing before them could be none other than—

'Varuna, Lord of the Sea,' Ravana cried out. 'I call upon you to honour your vow to serve me in my hour of need.'

A deep rumbling came from the standing body of water. Sita sensed banked anger in the sound, but also resentful obedience. 'What is your wish, Lord of Lanka?'

Ravana pointed towards the far horizon. 'There, upon the mainland, my nemesis Rama Chandra and his army of vanars and bears are building a bridge to cross the ocean and invade my kingdom. I command you, Varuna-deva, to raise a tidal storm great enough to destroy that bridge and decimate my foes.'

For several moments the wind howled, lightning flashed and thunder growled. The sound of the ocean god replying was like the voice of the ocean itself, a watery rasping. '*It shall be done.*'

And to Sita's horror, the watery effigy of Varuna turned away and began moving, taking the typhoon storm and wind and lightning and thunder with him, moving towards the mainland to where Ravana had pointed.

Ravana laughed then. Laughed at his own power and at Sita's horrified expression. He was looking at her with unbridled pleasure. 'Finally,' he said. 'Finally you begin to understand, princess. No power on earth, no being, can oppose me and survive. As you see, the devas themselves serve me. Forget Rama now. For once Varuna-deva pits the power of the ocean against him, neither Rama, nor his empowered vanar Hanuman, nor all the vanars and bears in the world can hope to win. Your hopes of rescue are doomed to end in a watery grave, my beloved Sita. Along with your husband and brother-in-law and all their forces. You have only one way left to ensure your survival and the survival of your unborn child. Relent now, repent, and be my bride. Refuse and I shall take you by force, ravaging you the way Lord Varuna's oceanic powers will ravage your husband's army.'

3

Vibhisena found Mandodhari in the old enclave. She had left her chariot and entourage at the corner of the avenue and gone ahead on foot. Charred refuse littered the roads, and the stench of burning was everywhere. He had to search through a score of narrow by-lanes before he found her in a small clearing, listening to a group of less fortunate citizens vent their woes. He saw her eyes find him and then look away, her mouth pursed disapprovingly, lips curled around her horn-teeth.

It took him several more moments to get her attention, and even when he did, she seemed to deliberately avoid him yet again. He knew then that her mind was already made up, and that once that happened, virtually nothing he could say would dissuade her. He had no choice but to try. There was too much at stake.

She was speaking to the angry citizenry about arming themselves and preparing for the coming conflict when she turned her attention suddenly, unexpectedly to him. 'And in case you still have doubts that the mortals will invade, then hear what Ravana's own brother, Pundit Vibhisena, has to say.' She gave him his priestly title with an underscoring of scorn, making her antagonism unmistakable.

Suddenly a hundred or more rakshasa heads turned to stare yellow-eyed and red-pupilled in his direction. Snouts sniffed the air, scenting him suspiciously. He took a step backwards, shocked at the wave of hostility he sensed.

'Go ahead then, brother-in-law,' Mandodhari declared, loudly enough for the entire neighbourhood to hear. 'Tell our fellow Lankans what you have been telling me these past few days. Tell them why we should lay down our arms and bow before the mortal invader Rama when he comes, and recant our crimes and transgressions against humanity. Tell them how we must grovel on our bellies and beg for his forgiveness.'

Snorts and chuffs of derision and anger sounded across the square. Vibhisena sought words that would calm the resentful crowd rather than inflame it further. 'I do not say that we should beg or grovel before mortals,' he said uncertainly. 'Only that we should accept our mistakes and attempt not to make new ones.'

Someone from the crowd said with a gruff growl, 'You spoke in favour of the vanar emissary too, did you not, brahmin? It was your meddling that stopped his execution and transmuted his sentence . . . which left him free to wreak havoc upon our kingdom! Are you still so full of mortal-love even now that you do not see what destruction your blessed Rama has wrought upon our lands?'

A chorus of angry voices ayed the unknown speaker. Vibhisena tried to keep his voice calm as he sought a reply. 'The vanar only did what he did in order to defend himself. It was we who were the original transgressors. He came here as a messenger of peace, offering terms. We chose instead to beat him, bind him, and then torture him inhumanely. After that, we cannot fault him for having done what he did to redress the wrong.'

Cries and howls of protest greeted this attempt at mollification. 'And what would you have us do now, then?' shouted another voice, this one female. 'Go run after him and kiss his scorched tail and beg his forgiveness?'

Angry laughs met that one.

Vibhisena looked around nervously. 'Violence begets violence. We were the original transgressors when our lord Ravana abducted the wife of the mortal Rama. If we appeal to him to

return her forthwith, we may yet prevent a terrible, tragic war.
You have seen what havoc a single vanar emissary could accom-
plish. Imagine what an entire army led by Rama would do to
Lanka.'

'So now you're speaking for the mortal, are you? It wasn't
enough that you stood up for the vanar; now you want to
betray your own people for a mortal barbarian who invades
our land through no fault of ours! How dare you!'

'He is not a barbarian,' Vibhisena protested. 'He is only
coming to retrieve his wife—'

Mandodhari's voice cut him off curtly. 'If Rama only wished
to retrieve his wife, he could have had the vanar do that for
him.' She gestured at the destruction around her. 'He seemed to
have power enough to do as he pleased here; how hard could
it have been for him to take the woman Sita back with him?
But instead of doing that, he rampaged and nearly destroyed
Lanka. I say that puts the lie to your words, Vibhisena. Neither
the vanar nor his mortal master wants peace. They want war.
And so we have no choice but to give them war. For Lanka will
not stand by and be attacked twice by such treacherous outsiders.
This time, when your mortal friends arrive at our shores, we
shall be ready to repel them, shall we not, my people?'

'AYE!' rose the resounding cry.

Vibhisena shook his head in dismay. He tried to find something to say that would counter Mandodhari's argument. But
when he opened his mouth to speak, Mandodhari cut him off
yet again.

'I think you have said enough already, brother-in-law. I
should not have listened to you yesterday when you came to
speak to me on behalf of the woman and the vanar. Nor should
the council have listened to you. We were fools, all of us, to
be taken in by your pleas at the vanar's helplessness, were we
not?' She indicated the damage wrought to the neighbourhood
in which they stood. 'Helpless enough to wreak havoc upon
our beautiful city-kingdom, it would appear.'

'You don't understand,' he said, keenly aware of the angry eyes glaring at him from every side. The mob would like nothing better than to take the cost of their demolished homes and property from his own skin. And they were already past the point of anger. 'We cannot blame the vanar for this.'

Mandodhari interrupted his next words. 'And now he cannot fault us for doing what we must to defend ourselves against such future insidious attacks. Nor should you, Vibhisena, defend him or the other enemies of Lanka any longer. Why do you insist on taking the side of the mortals? Do you not feel for your own scorched people? Do you not care about the plight of rakshasas? Are only mortals and their vanar supporters in the right always? Are we as nothing in your opinion?' Her eyes flashed with anger and pain. 'Have you forgotten that this same vanar emissary heinously murdered my younger son and your own nephew, Akshay Kumar?'

'Mandodhari,' he sighed, 'I have not come here to argue with you.'

Someone in the crowd shouted, 'Then why have you come, brahmin?'

He appealed to his sister-in-law one more time. 'If I could speak with you privately . . .'

'Anything you have to say to me, say to Lanka as well,' she said coldly. 'I am a servant of my people. As are you, brother of Ravana. Or have you forgotten that?'

He gathered up his courage and attempted one last time to breathe reason into the smouldering bonfire. 'Then hear me well, all of you. Queen Mandodhari asks me if I care for you all. Of course I care. I care for Lanka as nobody else does. My every waking moment is spent in prayer, invoking the blessings of the devas upon our land—'

'Prayer! As if that ever solved anything!' a rakshasa said scornfully.

'My friends, fellow Lankans,' he cried, 'You must believe me. I speak with concern for your welfare. We must cease this futile conflict here and now. We must make peace with the mortal Rama and his forces at once.'

Someone yelled an obscene suggestion as to what Vibhisena ought to do with his mortal friends.

Mandodhari folded her arms across her chest as she watched Vibhisena's discomfiture. A smile cut her formidable features. 'And why do you think we should do this?'

'Because if a single vanar can wreak such havoc, imagine what an entire army can do. Imagine what Rama himself is capable of. Do you really wish to see Lanka destroyed? Not just the bricks-and-mortar city-kingdom that you so lovingly rebuilt from the ashes fourteen years ago, but the very land you call home. Would you want to see all our people massacred?'

She laughed at him in disbelief, her eyes flashing jewels of cold fury. 'You are beyond belief, my brother-in-law. Do you truly believe this Rama and his army are capable of invading Lanka and wiping us out? And yet you speak of him as if he were some paragon of dharma. How do you reconcile committing genocide with upholding dharma?'

'What choice would he have? What choice are we giving him? Unless we appeal to Ravana to return Sita-devi at once and end this futile war before it begins.'

'*Sita-devi*?' She repeated the words with open contempt. 'You speak of her as if she were a goddess incarnate, not a mere trollop of a human.'

Vibhisena realised he might have gone too far in his enthusiasm. 'Mandodhari, I know how much you love Lanka. Do you really wish to see it wiped off the face of the world? Please, I beg of you, come with me now to Ravana before it is too late. Let us appeal to him one more time. Perhaps now he will see reason.'

She looked at him scornfully. 'Why do you need me at all? Why not go to him directly?'

He sighed. 'Because he will not give me an audience any more. His doors are shut to me.'

She looked at him for a long, silent moment, her eyes glinting, reflecting the embers of some distant fire still smouldering on a hilltop behind him. Finally, when she spoke, her voice was as ice shaped to form a dagger. It drove into his consciousness without resistance. 'Vibhisena, you are my husband's brother. For that reason you have been forgiven many things. But treason and betrayal are beyond forgiveness. I advise you to leave my side and go back to your brahmanical rituals and prayers. You are wasting your time here arguing your case. I do not wish to hear another word you have to say. And I do not think anyone here can bear to listen to your insidious words a moment longer.'

'Aye,' growled one of the rakshasas who had spoken out earlier. 'But give the word, my queen, and we shall tear him apart limb from limb.'

'Even Ravana's brother has no right to utter such treason in Lanka,' said another.

Several others voiced their assent loudly and shrilly. Some raised their snouts and roared their anger as well.

Vibhisena looked around. He could smell blood-rage now in the mob. If he tarried here any longer, they would not use words to attack him. It would be claws and jaws.

He turned and started back the way he had come. The crowd jostled and shoved him as he went, but grudgingly allowed him to pass. He knew this was because of Mandodhari's presence. Were she to but give the word, he would be ripped to shreds in moments. Furious silence engulfed him as he made his way out of the square and back to where he had left his chariot. As he boarded it, he heard Mandodhari's voice ring out, loud and clear across the packed square.

'There is no place left for you in Lanka now, Vibhisena. Go now. Go to your beloved Rama. Go! Lanka has no need of you any longer.'

He boarded the chariot and rode away without looking back.

*   *   *

Ravana gestured and dispelled the image in the standing water. The sheet of fluid, suspended in mid-air by his sorcery, fell back into the earthen bowl from which it had been summoned to rise. The three-dimensional image projected upon the particles of water vanished as well. Ravana turned to look at Supanakha, his faces beaming.

'I think my wife has finally found her mettle, cousin. Did you see how she defended me in that debate? Like a lioness protecting her wounded mate!'

'You brainwashed her well,' she said slyly.

All but one of Ravana's heads lost their smiles. Supanakha cowered and displayed an appropriately apologetic expression; Ravana had been sullen and withdrawn since returning from the long morning session with Rama's wife. She wished she had the water-curtain to see what had transpired between *them*. Whatever it was, it had not improved Ravana's temper, already visibly provoked by the devastation left behind by the vanar.

He controlled himself with an effort and continued brusquely, 'She has seen and heard all that transpired with her own senses, judged it herself, and come to her own conclusions. You call that brainwashing?'

She glanced up cautiously. 'Persuaded, then. You talked her out of her suspicions very effectively. I thought she was angry enough to turn traitor on you after that débâcle in the sabha hall.'

He snorted. 'Mandodhari? Never. My brother dear, though. That's another matter. What she said to him just now stung deep, you could see that from the look on his face. Because it is true. My brother was born wishing he was a mortal instead of a rakshasa. Sometimes I wish he *would* turn traitor on me.'

'You wish?' She leaped up on the edge of the large bowl, gripping it with her claws. 'Why? So you could kill him?'

'I can't kill my own brother, Supanakha. Whatever he says

or does, he is still my flesh and blood. It would be dishonourable.' He seemed distracted, as his heads turned their attention to other matters. The conference is over, she observed
silently. It was often like this with Ravana: all his heads would
come together briefly to confer on some matter which was of
greater importance than others, then some or most would go
back to other preoccupations. 'No. I wish he would realise
himself more completely.'

She cocked her head, not sure whether to ask or to wait for
his meaning to become clearer. Waiting seemed wiser. He was
never too patient when the heads were busy elsewhere.

He went on without noticing her lack of comprehension.

'He believes that I am the villain of this whole piece; he has
made that obvious from his actions in the tower when he went
to see Rama's wife, and from his confrontation with Mandodhari
afterwards. I love the way she threw his own philosophical
posturing back in his face. He always takes the high road, but
this time he's about to learn that the high road is a lonely one
that leads to only one place.'

When he didn't continue for several moments, she prompted
him cautiously. 'And which place is that?'

He glanced at her as if recalling suddenly that he had been
speaking to her and not simply airing his thoughts aloud.
'Banishment.'

Before she could ask a question, he clapped his hands and
sent a servant scurrying to fetch someone. Shortly afterwards,
General Vajradanta arrived. Supanakha perked up a little.
Vajradanta was a short, massively broad rakshasa who had one
strikingly unique feature: his teeth were diamantine. As the result
of a boon granted to his mother at his birth, he could bite
through anything. She had once seen him accept a challenge to
cut through a diamond. He had crunched the gem into bits,
then chewed up the pieces like any other rakshasa might chew
soft human marrow bones.

Ravana issued a series of precise instructions, then asked the general to repeat them back. Vajradanta did so, grinning his trademark smile all the while. His teeth flashed brilliantly, blindingly, against his greenish-white skin. He asked when Ravana wished the order to be carried out.

'At once,' Ravana replied tersely, already busy with other matters, his heads warring over some new issue, speaking a half-dozen different tongues at once, none of which Supanakha had ever heard spoken before, by rakshasa, human or animal.

She waited for a pause in the debate to ask carefully: 'Is that part of your plan? Or are you just upset with him because he tried to turn Mandodhari against you again?'

'He could no sooner turn Mandodhari against me than he could service a dozen kinkaras at once, cousin dearest. Everything you see unfolding before you, including Vibhisena's foolish posturings, is all part of the greater game that began long ago. Back when the world was young and none of us was what we are today.'

She had no idea what he meant, but she had a feeling it would not be advisable to ask him to explain. She satisfied herself by pointing a paw at the urn of water. 'Could I see?'

He sighed impatiently and gestured. The water flew up, hanging in mid-air like a sheer curtain. A flickering of colours ran through the mass, then particles of water rearranged themselves to form a solid-looking three-dimensional image. This picture was of Vibhisena, riding his chariot back to Lanka. He reached the main road leading into the city and saw General Vajradanta and the line of kinkaras blocking his way. Alighting from the chariot, he strode up to the general, who remained seated arrogantly on his broken-sur, leaving no doubt about who was in command here.

For some reason Ravana had neglected to provide sound for this scene, unlike earlier when they had been able to hear every word that Mandodhari and Vibhisena exchanged. Supanakha glanced around, but her cousin looked even more preoccupied, his heads engaged in some fierce unintelligible debate. She decided to watch and interpret the scene for herself. In any case, there was not much of a scene. Even as she watched, General Vajradanta spoke a few direct sentences to Vibhisena, who then reacted with visible shock. He tried to ask a question, or argue some point, upon which Vajradanta gestured to the kinkaras who strode forward in perfect formation, lowering their spears to attack position. Vibhisena, never a fighter, blanched and retreated hurriedly to his chariot. Vajradanta shouted something to him, the leer on his face suggesting that he was enjoying exercising such power over a member of the royal family, a pulastya rakshasa no less. His fellow clan-rakshasas, the other kinkaras, cracked mirroring leers as Vibhisena turned his chariot around and rode back the way he had come.

The images on the water flickered and vanished. The water fell back into the urn. Supanakha was much closer this time, and had to leap back three yards to avoid being splashed. Had even a drop of the sacred ganga-jal touched her . . . She had no wish to even know what the effect might be of such sanctified Ganges water upon an Asura like herself. She knew Ravana had deliberately tried to splash her for her impudence in demanding that he show her the encounter between Vibhisena and Vajradanta.

She did not mind. It was worth it to see Vibhisena sent into exile and yet another phase of Ravana's grand game unfold. She had played no small part in that game. And her role would continue, their little skirmishes and disagreements notwithstanding. In fact, their make-up sessions were often worth the fights themselves. Vibhisena, on the other hand, was out of the picture completely. She smiled a catty smile, licking her damp fur dry, relishing the memory of the look on his face when Vajradanta had told him that he had been banished from Lanka for conspiring against the king, and must leave its shores at once, never to return, on pain of death. Banishment from his homeland, for seeking to save it. Serve the self-righteous fool right. Where had he thought he was anyway? Ayodhya? Hah!

But the bigger question was why Ravana had let him go. It was not like the Lord of Lanka to spare even his own brother in the face of such treasonous rebellion. No, she thought craftily, twirling her bushy tail around the vessel of ganga-jal without actually daring to touch a drop of the sacred fluid, if Ravana had allowed Vibhisena to go and join his enemies, then surely that too was part of some greater plan. Ravana had a reason for everything. Even sparing his own brother's life.

Some time later, with a heavy heart and an even heavier conscience, Vibhisena made his way downhill to the narrow strait that bordered the northernmost shore of Lanka. Four trusted clansmen, rakshasas loyal to his branch of the family for generations, waited there. They had secured the boat he had requested, a simple fishing craft that bobbed up and down in the calm waters of the strait. It was well into morning by this time. He had tried fervently to secure an audience with Ravana, but the hostility that met his every effort spoke more eloquently than any angry refusal might have done. His brother's doors were closed to him, figuratively and literally. But more than that, he suspected, nobody knew exactly where the Lord of Lanka was just then. Ravana had last been seen travelling in a section of Pushpak with the mortal prisoner Sita. They had gone towards the cave-mountain sometime around dawn. Nobody had seen them since. Vibhisena had no means to follow them there, and even if he had, there was no guarantee that they might not return before he even descended into the mountain: he could hardly keep pace with the celestial vaahan.

Everywhere in Lanka there was frantic activity. On Ravana's instructions, his generals were overseeing the largest mobilisation of military forces on the island that Vibhisena had ever witnessed. Never before had Lanka been threatened by invasion. He shuddered to think of the coming war.

He paused now by the shore, looking back. Had he done

everything within his power to champion the cause of peace and dharma? Was there naught he could do to prevent the coming calamity? It seemed unlikely. Mandodhari's anger and the resentment of his own people had scorched him. If she, his closest ally, could threaten him thus, then he had no doubt that the ordinary rank and file would not hesitate to tear him apart. He had been a stranger in a strange land too long. It was time now to throw in his lot with those who understood the language he spoke, those who respected the value of dharma and all that was right and true in this world. Only thus could dharma be restored to Lanka and the island-kingdom returned to its former glory.

He climbed into the boat as the other rakshasas held it steady. Once he was aboard, they clambered in as well, and pushed off from the shore. Rowing strongly, they pulled away from the tide's grip, out to sea. In a short while they were upon the ocean, leaving Lanka behind and starting forth across the vast waters in the direction of the mainland. Vibhisena spoke a sloka ensuring safe passage, then tried to still the immense weeping of his heart. It filled him with anguish to do this, yet he had no other choice. He must leave Lanka in order to save it.

He was almost a full yojana out to sea, making good progress northwards, when the genial ocean wind suddenly fell still and their boat was becalmed. A chill foreboding filled his heart. He was reciting the Tataka maha-mantra when the gigantic shadow rose behind him in the distance, looming larger as it approached at juggernaut speed.

4

At dusk they had glimpsed the first ominous signs.

The western sky turned an angry red, slashes of crimson painting the horizon like a wound inflicted by an angry tiger. Clouds gathered in the south-west, black and brooding and threatening rain. Thunder growled in the distance and occasional glimpses of lightning flickered at the extremities of Rama's vision, too far to be seen directly. Wind dervishes sprang up, hurling rock dust and sand into their eyes, blinding them all and making the bears sneeze violently. The singing stopped here, then there, until finally all grew silent.

Various omens were spotted: a flock of a certain variety of birds flying in an inauspicious direction; dead fish floating on the surface of the sea; left eyes twitching – or was it right eyes?; an unseasonal star that could only be Rahu or Ketu, the two most feared stellar deities in the firmament. Someone came scurrying up, shouting about a wild elephant that had run amuck in the woods, trampling an entire unit of vanars. About bears who had been killed by vampire bats. The mood, so cheerful and optimistic until now, turned sour and gloomy.

Lakshman dismissed all harbingers of doom and sighters of omens point-blank, refusing to hear such superstitious talk. When they persisted, he grew somewhat irritated and told them to be rational. Rama kept his silence, knowing that people would believe what they desired, no matter how logical or illogical. But when Lakshman turned to him at last and asked him to speak aloud and dispel the unease that everyone was feeling, he was reluctant to do so. He felt something too, though he could not say what it was. A sense that something had changed during the course of the day. It was not only that he was waiting for Hanuman's return; it was something greater than the vanar's mission. Something that involved the forces that governed the universe itself. There was a disturbance at the most primordial level of existence, in the very ether.

Sundown found him standing on a ridge overlooking the part of the shore where the bridge-building was in progress. Workers were still passing on rocks, egged on by Nala, who leapt up and down in agitation, seeking to get every last moment's work while there was yet light enough to see by. Lakshman had stalked off to have a word with Sugreeva about calming down his vanars and quelling the rumours of ill omens.

As night fell, the weather worsened, as did the mood of the vanars and the bears. Petty squabbles broke out between vanar factions, between the two species, and even amongst close comrades. Insects filled the air, adding to the irritation and frustration. A dead kraunchya bird fell out of the sky and nobody would touch it. It attracted a riot of gulls, fighting over its pink innards. Its desolate mate wheeled overhead, wailing its throaty cry. The ocean grew angrier, the waves sloshing so high over the bridge that even Nala agreed dismally to call off the work for the day. They had made some progress despite all the distractions, but it was nowhere near what they ought to have accomplished.

Would it ever be enough? Rama had wondered, standing on a ridge overlooking the shore. Had he taken on a task that was foolish rather than just foolhardy? Building a bridge across the ocean? Taking an army of vanars and bears to Lanka? Invading the realm of rakshasas? The gathering storm mirrored his own inner turmoil, and like the storm he banked his anger, keeping a tight hold of the rage that lay always just beneath the surface.

What people failed to understand about him, even Lakshman, was not that he did not feel rage or grief or desire; he ruled these emotions, they did not rule him. Perhaps it was because so much excess had been committed in his childhood and youth, so much self-indulgence displayed, that he had learned from a very young age to keep his portions small, to eat and feel and live in little manageable increments, never taking on more than he could chew at one time, never demanding, never having more on his plate than he could comfortably eat.

But this was not one of those times. He felt overwhelmed by the sheer scale of what he had undertaken. An invasion? For what? To regain his lost love? But that was his loss, was it not? What did it have to do with all these innocents? If a queen was abducted by another king, did her husband have the right to wage war against the other's kingdom? To slaughter thousands, maybe hundreds of thousands, only to avenge his and his wife's honour? He knew the inevitable argument: that a queen's honour, or a king's, was the people's honour as well, the kingdom's honour. But here he had no kingdom. These were not his people. Yet they fought for him, pitted their lives against the forces of nature, against impossible odds, against stones and sea and storms, and for what? For honour? Was honour worth the cost of so many lives?

In an ideal world, he would call Ravana to arms and face him alone, resolving the issue once and for all. But that choice had not been given to him. To reach Ravana he needed to cross the ocean and wade through a kingdom full of rakshasas. To do that, he needed an army. This was that army. That was all there was to it. Shut up your conscience and fight, his sword-master had always told him. Morality belongs in the sabha hall, not on the battlefield. When a sword is drawn, the time for thinking is past.

Perhaps that was why Rama had always preferred the bow. One could think when using the bow. One could pause, or replace the arrow, unfired, into its quiver. An arrow could afford to have a conscience, up to a point. A sword had only a cutting edge.

When the evening star reached its zenith and began its downward descent, he felt the first prickings of despair. He had faith in Hanuman, but clearly there were forces at work here that were far greater than any one individual, however dedicated he might be.

The storm brewed like a cauldron of broth, clouds seething in the western sky, the fading twilight turning the rim of the world vermilion and purple. The air turned so electric with impending lightning that the hair on the back of his hands and the nape of his neck felt as if might burst into flame. Slowly, in angry, reluctant stages, night fell like a sullen youth performing a punitive chore.

Rama stood, wrapped in darkness, bound by the ropes of his own self-doubt, drawing the cloak of conscience close around him. Dharma was his only defence against an irrational, unreasoning world. In dharma he found solace; in karma, the commission of duty, he burned the vestiges of past misdeeds and rebuilt his store of brahman.

He lost track of time. Yet when a voice spoke in his right ear, he knew it was Jambavan. Even the wind and the angry sea and the brewing storm could not overwhelm the smell of bear sweat, fish and honey that pervaded the rksa.

'Hubris,' said the bear lord.

Rama looked at him. 'Hubris?'

'Defiance of the gods,' Jambavan explained. 'Daring to attempt a feat that rivals the actions of the devas themselves. Transgressing the limits of mortal or animal behaviour to achieve something miraculous, godlike.'

Rama thought of all the things he had done during his life that could be classified as such. He could think of several. But he had a feeling it was not his actions Jambavan was referring to. 'Hanuman?'

The dark snout dipped.

'Do you know how he fared?' Rama asked hopefully. 'Whether his journey was successful or no? Is he there in Lanka yet? Was he able to—'

Jambavan sighed and shook his head. 'That is beyond my powers, lad. Yet I know this much. He has faced many obstacles on the way to Lanka. It has not been as simple as leaping from branch to branch after all.' He snorted in self-derision. 'Not that I ever meant it would be.'

Rama's heart pounded. 'Obstacles? But he did—'

'Reach Lanka? I do not know, Rama. I would like to think so. But in attempting this leap, he provoked the powers that be. By calling upon his own hidden strengths, he has awakened great forces. Forces which may be jealous of his gifts. And other forces which may be more sympathetic to Lanka's cause than our own. These sleeping giants would no doubt have revealed themselves to us in due course. On the other hand, it is also possible that they might have gone on sleeping and never been called into play. Now their awakened shakti is formidable and far greater than what is needed to crush us all.'

The bear lord waved a hirsute paw at the beach swarming with vanars and bears bedding down for the night. Growls and snarls of discontent rippled through the camp, as the two species shared their mutual unhappiness at the inauspicious weather. 'But by invoking his celestial gifts, Hanuman has awakened them all at once. Challenged them unwittingly. The signs and omens our people speak of are not wild imaginings or superstitious illogic. They are signs of the struggle waged by our friend out there.' The bear indicated the open sea. 'He has fought many battles today. That much is certain. And yet the greatest battle of all remains to be fought. Tomorrow.'

'Tomorrow?' Rama's heart lurched. 'Then you believe he will not return tonight with Sita?'

Jambavan laid a paw on Rama's shoulder. The bear's paw was very warm to the touch, and very heavy. 'Have faith, Rama. Hanuman has faith in you. He believes that you are blessed by the devas. So in turn you must sustain your faith in him. Trust in him and believe that he will triumph over all odds. I only wish to warn you that all may not turn out as we would desire.'

Rama made to speak again, but the bear king raised a single talon. 'I do not know of Sita's fate. I speak of the forces that swirl around us all. You well know that this conflict is not simply a jealous lover seeking the return of his beloved, nor his desire for redressal. There are forces here at work that are beyond even my understanding . . .' He paused and scratched his loins a moment. 'Well, perhaps not beyond my understanding, but surely beyond anyone else's. This pot was first brewed long before you or Ravana or even I were placed upon this mortal realm. It is a game of gods and demons. Devas and Asura lords. We are only playing out our part in this one chapter of an epic history.'

Rama found little comfort in the bear king's words. 'Then . . . what am I to do?'

Jambavan's furry features twitched in a grunting smile. 'Do? Ever the kshatriya, eager to act. The time for action will come soon, Rama. Sooner than you expect. There is plenty to be done. And I have no doubt you will do your task well enough.'

'But?' Rama asked, for the word was implicit in the bear's tone.

Jambavan scratched his lower back and sighed with relief. 'What is to be is to be. What good will it serve us today to know we die tomorrow?'

He saw Rama's face and emitted a choked laugh. 'By that I do not mean that we will die tomorrow. I am speaking figuratively.'

Rama made no comment.

Jambavan sighed again, exuding a strong odour of crab meat. 'In any case, we must now await our champion Hanuman's return. I will keep vigil with you by going into the caves and making an offering to the devas. I have already asked my hunters to collect the necessary items. We shall pursue this course further when the lord of light returns to show us the world again.'

Thunder rumbled in the distance as he turned to go. He paused. 'The ocean deities are angry with us. Perhaps they were frustrated in their attempts to halt Hanuman on his epic journey. Soon I think they will turn their power upon us puny beings.'

Rama frowned. 'What must we do then?'

Jambavan's beady eyes flashed with a dark light. 'We will do what mortal beings must do when they commit hubris, my friend. We will die. But do not be alarmed, for in a sense our very existence is an act of hubris. All of us, feeble, futile mortal fleshbags, tempt the forces that be merely by staying alive. What else is life itself, living in the face of natural odds, if not the defiance of celestial power? It is the ultimate hubris.'

Rama remained on the ridge after Jambavan had gone. After a long while, Lakshman came and stood beside him, sharing his vigil. Together they waited as the night grew darker and colder. The storm brooded with them, mirroring the discontent simmering within their hearts.

Towards dawn, as the sky lightened again to an angry shade of deep blue streaked with vermilion, they saw something appear on the horizon. It grew steadily, and finally coalesced into the silhouette of a flying being without wings. The armies were already stirring, restless from an uneasy night's respite. A sleepy, questioning *cheeka* sounded from the beach, followed by a string of enthusiastic yelps and cries. The excitement built into a roar as the skies brightened and the approaching silhouette grew larger and closer.

It was almost sunrise when Hanuman became clearly discernible. He slowed his approach and reduced his size, hovering in mid-air with an ease that was wonderful to behold and which revealed the control he had acquired over his abilities since his departure. As easily as a feather drifting to earth, he descended softly to land upon the ridge where Rama and Lakshman stood. He was his normal size by this time.

His first act was to bend down and touch Rama's feet reverentially, taking his lord's blessings.

Rama took hold of his shoulders, pulled him up, and embraced him warmly.

5

The anxious crowd looked on as Hanuman prepared to speak. His eyes found his king, Sugreeva, Prince Angad, his brother Sakra, and so many other familiar faces. His heart ached at seeing them again. For a moment he wished he had stayed in Lanka, continuing to battle. It would be easier than explaining his failure. But his lord Rama's face was so calm and devoid of the anxiety that he saw on every other face that it shamed him. Rama had not asked him even once about Sita. His only queries thus far had been about Hanuman's own welfare, about the minor cuts and bruises his body displayed, the charred end of his tail.

'My lord Rama,' he said. 'As you can see from the fact that I return alone, unaccompanied, I have failed in my primary mission. I was unable to bring back the lady Sita. For this, I ask your forgiveness. I regret I could not do as you expected me to, my lord.'

Rama replied in a level voice. 'I know you must have done your best to save her, my friend. It is all I expected of you. Beyond that, a person's fate depends on his or her own karma. If Sita's karma decreed that she was not to be saved, then that is that. Neither you nor even I myself could have saved her then.'

Hanuman read the fatalism in his master's words and shook his head quickly. 'No, my lord. It is not as you fear. The lady Sita is alive and well. Not in the best of health perhaps, for she fasts out of choice, and has endured many hardships, but she is alive and in her wits yet. She has not been physically violated by man or weapon. I cannot claim to know for certain how she fared after I left Lanka, but I would warrant that she is yet alive and maintained carefully as a precious hostage. For if my understanding of his methods is correct, then Ravana intends to use her as a pawn in the war ahead, and it is for this reason that he shall keep her alive until the very end.'

The collective sigh of relief that rose from the assembled vanars and bears seemed to express Rama's own inexpressible joy at this news. For the first time since he had known the mortal yodha, Hanuman saw a bright light spark in Rama's deep brown eyes. 'Is it true then, my friend? She is safe and well? Unharmed and unhurt? My love, my wife, my Sita?'

Hanuman felt greatly reassured to see the light of joy in his lord's eyes. He hesitated, choosing his words carefully to avoid giving a falsely optimistic impression. 'I would not say unharmed and unhurt, my lord. Nor safe and well. For she has suffered great mental torture and agony at the hands of the rakshasas set to guard her, and far more psychological battering by Ravana, his wife, and the antics of the Lankan court.'

'The Lankan court?' It was Lakshman who asked this question. His eyes were as bright as Rama's but with a feverish glint that was absent in his brother's gaze.

'Aye, my lord Lakshman. It seems that when Vibhisena, brother of Ravana, an apparently pious brahmin rakshasa, attempted to defend her rights and see that the lady Sita was fed and better cared for, it created dissent and resulted in one of the more sympathetic rakshasas being murdered. But the lady Sita was falsely blamed for the murder.'

Cries of outrage rose from the assembled listeners.

'Tell us all,' Rama said. 'Start at the beginning, from the time you departed this shore, and tell us everything that befell you during your time in Lanka.'

Hanuman did as Rama said. He told the whole story: his

flight across the ocean, the encounters with the flying mountain Mainika, how he outwitted the sea serpent Surasa, his
landing at Lanka, tunnelling up through the labyrinthine cata-
combs, his first view of the golden city, resplendent and breath-
taking in its beauty, the appearance of the ethereal being whom
he believed at first to be a benign spirit, her leading him on a
tour of the city and its sights as he searched for Sita. He related
how he entered the great tower-palace, the wondrous sights he
beheld within that sorcerously created edifice, the endless magical
realms contained within, the wicked temptations and tricks
that sought to deprive him of his self-control and break his
brahmacharya vow of chastity, and the eventual exposure
of the ethereal spirit as a quite solid flesh-and-blood Asura,
a shape-shifting cousin of Ravana himself, sent to lead him
astray. At the mention of Supanakha's name, Rama and
Lakshman exchanged grim glances.

Hanuman went on to tell the rapt assemblage of his sighting
of Ravana himself, surrounded by exquisitely beautiful people
and things. Then of his sighting of the lady Sita, his conversation with her, her anguish at the lies that the Lankans had
poured upon Rama's good name, her determined resolve to have
Rama come to Lanka in person and fight to redress the wrong
done unto them both, to clear his name and prove his worth,
Hanuman's own impassioned pleas to her to come back with him
and her proud refusal. He then described the battles he had
fought with the rakshasas, the destruction he wrought, the champions he slaughtered. Cheers of exultation rose from his enraptured comrades, bears as well as vanars, and when he described
his capture by Ravana's eldest son, Indrajit, a great sigh of
disappointment rose from the beach. He described his trial in
the Lankan court, the passionate defence put up by Vibhisena,
the court's glee at the announcement of Hanuman's execution,
and Ravana's unexpected revision of the verdict and its trans-
mutation to the deceptively simple punishment of the burning
of his tail, actually intended to be no less than a death sentence

in itself. He narrated how he turned the tables and wreaked havoc on Lanka, burning and destroying, ending with the destruction of the great tower and his final appeal to the lady Sita. As he described his last sight of Sita, haggard from fasting and smirched by her imprisonment, yet proud and strong even in that time of ultimate crisis, the congregation was stone silent. He saw tears glinting in the eyes of Angad and Nala and Sakra, and even the bears sniffled.

A silence descended on the shore, broken only by the sound of the ocean. The sun had risen to a good height, and the warm sunlight bathing them all brought a welcome respite from the chill autumn air. The gloom of the evening and night before had passed, and the brewing storm seemed to have dissipated. Except for a discoloration on the western horizon, like a bruise on an otherwise flawless body, the sky was a perfect cerulean blue.

Rama was the first to speak. He rose to his feet so he could be seen by as many as possible. 'No one could have accomplished as much as Hanuman, not even in their wildest imaginations. Not only did he save the life of my beloved wife Sita and deflect the crisis she faced last night, but he wreaked more havoc in Lanka than an entire army! Let it always be known and remembered that his accomplishments on this mission went far above and beyond the call of his given task. As and when I return to my homeland, I will see to it that his exploits are enscribed and stored for posterity in the chronicles of our time. May his name be remembered even above my own, for by serving me, he made me, my brother, my wife, my entire dynasty proud. From now to time immemorial let it be known that the name Hanuman stands for the most loyal of servants and friends, he who risks his own life and does impossible things to show his fealty.

'Would that I had the wealth of a kingdom at my disposal, to reward him as I would wish to. Would that I possessed a whole nation's treasure, to gift him as a sign of my gratitude.

But for now, this affectionate embrace is all I have to give him. Hanuman, my friend, my loyal soldier, Sita's brave champion, my brother in heart and mind and spirit, take this embrace as a token of my immeasurable gratitude and love.'

Hanuman was surprised to find that his legs trembled when he stood. He felt hot tears spill from his eyes as he accepted Rama's tight embrace. 'My lord,' he said over and over again, 'my lord, my lord, my lord, would that I had served you better.'

Rama shook his head and wiped Hanuman's tears with his own fingers, gently, like an elder brother comforting a young sibling. 'You served me best of all when you returned safely.'

Lakshman embraced Hanuman as well. 'Truly, Maruti,' he said in a heartfelt tone, referring to Hanuman's paternal name, after the deva of wind, Marut, 'no one could have done more. The deeds you accomplished in Lanka shall never be forgotten. Never.'

Loud cheers greeted these words, and hoarse cries of support showed how moved the soldiers were as well. Hanuman was not surprised to find glistening eyes in the vanar ranks, for he knew his people were sentimental, but he was astonished at the copious tears flowing down the faces of the bears, dampening their fur and leaving streaks on their dust-covered cheeks. He scanned the scores of faces staring up at him, extending the length of the beach and far beyond, to the point where thousands could see neither him nor Rama and Lakshman and only knew what was transpiring because of their compatriots, who passed on descriptions of what was said and done here. He sensed that they desired him to say a word or two in response to Rama and Lakshman's effusive praises.

'All I did was in the name of Rama,' he said. 'I would do ten times as much in a trice. For my lord is a just and true man and he has been wronged.' He paused. 'Woefully wronged! My brothers and sisters, when I heard the lies they spoke against Rama, it made my blood turn to fire. Everything they have done against him and his loved ones, every transgression they have visited upon Rama's family, they blame him of doing against them! Imagine! They abduct his wife without cause or provocation and then they blame him for raising an army to get her back. Tell me, my comrades, are we wrong to go to Lanka and fight for our mortal friend's honour?'

The reply came in a multitude of vanar and bear dialects and varieties of grunts, all of which added up to one deafening 'Nay!' that made crowds of gulls rise up shrieking in protest and wheel about the sky.

'I tell you, rarely has such a righteous war been waged, against those deserving of the harshest penalties possible. I urge each and every one of you, do not be overly impressed by my accomplishments in Lanka. Yes, I slew a good many rakshasas, and will slay a good many more when the opportunity presents itself again. But what I did, you can each one of you do as well, in your own way, big or small, great or modest. For each of you is armed with the shield of righteousness and the sword of dharma, and our success is assured in the end. No matter what the cost, no matter how great the price, we will reach Lanka and battle the minions of Ravana until they yield or until they are all slain; the choice is theirs. Are you with me?'

'Aye!' came the response. The gulls kept flying, and shrieking.

'Then, my friends,' Hanuman declared solemnly, the pauses between his words filled with the sounds of the ocean and the birds and the waves of whispers that carried his pronouncements to the rear ranks, miles away, 'with my lord Rama's blessings, I urge you return to the work of bridge-building without delay. For the sooner we complete Nala's bridge, the sooner we shall reach Lankan shores. And the sooner our just cause will triumph. Let us raise our voices together and ask strength for our limbs and hearts by chanting thrice the name of our mortal lord . . . Say now, Jai Shri Rama!'

'JAI SHRI RAMA!' chorused the armies of Hanuman.

'Jai Shri Rama,' he repeated. And they echoed him. And once more.

Then, with a great inhalation of breath, Hanuman expanded himself. Still expanding, he leaped off the ridge, landing thirty feet below on the beach. He sprang forward at a run, racing on to the bridge, to the end of the promontory, growing even as he ran. In his wake, the vanars and bears followed, roaring like an ocean.

6

Hanuman was the first to sight the coming calamity. Expanded to a hundred times his normal size, he was working with feverish speed. Gathering enormous handfuls of rocks from the debris of Mount Mahendra, leaping out into the ocean, depositing the load into the sea as carefully as possible to avoid splashing his comrades on the promontory, then leaping back to the shore to collect more rocks, he had extended the bridge by more than a mile in the time it had taken the sun to rise a finger's width. The other vanars and the bears worked at filling the irregularities in the piles he dumped, evening out the surface to make traversing easier. His example was a great source of inspiration to them all, and everyone worked as if their lives depended on it. Never before had Hanuman seen his people labour with such discipline and dedication, more like ants than vanars. And the bears? They toiled in perfect collusion with their vanar comrades as if the two species had always been accustomed to working thus together, shoulder to shoulder. It warmed his heart to see such cooperation and camaraderie.

At the rate they were working, Nala was confident they would reach Lanka within a day or two at the most. Already, from his superior vantage point, Hanuman estimated that they would approach the halfway point by noon today. Which would leave perhaps fifty yojanas more to go. If he could fill in another twenty or twenty-five yojanas before nightfall, they would surely be in Lanka tomorrow.

He was depositing a load of rocks into the sea at the outer extremity of the promontory when he felt the disturbance. It came to him first as a kind of trembling. He sensed the very ground beneath the ocean, some four hundred feet below the surface at that point, shudder as if in the grip of an earthquake. He was waist deep in the brine, and had dropped half his load. He frowned, wondering if perhaps he was mistaking the impact of the rocks he was unloading for something else, and paused, waiting. Half a mile towards shore, the vanars and bears working on the promontory continued singing cheerily, suspecting nothing. He felt a tickling by his right calf, in the swirling silt of the ocean floor, as one of the ocean's many denizens brushed past him. The water at his waist waxed alternately warm and cold as currents intermingled. In the distance, a herd of sea giants spouted fountains of water.

Then it came again. This time the trembling was so intense he had to spread his feet wider to keep his balance. Some of the rocks he was holding trickled through his fingers, splashing into the water. On the promontory the singing faltered, then stopped, as his comrades sensed something amiss. He saw faces turning to look up at him, everyone assuming that he had done something to cause the phenomenon. But then came a shuddering so violent that even he was almost knocked off his feet. He flailed his arms to get back his balance, dropping the rocks. On the promontory, thousands of vanars and bears scurried like ants in confusion, trying to get back to the safety of solid land. He saw a few lose their footing and fall, splashing and gasping, into the sea. Their comrades stopped at once to help them.

He turned, sloshing water and sending a cluster of white-finned predators scuttling out of his way. Facing the western horizon, towards Lanka, he peered into the distance. He could see nothing alarming. Just the sunlit ocean, stretching endlessly. A faint tremor shook the earth underfoot again, the ocean sloshed against his waist, and he heard the startled cries from the promontory behind him. Several called out to him, asking what was happening. He had no answer to give them.

He continued to watch the western horizon until finally he saw something, a faint shadow, like a dusky ripple in a field of otherwise perfectly aligned kusa grass. On land that meant a predator lurking beneath the grass, but he could not fathom what it might mean here in the brine desert. It curled softly at the very limit of vision, like a shadow of the horizon line separating from its master. He watched it with growing bafflement, unable to relate it to anything in his store of knowledge. He felt something tickling his shoulder and looked around to see a cloud nudging past. He had inadvertently been expanding himself further while watching the horizon. He was now several hundreds of yards tall, and the ocean lapped around his thighs just above his knees.

He looked at the horizon again. The shadow-like curl had grown farther removed from the horizon, the distinction much clearer now. As he watched, it grew more pronounced, the separation between it and the horizon line wider and wider, until it began to resemble something so familiar that he wondered how he had not recognised it at once. It was a wave, nothing more, nothing less. Simply a wave. But in order for it to be visible at this great distance, it must be a wave of some magnitude. A wave great enough to—

He turned and looked back at the bridge. His fellows were still scurrying back to land. Good. A few had stopped to look back and were gawking at the horizon – they were able to glimpse the curl of the wave too. He saw Sakra among those watching.

'Get off the bridge,' he said, hearing his own voice booming. 'Everyone go into the woods. Hurry!'

Still some fools remained, staring dumbly up at him. 'Go!' he shouted.

The stragglers leaped up and down, squawking more out of fear of their giant brother than the coming tidal wave, and loped back across the bridge. Hanuman sloshed through the ocean, disrupting the schools of fish that were swimming around madly in confusion. It occurred to him that the wave was no natural phenomenon. Had it been so, then surely the marine life would have sensed it. Even land creatures would have known there was something amiss well in advance and sought cover. There were warning signs when such things came, little changes in weather and air and in the patterns of insect and bird life. The fact that nobody had sensed its coming left no doubt in his mind that this was no natural thing; it was the product of sorcerous intervention. And he did not have to think twice to know who was responsible.

When he was within hailing distance of the shore, he made out Rama and Lakshman standing on the ridge, attempting to bring some order to the chaos on the beach. Vanars and bears swarmed across the shore front in organised confusion.

'Rama,' Hanuman said, 'you must seek cover quickly. Ravana has sent the ocean to attack us.'

Even at this distance, he could read incredulity in Rama's response. He had to attune his hearing to catch Rama's words above the cacophony of his comrades.

'Sagara?' Rama said. 'But why would—'

'Not Sagara, Varuna,' Hanuman interjected. Sagara was the ancient one who dug up the cavities in the earth that were later filled by the great flood and became the oceans, making his name synonymous with the word ocean itself. While Varuna was the deva who ruled over the waters of the ocean world and all creatures residing within those waters. 'Varuna-deva is beholden to Ravana and must do his bidding. He sends a great tide now to destroy our bridge and thwart our attempts to cross to Lanka. You must save yourself. Perhaps if you go into the forest you may outrun the wave.'

But Rama remained standing still, staring out at the sea. Hanuman looked back over his shoulder. The curling shadow was much taller now. It was impossible to tell height and size accurately at this distance, but he thought that the wave might well be a hundred yards high or greater. What shocked him more was the distance it had travelled in the few moments he had turned his back on it.

He turned back to Rama. 'My lord, there is no time to run now. Let me carry you to safety. Climb upon my hands and I will bear you away high in the sky where even the tallest wave cannot reach.'

He knelt down in the sea, ignoring the gritty rocks of the undersea floor digging into his knees, and held out his hands, palms upward, for Rama and Lakshman to climb on to. The chaos on the beach grew cacophonic as the vanars and bears began to succumb to naked panic. Lakshman's stentorian voice cut through the noise, issuing stern, crisp orders to the generals and the clan and tribe chiefs. Rama's attention continued to remain on the mêlée even as Hanuman waited. The vanar stole a glance over his shoulder. The curl continued to rise higher as it approached at a relentless rate. The entire horizon was one thick undulating shadow now. Probing with his heightened senses, he could catch the sound now, a deep subsonic rumbling, like a great shuffling in the bowels of the earth. It made him feel sick to the stomach. What havoc would a wave of that size wreak once it struck the shore? How far inland would his vanar fellows and bear mates have to flee in order to reach safety?

'Rama,' he called out, loud enough to be heard over the cacophony. 'You must come now, while there is still time. I urge you, my lord. Let me save you.'

Rama finished speaking to Nala, a pale, stunned-looking Nala, who was trying his best to listen to the mortal leader while avoiding the sight of the oncoming peril visible behind Rama. Nala nodded briskly, then turned and loped away, calling out in the vanar tongue. Several of his bridge-builder chiefs listened to what he had to say and began calling out as well, passing on the words of Lord Rama. Hanuman did not know whether to feel touched by this show of obedience and faith in the face of certain disaster, or to admire the great loyalty that Rama had come to command in so short a time.

Only then did Rama turn to Hanuman. His care-worn face looked up at the vanar's towering visage. 'Maruti, my friend. Save as many as you can. Act now, quickly!'

'My lord, even at my largest size I cannot save them all. But if I save you, I may yet achieve something worthwhile. I beg you, Rama. Climb upon my hand and let me take you to the skies.'

Rama smiled wistfully, yet, Hanuman saw, his eyes remained hard and determined. This was Rama the master warrior he had glimpsed in the clearing before the battle of Janasthana, the Rama who would stand and fight to the death against impossible odds rather than flee and save himself. Rama, yodha among yodhas. 'I stand with my brethren, Anjaneya. It is my place.'

Hanuman looked back over his shoulder. The horizon was a dense charcoal scrawl drawn by an old vanar with a shaking paw. The wave was gathering more water mass as it came, as if it knew that the longer it took to reach the shore, the greater the destruction it would unleash. A wind began to blow without warning, driven towards them by the approaching juggernaut. He felt the chill of distant polar oceans in the touch of that wind, an unnatural chill that ought never to have reached these warm tropical climes. This was no mere wind; it reeked of Asura sorcery. He clenched his great teeth in chagrin at the thought of Ravana's vile act of cowardice: for was it not cowardice to unleash death and destruction from afar, anonymously, instead of showing your opponent your face before striking?

He turned back to face Rama, folding his hands entreatingly. 'My lord. Reconsider one last time. All these warriors,' he indicated the mêlée on the beach and in the palm groves beyond as his comrades fled in as orderly a fashion as they could muster, 'depend on your leadership. If something should happen to you, how would we go on? Who will rescue your hapless wife Sita from the clutches of Ravana? Who will avenge the wrong and dishonour done unto your family?'

The wind rose fiercely, buffeting Rama and Lakshman hard enough to make them sway. They spread their legs and stood their ground. Near their position, Hanuman saw Sakra struggling to hold his posture erect – in imitation of his brother, as usual – and failing. The little vanar tumbled several times, then regained his footing and crouched down, fighting to stay upright, issuing a string of outraged *cheekas* at the elements. The chaos on the beach had resolved into something resembling a battle plan, with a large number already vanished into the groves. Yet many remained. Far too many. Hanuman saw, unsurprised, that many of those still on the beach were simply standing firm, like Sakra, determined not to run so long as their lord and leader stayed. Angad and Sugreeva were among this number, as were Jambavan and his lieutenants. The bear king was closest to Rama's position, his dark face inscrutable, bear eyes glinting in the dull gloomy light. The wind roared, raising sand dervishes that swirled around them all.

Rama shouted to make himself heard above the roaring wind. 'We cannot all escape in time. And I will not abandon my soldiers to save myself.'

Hanuman stared down in dismay. 'But you may . . .' he could not bring himself to speak of Rama being killed, '. . . you may come to harm, my lord, if you stay here.'

Rama's answer was torn ragged by the storm, but Hanuman was able to catch the frayed words. 'We are at war, Anjaneya. We would not flee from an army of rakshasas. Why should we flee from the lord of the ocean?'

Hanuman was spellbound by the strength of Rama's resolve, struck speechless by his conviction in the face of imminent death.

Rama shouted again. 'Save as many as you can. I make my stand here.'

The pitch of the wind changed then, as if protesting Rama's unwillingness to bow down, and a veritable typhoon blew across the beach, raising a cloud of sand so blinding that all of them, mortal, vanar and bear, had to cover their eyes and mouths with the backs of their hands and struggle just to remain standing. The howls and cries of fleeing vanars and bears came to Hanuman on the wind, like the ghosts of departed souls screaming on their last journey down to the underworld. He was filled with great despair and frustration on one hand, and great pride and boundless love on the other.

He turned away from Rama and strode out into the ocean, now choppy and ragged in anticipation of the coming tidal wave. The water level had dropped to the extent that the bed of the ocean was bared for several hundred yards out, leaving gasping, thrashing fish and sea creatures beached. At the edge of the new tideline, still receding as he strode out, the foaming water teemed with frenzied sea beings, maddened by their awareness of the coming devastation. He stopped at the tideline, lowering himself to sit on the soft, yielding sand.

He expanded himself as far as he could, refusing to accept any limits. He ignored the banshee shriek of the typhoon, the fury of the ocean churning around him, the whitefins and sea serpents and other devilish creatures of the ocean that bit and stung and jabbed at his body underwater, whether on the command of the Lord of Lanka or simply maddened by the storm and chaos, he did not know.

He lay on his side, putting his back to the frothing ocean. He was large enough by then that the water level only bisected his chest. A good hundred feet of his body still rose above the surface. He did not think that would be enough to stop the tidal wave, but it would surely thwart it somewhat.

He could see the beach from where he lay, could just make out Rama and Lakshman's silhouettes in the garish crimson-and-cerulean-tinted light of the typhoon-shadowed sky. They stood like warriors at the head of an army. The way he had seen them stand on the mound at Janasthana, awaiting the arrival of the rakshasa hordes.

Then he was forced to shut his eyes to keep the wind-flung sand and salty brine from blinding him. The last thing he saw was the world growing dark. The roaring from behind grew too enormous to comprehend, a sound beyond deafening. His last prayer was that his gigantic body should be enough to protect Rama and the others from the worst of this calamity. Then the wave struck him with the force of a hundred thousand sledgehammers, and he saw no more.

7

Rama regained consciousness to find himself lying on a grassy patch, palm fronds scattered across his body and face, and sand in his nostrils, mouth, eyes and ears, a veritable dune formed against the side of his body. He plucked away the palm fronds from his face to find himself staring up at a charcoal-grey sky as clear as crystal. The sound of the ocean washed across the background of his mind, omnipresent, but the absence of other sounds was stark, chilling. No birds called out. No vanars *cheeka*-ed or chittered or yelled. No bears grunted or chuffed. No sounds of stones being thrown or sand crunching under a million paws. No sound at all, except the incessant washing of waves on the beach, and the kind of stillness that came after a bloody battle.

He raised himself slowly, seeking out any damage to his person. Apart from a bruised shoulder and several sore spots on his ribs, thighs and hip, he seemed unharmed. He pushed aside the palm fronds and debris and rose unsteadily to his feet.

The first thing that assailed him was the stench of fish. It came on the soft wind that blew from the sea as if this were just another late summer afternoon and he were rising from an unscheduled nap. The stench was unbearable. Rotten, putrefying, stomach-churning, it resembled the gassy smell from the decaying remains of the beached sea elephant they had come across some days earlier, multiplied a thousandfold.

He turned around, seeking to get his bearings by spying out the palm groves and the trampled debris of Mount Mahendra, then turned again a second time, until he was back where he had started, facing south. Only then did he understand that the entire landscape had been altered beyond recognition. The grassy patch where he had regained consciousness was in fact the spot where the palm grove had stood, the same bat-ridden grove in which he and Lakshman and the bear and vanar leaders had held their conferences. The grove was razed clear, every single tree uprooted or broken off close to the ground. Looking northwards, he saw that the entire shoreline with its waving masses of palms had been ravaged as well. Bare, denuded grassy patches lay open to the skies, covered with the broken remains of the trees that had once grown there.

And not all the broken remains were of trees.

Rama choked back a cry as he looked down the length of the beach. The sand was covered with corpses as far as the eye could see. It was no less than the aftermath of a battle. Vanars and bears lay alongside, upon and beneath the carcasses of a hundred different varieties of sea creatures. Some were merely fish of different sizes, shapes and colours; others were beasts he had no name for, had never known existed. They were the source of the stench. Their putrefaction was far quicker and more advanced than that of the mammalian corpses. With the sun beating down on the denuded shore, they were decomposing visibly.

Rama staggered across the ravaged beach, seeking out any who might still be alive. All he saw were the dead, shattered, broken, torn-open bodies of his faithful followers. His soldiers. These vanars and bears had dedicated their every waking minute to his work, had committed their very lives to his cause. They had been willing to venture across the most feared place of their legends – the great sea desert – to invade the most terrible place in all the known world: Lanka. They had been prepared to battle the demon races and face beings many times their size and strength, to wage war until they were all massacred, or until the other side yielded. They had chosen to live and die fighting for him. And now, instead of dying the deaths they deserved, as brave warriors on a battlefield, they had fallen before striking a single blow, struck down by a foe that had no soul, no motive, no cause.

It was not right.

He stood in the midst of that vast desolation, surrounded by more bodies than he could see at one glance, more death than he had seen before in his life, more casualties than were caused by most battles, and he knew that it was not right.

It was not right and he could not let it stand.

'*Varuna.*'

Lakshman almost dropped the stone he had been lifting off the body of a bear. The stone was one of several that had been separated from the bridge and washed ashore by the incoming tidal wave. He had not thought the bear could have survived such a weight falling upon it but he had seen the poor creature's hind paws twitch several times, and had thought that perhaps he or she might still be alive but unable to call for help. So he and a handful of vanars and bears, all ragged and each one injured in some way, had pitted their strength together to raise the slablike stone – only to find that the bear, poor thing, was quite dead, and the twitching had been caused by a sea creature thrashing in its last throes of life beneath the bear's corpse. It was the third such rescue attempt Lakshman had participated in, and all three had turned out thus. He was just about to lower the stone to the ground again when Rama's cry pierced the deathly still air. The vanar beside him *cheeka*-ed, and lost its grip on the stone. Lakshman's back strained as the extra burden shifted to him.

A moment later, bent over and straining with all his might, he released his hold on the stone at last, stood upright, and turned. His keen eyes easily found Rama's silhouette striding across the beach, backlit by a gloomy charcoal-grey sky. The air was still rent by the moans and whimpers of thousands of injured and dying creatures, and a veritable cloud of gulls was starting to collect overhead as well as on the fringes of the arc of destruction wrought by the tidal wave. The mindlessness of their cries, seeing the devastation below only in terms of their own selfish need for food, was a cruel requiem to the fallen dead. Lakshman made his way across the beach with grim purpose, his mood matched by the gloom that had fallen upon the world in the wake of the killing wave.

At the edge of the beach littered with countless corpses and the crawling bodies of grievously injured vanars and bears, Rama stood, staring out to sea, his profile windblown and dark, dark even against the stormy grey sky.

A corona of faintly blueish light seemed to shimmer around the outline of Rama's form, and Lakshman blinked, trying to clear his vision. When it persisted, he took it to be a trick of the erratic light. Rama's voice rose clear and strong, buoyed by a cold, relentless rage that Lakshman had not heard in his brother's voice for a long while.

'Varuna, lord of the ocean,' Rama called out, in a tone that was neither a shout nor a challenge, merely a command. 'Show yourself to me. I, Rama Chandra of Ayodhya, son of Dasaratha and grandson of Aja, of the line of Manu and Ikhswaku, going back to Surya himself . . . I command you, show yourself!'

Across the ravaged beach, and at the edges of the pathetically denuded land where thickets and groves had once stood, fallen vanars and bears began to stir. Still stunned by the disaster that had befallen them, still grieving for lost comrades and blood-kin, still reeling from the sheer scale of the calamity as well as its unexpectedness, nevertheless they all responded to the voice of their lord and leader. Perhaps some took comfort merely from knowing that Rama was alive and well, that he at least had survived the disaster. Others rallied their shaken morale around the unbowed strength of the mortal warrior.

All responded to the cold steel in Rama's voice, that tone

that could command armies and devastate entire realms, for the myth of Rama was already greater than the reality, and day by day the legends of his deeds grew, were embellished and enhanced with each repetition. Regaining their feet slowly, dragging injured limbs, shaking addled heads and gathering scattered wits, they shambled towards the mortal in whose service they had come here to the edge of the known world, to this place where death had decimated their beloved brethren without so much as a battle cry for warning. They shuffled, limped, gathering mutely around Rama, a funeral procession with no destination.

'Varuna,' Rama called, and this time Lakshman felt that the very sky responded, clouds overhead churning like curds in an earthen pot. Thunder growled somewhere far across the horizon, as if giants asleep beneath the ocean stirred uneasily at Rama's call. '*Show yourself!*'

And still the ocean remained empty.

Rama raised his hands to the sky in the universal gesture of supplication.

'If Varuna will not hear me, then you must, O Lord of Kailasa. Hear this plea of your servant and your devotee. I call upon you to mete out justice at this unholy act of cowardice. See for yourself, my lord Mahadev, what the ocean lord has wrought here upon this shore today. What destruction he has wreaked upon innocent lives. And at whose urging? Is this right, I ask? Is it meet that he be permitted to unleash such a heartless massacre on behalf of the Lord of Lanka? He must pay for this act of transgression! He must pay for it by the loss of his very power itself!'

The sky boiled, clouds churning, and the air around them all seemed to grow thick with fear. Lakshman stared at his brother in disbelief. Rama's aspect had turned so awful, he could barely look upon his own brother without blanching. There was an aura of power around him that was unmistakable now. That was no trick of the light, it was brahman shakti itself manifesting itself. He had seen it often enough before to know it for certain. Nor was Rama's anger mere mortal rage; it was a sacred fury. And the very elements were now responding to the righteousness of his appeal.

Rama went on, his voice the voice of death itself, his tone as cold as a sword's blade dipped into a glacial pool.

'Once, the lady Anasuya granted me a bow,' he said, in a voice that seemed to carry for yojanas, by what means Lakshman knew not. He listened, enraptured by the words, and by the force of Rama's will, speaking directly to the gods themselves. 'She gave me that great weapon that once belonged to the Lord of Vaikunta, great Vishnu. Use it as if it were your own, she said. And she granted me use of a single arrow as well. That missile that once belonged to the four-faced one who sees all, knows all, and *is* all: Brahma-dev. These weapons she gifted me, and told me to use them wisely in the service of dharma only, never for personal gain or revenge. Even when confronted with an army of fourteen thousand rakshasas in the wilds of Chitrakut, I did not use those weapons. I bade her take them back and keep them safe, so that I might not be tempted to use them for an unrighteous selfish cause.

'But today, seeing the heinous misuse of his power by Varuna and the grievous suffering of my innocent vanar and bear brethren, I call upon Anasuya the Wise and Beautiful to grant me use of those weapons again. If Varuna has done wrong, and my cause now is just and righteous, then in the name of dharma let me have the bow of Vishnu and the arrow of Brahma once again!'

He was answered by the twin forces of thunder and lightning. The one boomed deafeningly in the dusky sky, so as to make the assembled vanars and bears shudder and clap paws over eyes and ears in fright. The other snaked down like a living serpent of energy, to strike at a point on the sandy beach mere yards before Rama's feet. The impact blazed blindingly bright for an instant, searing Lakshman's mind with an imprint of the whole scene, as if the image were burned into the backs of his eyes themselves. The sky boiled and churned, and all grew so dark that Lakshman had to strain to keep sight of Rama. He saw his brother reach up at the instant the lightning struck, as if he *knew* it would strike, and when the flash had burned its brightest and faded away, leaving Lakshman dazed and dazzled, Rama stood bearing in one hand a great ancient bow and in the other a single arrow that gleamed and refracted light in diamantine hues, even though there was no light upon this dusk-enshrouded beach.

Rama raised the bow and arrow to the sky, and chanted a famous Sanskrit sloka praising the devas. Those of the assembled armies, bedraggled and shaken though they were, who knew the sloka in question chanted with him, their voices suffused with awe and wonder. Slowly the fear that had struck them senseless was being replaced by a fury that seemed to Lakshman to match Rama's own.

Then Rama took the bow and put the arrow to its string.

He directed the arrow out to sea.

Aiming it in the direction from which the killer wave had come.

'Varuna does not heed my calls,' he said. And his voice echoed the thunder itself now. 'Varuna is a coward who strikes at innocent vanars and bears and then scuttles back to his deep watery bed to hide. Varuna has performed an unrighteous act and aided the Lord of Lanka in executing a massacre that is against dharma itself. Therefore I shall have no sympathy for him as I use these weapons to unleash the wrath of the devas upon his marine world.'

Rama turned to look towards where Lakshman stood. His eyes found his brother at once, despite the dullness of the light and the hordes standing around him. Again Lakshman thought he saw the blue light of brahman shakti flash from Rama's pupils; but it could not be so – the power to channel the power of brahman had been lost to Rama after the unleashing of the

brahm-astra at Mithila. And yet Rama's voice, his form, his
entire aspect all blazed with the inner strength of divine shakti.

'Lakshman! My brother. Watch as I use the weapons of Brahma
and Vishnu to decimate the creatures of the ocean world just as
their lord decimated our noble followers. Today I shall declare
war upon this great ocean. I shall destroy all life within its
waters, render those waters poisonous and uninhabitable. And
after every creature has suffered and cried out in torment and
died a terrible painful death, I shall cause those waters to dry
up for ever. The ocean thinks that because I have respected his
territory, because we have laboured painstakingly these past
several days to build this bridge to span his vastness, we are
pathetic and puny. He mistakes our respect for weakness. Our
patience for pacifism. You know how patient I have been. How
I have sought peace rather than war. How I have used sweat
and muscle and hard work rather than resort to the easy power
of brahman shakti or even use of godly weapons. You have been
witness to my forbearance, Lakshman. Now bear witness to my
justice.'

And Rama raised the bow and unleashed the arrow. At that
very instant the sky turned utterly black, as if a light had been
snuffed out. In that preternatural darkness, the only thing left
visible was that single arrow, a yard's length of reed-thin wood
blazing white as lightning. It rent the darkness like a needle
piercing a finely woven black fabric, and Lakshman felt he
could *hear* its passage across the void. The arrow rose, arcing,
then fell far out to sea – or where the sea had been before the
world had turned black. It fell into the void and there was a
terrible tearing sound, as if the very fabric of the universe was
being ripped open.

8

The void was ablaze.

The darkness that had extinguished the view of the ocean was replaced by the illumination of numerous fires . . . countless fires.

Even though it had been barely noon when the tidal wave had struck, the sky was now pitch dark. Glancing up, Lakshman could see lightning webbing the cloud-enshrouded sky, like the flicking tongues of a hundred invisible serpents.

Below, in the place where a sunlit ocean had lain not long before, there was now a burning sea.

The armies of vanars and bears, reassembled to watch Rama wreak his ire upon the ocean lord, gasped with astonishment. They had never seen such shakti unleashed, such phenomena revealed. As Lakshman stared at the ocean, at the unnaturally shrouded and benighted sky, he realised that neither had he. Certainly, he had seen some amazing sights in the past fourteen years, but nothing quite like this.

Like some great city on a vast plain, torched by an invading army, some immeasurably vast metropolis sprawled across countless yojanas, the kingdom of the sea lord was burning in patches and pockets. Sea creatures threw themselves up out of the waters, seeking to escape the supernatural fire that scorched and charred them below, only to fall back helplessly, screaming their exotic cries and wails. Enormous sea elephants, frenzied white jagged-toothed predators, rainbow-hued fish of varied sizes, sea serpents,

fleshy tentacled creatures, orange-shelled crustaceans with claws
and feelers, all thrashed and churned in agony, caught in the many
pockets of divine fire that blazed phosphorescently, turning the
grey-blue ocean white as salt where it worked its cruel magic. He
saw one great charcoal-grey beast rise up, water pluming from a
spout-hole on the top of its head, wailing its distress. Then it fell
back and was engulfed by a pocket of greedy white flame.

Lakshman looked around in disbelief, sweeping the sea from
end to end, turning almost fully to either side to take in the
sheer scale of the spectacle unfolding before him. For as far as
his eyes could see, from one extreme to the other, from the
point nearest the shore to the farthest line of the horizon, the
ocean was afire.

Could all this be the work of one arrow? A single stick of wood?
But of course.

It was the arrow of Brahma. Fired from the bow of Vishnu.

These were dev-astras. Weapons of the gods. Once, he had
been given the power to wield such weapons too. He had felt
the unspeakable potency of their unleashing, the throbbing in
every cell and fibre of his being, the sheer intimacy that he
shared with the force of existence itself when he unleashed those
astras. He had felt as if he could accomplish anything, destroy
anyone, wreak any vengeance imaginable.

He believed. The sight before his eyes was no illusion. It was
the wrath of the devas unleashed upon the ocean as punishment for misusing its power in the service of the Lord of Lanka.

'*Varuna!*' Rama called again, and this time his voice was so
terrible, even his own armies shrank away from him. '*For the
last time, show yourself. Or reap the harvest of your misdeed!*'

And he raised the arrow of Brahma once more to the bow,
directing it at the tormented ocean. For no matter how many
times it was fired, the arrow would always reappear magically
in the sender's hand in an instant. This Lakshman knew without
being told, for it was the way of such dev-astras to be eternally
replenished.

Rama pulled back upon the arrow, stretching the cord of the bow to its limit. Even from where he stood, several yards distant, Lakshman could feel the shakti of the bow vibrating in the air. The energy winding up, thrumming with power, preparing to unleash another miasma of destruction. He looked out upon the blazing ocean and the torment of the sea denizens and almost felt sympathy for their plight. If a single loosing of the celestial arrow could wreak such havoc, what would a second loosing accomplish? Or three, or four, or more? Truly, it would be as Rama had threatened: the ocean world itself would be rendered desolate and devastated, uninhabitable for aeons to come.

At the very last instant before Rama was about to loose the arrow a second time, a great commotion occurred far out to sea. The waters boiled and seethed, great gouts exploding and splashing this way and that. The dying creatures around that spot thrashed and struggled pitifully to leave the region.

Then, with an immense rending sound, as if a mountain were being torn apart rather than an ocean split, a great mass rose up out of the ocean waters.

It rose and rose, filling the benighted sky with its hulking shape. Then it stopped rising, and stood, shaking.

Water cascaded from its form, splashing back into the sea. There were patches where it was afire too, white flames licking greedily at its upper torso and limbs, for they could not be called a chest and arms. Great sea serpents, their undulating lengths burnished gold, coiled around the being's limbs and body, hissing and screaming, for they too were tormented by the celestial flames ignited by Brahma's arrow. The body of the sea lord shimmered and shone with dazzling intensity, like a rainbow that could be seen and yet not seen wholly. It was smooth as an emerald and as translucent. It seemed to be clad in a variety of weeds such as might be found at the bottom of a river or ocean, except that they were brackish red rather than mulchy green. A colourful vine adorned its upper torso, like a garland of flowers. But the vine-garland moved, and Lakshman saw that it was also a variety of sea serpent, fat and thick with age and excess, like a favoured pet. Its multiple eyes glimmered like glowing coals in a bed of mud.

The sea lord himself was somewhat masculine in aspect, but Lakshman felt instinctively that to attribute mortal masculinity – or feminity – to such a being was impossible. It was more anima than creature. A being composed more of water and weed than blood and flesh. Its aspect was terrible to behold, like that of any deva manifesting itself. The assembled vanars and bears on the shore stared up, swaying slowly like drunken beings, mesmerised by the sight. They would have fled had it not been their own lord who had called upon the ocean lord to manifest itself.

Lakshman looked towards Rama and saw that he still held the arrow strung in the bow, the cord as tightly wound. Only a very faint tremble in Rama's shoulder and arm muscles betrayed the strain of holding that great weapon for so many moments. Lakshman could hardly imagine the strength that must be involved. And still Rama held it, pointing it directly at the top of the form of the being that stood towering above him in the blazing ocean.

'Varuna. So you deign to make yourself manifest at last. Speak then. Or suffer the effect of a second assault from this celestial arrow.'

The sea lord moved forward in such a manner that Lakshman almost cried out to warn Rama. Water sloshed before his shell-encrusted lower limbs. Lakshman opened his mouth to shout a warning, then watched in amazement as the sea lord bowed the top of his head and joined two of his many serpentine limbs in a manner that almost resembled a namaskaram. When he spoke, his voice was the voice of a thousand sea elephants, wailing and moaning and trumpeting their distress; it was the voice of water itself, gurgling and splashing and thundering like waves upon a rocky shore.

'Rama,' he said. 'I am but a force of nature. Like the sky, the earth, the wind . . . like fire. I am water itself made manifest. And

I too have my own nature. Just as fire will burn flesh that is put into it, so also must I embrace and engulf any thing that enters my body, swallowing it whole and digesting it slowly, more slowly than fire, yet much faster than earth, or wind, or sky.'

Rama lowered the bow slightly, loosening his grip upon the cord. Yet, Lakshman noted, he did not put the bow down, or release the arrow from the cord yet. He kept it lowered by his side, ready to be deployed again at a moment's desire.

'Varuna,' Rama said quietly, though that quiet tone somehow carried to the farthest vanar or bear in the great throng behind him. 'Do not justify your misdeeds as part of your nature. What you did earlier, when you unleashed that tidal wave of destruction upon my followers, that was no force of nature. It was the work of Asura sorcery. You obeyed the diktat of Ravana, Lord of Lanka, and in doing so you have brought my wrath upon yourself. You have already seen what I can accomplish with the loosing of this arrow but a single time. Tell me one reason why I should not unleash it again, and yet again, and again, until I have destroyed every last vestige of life in your vast holdings. Tell me why I should not wipe out the ocean itself from this world.'

Something thrashed in the ocean behind Varuna. Lakshman looked and made out an appendage like the fins that served fish as tails and feet both. Varuna's upper body trembled as well, and the serpents entwined around the sea lord's body writhed and hissed desperately. Even the ancient one coiled around Varuna's neck raised its thick head slowly, with great effort, and gazed upon Rama with its myriad eyes. Lakshman thought he could even guess what that ancient being must be thinking: who is this mortal who threatens my lord himself with extinction? What favour does he have with the devas that he possesses the shakti to unleash such destruction?

Almost as if sensing Lakshman's thoughts, the ancient one turned its head slightly, looking at him now. He felt a force probe his mind, alien tendrils of energy penetrating to his innermost thoughts. It was no less intrusive than if a real flesh-and-blood sea serpent had coiled its slippery length around his limbs and bared its venomous fangs at his face. He could almost smell the breath of the ancient serpent upon his face, the stench of the deepest oceans, of rotten fish that it took a thousand years to digest, of things he had no name for, nor words to describe.

Who? asked the ancient one directly to his mind. Just that one question, blindly probing, demanding with the arrogance of one whose power and wisdom were so great it had never needed to explain itself. *WHO?*

Rama, he heard himself respond defiantly, in the caverns of his mind. *He is Rama, dharma incarnate. And I am his brother Lakshmana. Underestimate us at your own peril.*

He felt the ancient one observe him for an instant more, then turn its head again to look at Rama once again. Lakshman sensed the passing of some wordless communication between it and Varuna. After a moment, when the sea lord spoke again, he sounded chastised.

'Rama, what you say is true. In your present state, you are omniscient. There is no use my denying anything to you. I did indeed obey the command of the Lord of Lanka and executed his will. I sent the wave to destroy your soldiers and your bridge. But I had no choice. I was powerless to disobey the king of rakshasas. For in another age he invaded the realms of the devas and defeated them in open battle. His Asura armies wreaked unspeakable horrors upon the devas and the other denizens of the heavenly realms. They were prepared to offer him anything to rid themselves of his foul presence. In return for leaving those realms, he secured several boons, including the services of many devas themselves. My service to him was part of that war-bond. When he commanded me, I had no choice but to fulfil his desire. I see now that I did wrong, that I have caused grievous harm to your people, and to your bridge, which now lies broken. I assure you, now that my bond to Ravana is fulfilled, he has no more power over me. I shall not cause another wave to rise. I will take no more steps to cause you harm.'

Rama laughed shortly. Lakshman frowned. He had heard that laugh before, when Rama had confronted the giantess Tataka in the wilds of Bhayanak-van, fourteen years ago. But Rama had been infused with the power of the maha-mantras Bala and Atibala then, an indestructible machine driven by the universal force of brahman shakti. How could he have regained that shakti?

'You will not dare harm me now, Varuna. For I wield the weapons of Vishnu and Brahma that can cause the destruction of your entire realm and all species that dwell within it. Do not offer me irrelevant assurances. Tell me instead why I should not punish you for your heinous massacre of my innocent followers. Why should I stay my hand? Answer me well, and wisely, lord of the seas, or you will soon have no power to form words at all!'

And Rama raised the bow once again, aiming it directly at Varuna himself.

Lakshman saw the ancient serpent's myriad eyes gleam darkly as it stared at the shocking impudence of this mortal. Varuna himself took a step back, the ocean sloshing like water in an arghya bowl. His followers screamed and wailed and thrashed, seeking to swim away from him, to distance themselves from the destruction that would certainly come if Rama loosed the arrow a second time.

'Pray hear my plea,' Varuna said, and his watery voice trembled audibly. 'Do not loose your arrow upon me, good Rama. I am repentant for my transgression. I have committed great wrong by taking the lives of your followers and destroying your bridge.'

'Mere apologies will not restore their lives, nor rebuild my bridge!' Rama shouted. Thunder echoed him, crashing in the skies above. Lightning flashed, striking the body of the ocean lord in three separate spots. Small fires burst out at each of the three places; one stroke of lightning cut a serpent in half, and both halves fell writhing, splashing into the ocean. 'You must do better than that, ocean lord! You must pay the price for your mistake!'

'Rama,' Varuna pleaded, 'I beseech you. Do not loose your arrow. It will destroy all ocean life on this mortal realm. It will end the lineage of countless species for all time. The very future of this realm will be altered, for the oceans are integral to the survival and sustenance of the realm itself, and of the other species that inhabit it, including your own mortal fellows.'

'You did not care how many vanars or bears or mortals you killed when you obeyed Ravana's order and unleashed your wave,' Rama replied. 'Where was your sympathy for living things then, Varuna? Why should you expect me to care now?'

'Wait, Rama!' Varuna cried. 'Wait but a moment! I will make amends for my wrongdoing. I will atone for it by aiding you in your mission. I have offended you grievously by acting on behalf of the Lord of Lanka. I did so under duress and unwillingly. Now I will act on your behalf and do ten times more for you than I did for him. I will be as your servant, and serve you loyally, and do your bidding. I will do so joyously and willingly. My powers are great. Use them. Use them to undo the destruction wrought by Ravana's diktat to me. Use the very same powers against him!'

At these words Rama cocked his head slowly to one side, deliberating. The armies of vanars and bears waited for his answer with bated breath. The ocean lord waited. The denizens of the sea waited. The sky, the clouds, the wind, the earth all waited.

After a long moment Rama lowered his bow and released the arrow from the cord.

9

Hanuman regained consciousness to find himself lying on an immense grey bed. The sun was shining in the sky again, wisps of clouds drifted lazily overhead, and high above the silhouette of a flock of birds resembled the shape of a mountain peak turned sideways. He sat up, and found himself reduced to his normal vanar size. He looked around, trying to get his bearings. How long had he been unconscious? Where was he now? What had happened when the wave struck? Rama! Lakshman! His lords Sugreeva and Angad!

~be calm land-being your friends are safe and well~

He started, unable to discern what being had spoken to him and by what means. The words seemed to enter into his mind directly without being uttered as sounds to be captured by his organs of hearing. Yet he did not feel alarmed, for the voice, if it could be called that, seemed benign and benevolent, much like a wise, ancient silverback elder of his own race.

~i am called greyback and it is upon my back that you are resting~

He looked down. And realised that the immense grey bed he was lying upon was in fact a living being. He recalled the great sea elephants he had seen in the ocean, spouting high plumes of water and calling out to each other in strange high-pitched tones. This was one of them, then. Still, he was cautious and suspicious. The lord of Asuras had many minions, and they could assume many forms and avatars.

'Where am I? Where is my lord Rama, and all my comrades?'

~you will see them very soon ~at the great rama chandra's command, my lord varuna asked me to bear you aloft and keep you here in the event that ravana attempts another assault upon your people ~rama wishes you to remain here until he orders otherwise~

At the mention of Rama, Hanuman allowed himself to relax somewhat. There was something in Greyback's tone that made him want to believe the sea beast's mind-speech.

'Then it was Ravana who unleashed the wave upon us?' Hanuman said angrily, clenching his fists and baring his teeth. 'The craven. To use Asura shakti to kill from afar instead of daring to face my lord in person. Only a coward would wreak havoc thus, without staining his hands with the blood of his foes.'

~indeed ~and for this same reason your lord rama was infuriated beyond measure ~he resorted to celestial weaponry and was about to wreak havoc upon the oceans as chastisement for killing so many of his followers~

Hanuman felt the great grey-backed being shudder, its entire body rippling as it trembled in fear of Rama's wrath. He felt his own heart shudder as well, not in fear of Rama but in empathy for his fellows. *Killing so many* . . . 'My people are in distress then,' he cried aloud. 'They are in need of my help. I must go to their aid at once.'

~ease your heart my friend ~i understand your pain ~ but there is nothing you can do now~

And in the same fashion, speaking directly to his mind, the ocean being explained to him all that had transpired since the arrival of the devastating wave.

Hanuman's heart ached to think of all those fallen comrades. How could he have lain unconscious when his fellows needed his help? He felt wretched and would have expanded himself and leaped off Greyback to fly back to the mainland shore at that very instant. But the wise sea creature reassured him that his efforts had saved countless lives, and that after taking the brunt of the great wave on his own person, it had been necessary for him to rest and recover his strength. Now there was no need for him to fly to the shore.

'But my lord will have need of me,' he protested. 'I am well enough now; I must go to Rama at once and do what I can to repair the broken bridge. We have lost precious time already, and must redouble our efforts if we are to reach Lanka and avenge my lady Sita's dishonour.'

~my brave and big-hearted friend ~go then fly up as high as you will and see for yourself ~see for yourself what your lord rama has achieved through showing mercy to lord varuna and us ocean denizens ~see how we are serving your lord's purpose in exchange for his sparing our lives and the ocean world~

Hanuman needed no further encouragement. He took a deep breath and expanded himself. As he grew, he crouched down and used the back of the grey being to launch himself up into the air. Had he waited too long and grown too large, he feared that he might injure Greyback with his weight and force. Even so, he felt the sea creature's immense body dip briefly beneath the surface and the ocean waters slosh noisily in his wake, then he was aloft and rising rapidly, up past the clouds and the high-flying flocks of birds – who squawked and broke their neat formation to disperse, protesting angrily – until he was high enough to see for yojanas in every direction. He looked towards the mainland, heart clenching at what he might witness.

And he saw an amazing sight.

Rama's bridge was indeed broken. Dislocated by the tsunami wave, the great rocks that he and his compatriots had laboured so long and hard, and at such terrible cost, to drag and drop into place were dispersed, fallen into the ocean, tumbled higgledy-piggledy here and there. It would be impossible for the vanars and bears to dive into the water and raise them up again. They would have to start anew, bringing new boulders and rebuilding the bridge almost from the start. It would be a daunting, near-impossible task.

But there was no need to do it.

For a new bridge had been constructed. A bridge of grey beings like the one which had borne Hanuman aloft just now lined up in the ocean from the mainland shore all the way to the spot where Hanuman's being was still floating and spouting water from the breathing hole in its head, and beyond, all the way to Lanka. Most were submerged beneath the surface of the water, waiting to be told to rise. But from his high vantage point in the sky, wafted by a gentle sea breeze, they looked like a great grey causeway across the ocean, as solid as any bridge of rock or wood. From time to time one of them would raise its head slightly and spout a fountain of water high into the air, issuing a deep, reverberating call that was answered by many other greybacks along the long line.

It was an astonishing, beautiful sight.

As he hovered, marvelling at this miracle of nature, Hanuman heard the creature on whose back he had been resting issue a high tone almost too intense for mortal ears to catch. To his vanar ears, familiar only with creatures of the jungle and the plains, the sound resembled the lowing of an elephant leader to its tribe. The long line of greybacks lowed back. Somehow he could follow the broad gist of their communication, if not every subtle nuance. There were cows and bulls among them, he understood then, just like among the warm-blooded creatures on land, and even young ones and elderly ones, although the eldest were of an age far greater than any vanar could ever hope to live . . . And the eldest, wisest and greatest of them all was the cow who had held him aloft, and from the tone of their response, he could tell that the great line of greybacks revered her and obeyed her every wish. She was the chief of the ocean tribe.

On the great matriarch's order, the entire line of greybacks elevated themselves out of the water, just high enough to make a natural bridge some two yards above the level of the ocean, a platform for vanars and bears and his lords to walk upon and cross as safely and comfortably as a rock bridge – nay, much more safely and comfortably, for unlike rocks, the backs of these creatures were smooth and flat, creating a perfect natural bridge all the way to Lanka.

Lakshman watched as the vanar forces lined up in an orderly fashion, their usual exuberance tempered somewhat by the ravages of the tidal wave and the loss of their fellows. Angad and the generals of the various armies were organising them into a queue of two abreast, for though the bridge of greybacks was wide and flat enough to make crossing easy, it was not wide enough for the armies to simply race across pell-mell, as they were clearly keen to do in their newfound anger. The bear chiefs were grunting and squealing at their forces to get them to form a similar queue.

A row of northern bears with their characteristic light-hued fur, almost silvery white in the sunlight, shambled to the fore, jostling past their fellows to forcibly make a third row, even though they knew quite well that the command had called for only two bears and two vanars to cross at one time. Lakshman succinctly but grimly spelled out to the chief of the northern bears the likely consequences of disobedience. The bear glowered down at him, his snarling jaws dripping threads of spittle, then turned and raised his head, issuing great grunting commands to his tribe-fellows. With lowing moans of protest they all turned and shuffled after him to the back of the long queue, stretching now far beyond the ragged line of debris that marked where the trees had stood before the wave struck.

Lakshman intervened in one or two other similar instances where vanars or bears who had lost companions to the killer wave were somewhat overeager to cross and have first strike at the rakshasa hordes, but on neither occasion did he have to use force. Simmering though their rage was at the unfair misuse of natural elements to strike down unsuspecting warriors, they knew better than to transfer that rage to the very mortal leaders who would grant them the revenge they now sought. After a few more carefully spoken stern commands and crisp orders passed down the lines, the vanars and bears subsided into an orderly routine, stepping down the beach in pairs. Lakshman turned and noted that the first line of four soldiers – two vanars and two bears abreast – was at the point where the first grey-back floated in the water, waiting. The ocean lord had stilled the waves nearest to the shore to allow the armies to board the bridge without mishap. Although Varuna was no longer in sight – Lakshman suspected that the deva could not maintain that physical form for long – his presence was palpable, keeping the elements of the sea and its environs tightly leashed and wholly benign to Rama's forces.

Rama.

Lakshman turned and sought out his brother. There he was, at the high northern end of the beach, conferring with Jambavan and Sugreeva and the other elder bears and vanars. His war council. He had asked Lakshman to join them too but Lakshman had answered gruffly that he would first oversee the preparations for the crossing. Rama had nodded without questioning him further, but Lakshman had seen him glance briefly in his direction as he walked away, his eyes seeing all, noting everything. Nothing escaped Rama's attention. Not even at a time like this. Certainly not the barely restrained resentment his brother was harbouring.

Lakshman clenched both his fists then released them along with an exhalation of breath, trying to rid himself of that very resentment. It was futile. He would have to have words with Rama. He needed to know certain things, to hear the answers to the questions that were eating him alive. He knew that this was not the time to pose these questions, to demand Rama's attention for even a brief moment, but he also knew that he could not concentrate on his duties until he had confronted his brother and received those answers to his fullest satisfaction.

Better then to do it now and get it over with.

He walked towards the knoll upon which Rama and his councillors were gathered. They were looking at the sand, where one of the vanar generals had been drawing lines and arrows to indicate strategy. It was Satabali. The elder vanar was crouched, pointing with a stick to various points on a crude map of what could only be Lanka, a rough indication of what they presumed to be the island-kingdom's layout. The other vanar generals, Nila, Susena and Vinata, crouched around the map while Angad stood by with a stick of his own and a frown marring his golden-furred features. Rama, Sugreeva and Jamabavan stood facing the map, listening carefully. Kambunara and the other bear generals were standing behind and around them, tall enough to be able to see over the heads of the vanars easily.

Lakshman spared the map a glance, walking around the knot of vanars and bears. He listened to Satabali's laboriously detailed war plan as he walked. It was a good plan, not unlike classic siege-breaking strategies that mortals also used, and which Lakshman and his brothers had studied back in Ayodhya during the military part of their education. But Lakshman could easily see the flaw in the plan, and knew that Rama saw it too; indeed, Rama must have seen the flaw within moments of Satabali starting to expound it, yet he had listened these past moments and was listening still, patiently and with evident interest. Lakshman did not understand how his brother could be so patient with what was clearly an irrelevant course of action. There was no point in discussing a siege-breaking strategy because there would be no siege. He restrained the urge to interrupt the elderly vanar in his droning, meticulous explanation, and stopped at the far end of the circle from Rama.

Now he could look across the map and see Rama directly, face to face.

Rama continued to listen intently to Satabali's explanation. Finally the general wound down and his flow of words petered out. He stood erect, the stick clutched by his side, like the military veteran he was, awaiting his commander's response to his suggestions.

Rama spoke a few well-chosen words of praise and admiration for the plan, and for Satabali's astuteness in applying it to the current scenario. He also thanked the other vanar and bear generals for laying out their excellent suggestions, and promised that he would take all their ideas into consideration when planning the actual assault on Lanka. He finished by saying, 'We shall make our final decision once we are on the far side of the ocean and have reviewed the lie of the land.'

The generals nodded approvingly, and Rama turned his attention to Lakshman. Although Lakshman knew that his brother had been aware of him from the very instant he had stepped into his field of view, if not before, it was only now that Rama permitted himself to raise his eyes and look directly at him. 'And now my brother would have words with me. If you will grant us a few moments in private . . .'

'We shall go and prepare for the crossing, Lord Rama. But we shall await your command to begin,' Sugreeva said. The vanar king looked wan and weary, his injuries from the wave no doubt adding to his age and ailing health. Still he bore himself proudly as he walked stiffly with his son and the others towards the quadruple lines snaking up the beach.

Lakshman walked slowly around the map, keeping his eyes on the sketch of Lanka. 'I apologise if I am distracting you at this crucial time, Rama,' he said softly.

Rama shook his head. 'You have nothing to apologise for. You are my brother. We command this army, this campaign, together. Whatever you have to say is not a distraction, it is a necessity. Speak your mind, Lakshman, my brother.'

Lakshman stopped and looked up at Rama. Suddenly, without warning, the anger he had been suppressing the past several hours flared into flame. He fought to restrain it, but it was hard not to raise his voice and howl his anguish. When at last he spoke, his voice was pitched evenly, just loud enough to be heard above the inevitable background sound of a million-plus vanars and bears jostling and preparing for the great crossing. But he could hear the pain and confusion in his own tone, and knew that Rama heard every nuance as well.

'Why, Rama?' he asked. 'Why did you do it? Why did you betray Sita and me and yourself? Why did you deceive us all these years?'

Rama regarded Lakshman calmly. He had expected this very outburst from his brother. It was testimony to Lakshman's age and maturity that he had waited this long to broach the topic. Now he could wait no longer. It would do no good to suggest to him, however gently, that they should speak of this later, that there was a great deal of arduous work ahead, or that it would not help the vanars and bears to see their mortal devas – for, like it or not, they now regarded himself and Lakshman as nothing less than demigods or avatars – bickering thus. He knew his brother well enough to know that Lakshman could not be persuaded to wait. Best to deal with this quickly and be done with it.

'Lakshman,' he said gently, 'I understand your ire. You wonder how I was able to summon the shakti to call up Varuna-deva, and challenge him with annihilation. That is what troubles you, is it not? How did I come by such power? For after unleashing the brahm-astra at Mithila, to repel the Asura armies of Ravana, both you and I were divested of the maha-shakti of Bala and Atibala which Brahmarishi Vishwamitra had infused into us, as well as the several dev-astras he imparted to us. Indeed, we were denuded of all brahman shakti for ever. For that was the heavy price we had to pay for unleashing the ultimate weapon of all, the weapon of mighty Brahma the Creator. So how was it that today, long years after that divestment at Mithila, I was able to summon up such shakti as would compel the lord of the oceans himself to take physical form and show himself to me, and enable me threaten his vastness with destruction on a scale so terrible that it would be beyond even his divine powers to prevent? This is the question that burns within your breast, is it not? How was it that I was able to summon up such great power at will today, when Brahmarishi Vishwamitra said quite explicitly that we would not be able to do so for the rest of our mortal lives?'

Lakshman's face, drawn and angular from years of hard forest living, stared back at him with blazing eyes. 'Yes, Rama. That is the *first* question that I wish to hear answered. How? How did you come by such immense shakti?'

Rama was about to answer when Lakshman held up his hand.

'No, brother.' He shook his head grimly. 'Do not speak just yet. For I fear that once your words flow, they will sweep away all my objections the way the Sarayu in spate carries away a sapling torn from its roots. Allow me to speak a few moments longer. You have already asked my question for me. Now allow me, if you will, to attempt to voice your answer.'

Rama inclined his head in acquiescence.

Lakshman went on. 'The answer that I propose, for I have thought this over carefully these past hours as the ocean lord's great greybacks arranged themselves to form the bridge that awaits our armies . . . the answer I propose to my own question is itself a question. Bear with me as I speak my thoughts aloud, for I have not your skill at wordcraft, my older and wiser brother.' He paused, staring out at the horizon for a moment before going on. 'At first, when I saw you unleash such great power, not just shakti but *maha*-shakti, I was dumbstruck. I could not believe my eyes. Then, when I saw you wield that celestial bow and arrow, I recalled their shaping and form at once.'

Rama nodded. Weaponry had always been Lakshman's strong point; even as a youth he had been able to point out subtle differences in the crafting of weapons and gauge the possible effect those could make to the eventual deployment. And the celestial bow and arrow he spoke of were truly distinctive – their like did not exist anywhere else in the universe. Rama could imagine the shock Lakshman must have felt on seeing Rama wield those great weapons unexpectedly.

Lakshman turned to look at him, his eyes penetrating, accusing. 'I knew immediately where I had seen those weapons before. Which raised the question in my mind . . . nay, not a question, but a conjecture, a theory . . . Could it be possible, my brother – and correct me if I err – could it be possible that you have been in possession of this maha-shakti all along? That it was in fact given to you by the sage Anasuya fourteen long years ago, in the wilderness of Chitrakut? At the very beginning of our exile, when we encountered her in the guise of an old low-caste woman and you gladly shared her half-bitten berries with her, unwittingly earning her love and admiration and passing the test she had devised to judge you by? Could it be that the gifts she rendered unto you as a reward for your passing her test, that celestially endowed bow of Vishnu and the arrow of Shiva, those weapons which you then claimed to have returned to her, and which you refused to use against the hordes of rakshasas in Chitrakut who were hellbent on destroying us to avenge the alleged humiliation we inflicted upon their sister Supanakha the seductress . . . could it be that you never truly returned those weapons at all? That they remained with you all this while, invisible, suspended in the celestial realm beyond the vision or reach of any physical being yet accessible to you at any instant through a mere exertion of your will? That these weapons, which all these assembled armies,' sweeping his arm to take in the vanars and bears lined up for miles along the shoreline, 'and I saw you use but a few hours ago, these weapons of divine shakti, were within your reach all these years?'

Rama knew that the more he resisted Lakshman's anger, the

more he would fuel it, just as a strong wind only whips a forest fire into greater ferocity. So he replied quietly, simply, 'Yes. Everything you say is true.'

Lakshman stared at him a moment longer. Then he turned away and looked up at the sky, then out to sea, then down at the sea. He started to turn away, as if he would walk down the length of the beach, then stopped and turned back. He shook his head, in bewilderment and in sorrow – for Rama could see that Lakshman took this to be a betrayal of sorts, a betrayal of the close bond that existed between them, of the immutable trust they had for each other. When he spoke, his voice had no anger in it any more, only sorrow and hurt. 'Why, Rama? Why did you not confide in me back at Chitrakut? Why did you keep this a secret from me for these fourteen long years? All those battles and conflicts, all those endless days and nights spent crawling around on our bellies in the dank wilderness, watching our fellows slaughtered by hideous fiends, never knowing a moment's rest, a night's sleep, a day's peace, watching children – mere babes, some – die needlessly, uselessly . . . Why? We could have decimated the rakshasas . . . wiped them out, and passed the years of our exile in lazy indolence.' A spark of memory flashed in his eyes, causing him to raise his voice slightly, angrily. 'We could have saved Sita! She would not be in Ravana's clutches today. Nor would we have had to raise this army and suffer this new set of tortuous challenges, building a bridge, crossing the ocean, waging war with the entire rakshasa race. We would still be in peaceful Panchvati, passing the last of our days in blissful harmony with the creatures of the forest, and in a few weeks, days barely now, we would be on our way home to Ayodhya. None of this needed to have happened. It could all have been prevented. You had the power, Rama. You had it in the palm of your hands. You possessed such great, immense maha-shakti, and yet you concealed it from me. From Sita even. From everyone. And instead of sparing us all that fighting, those many battles, and now this war that lies ahead, you chose to keep this a secret. Why, Rama? Why did you let us undergo all this suffering when it could have been prevented?'

Rama's heart ached to see his brother's anguish. He wanted to embrace Lakshman, to put his heart against his heart and calm his anger, soothe his pain. He wanted to do as he had done when they were little children, striplings, and he would simply hug Lakshman and hold him until his tears ceased, when words had not been needed to explain things, and their eyes had voiced the feelings that language could never transport. But such was the burden of adulthood, of maturity, that he was compelled to attempt to use that very inconsistent mode of communication to convey his reasons to Lakshman, to put those inexpressible emotions into clumsy words, and try to convey a lifetime of love in a few quick utterances of sounds and pauses. Language was not invented to convey such things, and still language was the only mode he could use.

'Brother,' he said softly, 'you know that I love you more than life itself. You are not merely my brother but my soul brother, half-moon to my own half-moon, without whom I am no more complete than day can be complete without the sun, nor night without the stars. I would sooner hurt myself than hurt you.'

Lakshman looked at him, tears welling up in his eyes, yet none spilling. He exhaled and said sadly, 'And yet you did hurt me. You lied to me. You betrayed me.'

'No! I never lied. I told you something that day in Chitrakut, fourteen years ago, at the river, when we were making our stand together against the hordes who were seeking to cross, led by Khara and Dushana at the time, if you recall.'

Lakshman snorted. 'Of course I recall. I recall it by the scars on my body, and by the scars on your own self. I recall it because had Ratnakara and the other bandits and outlaws come when they did, we would have been overwhelmed by the sheer numbers of the enemy. And now I shall recall it always as the fight we fought even though we did not need to, but were compelled to because you deceived me, by not using your celestial gifts, and by lying to me that you did not have them any more.'

'Then you must recall that I did not lie to you, Lakshman. I told you then that those weapons were given to me strictly for use in enforcing dharma. Not for personal protection or whim. I told you these things then. Perhaps I did not emphasise that as and when the day came that I was called upon to enforce dharma, those weapons would be made available to me again. In that conflict, we were weaponless. I could no more resort to those weapons for that battle, or any of the battles in the wilderness during our years of exile, than I could summon the armies of the Kosala nation to aid us. Surely you understand that?'

'I understand that you had access to a means that could have saved untold bloodshed, life-loss and suffering. Yet you chose not to resort to those means.'

'For the sake of dharma, I could not!' Rama forced his voice to remain even, hard though it was. 'That was a personal fight for personal reasons. You and I attacked Supanakha and mutilated her. For a rakshasi of her breed, it was a greater humiliation than death itself. She called upon her brethren to avenge her humiliation. There was no law of dharma to defend or uphold. It was merely a disagreement between two parties acting for their own selfish reasons.'

'Selfish? Personal? If that was selfish and personal, then what was it that made today's display an act of dharma? If you could not use it to defend us against the hordes in Chitrakut and Janasthana, then why did you use it today?'

'Because it was not to protect myself or my loved ones. It was to protect these hundreds of thousands of innocent vanars and bears, to defend them against a force too great for them to face and survive. Varuna-deva violated dharma by using his immense shakti to attack these innocents. Had he only sunk the bridge, perhaps it would have been acceptable. But by taking innocent lives . . . Why do you shake your head, Lakshman? Do you not see the point I am trying to make?'

'How is it dharma to protect these vanars and bears . . . these *innocent* vanars and bears who have come knowingly and wilfully to wage war upon the rakshasa race . . . but not to protect those innocent outlaws who stood by us at Janasthana and died fighting the same race of rakshasas?'

Rama sighed. 'Because the cause these armies are assembled here to fight today is a struggle to uphold dharma, whereas our cause back in Janasthana was merely our personal survival.'

Lakshman shook his head. 'I do not follow you, Rama. If we are upholders of dharma, if we and our followers are soldiers of dharma, then even our personal survival is righteous under dharma, is it not?'

Rama said slowly, 'It is our duty to defend dharma. It is not dharma's task to defend us.' He added sadly, 'I agree, it is a hard bargain. But it is the one we swore to uphold from the moment we were born kshatriyas.'

Lakshman was silent a long moment. He looked out to sea, the wind rippling his matted hair, loosed from its usual knotted pile and set free by his exertions after the striking of the wave. A number of cuts and bruises marked where he had been scored or scraped, some crusted with dried blood. His face was as stony as the statue of Manu the Lawmaker, forebear of the Ikshwaku dynasty, back in the great hall at Ayodhya. Some day, Rama thought, Lakshman's likeness would be carved into a statue as well, and placed among those effigies of their ancestors. He would ask the stone-carver to attempt to capture this expression, this look of great strength and great frustration. For that was Lakshman: a brother compelled to leave his wife, his mother, his kingdom, everything he loved and possessed, and to go into exile for fourteen long, hard years in the wilderness, and to fight endless wars against hideous beasts. This was the life he had endured for Rama's sake. And yet all this while Rama had had to artfully conceal from him the truth about the celestial weapons, for had Lakshman known that he still possessed them, he would have demanded that Rama use them

– nay, beseeched him, even. And it would have torn Rama's heart to refuse him. As it tore his heart now to see Lakshman accept even this revelation that his brother had kept this great secret from him for nigh on fourteen years, for Lakshman had accepted it now, he saw, accepted and absorbed it, and was preparing himself to continue being the brother he always was: loyal, and unshakeable as a rock.

Lakshman turned to him at last, his eyes reflecting the glacial depths of the Sarayu in winter, when great spears of ice floated downriver from the Himalayan heights and gnashed and crashed their way past the rolling hills around Ayodhya. He folded his hands and inclined his head to Rama. 'Rama, you did as you saw fit. You upheld dharma, as you always do. How can I find fault with you when you did nothing wrong? I apologise for questioning your motives. Please forgive my impudence. I shall go and see to the crossing and await your further orders.'

And without another word he turned and began walking down to the shoreline, to where the ranks of vanars and bears were waiting impatiently.

Rama started to call out to him. He heard the word 'Lakshman' escape his lips once, only to be torn away by the wind that had sprung up. But Lakshman kept walking. And Rama held his silence. He waited a moment or two, willing the cry in his heart's cave to quiet itself. Then he began walking down to the head of the lines, to give the order they were all waiting to hear.

After so much herculean effort and struggle, after so many lives expended – first in the bridge-building, and then taken by the tsunami – the long-awaited crossing itself began without any further difficulty. Under Rama's crisply issued instructions, and the watchful gaze of Hanuman above, the vanars and bears went forth upon the line of greybacks four abreast, and made their way steadily across the ocean.

Both species were uneasy and nervous at first. But they had had many days to grow accustomed to the idea that this crossing would be made, and the toll their fallen comrades had paid made it seem like a victory in itself. The bears were somewhat more confident than the vanars, since they were used to crossing rivers and streams in search of fresh fish, and after a few uneasy moments spent testing their footing upon the very smooth backs of the great sea beasts – a process which involved dropping to all fours and sniffing suspiciously, perhaps even eagerly, at the greybacks, who of course reeked of fish – the first score of bears turned and bellowed encouragement to their comrades. The bellows were passed up the bear lines, all the way up the beach and miles inland, echoing for several minutes. Then the first bears grunted and ambled forward. After a while, they dropped to all fours again and galloped merrily, racing across the ocean as if they had done this all their lives.

The vanars were more skittish. The first ones in the lines spent many moments peering over this side and that at the ocean that lay only a few yards below the surface upon which they stood, then *cheeka*-hed in mortification when a wave crashed into the side of the greybacks and a little foam splashed on to them. It took stern orders from their generals to get them to emulate their bear comrades and move across the ocean. Finally Rama himself came forward to speak. He reminded them that he had offered prayers to Lord Ganesha, the elephant-headed deva of auspicious beginnings, remover of obstacles, and pointed to the spot in the ocean where he had floated a mud effigy that Nala had quickly but expertly shaped despite his injured foot and broken arm. The effigy was all but vanished by then, dissolved in the water, but it so chanced that the spot where Rama had immersed it was calm and in the lee of the greyback line. He pointed this out as proof that the Tusked One had blessed their crossing and would grant them safe passage without hindrances. That breathed great courage into the vanars' hearts, and when Rama spoke quietly to Angad, the prince of Kiskindha took up a familiar vanar travelling chant praising their great ancestors. The nervous vanars in the front lines immediately took up the chant and in a few moments were tramping their way across the sea, still watchful of the licking waves to either side. They soon fell into a rhythm and in only a few more minutes had caught up with their bear comrades.

After that, it was nothing but rote repetition. Those behind were reassured by the knowledge that their fellows had already gone forth and were crossing safely. And with each tribe that crossed, the ones behind made it a matter of pride to show that they were just as brave. In a few hours the crossing was proceeding exceedingly well. Varuna-deva lived up to his promise: the ocean remained sedate and calm, with only the natural move-ment of the tides stirring its immense vastness; the air was cool and refreshing; the sky above stayed clear cerulean blue, with only an occasional cloud to be glimpsed. The chanting of the vanars filled the air for miles, counterpointed by the almost musical grunting and snorting of the bears – at times almost seeming like a song of their own – and the gentle high-pitched lowing of the greybacks was a beautiful exotic accompaniment to the orchestra of sounds that lent an auspicious air to the crossing of the armies.

Rama and Lakshman, once they had made sure the crossing was proceeding efficiently, made their way to the head of the lines, sprinting to easily overtake the bears and vanars, their long-legged strides carrying them with the speed of the wind, according to the awed vanars and bears. Rama heard this comment and many others and hardly knew whether to smile or to sigh; he was resigned to the knowledge that virtually everything they did would be turned into lore and legend, with all the accompanying flights of imagination and exaggeration that poetic licence allowed.

As they ran steadily alongside the quadruple lines, a little water that had sloshed over the top of the bridge splashed underfoot – apparently the greybacks needed to remain as deeply immersed as possible, which meant that the bridge would dip slowly upwards and downwards from time to time, in sections. But it was done so cautiously that even the vanars did not heed it . . . much.

Rama glanced briefly at Lakshman as they ran. Lakshman's face, hardened and intensified to the point where he barely resembled the brother Rama recalled from Ayodhya – just as Rama himself barely resembled his own earlier self, no doubt – did not display any anger or resentment outwardly; but then again, these past several years he too had learned to control his emotions well. Rama thought Lakshman had accepted his explanation about his concealing his brahmanic shakti for so many years, but he still worried that his brother harboured some small unvoiced resentment. Once the war was over, he would try to make amends. *Once the war was over . . .* There was so much he wished to do once the war was over. But now was not the time to think of that. Now he must keep his attention focused on the task at hand. Clear his mind of all extraneous distractions and concentrate his energies only upon the here and now. Most of all he must allow himself to celebrate this small but significant progress: finally, they were crossing! Soon they would set foot on Lankan soil . . . and then the final conflict would be joined. He bit back the image of Sita, bound and trussed and scored with multiple injuries, the way Hanuman had seen her last, before it threatened to overwhelm his natural resolve.

He and Lakshman reached the head of the line and slowed just enough to set a strong pace without taxing the vanars and bears. It was a long crossing, and it would be better accomplished if they paced themselves. After the first yojana or so, the vanars and bears perhaps realised this as well, for the chanting faded out gradually, and in time the gentle lapping of the waves against the sides of the greybacks and the occa- sional lowing of the sea beasts themselves were the only sounds audible – those, and the relentless chuffing of the bears' breathing, of course.

There were few birds visible this far out, and for as far as one could see in every direction there was only ocean, ocean and more ocean. The sunlight glittered off distant waves, turning them into patches of gold and silver, and occasionally the watery expanse was broken by the presence of other sea creatures, akin to the greybacks but much smaller and with tapered snouts and finned backs, that appeared and disappeared alongside the bridge, their large black eyes staring curiously at this odd procession traversing the surface of their world. They seemed far too intel- ligent to be mere fish, Rama thought, and he suspected they were a higher species of ocean-dweller, more akin to the grey- backs than to the vast schools of silvery fish that darted under the surface. Neither the vanars nor the bears made any comment on these snouted sea bulls – for that was how Rama thought of them – but on glancing back once, he caught a large brown bear licking his lips hungrily as he gazed at the snouted bulls dipping into and out of the ocean. This despite the fact that the bears had found enough drowned fish after the tsunami to feed them for a week. He shook his head, smiling to himself. Bears would be bears.

He caught Lakshman glancing at him curiously and turned to share the smile and the thought with him. But Lakshman turned away at once, looking in the other direction, and the smile fell from Rama's face. He resigned himself to a silent crossing.

They had covered perhaps a yojana and a half thus when Lakshman slowed to a halt, pointing. He said sharply, 'Rama.'

Rama was already alert. He had known something was potentially amiss by the reaction of Hanuman. Until just now the vanar had flown back and forth along the length of the bridge – or rather, that part of the bridge which his comrades had covered already – making sure that nothing untoward happened to delay their progress. Once or twice Rama had seen him swoop down, like a hawk falling out of the sky in pursuit of a long-watched prey, and pluck some unfortunate, or mischievous, vanar from the ocean into which he'd fallen, restoring him to the line. But mostly the vanar had only had to patrol the bridge, remaining at a height of about a mile above sea level, visible only as a speck from down here. But a fraction before Lakshman had slowed and pointed, Rama had glimpsed Hanuman swooping down out of the sky. From the trajectory of his descent, he was not diving to rescue another fallen soldier; rather he was heading for a point some few hundred yards away from the bridge, far to their right, out in the open sea.

Rama acknowledged his brother's warning and indicated the diving speck that was Hanuman. He slowed down, gesturing to the lines behind to slow as well. The orders were passed down the line by the generals and tribe captains, positioned a few dozen yards apart to make conveyance of such instructions easy, and slowly the juggernaut of Rama's army ground to a gradual halt. There were eager queries and grunts of curiosity down the line, answered only by firm admonishments from the leaders to maintain silence and hold positions. A few of the bolder vanars, filled with a false confidence from their hours of traversing the salt desert, used the opportunity to peek over the edge of the bridge. 'See there,' Rama heard one of them tell the others, 'I told you, there are no sea serpents waiting to swallow us. Those were just things our mothers told us to get us to keep away!'

Just then something surged up out of the water, and the trio of vanars screeched and fell back over themselves. It was only one of the snouted sea bulls hoping to make friends with the land beings, but the vanars thought it was a sea serpent come to swallow them all whole. Rama admonished them with an upheld hand and a stern glance, and they subsided at once, scrambling back into formation in their lines, still trembling from their encounter. The friendly sea bull uttered an enquiring honk, peering over the top of the greyback, then, when nobody responded to its overture, sank back with a disappointed bleat.

Rama ignored this trivial distraction and focused his gaze upon the part of the ocean where Hanuman was descending with great speed. He could see something there now that he knew where to look. Something that was not a trick of the sunlight and cloud shadow, but an object suspended upon the water itself. Some kind of craft floating on the sea. And where there was a craft, it stood to reason there would be someone aboard it.

His pulse quickened slightly. Had Ravana launched an armada to repel their crossing, it would have been far greater than that single small speck. And the ocean denizens, if not Hanuman himself, would have warned them against it long before now. Whatever that craft was, it was isolated, and posed them no harm.

Or so he hoped.

At first Hanuman took the object to be a piece of driftwood. And indeed, it was not much more than driftwood. As he descended, he saw that it was a boat of Lankan design. He had seen many such on his trip to the island-kingdom, but none so small or pathetic. Its ribbing was visible, ocean water sloshing through to fill the bottom of the craft, and its single sail was tattered to shreds. It appeared to be occupied by five persons, but even from here he could see only one of them showing any signs of life. The other four lay sprawled in postures so decrepit, he felt certain they must be dead. There were a few scavenger birds floating on the waves nearby, crying out occasionally. It was the presence of these birds and their calls that had alerted him a moment earlier. From the looks of it, the craft appeared to have survived some terrible sea storm, perhaps even the very tsunami that had devastated his comrades on the beach.

He reduced himself until he was only three or four times more than his normal size and slowed his descent until he was hovering perhaps a dozen yards above the water, examining the battered craft intently for signs of deceit. After all, those were rakshasas in the boat, and for all he knew, this could be some new ploy by Ravana to obstruct their crossing. He set his jaw firmly. If this was indeed another ploy by the lord of rakshasas, he would not have a chance to do more than show his hand. At the first sign of peril, Hanuman would crush this boat and its occupants like . . .

One of the rakshasas stirred.

Hanuman dropped a yard or two lower, examining the Lankan, his fists ready to pound anything that posed a threat. But the creature only turned its head and moaned groggily. It seemed to be half out of its senses, weakened from exposure or injury, he could not tell which, and despite his best efforts he could not find any weapon upon the rakshasa's person, nor upon any of the other four wretches lying around him in the half-sunken craft. The rakshasa moaned a second time, turning his head upward, eyes shut tightly against the relentless sun, and it was with a small frisson of surprise that Hanuman realised he understood the Lankan word the creature was speaking: it was asking for water. With another small start, he found that he recognised the rakshasa.

He flew around the craft a few times, circling it and examining it from every angle. He could find no evidence of weaponry or subterfuge. The craft was what it appeared to be: a damaged Lankan fishing boat with four dead rakshasas and one barely alive.

Certain that there was nothing in the craft that could endanger his lords Rama and Lakshman, he dropped down to the level of the ocean, waves licking briefly at his bare feet, the water surprisingly cool even in the noonday sun, and hefted up the entire craft, rakshasas and all. Water splashed as the craft broke free of the ocean, pouring down his arms and body as he lifted the boat and flew it to Rama.

12

Angad called for the section leaders to maintain order in the ranks. The flurry of excitement that had broken out when Hanuman brought the Lankan boat with its passengers died down reluctantly. As the vanar prince saw to it that discipline was maintained, Rama and Lakshman conferred with the other generals and chiefs about what Hanuman had found.

The four dead rakshasas had been consigned to watery graves along with the battered craft in which the vanar had found them, while the lone survivor had been given the water he was moaning for so pathetically, and made somewhat more comfortable. He now sat propped up on the bridge, where Hanuman had deposited him gently several moments ago.

The vanars shot baleful glances in his direction. 'He is a spy sent to assassinate you, Lord Rama,' General Sarabha said. 'Do not go within ten yards of him.'

The other generals also concurred, with varying degrees of suspicion. Only Sugreeva held his silence. Rama looked at him. 'Your majesty? What is your advice?'

Sugreeva looked at him wearily. 'You are wiser than I, Rama. You must trust your own judgement in this matter, as in all else. Bear in mind that we vanars are greatly biased against rakshasas.'

'And yet Hanuman speaks in this rakshasa's favour,' Jambavan said gruffly. The king of bears regarded the prone form of the survivor, looking more like a washed-up piece of debris than a dangerous assassin. Hanuman was squatting beside him, holding a skin of water for him to sip on slowly. 'No vanar has as much cause to hate them as he does. Nor knows them better. Yet he calls this one a friend and an honourable brahmin!'

Rama looked at the albino Lankan sipping water with obvious gratitude from Hanuman's hands. A cordon of vanars and bears stood around them, spears held at the ready. They seemed somewhat overzealous. The lone rakshasa, battered and exhausted as he was, looked as if he could barely stand, let alone pose any threat to anyone. He had told Hanuman that he had set out for the mainland shore in the first boat he could get his hands on, accompanied by four good rakshasas to man the vessel. They were caught almost at once in the tsunami sent to destroy Rama's bridge and battered by the unnatural fury of the ocean. The four others had drowned despite being on the boat, for such was the quantity of water that had fallen upon them. The albino had survived miraculously but had no means to row himself to either shore.

Rama came to a decision.

'I will have words with the rakshasa,' he said. 'I request you all to stand back and let me speak with him. Lakshman, you alone will come with me. This is a task better suited to two than ten.'

Nobody argued, although the vanars were unhappy and General Sarabha looked as if he would rather run the rakshasa through with a spear than talk with him. Rama and Lakshman went towards the head of the lines where the rakshasa was now sitting up, assisted by Hanuman. They both looked up as Rama and Lakshman approached. At once the rakshasa joined his hands together in a namaskaram of greeting. Hanuman stood to receive them.

'His name is Vibhisena,' Hanuman said. He pronounced the name *Vibhishun*, which was probably the way he had heard it spoken back in Lanka, Rama guessed. 'He is the brother of Ravana. And the one I spoke of to you upon my return, Lord

Rama. The one who championed my lady Sita's cause with such dedication, opposing even the King of Lanka in his own court to the point of endangering his own life. I believe him to be an ally and a man of honour, perhaps the most honourable rakshasa in Lanka.'

Rama nodded. 'Then I shall treat him with the respect he deserves. The enemy who supports us at a time of great crisis is preferable to the friend who turns his back upon us at the first sign of trouble.'

At these words, the pale-skinned rakshasa looked up at Rama with a strange light in his watery eyes. 'Truly,' he said weakly, his rakshasa mouth and tongue forming the words oddly but lucidly enough, 'I expected no less from the great warrior of dharma. It is my everlasting privilege to meet you, great and virtuous Rama Chandra of Ayodhya. And this must surely be your equally renowned brother, Sumitra-putra Lakshmana, who sacrificed all to accompany you into exile fourteen years ago.'

Lakshman's eyes narrowed. 'It seems you know a great deal about us, Lankan.'

Vibhisena shrugged weakly. 'Who does not know the tale of Rama's great sacrifice and unjust banishment? It is the misfortune of the rakshasa race that we are relegated to playing the role of the villains in your great life history.'

Lakshman frowned. 'Tell us then, why did one of you villains suddenly leave Lanka and come seeking us?'

Rama said softly, 'Lakshman, if Hanuman has vouched for him, then that is reason enough for us to trust him. We should not question him so roughly.'

Vibhisena's eyes gazed up at Rama. 'Permit me to answer, Lord Rama. Your brother is fully justified in questioning me. I know full well he means no offence by these questions, but seeks only to appraise himself of my motives.' He turned to Lakshman. 'My lord Lakshman. I am but a devout brahmin-rakshasa seeking to find peace in this time of great madness and war. My only mission is to aid you and your illustrious brother in your righteous effort.'

Lakshman looked suspiciously at the rakshasa. 'You pick a strange time and place to show your support, Lankan. How do we know you are not here to delay us in our crossing? Perhaps you were sent here to stall us, and give your brother time to put some fiendish new plan into effect?'

Vibhisena shook his head in denial. 'My lords, my brother and I have always held widely different views on many matters; this is no secret. Hanuman here has witnessed how fiercely I opposed him in his own council. The only reason Ravana tolerated me this long was because even he has not sunk so deeply into arrogance that he would execute his own flesh and blood. But on the matter of the abduction of Sita, he and I have finally parted ways. I have sworn to remain in exile for ever rather than live in a land where such acts are tolerated. So it was that after Hanuman departed Lanka, I too resolved to leave and to offer my services to Lord Rama. For I was greatly impressed by Hanuman's valour and the manner in which he bore himself while in our kingdom. If the messenger is such a great being, I thought, what might his master be like? Had I intended you any harm, why would I have set sail on the very sea upon which Ravana was about to wreak his sorcerous havoc? It was perhaps an ill-thought-out voyage, for I am no shrewd planner of such jaunts, but the devas have seen fit to spare my life and bring me to your feet. And here I lie, prepared to serve you as best I can.'

Still Lakshman persisted. 'Even so, how can we trust you? A brother who betrays his own flesh and blood. A rakshasa who joins with his enemies against his own race. A traitor and a turncoat.'

Vibhisena bowed his head sadly. 'What you say is all true, and it shames me to admit it. But Ravana violated dharma by abducting Sita, and after that great transgression he has continued to violate dharma in one misdeed after another. I cannot stand by and watch him without doing anything.' He looked away for a moment, his eyes distant. 'I have stood by silently for far too long as it is.'

Lakshman looked at him sceptically. 'So you are doing this in order to uphold dharma?'

'Yes,' the rakshasa answered simply. 'For dharma is above relationships, above brotherhood even, above race and caste and creed and community. It is my sense of dharma that makes me now turn against my people and my own brother.'

Lakshman was silent for a moment. Then he glanced up at Rama as if to say, *Well? What next?*

Rama addressed the rakshasa gently. 'You seek sanctuary then? Protection from your brother's ire?'

'Nay, my lord. I seek to aid you in your war. I ask for no sanctuary or favours. I wish only to help you win your righteous cause.'

'How so?'

'My lord, you are unfamiliar with Lanka, and unfamiliar with Ravana's military wiles. I have watched him wage war many times. I can impart to you a great deal of insight regarding the lie of the land and his strategies of war.'

Rama forced himself to inject a modicum of doubt into his next query: 'You would aid us in killing your own countrymen and overrunning your kingdom?'

'Only in the hope that by bringing this ill-desired conflict to a swift close, I may spare much needless bloodshed. The sooner peace is restored to Lanka, the happier I shall be. Ravana does not seek an early peace. In his current state of mind, he would desire war to be the only condition of existence. If left to him, he would sooner let every last rakshasa in Lanka die fighting than allow peace to reclaim the land. I hope that by aiding you I shall break this endless cycle of violence and restore Lanka to the beautiful, peaceful land it once used to be.'

Rama was silent for a moment, contemplating what the rakshasa had said. He looked at Hanuman. Then at Lakshman.

Then back at the long lines of vanars and bears stretching out across the ocean, waiting for his command. This decision could not take all day. He had to choose swiftly and decisively. He knew already what he must do. He spoke once more to the rakshasa, this time without any trace of suspicion or doubt.

'My good Vibhisena, I apologise if my brother's questioning was somewhat harsh. We are at war with your race and your appearance here was most unexpected. We would be foolish not to suspect something amiss.'

Vibhisena shook his head in dismay. 'Nay, my lord Rama. You owe me no apologies. Lakshman was well within his rights to question me. After all you have endured at the hands of my brother and his fellow rakshasas, I am astonished at how graciously you have treated me. In contrast, I am ashamed of how my people treated your own emissary Hanuman in Lanka. Sadly, it is such misdeeds that bring shame to the name of rakshasas.'

Rama held out his hand. 'Then let us make a fresh start towards a new era of peaceful friendship. Perhaps all rakshasas and mortals cannot be friends, but we can prove the exception. I accept the hand of friendship you offer so graciously.'

Vibhisena clasped the hand Rama proffered him, tears streaking down the sides of his face. 'I thank you, Rama. And I salute your greatness. Truly, all the great praises Hanuman heaped upon your name in my brother's court were no more than the honest truth. You are truly a deva among mortals.'

Rama brushed aside the compliments, continuing hurriedly, 'You are now a part of my forces, and will travel with us. However, I do not wish to delay the crossing of my armies any longer. Let us proceed to Lanka and we may speak further once we reach those shores.'

Vibhisena nodded. 'That is wise. The sooner we reach Lanka, the better your chances of victory. Come then. I do not wish to be the cause of any further delay to you.' He struggled to raise himself to his feet, his nether limbs wobbling unsteadily with the effort.

Rama turned to Hanuman. 'My friend, our new friend and ally is clearly in no condition to keep pace with us on our march. If you will do me the courtesy of carrying the noble Lankan, we shall make better time. Vibhisena, my new friend, please accept this support. You are drained of strength, and incapable of running at the speed we must maintain to reach Lanka before nightfall.'

Vibhisena raised no objection. Hanuman bent down and hefted the prone rakshasa as easily as he might have picked up a small child. He placed Vibhisena on his shoulder, making him comfortable. Vibhisena's pale face reflected his gratitude and pleasure at being accepted as well as at the mode of conveyance.

Rama turned back to the others. From the look on Jambavan's face, the bear king seemed pleased at his decision. Only General Sarabha still looked sour, but Rama dismissed that as the inbred vanar distrust of all rakshasas. 'Lakshman,' he said quietly, 'give the order to resume the march.'

Lakshman issued the order smartly. It was taken up by Prince Angad, then passed along the line. Rama could hear the shouts proceeding in stages down the yojanas-long ranks. Finally, slowly, like a juggernaut starting up, the procession began to resume its forward motion. In a few more moments it had achieved a pace akin to a man walking steadily. And in another several moments Rama and Lakshman were running, then sprinting. Rama found the rhythm he had been marking before, just enough to keep the armies moving briskly, yet not so great that the bears and vanars would tire and fall behind. Soon the great procession was proceeding at a swift pace across the bridge. In the water, the greybacks lowed and called down the line, passing on the word: the army was on the move again.

13

Lanka.

The island-kingdom loomed before them on the horizon, proud and magnificent, a pearl set in a bed of lush green velvet surrounded by a perfect azure sea. Even from miles away, its beauty was unmistakable. Rama allowed his pace to slacken, Lakshman slowing beside him. The generals passed on the word that they were halting, while the rank and file muttered in awed consternation at the sight of their dreaded destination. Below their feet, the greybacks lowed. The sun, low in the western sky, illuminated the island-kingdom in a beatific golden light, the ocean calm and still around it, glistening peacefully in the slanting sunshine. Birds flew around the crown of cliffs that ringed the northern shores, and the lush green flora on the hills was dotted with patches of red palas flowers in bloom.

It looked so tranquil, so alluring, like a haven of respite, rather than a lair of rakshasas.

'It must be Ravana's vile sorcery,' Lakshman said doubtfully. 'He has altered the aspect of the land to appear beautiful and inviting, in order to deceive us.'

'Nay, Lakshman,' Rama said. 'I do not think this is Ravana's doing. I think this is Lanka's own natural beauty. After all, do not forget, the legends say that Lanka was a great and beautiful land long before Ravana made it his home. We are so accustomed to thinking of it as a den of Asuras that it is easy to forget that the land itself is not evil, only those who occupy it presently.'

Hanuman came up, bearing his passenger upon his shoulders. Vibhisena, who had heard Rama's last words, said, 'Indeed, Rama. You speak truly. Lanka is a great and beautiful land, rich in resources and bountiful in harvest. If you think it beautiful now, what might you have thought had you seen it a few thousand years earlier, when my half-brother Kuber ruled it.'

'Kuber,' Lakshman said thoughtfully. 'He is the treasurer of the devas, is he not?'

'He is. A veritable lord of wealth. Ravana invaded his inner sanctum in the realm of the devas, decimating his army of yaksas, and stole from him his celestial vehicle Pushpak as well as a large share of his great treasure trove of wealth. Then he usurped Lanka, which Kuber had been given as a gift by the devas for his many services, and proceeded to turn it into a living hell on the mortal plane.' He sighed. 'It was only after Ravana was incapacitated during the last fourteen years that my sister-in-law Mandodhari was able to repair some of the damage he had wrought to its natural beauty. What you see before you now is only a pale shadow of the Lanka that once used to be.'

'And shall be again,' Rama said quietly.

Lakshman looked at him.

Rama looked back, nodding. 'We come not to destroy, but to reclaim. Our quarrel is only with Ravana and those rakshasas who make the error of supporting his vile ways. Once we have secured what we have come here for, we shall leave Lanka better than we found it. That is how we shall show the Lankans that we Ayodhyans are builders, not destroyers. And that their true enemy was Ravana himself, for leading them so far down the path of unrighteousness.'

Lakshman frowned doubtfully but spoke no objection.

Vibhisena's eyes filled with tears. 'My lord, if you could truly achieve such a thing you would be blessed for a thousand lifetimes.'

'It shall be so, my rakshasa friend. We did not choose to start this war. But we shall be the ones to end it.'

Lakshman inclined his head at the sun, low on the western horizon. 'We should try to make land before nightfall. It will be harder for the vanars and bears to cross in the dark.'

Rama nodded. 'Yes. Let us make speed. Give the word to the lines behind that we shall not stop now until every last soldier is safely on land. To Lanka!'

'TO LANKA!' came the thundering, excited response.

Supanakha prowled the walls and ceiling of the cavern where Ravana had commanded the generals to assemble. The chamber had been carved out of rock by Ravana's Asura sorcery, along with the labyrinthine network of caverns that riddled Mount Nikumbhila. Ravana's fiendish imagination, never at a loss for creativity, had shaped some of the natural rock protuberances in the ceiling and walls to make them resemble anthropomorphic shapes and outlines. The one she was clinging to with feline grace was shaped to resemble an apsara and a deva in the throes of copulation. She wondered if the deva depicted in the act of kama was Indra himself. The thousand-eyed one was renowned for his carnal appetites. He was also renowned for a certain peculiarity of his anatomy. She probed the recesses of the carving, seeking to ascertain the accuracy of the anatomical depiction, but was distracted by a flurry of activity on the floor of the chamber, some ten or fifteen yards below the ceiling from which she was suspended upside down.

The score or so of assembled rakshasas gathered below looked unhappy and angry. The garish light of the sorcerously illuminated stones set upon the walls at regular intervals did nothing to enhance the fierce monstrosity of their natural unattractiveness. Their furred limbs and tusked faces were richly clad, as befitted the highest clan lords and generals of Lanka, but even from the high shadows in which she was concealed she could spy a burnt patch in a tunic, a jagged rent in a waistband stitched from priceless tanned human leather, a crack in a polished breastplate carved from the bone of some extinct Asura species – almost every one of these proud rakshasas was marked in some fashion or other, testimony to how narrowly they had survived the burning of Lanka and the damage wrought by the rampaging vanar emissary. Supanakha licked her chops in recollection of the night of wanton destruction. Ah, had she known the vanar was possessed of such great powers, she would have focused her energies more on seducing him rather than merely deceiving him. What a rampage! Never before had she heard of any creature wreaking such havoc in a rakshasa lair. For that night of unbridled destruction she could almost forgive him killing the handsome Akshay Kumar. Watching him expanded to a thousand times his natural size, pounding the great golden-white tower of Pushpak to smithereens, his lightly furred limbs working with powerful ease, she had been overcome by lust. Even now she purred silently just to recall the scene. Would that he had wreaked his havoc upon her person. She would have burned more willingly for him than Lanka had!

She was distracted from her self-indulgent fantasies by another outbreak of growls and grunts from the cavern floor below. The generals were growing restless. They had been waiting here a long while, on Ravana's instructions. And there was neither sign of the Lord of Lanka, nor word from him. Come to think of it, Supanakha herself hadn't seen Ravana since early this morning either – and that had been barely a glimpse of him riding in Pushpak with that wretched woman. Her lips curled at the thought of Sita. She didn't understand why Ravana didn't just have his way with the woman or else do away with her. At the very least he could hand her over to Supanakha. There were a few delicious torments she could think of to visit upon that wench . . .

'Where is he?' asked a kumbha-rakshasa loudly. 'How much longer are we to wait around here? There are important decisions to be taken, pressing matters to be seen to. We cannot spend all day waiting here for Lanka-naresh to show himself when he pleases.'

The other clan chiefs echoed his complaints with noises of their own. Some had to see to arming their forces, others to transporting soldiers and supplies to various sites where they were to be stationed; one general had to see to fortifications that had been destroyed by the vanar's rampaging spree . . . In moments the chamber echoed noisily with the complaints of impatient rakshasas. Supanakha watched with amusement as the complaints soon turned to a venting of opinions on the previous day's disaster and how it could have been prevented – or at least stopped.

'*Enough*,' said a familiar voice.

The cacophony ended abruptly. The generals and clan chiefs looked around, startled. The voice had been unmistakably Ravana's, yet the Lord of Lanka was nowhere to be seen. One of the chiefs pointed with a taloned claw at a wall of the chamber. A greenish light had begun to glow there. Supanakha moved across the carving to give herself a better view of that part of the cavern.

The greenish glow resolved slowly into an image of the northern shore of Lanka. It was similar to the water-illusion Ravana had conjured up earlier, she realised, projecting the image of a scene occurring in some distant location upon the wall of the cavern. As everyone watched silently, the image sharpened by degrees, until the ocean and the palisade cliffs ringing the northern end of the island were recognisable. Everything was greatly reduced in scale, in order to fit upon the section of the cave wall on which the image was sorcerously projected, but it was clear enough overall to make out the familiar geographical features. It was also clear enough to depict the objects floating in the ocean off the northern shore: enormous sea beasts arrayed in a continuous line that extended well beyond the periphery of the image projected – to the end of the horizon itself, it seemed.

This extraordinary living bridge across the ocean, joining Lanka to the northern mainland, was covered with countless tiny living creatures, scurrying across it like ants upon a rotted tree trunk. The creatures were coming from the north, across the ocean, and as Supanakha watched with fascinated interest, creeping lower to gain a better view, they reached the end of the bridge and began leaping to the thin sandy beach that bordered the northern shore. In mere moments, scores of the creatures began pouring upon the beach, spreading out in all directions with astonishing speed.

'This is Rama's army,' said the disembodied voice of Ravana, seeming to issue from nowhere and everywhere at once. 'They are setting foot upon our shores at this very minute as you can see. Hundreds of thousands of vanars and bears, perhaps even millions – even I do not know how many exactly, and I doubt the mortal himself does!'

Her cousin sounded almost gleeful, Supanakha thought curiously. Instead of being furious at the sight of his enemy arriving and setting foot upon his land with such a vast host, Ravana was amused!

His rakshasa leaders didn't share his amusement. Several of them were scowling, others grunting and chuffing angrily, a few even snorting nervously and spraying spittle and nasal fluids as they sought to vent their feelings of fear and panic. 'There are too many, Lord Ravana,' cried one of these, his boar-like tusks glistening with the fluids he was exuding with nervous haste. 'How will we combat such large numbers?'

Ravana's laughter echoed through the chamber. Supanakha started. It sounded as if he was right here beside her, high up on the wall of the cavern – as well as down there, and there . . . Where was he really? Why was he not showing himself? Those fools were losing their nerve just at the sight of Rama's army landing on the unassailable shores of Lanka. No army had ever invaded the island before. None had even dared try. The very fact that Rama had brought such a vast host to Ravana's threshold, in the wake of the unprecedented destruction wreaked by his vanar emissary, was enough to make any rakshasa lose a few fluids. She was interested in seeing how Ravana calmed his generals long enough for them to listen to his war plan. At least, she assumed he *had* a war plan.

'*Kambhakhatar*,' Ravana boomed, the rakshasa word for fool echoing around the chamber. And this time Supanakha felt as if he were addressing her as well, mocking her for daring to doubt his power. She licked her lips: Ravana was wont to deal with any doubters swiftly and brutally. She tensed herself, anticipating that the boar-clan idiot who had questioned his lord would find himself rendered to fat and gristle in a sorcerous flash.

Instead, to her mounting surprise, Ravana responded with more words. Not even angry words at that, but the same amused tone, as if he were speaking to a roomful of children rather than the most powerful rakshasa leaders in all Lanka.

'Do you really think any of this could have happened without my consent? Do you think that army of bears and baboons could have landed here had I not wished it? Nothing happens in Lanka that I do not permit to happen. Not a blade of grass dares arise from the ground without my willing it. I am Ravana, Lord of Lanka. This land is wedded to me as flesh is to bone. My Asura maya permeates every fibre of this island-nation. I have permitted the mortal Rama to bring his army of monkeys and coons here only so that I may teach him a lesson. A lesson in warcraft. It is a lesson you should heed as well. For in the hours ahead you will see Lanka restored to the time of its greatest glory. A Lanka that is the supreme purveyor of war and holocaust. Once again we shall be feared in the three worlds, by every species, every race of living being. We shall crush the mortal Rama and his minions like the insectile hordes that they are, the way a kumbha-rakshasa's heel crushes an anthill into the ground without even knowing that the anthill existed, and when we are done, all shall know and fear us once again. For the past several years you have grown soft and accustomed to luxury and indolence. Peace and prosperity have made fat-bellied dogs of you all. It was good that the vanar came and shook you out of your complacency. Now you are awake and alert. Now you will prepare yourselves and fight like the rakshasas you are, and when this war is over, you will follow me across the ocean to the mortal realm and we shall conquer the nations of Aryavarta. Once we were halted at Mithila by the use of a celestial weapon that none could resist. Today, after we have killed the mortal who wielded that weapon, we shall have avenged the massacre of our fellow Asuras at Mithila, and none will remain to oppose us on our new campaign of conquest. Today we reclaim Lanka and wipe out Rama and his forces. Tomorrow we conquer the world!'

After this extraordinary speech, even Supanakha felt like cheering. The clan chiefs gathered in the chamber raised their guttural voices in throaty exuberance, their fear and panic subsumed by the war-lust Ravana's words had awoken in their warrior breasts. They cheered and roared their approval of his rallying speech.

At last they fell silent again. Finally, as she had known they would, they asked the question she had wanted to ask as well.

'My lord, what are your orders? How are we to accomplish this victory? Will you not show yourself and lead us to triumph in person?'

In response, Ravana's voice chuckled softly. 'My orders for the nonce are that you rest and prepare yourselves for battle on the morrow. We shall convene here again at dawn, and I shall tell you what is to be done next. Meanwhile, tonight, I am already at work, laying the seeds of the victory we shall reap tomorrow. For as you sleep, I shall be turning our island-kingdom into the great unassailable fortress she once was. Tomorrow, when you arise, you shall see for yourself the result of my invocations. You shall awaken to a new Lanka.'

They looked at one another in puzzlement. 'But my lord,'

said the leader of the kumbha clans, 'the enemy has landed on our shores. Should we not make efforts to repel them at least? Left to their own devices, they could encroach upon a great part of our kingdom by the morning. We should immediately lead a foray to push them back into the sea whence they came.'

Again that amused chuckle. But now it sounded a trifle impatient, as if Ravana was done with talking and explaining himself. Sooner or later, Supanakha knew, that tone of impatience always crept into his voice – or voices, for Ravana had ten tongues in his heads – but it was a matter of surprise to her that he had been so patient so long. 'They shall not encroach upon a single yard of Lankan ground tonight. And many of them will not live to see the morning light. While all will rue the moment they stepped upon the shores of our land, and shall long for nothing but to return across the ocean. This will happen even as you sleep tonight. Now, enough has been said. Go and rest yourselves and your forces, and we shall meet again at dawn to face the armies of the invader and reclaim our lost glory.'

They looked at one another, awe and amazement writ large upon their snouted faces. But all knew better than to press their luck further. The next few moments were spent in bowing and scraping and calling out the praises of the great Lord of Lanka. Then, one by one, they all filed out of the chamber until Supanakha was left alone once more, with only the flickering green image upon the wall for company. She crept down the wall, peering at the image of the invaders pouring across the bridge still, flooding the northern shore of the island. What had Ravana meant? *Even as you sleep tonight.* How?

Suddenly she knew she had to go to the northern cliffs. She would take the caverns, the way she had entered Lanka months earlier, when she had brought with her the means to resurrect her cousin. She would go and watch for herself as Ravana's sorcery assailed Rama and his armies by night. It promised to be a massacre worth a ringside seat!

With a flick of her tail, she bounded out of the cavern.

KAAND 2

ISLE OF THE DEAD

I

The greybacks were too large to come on to the beach itself. The closest one to land had positioned itself in such a manner that the travellers could leap from the end of its back to the edge of the shoreline. It meant a little wading through knee-deep foamy water. Rama watched as the bears jumped into the water and waded up the beach, splashing sand and water carelessly. They roared and flailed their arms happily, pleased to have reached their destination at last. The vanars were apprehensive at first, but under their commander's watchful gaze they plucked up the courage to jump and waded after the bears, wincing as water splashed around them and new waves soughed softly inwards. The first bears swept up the first vanars in happy bear hugs, and both species roared and *cheeka*-ed their delight at having been the first to reach Lanka. The vanars seemed a little the worse for wear after being hugged so enthusiastically, but soon recovered, coughing and grinning cheerfully enough. Some even splashed around in the shallow water, but that ended once one of them spied crabs scuttling underfoot, causing a mass exodus up to dry sand.

Rama noted that the tide was coming in and the tidemark was several yards further up the sharply sloping beach. Once it was in fully, there would barely be room left to stand here on this narrow strip of a beach. He issued orders to speed up the crossing, then turned to look at the land upon which they had arrived.

Enormous blackstone cliffs rose in sheer daunting lines above

the narrow strip of beach. They ran in either direction as far
as his eyes could see.

He turned to look at Vibhisena, who stood beside him and
Lakshman. The vanar and bear generals were seeing to the
disembarkment of the troops, but King Sugreeva came up to
join them in their conference at Rama's request. Jambavan was
still on the bridge, making sure that there were no laggers and
that the troops did not panic once the sun went down, which
would be in a short while.

'These are the cliffs you named palisades,' Rama asked
Vibhisena.

'Indeed they are, Rama. They are so named for they are great
natural walls of defence guarding Lanka from intruders upon
this coast.' He added slowly, 'Although there have never been
intruders upon this or any other coast of Lanka before.'

Rama indicated the narrow sandy line running to either side
of the cliffs. 'How far inland could we travel along the beach?'

Vibhisena's forehead creased with thought. 'Perhaps less than
a mile either way. But that would be at low tide,' he glanced
around, 'which is now. After the tide rises, it would engulf most
of this sandy strip.'

It was as Rama had feared. He exchanged a glance with
Lakshman, who understood the problem without needing it
spelled out. 'We need to get as many of our troops as possible
off this beach before the tide turns,' Lakshman said. 'As it is,
there's barely room to accommodate a few tens of thousands
here, and even they would have to be packed together like too
many teeth in a small mouth.'

Everybody glanced around. The disembarkment was proceeding at a brisk pace now, vanars and bears leaping off the
last greyback into the shallows by the score, raising a great
ruckus in their excitement. Already this portion of the beach
was growing overcrowded. Several of the new arrivals were
stopping once they reached the dry sand, looking around in
bemusement at the place they had feared so long in their dreams

and tales. Several vanars and bears milled around Rama and his cohorts, looking dazed and disoriented now that the long-desired crossing was finally over. Someone jostled Vibhisena accidentally.

Rama wasted no time. 'Lakshman, tell the chiefs to send the troops up the beach on either side, to make room for new arrivals. Fan out as far as possible. Keep runners ready to carry messages and keep the lines of communication working efficiently.'

Lakshman was already off and issuing the orders even before the words were out of Rama's mouth. He passed on the instructions to Prince Angad, who had disembarked a moment earlier and was standing in knee-deep water, shouting orders to the rank and file. Angad listened briefly to Lakshman's orders, nodded once briskly, then began shouting new commands to the chiefs who were arriving. Lakshman rejoined Rama and the others up the beach.

'There is no other way around the palisades, then?' asked Rama.

Vibhisena shook his head slowly. 'That is why all quays and docks on Lanka are built further south.' He frowned, looking at the line of greybacks stretching back to the horizon in the fading sunlight. 'Perhaps if your bridge could be extended around the periphery of the island . . . A few miles upland and there are many good landing points where you can have direct access to the inland routes.' He sucked in a breath. 'Of course, my brother's forces would certainly be guarding those points, but nevertheless . . .'

Rama looked at Hanuman, who was waiting just behind him for his instructions. 'My friend, you understand the language of the greybacks. Would you enquire with them if they could do as our rakshasa friend suggests?'

Hanuman shook his head regretfully. 'Rama, they have already told me they have risked much to bring us so close to land. You see, there are sharp reefs below the water here, and they are already injuring themselves holding the line until our forces disembark. To go further along the coast would mean certain injury, even death to many of their numbers. Even so, they would not hesitate to sacrifice their lives, but there is another problem. Every available greyback in this part of the world has been conscripted to form the bridge to Lanka. There are none to spare to extend it further upland.'

Lakshman looked at Hanuman thoughtfully. 'What if we have the greybacks at the mainland end of the line come up here and form the extension? Surely our people have come far enough up the bridge to leave a few score greybacks free at the other end?'

Hanuman cocked his head, listening to the greybacks lowing mournfully in the fading light. 'They have discussed that option as well, my lord Lakshman. The time required for those greybacks to swim all the way here and then re-form into a new line might not suit our purpose. It would take until morning at least. And even then, they say it would be treacherous going, for the tides are fierce this close to Lanka, and are particularly bad at this time of year. The greybacks forming such an extension to the bridge would have to be moving constantly to keep themselves from being thrown against the reefs.' He paused, listening to the greybacks before going on. 'The risk would be great to us as well. Were even a single greyback to be pushed out of line by a riptide or undercurrent, it would cause scores of our troops to drown.' He listened a while more before shaking his head decisively. 'They have sent a scout to investigate and she answers saying that the tides are too savage to enable such an undertaking. It would be suicidal to risk it. Perhaps a few weeks hence, when the summer tides turn once more . . .' He dismissed the rest with a shrug of his powerful shoulders. 'Nay, my lords. It cannot be done that way. The greybacks have done as much as they can to aid us. We must find some other means of getting our troops inland.'

Rama was silent for a long moment, thinking. The cacophony from around them continued as clan chiefs yelled and bellowed at their troops to form lines and march post-haste up the beach.

Several platoons went sprinting across the sandy strip, disappearing out of sight around the curve of the cliffs. Rama followed them, keeping his gaze fixed on the cliffs, then raising it to the top of the palisades.

He sighed and pointed with his chin. 'Then that is the only way.'

Lakshman nodded. 'We shall have to send them up the cliffs.'

King Sugreeva sucked in his breath. 'It will not be an easy ascent. There is no sign of any shrubbery to cling to. Vanars are accustomed to climbing steep hills if they have growth to clutch at, but these are sheer stone cliffs, moistened by the spray of the ocean.' He licked his thick vanar lips. 'Everything on this coast is already liberally coated with the moisture and salt we taste on our faces. It will make the ascent very treacherous.'

Rama nodded. 'You are right, my friend, but we have no other choice. If we go around by the beach, then when the tide comes up we shall be stranded on those sharp wet rocks until it goes out again.' He pointed to the craggy black monstrosities that clung to the bottom of the cliffs like teeth at the base of a gaping black maw. 'And there are too many of us to be accommodated that way.' He gestured back at the lines upon lines of vanars and bears now streaming on to the shore. 'We can hardly expect the bulk of our forces to wait on the greybacks either. It will be hard enough to keep their footing out there once darkness falls. Nay. We must climb the cliffs, difficult though it may be. And we must start doing so now, before too many of us are ashore. Lakshman, call Angad.'

Lakshman put his fingers to his mouth and issued a sharp, piercing whistle. He called out a single word, 'Angadia!' A messenger vanar waiting nearby gave a shrill *cheeka* in response and scampered to call the prince, who was only a few dozen yards away.

Prince Angad came up, breathless from shouting commands at the troops and their chiefs. 'We are making good progress, my lord Rama. By the middle watch of the night we should have all our troops ashore.'

'Very good, Prince,' Rama said. 'But now we have another great challenge facing us.'

'Angad, my son,' Sugreeva said with his customary sorrowful expression. 'It appears we shall have to climb these stone walls.'

Angad looked up sharply at the cliffs. 'Those?'

'Yes, those,' said Lakshman laconically. 'Can your vanars do it?'

Angad looked at Lakshman, then at Rama, then at the scores of troops splashing into the shallows and up the beach. 'My vanars? Surely. But can your bears do it?'

Lakshman folded his arms across his chest and looked questioningly at Rama. 'A good point. Can the bears climb those cliffs?'

Rama thought about it briefly. 'There's only one way to find out.'

Supanakha peered cautiously out of the narrow mouth of the cave, high on the face of the cliff overlooking the northern shore of Lanka. She looked out at a sight every bit as amazing as she had expected. At first it appeared much like the sorcerous image projected on the wall of Ravana's chambers.

A great line of immense grey sea beasts extended from the shore of Lanka out to the farthest horizon. The living bridge of floating sea beasts was covered with tens of thousands of vanars and bears, all marching – nay, running really – with the efficient brisk pace of a military juggernaut on the move. From her point of view, some three hundred feet above the ground, it was a formidable sight. Line upon line of furry vanars and burly bears scampered, sprinted, jogged and ran, bellowing, shouting, *cheeka*-ing, grunting, chuffing and otherwise venting their enthusiasm as they made their way across the ocean. And here, at the shore of Lanka, they were leaping off the end of the last sea beast, splashing through the shallow water and making their way up the narrow strip of sandy beach, from where they were dispatched in neat squads up the beach, disappearing out of her narrow range of vision. It took her a moment to understand that they were being directed away in order to make space for their fellows who were arriving after them. She wondered how they intended to get inland though; there was no ingress to be had further up the beach. The entire north coast of Lanka was lined by these palisade cliffs. She knew that from bitter personal experience; it was not that long ago that she had made the same ocean crossing to reach Lanka. And she had had no bridge of sea beasts to keep her dry.

She marvelled at Rama's ability to command such an extra-ordinary army, as well as his ingenuity in conceiving of such a means to cross the ocean. How had he accomplished such a task? Did he know the lord of the sea beasts then? She would have to ask Ravana how Rama had done it – or then again, perhaps it would be best not to ask. Despite his apparent good humour when addressing his clan chiefs earlier, she could not fathom how Ravana could find this latest accomplishment of Rama's amusing. She watched as the lines of bears and vanars continued to arrive, a seemingly endless parade of eager soldiers ready to fight for Rama and his cause, filling up the narrow beach until it seemed there would be no more room to stand. The sun was almost down now, and she wondered how they would cope with the darkness. It was astonishing enough to see vanars crossing the vast body of water, let alone organising themselves into such an efficient army. She did not think they posed any threat to Lanka's rakshasa hordes – although those bears looked fairly threatening, especially the large darker-pelted ones that were arriving now, grunting and bellowing loudly – but there were so many of them! How large was Rama's army anyway? A million? Two million? More? It was hard to tell for sure, with the bulk of them still spread across the ocean along that long line of sea beasts, but there were certainly enough to mount a formidable invasion. Perhaps this would be a war worth the fighting after all. She flicked her tail in glee.

She was looking for Rama himself, searching for his familiar form amongst the furry crowds below, when she happened upon a small cluster of creatures standing directly below her on the beach, pointing up the cliff in her very direction. She cringed, thinking they had spotted her, and prepared to retreat hastily into the cavern. But then she realised that they were pointing not at her but at the cliffs. They had not even spotted the cave's mouth. In this slanting evening light they were unlikely to spot it unless they climbed within a few yards' reach of it. She had been lucky to find it herself when she had landed on the same shore, months earlier.

She looked closely at the group pointing at the cliffs, and with a frisson of sensual pleasure recognised Rama's beautiful visage among them. Ah. Her prince. He had grown leaner, more rugged and craggy than when she had seen him last in person, at the battle of Janasthana. His body, never given to softness, had grown harder, more sharply defined, like a sculpture chis-elled minutely to the very limit of the artist's abilities. Surely no further improvement was possible now. He was a beautiful, lithe, savagely muscled fighting machine. Her Rama. The mortal she still longed to possess with every fibre of her being.

She soughed softly, feeling the warmth of her own breath upon her front paws. It was futile to dwell thus on past desires, lost lusts. But she could not help the feelings that the very sight of Rama evoked in her. It was all she could do not to clamber down the cliffside and bound up to him, to embrace him in her limbs, feeling his hard, masculine strength against her furry pelt, entwine herself around his torso and—

Rama was coming towards the cliff.

She snapped herself out of her daydream and watched as the mortal for whom she had lusted so long and so hopelessly came to the foot of the very cliff upon which she was standing and, with a last brief word to his companions, began climbing the sheer rock face.

2

'My lord.'

Rama paused at the sound of Hanuman's voice. Standing at the foot of the cliff, looking up in preparation for starting his climb, he glanced around. The vanar was walking towards him up the sandy slope of the upper beach. 'Yes, my friend?'

'My lord, there is an easier and speedier way to broach these cliffs.'

Rama turned to face him fully. 'How?'

Hanuman bent low, prostrated himself, and touched Rama's feet. 'With your ashirwaad, my lord.'

'You always have my blessings, Hanuman. Rise and show me this solution you propose.'

Hanuman regained his feet, inhaled a deep breath, then began to expand himself. As with the earlier times, it was no less amazing a sight to behold. The vanar's body appeared to magnify rapidly, growing evenly and proportionately. In seconds he was the height of a tall tree, then a hundred feet. He stepped aside to avoid inconveniencing Rama and the others on the beach as his feet grew to the size of large boulders. He continued to grow until very shortly he was as tall as the cliff itself – and then even taller.

When he was half as tall again as the top of the cliff, he paused, ceasing to grow, and moved forward very carefully, taking great pains not to touch any of his comrades or masters on the beach far below. Bending over the cliff, he placed his hands firmly on the edge, taking a hold of it, then pressed down hard.

The muscles in his shoulders and back and arms began to bulge and stand out in clear relief, each corded group individually distinguishable. Rama saw that this immense strain was not due to any great use of effort on Hanuman's part; rather, it was due to his desire not to cause any sudden avalanches which would endanger those below. The crowds thronging the beach raised a great roar of excitement as Hanuman began to work the edge of the cliff. They grew silent in awe as they watched the gigantic vanar strain and sweat, using his powerful hands to mould the very rock of which the cliff was composed. The troops still on the bridge began calling out from the ocean, for Hanuman must have been visible from miles away. Then they grew silent too as the sounds of rock cracking and bursting travelled on the balmy evening breeze that was blowing from the south-west. Rama could see the dust of shattered rocks rise in a small cloud, but Hanuman's immense body obscured most of what he was doing. He saw the vanar's right knee rise as he placed it against the cliff, the way a man might press his knee upon a mattress or a load to keep it in place. Hanuman's powerful back muscles tensed and bulged as he worked his will upon the palisade cliffs. Glancing to one side, Rama saw the rakshasa Vibhisena staring open-mouthed at the sight. Even the others, familiar by now with their vanar compatriot's magical ability, watched in awe.

After several moments Hanuman issued a great sigh of satisfaction and moved aside, allowing them a clearer view of the cliff face. Or what had been the cliff face only moments ago. Now, where a sheer wall of black rock had risen to obstruct their way, a sloping passage had been formed, rising from the beach at a steep but perfectly negotiable gradient, no less than a rough ramp leading to the top.

As the massed soldiers took in the implications of what their fellow vanar had wrought with his bare hands and brute strength, a great roar of approval rose up from their combined throats. Rama joined in with his own voice, raising his hands and cheering Hanuman's achievement.

Hanuman bowed low before his lord, reaching out to touch Rama's feet. His enormous fingers embedded themselves a full yard deep into the sand, creating a veritable pit. Rama had to step back to keep his balance. The tips of the fingers that sought out his feet were each the size of an oak trunk. He touched the fingers with his own hands, feeling the way an ant must feel when faced with an elephant. 'Bless you always, my soul friend. Once again you earn your own shakti through the greatness of your karma.'

Then he turned with a great smile and addressed his company. 'Start the ascent in orderly fashion.'

Supanakha thought she was doomed for certain. It took her a moment to understand what the vanar intended when he began to expand himself. She turned and scampered away down the cave tunnel, not a moment too soon. A moment later the cave mouth behind her began to close shut with a grinding of rock, and the tunnel went pitch dark as the vanar pressed the rock itself inwards. She felt the thumping vibrations of sections of the tunnel's roof caving in and the pricks of fragments striking her furred back and haunches. She raced down the tunnel until finally, several moments later, she discerned it was safe to stop and look back. There was nothing to see. The tunnel had collapsed, the very cliffside moulded by the vanar into gods alone knew what – although it was not hard to guess. The vanar had obviously pressed the rock into a more negotiable slope, so that Rama's soldiers could climb it.

She padded on all fours down the dark tunnel, pausing to sneeze out some of the dust raised by the vanar's manipulation of the rock, and seethed silently.

She didn't know whether to curse the vanar for almost killing her accidentally or marvel at his brute power. A little of both, probably. Fortunately for her, she had seen his amazing size-altering ability first hand the previous night, and knew well enough to get out of the way. He was a fool, though. Had he been sharp enough to see this cave, they would have had another ingress into the heart of Ravana's sanctum. For this network of tunnels led all the way to the heart of Mount Nikumbhila, yojanas from the northern shore. And as far as she could tell, even the normally paranoid Lord of Lanka had not seen fit to post guards in them. Come to think of it, how careless could her cousin be, to have neglected to send a horde or two to repel the invaders as they arrived on the beach? It would have been easy enough for the kumbha-rakshasas to roll a few boulders down from the clifftop, or vats of boiling oil. Or better still, use some of his high-falutin rakshasa maya to smash those arriving vanars and bears before they could even land on Lankan soil. She had not thought herself a patriot, and irreverence and rebellion had been her lifelong trademarks, but for better or worse, this land was her home, the last bastion of rakshasa life upon the mortal plane – upon all the planes, for that matter – and it rankled with her to see the invaders land on its shores and start their campaign of ingress without so much as a rakshasa claw raised to obstruct them.

Is that what you think, cousin dearest? That I would stand aside and let the mortal and his furry friends land upon our shores like holidaymakers arriving for a friendly visit? Do you take me to be that much of a fool?

She stopped short, sniffing the darkness sharply. There. She could smell the unmistakable odour of the lord of rakshasas: that stench as of vegetation rotting in a deep jungle, a reek like long-decomposed boar or bull lying fly-laden in the hot summer sun, a sharp tang redolent of freshly spilled blood . . . and a pungent smell pervading the whole mix, like semen from an elephant in masth-heat. Only Ravana smelled like that. She relaxed, not wasting her time trying to figure out whether he was present here in flesh or merely in presence. Here in Lanka, Ravana was the very air you breathed. Reeking and omnipresent.

'I thought you were spending too much time in the palace of pleasures indulging your carnal lusts, cousin,' she said mockingly.

'Why else would you not take steps to repel the invaders? Why else would you allow them to land on our shores in the first place? And why else would you send your generals to their beds for the night while Rama and his vaulting vanar heroes cover your land like a pestilence of locusts? Yes, cousin. I thought you must be surely slaking your lust between the haunches of some new rakshasi plaything – or some two dozen new playthings. Too lost in your own sensual gratification to even take this menace seriously. Either that, or . . .' She paused.

Go on, my sweet cat-sister. Don't hold back now when you're enjoying a rare moment of perfect eloquence. Finish that last thought as well.

She barely hesitated. She had said enough to rouse his ire already. She might as well carry on. 'Either that, or I thought you were so shaken by the vanar's display of strength last night that you were cowering and cringing in some haunted corner, intending to stay there while Rama overran our country and came to drag you out by your hair – by your ten heads of hair! – and put an end to your misery.'

There was utter silence after she had finished. She could hear the steady thrumming of blood in her veins. Had she gone too far? Calling Ravana a coward was somewhat beyond the bounds of good taste. But she had been genuinely angry. She shrugged. Someone had to say it. And his generals were hardly man enough to stand up and tell him such things to his face – to his faces. Or even to whisper it behind his back, for that matter.

A soft chuckle came back from the darkness. It was the most unexpected response imaginable. But in a way, she felt a sparking of hope. If he was that confident that he could laugh away such bitchy criticism, then he must be more in control of the situation than she had thought. Only a king who had completely lost his senses would laugh like that at such a time – or a king who possessed secret knowledge that nobody else had.

Bravo, cousin, bravo. It would appear you have become something of a loyalist after all. Who would have thought it?

Just a few months here in the homeland and you are a Lankan through and through. Simply amazing! I had no idea you had become this patriotic.

She sniffed out a suitable spot in a corner of the tunnel and raised her hind leg, relieving herself copiously. After she was done, she shook herself. 'I care nothing for Lanka,' she said brusquely. 'But this matter concerns my rakshasa honour as well. I want to see the mortal crushed and broken like a smashed beetle under a boot heel, not running unobstructed across the countryside with an army. It is not right for mortals and vanars and bears to dare to encroach upon rakshasa land this way. Why do you stand aside and do nothing? I heard you tell your generals to go to bed. Why are you not repelling the invaders? Why did you let them land here at all? That is what I understand least of all! Why could you not stop them before they even reached Lankan shores?'

Ravana's voice, still rich with the amusement he had found in her last remarks, was tinged with steel this time. 'Because this is an endgame, cousin. Not a skirmish. Not another battle. Not even a war. It is the end of all wars. The culmination of a long and ancient conflict, the last of many campaigns waged over more than one era. I do not seek merely to win this time, nor to repel, or crush. I seek to triumph.'

She realised that his voice was no longer in her head; it had assumed physical form. He was here in the tunnel, she sensed, not far from where she stood. She sniffed, seeking him out, and her senses told her that he was less than three yards ahead, to the right. Slowly, as if locating him had made it happen, he began to emerge from the darkness, his sorcerous shakti illuminating the very pores of his leathery skin, until he stood revealed before her in all his rakshasa splendour, nine of his ten heads engaged as always in their individual bickering and constant dialogue, while the central head addressed her, its eyes glittering like jewels lit by their own inner light.

'Cousin. You asked me why I permitted Rama to land his

forces here. It was because this is rakshasa territory. This is my land. And by coming here, he has played right into my hands. Now, I have only to reach out,' his hands did as his words promised, reaching out with the palms facing upwards, then closing into mighty fists, the bones crunching harshly, 'and crush them. Back on the mainland, they might have been able to run or hide or evade me somehow. On the open seas they might have found help from their oceanic allies. But here on Lanka they are within my grasp, naked. They have nowhere to go from here. There is nothing they can do to resist my power. Nothing they can do now . . . except die.'

She stared, mesmerised. His vitality was so overwhelming, his power rolling off him in thick, palpable waves, that she was compelled to believe every syllable. If any creature possessed the ability to do as he willed, it was Ravana. All her doubts and resentments melted away, seeming foolish now in the presence of such potent shakti. How could she ever have doubted him? How could she have accused him of neglect, of cowardice even? Look at him! Magnificent, omnipotent, conqueror of the over-world and the underworld both, defeater of the devas them-selves, master of all he surveyed. What fool would dare oppose him? Of course he had a plan. Brilliant strategist that he was, he had chosen to allow the armies of Rama to land on the shores of Lanka, to lure them here just as a predator lures prey into its sanctuary, the better to pounce on it and savage it at its leisure.

In a single moment she went from blustering resentment to reverential ecstasy. She gazed up adoringly at the ten-headed master of her race, quivering with pleasure and sensual delight at merely being within his virile presence. She knew she was allowing herself to be hypnotised by the sorcery he wielded to subjugate those who encountered him, but she did not care. He was Lanka. And he was indomitable. This was the Ravana she had admired and feared for so long. Who was so named *Ra-va-na* because his aspect and his deeds were fearsome enough to make the universe scream.

Only one question occurred to her.

'How?' she asked, lowering her eyes to show him subservience.
'How will you do it, my lord?'

She asked it not as a form of censure or objection, only out
of curiosity. How would he choose to dispatch the forces of Rama?
What devious intent did he have in store for them? The sadistic
part of her relished the revelation of some grotesque new means
of taking life, the one act that gave her most pleasure, more than
even the act of procreation, which, after all, was only a means
of defying one's own mortality. She preferred to embrace the dark
descent. To lick the loins of the deepest, most secret craving of
all living beings – the ultimate mating of all, the coupling of living
flesh with sudden, unforeseen, brutally violent death.

Ravana's faces shared one of those rare moments of concaten-
ation, those brief instants when all ten heads were united in a
common thought, joining their formidable individual powers
to form one great chain of mental prowess. All heads smiled,
displaying a variety of teeth, glistening with the saliva of predatory anticipation. The lion was hot for the hunt.

'Come,' he said, his ten tongues speaking in ten mouths all
at once, writhing glossily like serpents in the mouths of sub-
oceanic sea caves. 'Let me show you.'

He clapped his hands together.

And in a winking of an eye she found herself elsewhere. She
gasped as she teetered on the edge of an abyss, her claws scrab-
bling for purchase on a gravelly slope, then ceased her struggles as she realised that she was not present here in physical
form. Ravana had brought only her consciousness with him,
though he was here in all his corporeal glory, naked body weeping
perspiration that roiled and dripped like hot oil through the
crevices and contours of his acutely define musculature. But she
had no time to lust at the sight of his magnificent anatomy, for
the thing he had brought her here to see lay below, far below,
in the great abyss that she guessed was within the labyrinthine
network of cavernous tunnels leading ultimately to the volcano

that had once birthed Lanka and formed the island-kingdom itself. The volcano had lain silent and still for nigh on fourteen years, as had Ravana himself under the influence of the brahm-astra cage in which he had been imprisoned at Mithila. But she saw now that it was not truly dead, only dormant, and even in this dormant state the heat it gave off was immense, in-tolerable. She cringed at the rim of the ledge as waves of searing heat rolled up and over her. Had she been present here in the flesh, it would have been roasting now, and her fur singed and evaporated. Even incorporeal as she was, she crouched in reflex, fearful of the power of the sleeping titan.

Ravana was chanting slokas in that rhythmic incantation that she loathed: every time she heard a rishi or tapasvi sadhu in a forest muttering those Sanskrit verses, she felt inclined to leap upon them and tear out their throats – and she had done exactly that innumerable times. Every rakshasa hated the sound of those incantations, that smooth, perfect Sanskrit that seemed to carry the motes of energy of brahman itself in every syllable. Except that Ravana was chanting them backwards, perfectly inverting every syllable, every word, every sloka, to reverse the energies of brahman. And the effect was galvanising to a rakshasi ear. It was the sound of roaring blood and cracking bone and brutal agony, the very antithesis of the peace and beauty of their original meaning.

Revelling in the sound, she persuaded herself to peek once more over the rim of the crater. And saw a sight astonishing enough to hold her attention despite the terrible maw of the volcano far below. From a ledge at the tip of another tunnel much like this one but a few dozen yards below and to the right of where she crouched, a line of rakshasas of both sexes were emerging. From their white and red-ochre robes she knew them to be the followers of the same brahmanical cult that Vibhisena had espoused. Indeed, every one of them was anointed on the forehead with the ash markings of brahmins. They were lined up in neat rows extending far back into the dimly lit tunnel.

From the glazed absence of intelligence in their half-shut eyes, she guessed that Ravana had mesmerised them somehow. And compelled them to do what they were about to do. For as she watched, the first brahmin rakshasas stepped off the ledge they were standing on, and fell to certain destruction far below. She followed their plummeting bodies for a long moment until they struck the dark surface of the volcano's pool of searing magma. Their flesh ignited instantly on impact and burst into flame. More bodies followed in an unending procession, until the belly of the volcano was a hotbed of flaming spots.

As the brahmins continued to fall, and Ravana continued to chant his obscenely inverted mantras, she felt a trembling beneath her insubstantial paws. Or perhaps she felt it beneath her real paws, still back in the cavern where Ravana had found her. For she sensed that this potent vibration was reverberating not just through the maw of the volcano, but throughout the length and breadth of Lanka itself. She had no clue what dark ritual Ravana was performing here, but it was obvious that it was some form of power-enhancement. He was clearly using the fire sacrifice of these hundreds upon hundreds of pious souls to create a power well of brahman with which he intended to work some monstrous sorcery.

Just what that sorcery might be, she shuddered to imagine. As the rumbling increased, growing deafening and causing her every nerve to shudder painfully, she was transported back to the cavern. Just before she was pushed away by Ravana – for she knew it was he who had magically removed her in the nick of time – she caught a tantalisingly brief glimpse of a pillar of fire rising up from the depths of the volcano far below. She barely had time to see it, but she could have sworn on her own black soul that the unnatural fire had faces and features that strongly resembled the being responsible for its creation.

3

Rama felt a faint trembling beneath his feet and frowned. Perhaps it was caused by the tramping of his enormous army. As suddenly as it had begun, it faded away. He dismissed it and refocused on the task at hand, overseeing the transfer of the armies from the sea-bridge to land.

After Hanuman's dramatic alteration of the cliffside, the ascent posed no challenge. Rama and Lakshman led the first wave to the top, deafened by the cheering of the troops in celebration of their crossing as well as at entering Lanka so easily. The top of the cliff was a plateau stretching for many miles, rolling grassland dotted with clumps of wooded areas. Vibhisena had said that Lanka was shaped like a teardrop suspended just below the mainland. It was some hundred and twenty yojanas in length from shore to shore, and at its widest point, at its waist, some forty-five yojanas across. That was both larger and smaller than Rama had expected. All he had learned of Lanka before today were stray bits of information gleaned from legends and myths. Like all such scraps of information, they had ranged wildly from fantastical descriptions of a hellish Asura-infested landscape with a great black castle set in the heart of a seething, exploding volcano, to a vapid desert island barely a mile from end to end. Like all realities, the truth was to be found in neither extreme. It was a country much like the southern tip of the mainland they had left behind, the flora and fauna appearing almost identical to that one, for at some point in its geographical past this island had certainly been attached to that mainland. Its lushness was unexpected, yet welcome. For his first concern had been how to feed such a large army with an ocean separating them from their familiar sources of sustenance. Now, he saw, he would not have to concern himself with such mundane matters; the troops could easily find forage in these fecund grasslands and forests. He and his generals could concentrate on the real issues at hand: the strategies of war.

He called a meeting of the leaders at a suitable spot on the plateau, close enough to the edge that they might oversee the beach, where troops were still arriving in a steady stream, as well as spy the lie of the land and plan their next moves. Twilight had fallen by now, a quiet, luminous pallor falling upon the world, with birdsong and the soft shurring of the ocean providing a placid backdrop. It was hard to believe this was the dreaded lair of rakshasas. He noticed the disbelieving look on the faces of each new wave of troops that ascended to the plateau: surely this could not be Lanka? Land of rakshasas? Lair of Asuras? Impossible!

For some reason, the impossibility of it troubled him too. He could not easily express why, but it bothered him that the land seemed so peaceful and verdant. That their landing had been unopposed, their ingress unobstructed. Others had voiced these same concerns, but they had been answered, doubtfully. After all, it was not for nothing that these cliffs had been named palisades. Had they not had Hanuman's prodigious talents to simplify their ascent, these rock walls would have daunted them for hours, perhaps even an entire night and a day, for it would have been no joke to have such great numbers climb such steep faces. As it was, the only thing they had to contend with now was keeping the lines moving up from the beach in orderly fashion, making sure that the flow remained as continuous and unobstructed as a river flowing uphill. Already a goodly percentage of their numbers were upon the plateau, and at this present rate, a few minutes after the last vanars and bears came ashore, at around midnight, they would all be up here, assembled and ready for war.

He turned his attention to the gathering of chiefs. They were all here: Jambavan, Kambunara and their generals of varying pelt shades – fawn, light brown, dark brown, jet black, and black with white streaks. King Sugreeva, Prince Angad, Hanuman and the five vanar generals. And Vibhisena, Lakshman and himself. The troops were being managed by the clan chiefs, who had gained immeasurable confidence after the successful crossing and the absence of opposition on the Lankan shore. This unwieldy mass of furry friends was finally starting to resemble an army that could give Lanka's rakshasas cause to fear. If nothing else, their sheer numbers would count for a great advantage: from Hanuman's keen observations of Lanka's forces, the rakshasas would be outnumbered by a factor of three to one. Now it was up to Rama to ensure that this weight of numbers was utilised in the most effective manner possible.

'The key is speed,' he said. 'We must strike like the cobra, swift and unhesitant. And continue striking, in unending waves.' He indicated Vibhisena. 'As you can see from this solitary example, the average rakshasa is thrice as large as the average vanar. And with a hide that is almost akin to armour. Even if three vanars were to attack a single rakshasa at a time, the enemy would still have the advantage of weight and strength.'

He noticed the frown on Vibhisena's face and paused. 'Do you wish to add something to that, my lord Vibhisena?' he asked politely.

The rakshasa nodded thankfully. 'By your leave, Rama. I am not a typical example of my brother's warrior forces. As I am sure Hanuman can tell you. But even the sturdiest pulastyas – which is my clan – are pygmies compared to the kumbhas.'

'Kumbhas?' Lakshman asked.

'Indeed, Lord Lakshman. The kumbha-rakshasas are related to our other brother, Kumbhakarna. While they do not possess his extraordinary stature, for he is quite unique in that way, they are considerably larger than the average warrior rakshasa.'

'How large are they then?' Prince Angad demanded with uncharacteristic churlishness. Both the vanar prince and his father were still openly suspicious of the rakshasa collaborator and his motives. King Sugreeva felt strongly about the wisdom of discussing vital military strategy with a member of the enemy; it was only his respect for Rama that had compelled him to swallow his objections. Angad, of course, had followed his father's example and bitten his own tongue as well.

Vibhisena shrugged. 'At least thrice as large as I am, in height as well as weight.'

Everybody exclaimed. Even the bears glowered. 'And how many of these kambos are there?' asked Kambunara angrily, as if Vibhisena was personally responsible for birthing the whole sub-species.

'A full rakshasa garrison,' he said. 'Roughly equivalent to two of your akshohini.' He addressed the last to Rama and Lakshman. They exchanged tense glances. An akshohini was over sixty thousand soldiers. Two akshohini would mean a lakh and twenty thousand kumbha-rakshasas, each thrice as large as an ordinary rakshasa, which meant they were about four times as large as the bears.

Sugreeva stared coldly at Vibhisena. The vanars did not take disappointment well, and the king's response at hearing about the kumbhas was writ clearly on his sorrowful features. 'How do we know that these beasts even exist?' he asked. 'In all my years I have never heard of rakshasas that large.'

Hanuman spoke up. 'They exist,' he said simply. 'I fought them only yesterday.'

Lakshman turned to Vibhisena suddenly. 'You mentioned your other brother. Kumbhakarna? Who is this person?'

Vibhisena passed a hand across his eyes. 'He is not someone any of you would wish to face in battle, Lord Lakshman. Fortunately, I do not think you will have to.'

'Why is that?' asked the vanar general Sarabha. 'Does he not fight on the side of Ravana? Is he a dissenter like yourself?'

'Nay, nay,' Vibhisena said. 'Would that he was. He is a partner with Ravana in every vile act he has ever committed. Together they have ravaged the realm of the devas and wreaked havoc in the underworld. Kumbhakarna unleashed in battle is an army unto himself.' He shuddered and shook his head. 'If he were in this fray, we would not be standing here debating sizes and weights. All our strategies would be devoted solely to defending ourselves against his onslaught. And I honestly would not know how that could be done. Nothing can face my brother and survive. Nothing that I have ever seen or heard of before.'

Everybody looked at the rakshasa with dubious expressions.

Prince Angad seemed the least willing to take Vibhisena's words at face value. 'What exactly makes this Kumbhakarna so formidable? He is a rakshasa, yes? A large rakshasa? Well, even the largest can be downed in battle.'

Vibhisena looked pityingly at the young vanar. 'Nay, Prince Angad. He is not merely large. He is the thing against which all other things are measured, and found wanting. A long time ago, Kumbhakarna was given a boon by the devas. He had only to speak his wish and it would be granted. But he was clumsy and mis-uttered the Sanskrit sloka. So instead of asking to be able to wage war all year round, which was what he desired, he asked to be able to wage *sleep* all year round! Lord Brahma, taking advantage of the verbal slip, immediately granted the boon. And so Kumbhakarna, who loved nothing more than to do violence every waking minute, was cursed to sleep for six months at a stretch. He awakens for a single day, during which he eats prodigious quantities of food and consumes great volumes of liquor, and only then is he ready to fight. But since there are rarely any foes worthy of facing him and surviving more than a few moments, let alone an entire day, he has taken to eating nonstop until he falls asleep once again. That may be a day, or a month, or six months later. As long as he is awake, he eats and drinks, and then, soon enough, he sleeps again. And once he sleeps, nothing can awaken him.' He sighed, and made a rakshasa gesture that suggested relief. 'He is in the middle of a sleep cycle right now. Which is why I know for certain that he will not take the field of battle in this conflict.'

Everybody looked around at each other, unsure of how to take this extraordinary story. 'How large exactly is he then?' Lakshman asked curiously. 'I mean, if he is of the same clan as the kumbha-rakshasas, then he must be also—'

He paused as the ground beneath them vibrated briefly, like the floor of a canyon beneath an oncoming landslide. But they were standing at the highest point in sight, and the tremor passed as suddenly as it had begun. Vibhisena frowned as if about to comment on it, then shook his head and addressed Lakshman's comment.

'No, no, no, Lord Lakshman. The kumbhas are like ants before him. He is of a stature that cannot be measured.' Vibhisena indicated Hanuman. 'You have seen our vanar friend when he expands himself to his greatest size? As he did yesterday when he pounded the Tower of Lanka into the ground. Kumbhakarna would be taller than that, and much, much more powerful. For he retains every morsel and every drop that he consumes. That is part of the boon that Brahma inflicted upon him . . . a curse really.'

Lakshman turned his head slowly to look at Hanuman, then raised his eyes to the sky, trying to imagine a rakshasa taller than Hanuman's greatest height, and stronger as well.

Rama saw that this line of discussion was making the vanars nervous and irritable. It was time to divert the conversation back to the original line of discussion. 'In any event,' he said, 'if he is not able to take to the field, then we need not concern ourselves with him. Let us discuss our first assault now.'

He squatted on the ground and began pointing with a long stick Lakshman had cut for him for this purpose, indicating the stones they had placed in rows to suggest the formations of the two forces. He had based his plan on Vibhisena and Hanuman's descriptions of Lanka's geography as well as the likely defensive formations that Ravana's army would mount. Lakshman had lit a small fire to illuminate the space in which they had convened. The vanar and bear leaders had learned to steel themselves in the presence of agni for the sake of their mortal friends, but a few of them still blanched and winced as the hastily assembled sticks crackled and hissed in the flames.

Beyond the circle of light, Rama glimpsed the partially illuminated outlines of the troops bounding past in the darkness, eyes glistening red in the moonless night. They had fallen silent out of deference to the war council that was in progress, as the landing progressed beyond the initial euphoria to a stage of grim consolidation. Nightfall had darkened the mood as well. The entire landscape seemed different by darkness. Rama was glad that there would be a moon tonight and the next few nights; they had spied the new moon eight nights before, which meant it was waxing and would be full in another six or seven nights. They ought to have enough light to see by once the moon rose in another watch or two.

He resumed the description of his plans, using the stick and the stones to illustrate his strategy.

'As I was saying earlier, our greatest ally is speed. The vanars shall line themselves up in waves, thus. After three waves of vanars there will be one wave of bears. Which means that three vanars shall attack each rakshasa, and inflict as much damage as they can, and before the rakshasas have time to tear them apart or cut them down, the bears will follow, slamming into them with all their strength and weight. When the bear wave strikes, the first line of rakshasas should fall back. Then we repeat the formation. And so on, until we break through the rakshasa lines and crack their defences. At that point . . .'

He paused. Was it just his hand that was trembling? Or was the very ground on which the stick was resting starting to shudder? He looked around at the troops still pouring on to the plateau from the beach. Could their footfalls be causing the ground to shake? But why should it start of a sudden? Perhaps—

'My lords!'

The shout rose from the edge of the plateau. It was Nala, entrusted with channelling the various vanar troops into the formation decided by Rama earlier, telling this tribe to go there, and that one here, and so on. He was a dimly glimpsed furry smear in the near-darkness. Only the faint spill of light from the fire made it possible to see him at all. He was waving frantically, leaping up and down in true vanar fashion.

'My lords!' he cried again. 'The land! The land, it—'

He got no further. Chaos erupted all around, as the earth itself heaved up and began to attack them.

In the deep cavern in which Ravana had caged her, Sita felt the earth shuddering and opened her eyes. She had been seated cross-legged, meditating to calm her senses and reduce her bodily metabolism to a minimum. After the morning's display of shakti, Ravana had flown her into this cavern lit by the ghostly illumination of his sorcerous stones, and warded the entrance with a guard of rakshasas. The interior of the cavern was curiously similar to the place where she had been imprisoned when first brought to Lanka; she even thought she could recognise some of the same trees, with the markings of the rakshasas who had tormented her then. They had used their talons to scratch out obscene drawings and markings on the trunks of the trees, and the trees in this place had similar scratches and markings – similar but not the same. She knew this because these markings made no sense whatsoever. It was as if an artist had attempted to hurriedly copy them and had only roughly replicated them, without understanding what they actually stood for. She wondered if this was a consquence of the damage that Hanuman had inflicted upon Pushpak. This thought made her rejoice ever so slightly, for it proved that even the great and shakti-shaali, omnipotent Ravana had his flaws. Even his maha-shakti had its limits. An imperfectly rendered obscenity upon the trunk of a sala tree, an ashoka sapling which was bent to the right instead of to the left as it had been in that earlier grove . . . these were tiny suggestions that Ravana's sorcery was not infallible. Hopefully, neither was Ravana himself.

The cavern was vast, the ashoka grove the most peaceful part of it. She had enough space to wander around, even a little brook and a garden with trees and a shrubbery. Yet she knew that she was no less a prisoner here than she had been in the tower.

She had immersed herself in meditation all morning, knowing that the only thing she could do now was wait – wait until Rama arrived and saved her, or until Ravana finally lost patience and she was forced to end her life. His limits had been tested to the extreme, she knew, and this morning's outburst and display had been to intimidate her into succumbing to his will. She had resisted not by pitting her strength of will against his, but by simply negating his use of force. If one did not accept an abuse flung at oneself by another person, that abuse continued to belong to the person who had uttered it; by simply rejecting it, one brushed it off without any effect. Ravana's lust and his growing desperation were his problems to deal with, not hers.

And yet she knew that even the most disciplined application of yogic endurance would not help her survive much longer. Ravana's use of force could easily become physical at any moment, and while she might be able to combat him mentally, she had no defences against his great physical powers, let alone his sorcerously enhanced strength.

If that happened, she would not live long.

For she would sooner kill herself and her unborn child than succumb to the rakhshasa's will. There were no circumstances under which she would yield to his demands or even provide him with the smallest modicum of the legitimacy he desired. Perhaps the greatest advantage she still possessed was the knowledge that he wished her to yield willingly. To attack her would be an admission of his own failure – and her triumph. Either way, all she could do was wait him out.

And so she sat here on the grassy floor of the artificial garden, lost in meditation. Seeking that yoganidra state the devas were so famous for: if she could lose herself the way Shiva had, perhaps all this would pass in the wink of a third eye, and when she regained her consciousness, Rama—

That was when the earth began shuddering.

She unwound her limbs and rose slowly to her feet as the ground vibrated with increasing urgency. The walls and ceiling of the cavern, far and high though they were, shook as well, and fine powdery rock dust trickled down around her. In moments she was compelled to stand with her legs spread to maintain her balance, clutching the trunk of the nearest ashoka tree for support. The shudders increased, as if the island were in the throes of an earthquake. The light in the cavern flickered, dimmed to pinpoints, and then grew suddenly brighter, dazzlingly bright, too bright to look at. She shielded her face and clung to the trunk of an ashoka tree, alert to any falling debris – for now the tremors were great enough that she feared the cave ceiling itself might crash down upon her.

Instead, the floor rose up.

She gasped as the grassy ground on which she stood lifted without warning, carrying her with it. The tree she was clinging to remained steady, her only support, but everything else was rising and falling, moving, morphing, reshaping . . . She could actually see the walls bulge inwards, and then change texture, as if some magical force were altering their very substance. She saw the chiselled rock of the cave wall darken, then smooth out, then develop a network of indented lines . . . The pattern that was developing seemed almost familiar. As if she had seen it often before. She sent up a silent prayer as a great and terrible grinding and gnashing echoed up the length of the chamber, and then the cavern was plunged into pitch darkness.

4

The ground beneath Rama's feet rose up with a roar, flinging him upwards and backwards so suddenly he had no chance to react in any way. It was as if the earth had reached out with an angry palm, shoving him viciously. He felt himself falling through blackness – no, not falling, rising! Rising up, up, up into the air, upon the fist of earth that had erupted beneath his feet. He was transported upwards against his will, too rapidly to do anything more than lie still and try to catch his stolen breath. As he moved swiftly through the darkness, he heard an angry spitting and hissing, like a nest of uragas woken by an enemy, and saw a shower of sparks explode in the air somewhere far to the left, dispelling the darkness momentarily and filling the night with a cascade of blazing sticks and fragments – the remnants of the fire Lakshman had lit – and illuminating the plateau for a goodly distance for a few shocking moments.

It was a scene like nothing he had ever seen before. The ground heaved and rose and fell all around, twisting and writhing into a variety of tortured, contorted forms and planes. Like a living beast, it moved and turned and rose and fell, crushing vanars and bears here, tossing others remorselessly, sucking some down. The air was rent with the shrill screeches of vanars and the lowing rage of impotent bears. Once again, as with the wall of water, nature itself had turned against them.

He was flung so high that for an instant he could even look over the edge of the cliff, down to the very beach itself. He glimpsed the line of greybacks, ragged and heaving in the choppy ocean. It was too brief a glimpse to tell for sure, but he thought that the ocean itself was not churning – it was only the effect of the land mass moving that was affecting the water somewhat. He glimpsed also the lines of troops still pouring on to the beach, slowed to a shocked crawl, stunned by the sudden eruption of the land. He heard the frightened *cheeka*s of vanars on the beach, just landed and finding the solid sand suddenly exploding and imploding around them as if fired upon by astras, except that even celestial weapons would not operate in such a manic, frenzied fashion. It was as if an invisible army of crabs were scurrying up out of and down into the sand of the beach, tossing some vanars and bears in the air as they rose, sucking others down as they descended again, in an insane dance of sand and beast – and blood.

Then he reached the peak of his ascent, or as high as the fist of earth holding him aloft wished to go, and gasped in shocked wonder, experiencing a moment of perfect weightlessness, like a bird pausing in its flapping to allow a current of air to bear it along. But this was no current holding him a hundred yards aloft; it was the ground itself, risen up. And he knew that what rose up must surely fall. He braced his body, curling himself up into a ball and awaiting the impact. He would survive it, no matter what; he would survive it and then he would—

The ground shifted beneath him, scraping his bare back, moving under his limbs, tearing itself apart and putting itself together anew, reshaping itself. Great groaning and grinding sounds came from beneath him. He dared to open his eyes once more and tried to orient himself. There was almost no light to see by up here, but he could sense the transformation taking place by the sound and vibration itself. The finger that had raised him up was not falling back – apparently, tonight on Lanka, the natural laws of the world would not be entertained. Instead, it was growing, expanding. He uncurled himself slowly, cautiously, rising to his feet. And instantly wished he had not done so.

The burning debris from the fire, flung across the plateau for tens of yards in every direction, served to illuminate isolated patches of land. Seen from this vantage point, a hundred or more yards above the ground, it was like a map laid out before him, drawn upon parchment by some obscene, twisted artist.

The ground was re-forming itself into a new shape. He could already guess what that shape might possibly be, for the progress was swift. It was as if the island of Lanka itself had been commanded by the lord of rakshasas to alter its appearance according to his desires. And in doing so, it was moving of its own volition, rising, falling, squaring off, elongating, accomplishing what ten thousand artisans could not do in a dozen years – within a single night. For at the pace at which the reshaping was proceeding, it was evident that this devil's work would be done before dawn. The fact that they, Rama and his fellows, his troops, had been present here at the time of the earth's reshaping was no doubt part of the Lord of Lanka's plan. For while accomplishing his epic feat of sorcerous engineering, he was also launching the first major assault upon Rama's armies. Rama could see dead beasts everywhere: some torn apart by the earth separating, others crushed beyond recognition when two sections hammered themselves together, yet others tossed high, over the edge of the cliff perhaps, to fall on the jagged rocks far below, or even here on the plateau.

He saw a cluster of vanars, bunched together as was their tendency under crisis, thrown mercifully upon the upper branches of a tree, clinging desperately with limbs and tails. Another group, not as fortunate, were tossed high and then left to fall back upon naked rock, their bodies shattering, skulls smashing open to spill splatters of gore, the survivors dying slow, agonising deaths as they lay there helplessly, spines and limbs broken to fragments. Bears were worse off, by and large, for even when thrown down on to trees, they could hardly be expected to cling on to passing branches. They hit the ground with heavy thuds, many never to rise again. Those who did rise were thrown down once more, for the earth continued to shake and shudder and split open, hiving off in unexpected directions. There was no way to predict which way it would go next, up, down or sideways. In places he saw the earth split open, swallowing entire companies of his troops, the poor creatures falling silently into the dark maw of a crevice so deep, he could not hear their bodies strike the bottom.

As he watched, stunned and helpless for the moment, he began to discern the rough outline of the new shape the land was taking, and to guess at the ultimate form this sorcerous redesigning was aimed at producing. His fists tightened with cold, impotent fury, and he began reaching for the celestial weapons. Then he stopped, fingers curling in upon themselves, knowing that there was nothing he could do to stop this particular assault. Here, even the weapons of Brahma and Vishnu and Shiva would have no effect upon the sorcery of Ravana. For this was the rakshasa's domain. He had prepared for this very moment ingeniously, infusing the earth with his sorcery in some fashion, waiting until enough of Rama's troops were on the island – yet before they were ready to launch their own assault – and then he had struck. Now all Rama and his armies could do was wait out the attack. Attempt to survive it somehow. And when it was over . . .

He sat down cross-legged upon the spur of ground that had borne him up. It continued to shudder and writhe beneath him, as the sorcerous reshaping continued. Had it been possible, he would have climbed down and attempted to do something, anything. But there was nothing to be done. They were an army at war, and the enemy had launched the first assault. A treacherous, cowardly assault, for not one soldier of the enemy's ranks was here to spill blood or even offer a target. An unbalanced, unfair, uneven assault by an invisible, greatly superior force, upon a relatively helpless one. But an assault nevertheless. And faced by such an assault, he could do only what any commander did at such a time: wait it out and pray that his soldiers survived.

He tried to calm himself, regain control of his senses, and prepare himself for the war ahead. To form in his mind a strategy by which he could strike Ravana a blow as intense and unexpected as this one he had struck Rama. He sought the calm of meditation that had always come to him easily, like a flower yielding its fragrance to a kiss of the breeze.

This time, calm was hard to come by.

The screams and cries of dying and suffering vanars and bears kept battering his senses all night long.

Hanuman was filled with chagrin. He had come to the same conclusion that Rama had: there was nothing he could do. He tried to leap to save some troops from a falling mound of earth, to catch others who were flung up by another heaving section, to do what he could here and there. But the entire island was writhing and churning, and there was only so much he could do at one time, only so many he could reach. He worked all night long, refusing to give up, using every ounce of his strength and ability to try to save whomever he could. But as the long, terrible night wound on, and more and more vanars and bears died in his arms, he began to realise that it was a hopeless task. It was akin to trying to rush around a battlefield saving one's fellow soldiers from the attacks of the enemy. A battle could not be fought in such a way; not even by a soldier possessed of the powers that he possessed. It was futile. Ultimately, if he saved someone here, someone else died there. If he flew and picked up a cluster of vanars and carried them out of harm's way in one place, moments after he had left them there the earth would rise up and fold itself upon them where they stood, crushing them all without a second's warning. Soon, he was so covered with gore and gristle that he could barely get a grip on anything, his entire body slick with bodily fluids and dust and dirt.

He flew up as high as he could, trying to see as far as possible and spy out the land. It was towards midnight now, and the last of the troops had arrived as expected, for the greybacks had held their line for as long as it was physically possible; no sooner had the last of the vanars and bears leaped on to the killing sands of Lanka, the greybacks moved away with a great lowing and mooing, offering their heartfelt commiseration for the terror that was befalling his compatriots. He sent back thoughts of great sadness and grief, as well as sentiments of gratitude and love, for the greybacks had done their task admirably; what transpired after his people arrived on Lanka was not within their control. Even so, he heard their voices all night long, lowing and calling in the dark ocean, offering support and encouragement to their new landlocked friends, as well as the occasional siren of rage against those inflicting such suffering upon them. It tore at his heart then, that despite his great shakti he could do so little to help others. He opened his mouth and bellowed his anguish, beating his fists upon his chest.

Lakshman survived a flailing of earth, a mad frenzy of dust and dirt and shrubbery that blinded him for several moments and caused him to lose all sense of direction – or even orientation. For how could you tell which way was up or down when the very earth itself was surging to and fro in impossible patterns? One moment he was being pushed from behind by a wall of earth that rose out of the ground and continued to rise until it had gone too high in the darkness for him to see the top of it; another moment he was dodging a row of protrusions that shot forward from the wall with alarming speed. Despite being made only of mud, they were hard enough and pointed enough to pierce flesh, as he saw happen to one unfortunate bear who did not dodge them quickly enough. Three separate spears penetrated the bear's shoulder, chest and ribs, and even as Lakshman lunged forward to try to aid the poor creature, the points of the mud spears emerged from its back,

bursting out of the fur with bloody precision, and continued
their forward motion. They were no more aware of their ability
to kill than any force of nature, but they were no less deadly
for that. Lakshman roared with fury as he struggled to wrest
the bear's gasping body off the spears, and in the dust and
confusion he almost failed to see the second row of protrusions
emerging from a lower point on the same wall. These were
thicker, blunter, but they looked ugly and hard enough to break
leg bones. He spun around and began shouting warnings to
everyone within range. But despite hearing his cries, several of
the troops continued to mill around in dazed bewilderment.
Their terror and confusion was compounded by the holes
appearing in the ground around them, in a pattern that made
no sense at first, but gradually assumed a meaningful purpose
to Lakshman. One of the soldiers found his foot caught in
a hole that suddenly dropped out from beneath him, and
screamed. His vanar and bear friends nearby tried to pull him
out, while he kept screaming that the ground was trying to
swallow him whole. Lakshman saw to his horror what none
of the rest of them was aware of: the lower row of blunt spikes
were approaching them at a remorseless pace. He shouted to
warn them and they turned, looking at the wall. But they were
too late. The spikes struck them, punching through the bones
of their feet and thighs with sickening force, and knocked them
over en masse. Even as they struggled to break free, the ground
shuddered nearby, and a pile of earth flew up in an arching
swoop, landing right on top of the hapless band of trapped soldiers. The thud of the earthfall striking ground again cut off
their dying screams.

Lakshman saw many more such scenes of sickening, mean-
ingless violence all around him. At one point he began searching
for Rama, and when he could not find him anywhere, nor find
anyone who had seen him, he began to feel his gorge rise up
in his throat. The thought of Rama being brought down by
mud spears or spikes or holes in the ground sickened him.

Surely they had not come through so much, survived so many battles and fights, just so the future King of Ayodhya could die here on this plateau in Lanka, killed by nothing more vicious than mindless mud manipulated by an absent rakshasa's sorcery? He searched desperately for hours, passing grotesque tableaux of carnage, until, with an immense bone-shivering, grinding sensation, the first phase of the reshaping ended and a pause more terrible than all the dusty chaos descended briefly upon the battlefield – for it was nothing less than a battlefield. As he waited, not knowing what new horror might erupt next, he looked around and took stock. Immense vaulting walls of earth had sprung up all around the plateau, running along its rim in a pattern that his mind dimly recognised but did not wish to stop to name right now.

As the dust settled at last, he raised his eyes, wiping grime and blood from his forehead with equally gore- and dust-smeared hands. Holding his head up to keep a trickle from rolling into his eyes, he saw that a solitary figure was perched on top of one great wall, perhaps a hundred or a hundred and fifty yards high – it was hard to tell exactly in this dust-bedevilled darkness. He tried to find a better angle to see by, and when he looked up again he saw the figure move, rising to stand in a manner that suggested a man looking down. There was a moon out by now, and it emerged from behind a bank of cloud just then, silhouetting the lone figure on top of the wall. Then he was sure. There was no mistaking a mortal man's outline, and that was certainly no vanar or bear.

'Rama,' he said with a sense of relief so great, tears welled up in his eyes. He dabbed at them fiercely, forgetting his blood- and dust-smeared hands. 'Rama is alive.'

Then the next phase of reconstruction began, and he leaped aside just as the ground on which he had been standing began to ripple and slide slowly from side to side. It was not moving quickly or forcefully enough to smash or batter, and he saw that the troops across the field were easily able to sidestep these new developments, although they remained fearful and mistrustful of Ravana's sorcery. He called out to those captains and other tribe and clan chiefs within hailing range to remain alert and not to band too closely together, the better to dodge whatever hellish new thing came bursting out next. But now that they were forewarned and alert, nothing happened of course. The shifting plates and sections of the great scheme that had been put into place earlier merely adjusted and slid a few inches this way and that, the sounds of groaning rock and protesting piles of packed earth more eerie than any actual threat.

And so began a new stage in the battle, one in which the enemy continued to shape its mysterious design, working with the elements of soil and rock and tree, crafting them with invisible forces into a design that was clear even to the most dull-headed vanar or bear on the plateau now, while Rama's army continued to do the only thing it possibly could, faced with such a foe: survive until morning.

It was a long night.

5

It was dawn when the sorcery finally ceased. First light was creeping across the sky, patches of indigo, violet, purple, crimson and lime green seeping into one another, streaking across the world like coloured water flung across a parquet floor or like some bizarre after-effect of Ravana's maya. Everyone glanced suspiciously around, doubting that things were as they seemed, doubting their companions, their fellows, their leaders, even doubting themselves. For where only last evening they had stood upon a lush green plateau, undulating into rolling meadows, quiet brooks, placid flower fields, dense thickets rife with life and growth, stretching farther to the foothills of distant mountains, now in the place of all this picturesque natural beauty stood a terrible, heart-chilling vision. A dark nightmare made real through Asura maya.

Rama rose slowly to his feet, staring in first one direction then another, seeing with disbelieving eyes what the early slanting light unveiled. He had formed some notion of what was being wrought this long, dark and awful night. But it was still a shock to see it rendered complete even before morning was full-blown. And to know that all this had been achieved through the manipulating of mere earth, rock, trees and water, the natural materials of the land. Manipulated, reshaped, coagulated, hardened, baked and chiselled until the startlingly effective result lay before his very eyes, only a night's watch later.

The raised tower of packed earth which had carried him

aloft was now a solid wall of piled stone. The wall rose much higher than he had thought last evening. He had felt it shudder and move all night long, no doubt increasing by steadier, slower degrees. It rose now to a height of some three hundred yards, at least thrice as high as it had first stood. The surface was not dry earth packed together, but solid blocks of cut stone, as if carved in great chunks from living rock and then shaped into identical regular shapes, which then appeared to have been placed upon one another to form a piled wall. There were fortresses like this across the Arya nations, although none this high or thick, and surely none that had been erected in a single night. He bent and pressed his palm upon the stone on which he stood, feeling a familiar roughly chiselled texture. The grooves where the individual stones met were lined with a thin glue of mortar, as if living hands had applied the mortar before each new stone was lowered into place by teams of horses or men using ropes and pulleys. Yet no ropes had lowered these stones, no hands, mortal or rakshasa, had applied any mortar, no engineer had supervised the placement of the stones and the chiselling of their planes. Despite the absence of these normal essentials, the wall felt perfectly solid and real. After all, he realised, it *was* real, made from the same materials that would otherwise have been used in a normal construction. Only the means by which it had been constructed was unreal.

The wall's top was several yards wide, with crenellations running along the edge of each side for the entire length of the wall. And, he saw as the light illuminated more and more of the island, the wall itself ran across what seemed to be the entire length of Lanka itself. Or as much of Lanka as he could glimpse from where he was, and from this height he could see for a full yojana at least, any further view blocked only by the range of mountains that rose gradually, topped by a single great peak, the one that Vibhisena had named Mount Nikumbhila. Up to that point, and possibly beyond it as well, this wall ran like a great fortification, looking as if it had stood here a thousand years and would stand a thousand more. It rose and fell with the land's natural slope, dipping down to the valley where he could see brooks and thickets and glades that remained as they were the day before, then rising again toward the foothills of the mountain range, dwarfed only by Nikumbhila. Beyond the mountain, he glimpsed a reddish glow that seemed not to belong to the scarlet flares of the coming dawn. For one thing, it was in the south-west. It appeared like a great fire dimly glimpsed far beyond the mountain itself, perhaps several yojanas farther south. But surely no fire, however great, could send up a glow that would be visible beyond the height of such a mountain? It was something else, he could almost name it, but the name eluded him. He dismissed it for the moment. Right now, he wished only to return to the ground below, to join his armies once more. If these were ramparts, there must be steps cut through the heart of the wall, for defending soldiers to come up and go down. He began walking the length of the wall, searching for such a stairway.

Hanuman floated in mid-air, a thousand yards above the island of Lanka. He was standing in the position of an ascetic, with the sole of his left foot placed against the inside of his right thigh. Were he on the ground, he would be standing on one foot, a posture conducive to concentrating and channelling one's energies. His arms were folded across his chest. He was his normal size, for expansion used up energy and the strain of the long night had taken its toll, sapping him of strength as well as purpose. He stared mutely at what Ravana's sorcery had wrought, in a single night no less, and forced himself to remain calm as he examined and studied it in the same way that a hawk might study a nest of serpents a mile below, anticipating when and how he would swoop down to attack and kill the brood.

Ravana had turned Lanka into a fortress. The entire island

had been overrun by the rakshasa lord's devilish sorcery. From this vantage point, he could see a pattern of thousand-foot-high walls running along the coastline for as far as could be seen. The walls ran for a few yojanas south before crisscrossing the breadth of the island. Up to there, some of the natural landscape was still present, contained within the vaulting walls. Beyond that point, the very landscape had been altered. He could not tell exactly what purpose some of the newly designed features would serve, but they seemed warlike and aggressive. The entire island's aspect, so green and lush and beautiful, a veritable paradise as Rama himself had called it at his first glimpse, had now taken on the aspect of a dark country dedicated solely to war. Ravana had turned it into a giant fortress overnight.

And far to the south, he had done more than that. Hanuman could see a reddish glow, as if from a great fire blazing fiercely. But he knew that was no fire, for even an entire forest could not feed such an enormous flame. It was a volcano. Lanka had once been a volcanic isle, raised up from the bottom of the ocean in a series of gargantuan eruptions many millions of years ago. Now Ravana had tapped the volcano once again, reviving it, and had structured the heart of his fortress around the fires of that hellmouth. The searing heat and intensity of the glow exuded by the volcano was too great for even Hanuman's sharp vision to pierce its surrounding area. All he could tell was that a vast black pile of stone had arisen on that section of the island, occupying a substantial area of perhaps ten square yojanas at the south-western tip of Lanka. The devas alone knew what Ravana had built there during this long dark night of blood and terror. But it boded no good, of that he was certain.

His fists had tightened, despite his best efforts at self-control, and he desired nothing more than to expand himself to his limits and then swoop down in a rampage of destruction, wiping out all that Ravana had raised through his sorcery, smashing those fortress walls and ramparts, shattering those long spindly spikes that had taken so many of his comrades' lives, destroying, shattering, pounding . . . the way he had pounded and smashed and burned Lanka not two days ago.

But this was not that Lanka any more. This was a new Lanka. Or a very old and ancient one, resurrected by Asura sorcery to serve Ravana's purpose. Perhaps everything that had happened had served Ravana's purpose – even Hanuman's own rampage of destruction. For what good had it really done? Look at his people now. Look at how many lay dead on the ground below. Look at the beach – he could not bear to see those golden sands in the first flush of dawn. For thousands upon thousands had perished there, crushed by the alterations of the rocky cliffs, the palisades, that had formed the bulk of the material manipulated by Ravana's sorcery to raise those great rampart walls. So many bodies lay adrift there, tugged and released by the outgoing tide, that the ocean skirting the island was stained red with their blood. Senseless, futile, awful deaths. And none of them had been able to do anything to prevent it. Not even he, with his great powers and abilities.

Even now, if he expanded himself and flew down and began pounding and smashing, he would endanger his own fellow vanars and bears. These were not rakshasas that he would be harming, but his own comrades in arms. And who was to say that even if he flew yojanas further south and began smashing through the sorcerously erected defences he could glimpse there, Ravana would not erect new defences in a matter of hours, and that the process of reconstruction would not endanger the lives of Hanuman's comrades yet again?

What could he do then? Nothing. Nothing! He was helpless. All this strength and power, futile. Pathetic. He was nothing but a foolish vanar with an ego too large for his own skull. He belonged not here in the land of rakshasas, but back in the red-mist mountains, foraging for fruit, then stealing a little honey wine and falling asleep drunk and content under the starry sky, as he had done so many nights of his life while a young monkey.

That was all he was good for. He could not shoulder this great responsibility. He was no champion. He was only a vanar . . . no, not even a vanar. A monkey! A baboon! A langur! He ought to fly back home right now, for he was no use on this great quest, no use to anybody at all . . . Stupid, foolish idiot of a monkey!

Ravana laughed. A rich, deep-throated laugh that was echoed by most of his heads with varying degrees of humour. Only two heads remained unamused, one looking bored and distracted, another appearing to be quite fast asleep, its nostrils flaring as it snored gently. Supanakha laughed with him. They were in Ravana's palace. His new palace really. For while it was similar to the old one, the one he had occupied until the reconstruction of Lanka fourteen years ago, it was different as well. Grander. Enormous. Built on an epic scale that dwarfed anything and everything Supanakha had ever seen in her five-hundred-and-something years of existence.

This particular chamber, for instance, was a vast cavernous space whose walls and ceiling were constructed of the same black rock of which the new fortress Lanka had been built, using the same sorcerous maya. She had watched the night before as Ravana's sorcery had begun its menacing work, had seen a projected image of the chaos and bloodshed on the northern tip of the island as Rama and his forces were routed by invisible forces, decimated without even a chance to defend themselves. She had enjoyed that showing hugely. Had wished she were there to see it with her own eyes, hear the screams and howls of anguish and agony, perhaps sip a little fresh blood as it gushed from shattered limbs and severed arteries, munch on some vanar flesh, even taste bear – it had been a long time since she had feasted on bear flesh. But she had also seen that to go out there while Ravana's sorcery was working its wicked way might be less than sensible, and besides, she wanted to be with the one wielding this power, see what devilish new scheme he had cooked up, and how he implemented it. That was the thing she admired about her cousin. He always had another plan, and another, and another . . . It was the reason why he would win in the end, she had no doubt. Why he would triumph over Rama and all his determined might. Because in the end, Ravana was a juggernaut, as remorseless, relentless as the forces of nature he commanded and manipulated. He was shakti itself, incarnate.

He laughed for several moments, his muscled torso quivering with each expulsion of breath and sound. Even though he was dwarfed by the sheer scale and majesty of the immense chamber in which he stood, he looked as if he owned it, as if none other than he could stand here and laugh with this much abandon and energy, as if he were celebrating the greatest triumph of his entire life. His laughter slowed in stages, his heads switching to other occupations briefly, new thoughts, dialogues, concerns skitting across the rack, and when he turned his eyes to her again, only two heads were actually smiling, only two mouths still chuckling with glee. But his overall mood was one of great joy and triumph. For this was his moment to savour.

'Do you see now, cousin,' he asked, chuckling, 'how I decimated the enemy's troops without committing a single rakshasa's life to the fray? And in the process, rebuilt Lanka as I desired it, all in the space of a single night.'

'Not to mention eliminating virtually all the brahmin population of Lanka as well,' she added sweetly, batting her eyelids provocatively at him.

A head on his right-hand rack winked back at her. 'That too, my devilish one. It would not do to have Vibhisena's moral sena running about spreading their messages of peace and brotherhood when there's a war to be fought.'

'Most certainly not,' she agreed. 'And the sorcery you wrought with the brahman power unlocked by their sacrifice to the volcano . . .' She shook her head with amazement that was only slightly exaggerated. 'It was a miraculous feat,' she acknowledged with almost no irony. For once she did not have to summon up false sentiments to pander to his massive tenfold ego. She was genuinely awed by his show of power and his wily use of it. 'You have won the war in a few hours, without risking the lives of any of Lanka's rakhsasas.'

Ravana's smiles faded abruptly. 'The war? You must be jesting. The war has not yet begun! This was but a demonstration. To let Rama and his ragtag bunch of animals know what they are up against. Now, if he is wise, he will turn around and go back home with his tail between his legs.'

Supanakha leaped up on the lower part of an obsidian statue, shaped to resemble a naga feasting on a mortal warrior. She perched on the feet of the mortal, whose eyes bulged in anguish as the giant serpentine Asura tore open his belly to lay her chitinous black eggs within its warmth, then closed up the rift with her gooey saliva, sealing it until it was time for her young to hatch in a few hours. Supanakha wondered at how exquisitely Ravana's sorcery had constructed this entire palace, complete with vaulting façades, intricate pillars, polished floors, beautifully carved statues, and all in the space of a few hours. What had he said to her by way of explanation the night before? Ah yes. 'In sorcery, as in life, it is the design that takes time and effort and talent – once conceived, it is child's play to execute that conception into reality.' She had not understood him completely at that time; now she knew just what he had meant. The level of artistry in this statue alone was awe-inspiring. With all his many talents and gifts, he was a great artist, not to mention a talented poet and musician as well, a connoisseur of all arts. This overnight reconstruction had required a phenomenal exertion of sorcery. But the detail and perfection in execution had taken great creative brilliance. Ravana had supplied both in abundant measure.

Now she said aloud in response to his statement: 'Do you really think he will?'

He smiled at her with a head or two, while the others debated intently about some new matter in a tongue she did not recognise. 'No. Rama is not one to quit. Besides, he still has not recovered Sita. He will not leave until he has done that, even if it costs the lives of every last one of his followers. That is what the fools will now learn to their dying dismay.'

She flicked her tail at the gaping maw and dripping fangs of the naga above her. The realism of the detail was unnervingly accurate. 'So you will use sorcery to defeat him and his forces? As you did last night?'

Ravana stepped with slow, undulating strides to the foot of the dais that housed his new throne, a great black-stone seat carved with the entwined figures of countless lunging Asura shapes, some engaged in battle, others in copulation, to the point where it was impossible to tell which was doing what to whom. He stood with one foot resting on the first step of the dais. The onyx floor gleamed underfoot, reflecting as perfectly as a silver-backed mirror, and she gazed at the inverted black Ravana depicted there, the black dome of the ceiling a hundred yards overhead glistening faintly above him in the reflection, a thin tracery of veins in the texture of the dome pulsing with a reddish glow that indicated the maya shakti used to build and then keep this whole edifice erect.

'What would be the sport in that?' he said. 'No, my blood-lusting beauty, I will take the field against Rama before he has had time to recover fully from last night's losses, before his armies have a chance to re-form and prepare themselves, before his captains are ready to lead. It will be a battle to behold, because despite their long night of suffering, or because of it, his forces will fight fiercely and boldly, even bravely, eager to vent their frustration and anger upon our rakshasas, to face living foes and feel the bite of their weapons and claws and fangs in our living flesh. And we shall give them that satisfaction . . . at first.'

'And then?' she asked eagerly.

'And then we shall slaughter them like meat for our fires, and food for our tables, for that is all they are. Flesh to feed on, nothing more.' He climbed the steps to the throne, ten yards above the floor of the chamber. Even seated, he now looked down upon everything and everyone. Supanakha noted slyly that he had designed even the tallest statues – like the one she was perched on – to be below the level of his sight line when seated on the throne. Truly a master of detail! He looked down at her, eyes glistening chitinously – or perhaps that was only the reflection of all those gleaming black surfaces. 'Before night falls again upon Lanka, my victory over Rama will be complete.'

He clapped two of his hands together, calling out in a booming voice that echoed through the vast palace. 'Bring in my generals. I am ready to begin the war council.'

Supanakha licked the screaming, goggle-eyed face of the mortal in the statue with a little sympathy and a great deal of relish. The day of her reckoning had come at last. Finally she would have the revenge on Rama and his brother for which she had waited fourteen long years. Before nightfall. She could practically taste their rich, tangy blood already.

6

'*Anjaneya.*'

The voice was a distant echo in the background of his crowded mind. He marked it only as a futile intrusion into his private grief, and dismissed it outright. In his anger and remorse, he had drifted far to the south. Miles farther, even yojanas perhaps. He no longer cared; he had lost his bearings, both physical and spiritual. He no longer understood who he was, or what purpose he served in this life. What good was all the power in the world if you could not save your comrades when they needed you most? The cries of his fellow vanars still rang in his ears. Usually on battlefields, when soldiers died, the severely wounded and dying called out a single word: *maa*. Or a variation thereof; whatever word meant 'mother' in their language. So it had been since the beginning of time and the first violent conflicts, and so it would probably be until the end of days. But last night, apart from the many cries of 'mother' and 'mother, save me' and similar variations, there were two words that were constantly called out on the plateau of Lanka's northern coast. Those were the names Rama and Maruti. Vanars had died calling out his name, over and over again, and he had been able to do nothing to save them. Yes, he had saved a few dozen, perhaps even a few hundred. But it was not enough. Thousands had died. Tens of thousands even. The carnage was unspeakable. And he, the great Hanuman, the omnipotent Bajrangbali, leveller of Lanka, burner of the city of the Asuras, champion of Lord Rama the mightiest yodha of all, had been able to do nothing to stop it.

'*Anjaneya, control yourself.*'

He paused in his self-pitying misery to glance around. He was still flying, and somehow in his grief he had drifted even higher above the island-kingdom. Lanka lay far below now, a map perfectly drawn by a malicious artist to mock him. Only two days ago he had demolished this very city. And in a single night it had risen up once more to mock him, taunt him, show him that his power was worthless; Ravana's sorcerous shakti was supreme.

'*Stop it, Maruti. You will cease this line of thought and return to your lords at once.*'

A spark of unreasonable anger flashed within him. Who was it who berated him thus? Who dared to command him? None but his lord Rama had the right to—

'*I speak on behalf of your lord Rama. He has need of your services. Gain control of your wits and go to him at once.*'

His flash of anger was abruptly replaced by suspicion. 'Who are you?' he asked aloud. He had been duped before in Lanka, by that demoness—

'*Enough! This has gone too far. You need not obey my commands, or trust me. But trust your inner soul. You know that your lord has greater need of you in this hour than ever before. Desist in your rambling and go to him at once.*'

He wanted to argue, to lash out at the speaker of those words. But his anger shrank within him, humbled by the knowledge that whatever the source, the words themselves were true enough. Rama must be seeking him out at this moment, if only to berate him for not doing enough to stem the loss of life the night before. He felt ashamed and humiliated. How could he face his lord? How could he go before him and admit that—

'*There is nothing to be ashamed of.*' The voice was gentler, yet retained a tone of steel. '*You know your lord better than that. He is not Ravana. He is Rama. You do him a disservice by thinking on his behalf. Your duty is only to go to him and place yourself at his command. Go to him now. Fly.'*

He dabbed at his face, wiping away the tears that had trickled down his cheeks. His puffed mouth was damp and sticky with the residue of his weeping, and he turned abruptly, flying faster and then faster still, until he was speeding like a crow, then a hawk, then like an arrow shot from a longbow, then faster than any object in existence, living or otherwise. He swooped in a wide undulating arc, down, down, down, and cut the surface of the ocean at an angle so sharp, he barely raised a splash. He travelled underwater at the same swift speed, the cool salty water shocking his body, then calming him, then reviving him. When he emerged a mile further north, he was refreshed. Water cascaded from his body as he leaped from the ocean, shooting up to the sky again, rising high now, higher and higher, until he could glimpse the curve of the world beyond the horizon, and the risen sun already beaming down brightly upon lands far to the east where the day had begun hours earlier. The red-mist mountains were to the east. The home of his people. He reached the apogee of his rising arc and hung suspended momentarily, the rays of the sun warming him, enlivening him, then he folded his palms and feet together in a Surya namaskaram, holding the yogic asana until gravity began pulling insistently at his body once more, Mother Prithvi calling to him to return home to her.

Up here, everything was so calm, so serene, the earth herself undulating like the curved belly of a mother-to-be, seeded with untold generations of future lives, that he had a brief moment when he wished he could simply fly away, perhaps fly back home, or simply *fly*. As a young vanar, he had always dreamed of flying like the magnificent swans he saw crossing the skies above Kiskindha twice a year, going south in winter, north in summer. He had always wondered what it might be like to fly like that, beautiful and graceful and supremely elevated above all the petty grime and dirt and dust, the scrabble and squabble, the shrieking and the shrilling of land-bound existence. To soar amongst the clouds, eye to eye with the sun, lord of all you surveyed, free to travel anywhere you wished.

If he wished, he could go anywhere now. Fly anywhere. Away from here. Away from more bloodshed, more pain, more agony – all the strife and struggle that he knew with sickening certainty lay ahead. The deaths of friends and comrades and beloved ones. For what else was war but loss, loss, and more loss? Until finally, one party cried enough, I can bear no more, and surrendered. He had had enough of losing. There was no end to it. As long as you possessed something, it could be taken from you. Better then to possess nothing, to simply soar through the air like a bird, to fly through empty airways for ever, to reduce the troubles of earthbound living to a distantly viewed panorama, like a game where thousands scurried like ants to live and die, and fight and kill, like his compatriots and their enemies now scattered far below upon the hills and valleys and plains of Lanka. Fly far away, away from it all. And never come back. Fly away and forget.

He hung suspended, weightless, windborne, neither gravity's child nor the ether's possession. And dreamed. For a moment that seemed like an aeon, he dreamed and lost himself, and forgot all. A condor floating far below him wondered at the being that could soar higher than she, and how that being could stay thus so long. Where was the wind that bore that creature aloft? Or was it the hand of a deva that held him there?

The condor called out, mournfully, longingly. Cried for the losses she had suffered through a long and strife-fraught life: a fledgling lost to a storm, a yearling torn to bits by a rival, a mate caught by a wildcat when feeding upon a snake; all her life was contained in that cry.

High above, the cry penetrated through the dream-fog that obscured Hanuman's mind.

The cry seemed to be echoing, or mocking, a mortal word. A single name.

Rama.

Rama needs me. I must go to Rama at once.

He repeated the words to himself like a rote recitation.

He spared a moment of brief, fleeting regret for the emptiness and mystery of the high spaces, the freedom and glory of flight. Then he wiped all dreams clear and eliminated all thought, desire and emotion from his senses.

He straightened himself and plunged downwards again. So great was the rush of air against his speeding body that every last drop of water was cast away from his skin and his clothing. Lanka grew steadily beneath him, expanding until he was able to see the tiny ant-like figures of his lord's forces, covering the entire northern tip of the island. A final twinge of sadness stroked his heart, then he was close enough to see individual vanars and bears, and then close enough to tell the various tribes and clans apart.

He slowed as he descended to the height of the rampart wall, flying along its length until he reached the lone figure atop the fortification, standing and looking southwards. Rama turned to him as he descended to land.

'My friend,' Rama said as he came to rest softly upon the rampart. 'There you are. I was beginning to worry . . .'

He prostrated himself before his lord, laying himself flat upon the rampart. The black stone blocks were unnaturally warm to the touch, suffused with the energy of the Asura sorcery that had created them, but he ignored that. He kissed Rama's feet, not caring that they were dusty and crusted with dried blood. 'My lord,' he cried aloud. 'My lord, forgive me . . . I could do no more . . . I tried . . .'

His voice broke off helplessly. Despite his attempt to bathe and revive himself, to appear presentable before he faced his lord once more, he was stricken by a great and searing emotion when faced with Rama in person. He broke down and began crying helplessly, great sobs racking his body.

'Maruti!' Rama said in distress. 'My friend. Do not lose hope thus. Come, rise up, rise up . . .' Gently Rama raised him off the ground and helped him to his feet again. He put his arm around him, comforting him. 'I understand your pain. But this is not the time to give in to guilt and regret. There is a great deal of work yet to be done. The only remedy is to do one's duty, to execute one's dharma. In the end, that is all a warrior can do.'

Hanuman shook his head, unable to stop the sobs that tore at his being. 'But my lord, I let you down ... I let my people down ... I could do nothing to stop the sorcery ...'

Rama looked at him, his voice steady and strong as the arms that held him. 'I could do nothing either last night. But there is much that we can do now, together. Remember, my friend. Not every battle can be won, not every day brings a victory. Loss is a part of life itself. Respect it, and respect its power over us, but then move on. Loss suffered is natural and inevitable; loss dwelt on and obsessed over destroys us. Yes, we failed yesterday, and lost greatly. But today has dawned anew. Now the question is not what we could not do yesterday, but what we can do today. Will you squander the opportunities of the present to moan and weep about the lost chances of the past? You are a better man than that, Bajrangbali. You are the son of Marut, the child of Anjaneya. Your ancestors look down upon you and mark your deeds. The devas in the upper realms admire your prowess. Your friends will fight today whether you join them or not. You cannot bring back those who fell, no kshatriya can. They died fulfilling their dharma. All you can do is fight on, and fulfil your own dharma. I have need of you now. Will you help me?'

And Rama raised his hand to him.

Hanuman ceased his weeping. He looked at the figures on the ground far below, collecting now in neat lines and regiments as they had been taught to do by their mortal leaders and their own generals and captains and clan chiefs. It broke his heart to see them rallying so valiantly even after the carnage of the night before. He looked back at Rama, at the strong, handsome face of his mortal lord. And was moved beyond words to see the unshakeable resolve on those handsome features. The voice that he had heard earlier – he knew now that it was Jambavan, speaking to his mind as he had done before – had spoken truly. This was not Ravana. This was Rama. And Rama was not angered with him. Rama believed in him still. Rama had need of him.

He took the hand that was proffered, but instead of clasping it in the fashion that he had seen mortals do, he kissed it lovingly, then touched it to his own head, palm downwards. He could feel the heat from Rama's flesh seep into his brain. 'My lord,' he said in a voice that was as deep and strong as the voice of thunder in the heart of a stormcloud. 'I am yours to command.'

Lakshman watched as Hanuman descended from the wall, bearing Rama upon his shoulder. He landed gently, bending down so that Rama might alight easily. Rama turned, looking this way and that, then caught sight of Lakshman amidst the crowd of vanar and bear generals that had assembled, and came quickly towards him. The ranks parted to let him pass but he stepped around them rather than disturb their formations.

'Sumitra-putra,' he said softly as he came within hailing distance, almost too softly to be heard. 'My brother, you are well?'

'Yes, Rama, I—'

Lakshman barely had a chance to respond. Rama embraced him so fiercely, Lakshman almost cried out at the pain in his ribs where he had been bruised by a fall in the early hours of the morning, while attempting to save a stricken bear. Then he embraced his brother back just as fiercely, surprised at the tears that sprang up in his own eyes. 'I am here, Rama,' he heard himself say. 'Still alive. Still ready to go to war.'

Rama released him, keeping one arm around his back. His

eyes glistened in the early light, filled with a look Lakshman knew well from previous battles. He had had that look the day they had entered the Bhayanak-van to face Tataka and her demon-hybrid hordes; the evening they had made their stand in the Sage's Brow at Mithila immediately before unleashing the brahm-astra; the morning before the final battle at Janasthana. He pitied anyone who stood in Rama's way now, mortal, rakshasa or deva. Once that look came into his brother's eyes, no force could stop him.

Maryada Purshottam . . .

The words sprang up unbidden in his mind.

Maryada Purshottam Rama.

He Who Fulfils His Vow . . . Against All Odds. The last bit he added himself. Because the odds were truly against them now. Impossibly stacked. And yet. And yet. They had been stacked as high before, higher even. It had never daunted Rama then; it did not daunt him now.

'And war it shall be, my brother,' Rama said with a voice of iron.

7

Lying upon the grass of the ashoka grove, Sita felt the ground vibrating beneath her, and thought to her dismay that it was yet another wave of sorcery unleashed by Ravana. All night she had lain awake in anxious trepidation as the very island itself seemed to rumble and boom and grind its way through a series of inexplicable changes. Only in the morning – for Ravana's sorcery ensured that she enjoyed a simulation of day and night even within the bowels of this subterranean cavern – had the clamour ceased. She could not tell exactly what had been wrought by Ravana during the night, but she suspected that it was something epic.

And now it had begun again. She could feel the vibration through the kusalavya grass on which she lay, through the earth below the grass. Like giants pounding their enormous hammers deep within the bowels of the earth.

Then she realised that this trembling of the earth was caused not by sorcery, but by the pounding of feet. Thousands upon thousands of feet, racing through the belly of the island, racing through the cavernous tunnels that riddled Lanka.

She rose slowly to her feet, ignoring the throbbing in her skull, and walked to the far side of the grove. The pounding continued as she walked, now seeming to come from all sides at once. But it was loudest on this side, and she had found before that if she went to the very edge of the rivulet that wound its way through the grove, and stood upon this rock here, and looked through the gap between two sala trees in the far distance, she could just about glimpse the end of this cave tunnel and the place where it intersected with one or more other tunnels. Somewhere in that direction were the great underground chambers where Ravana had taken her yesterday morning – or was it this morning? Where he had taken her in the flying vaahan and shown her his prized secret: those hideous rakshasas hatching from stones like eggs, or eggs like stones . . . It was hard to concentrate or remember now. She was very tired.

She stood upon the rock and peered groggily through the gap in the trees, trying to position herself so that she could see the place where the tunnels met. She had glimpsed a rakshasa guard earlier from here, or at least she had glimpsed the top of his gleaming spear as he strolled this way, then that, conversing with his fellow guards. She had heard their guttural voices and harsh barking laughter, distantly and obscurely, amplified and echoing through the caverns. Now she could hear only the pounding, and as she approached this listening spot, it grew louder and came into clearer focus, until there was no mistaking it. That sound was the pounding of thousands of pairs of cloven-hooved feet. The feet of those beings that Ravana had bred in secret in the subterranean chambers.

She craned her neck and crooked her head and arched her back until she found a suitable angle and was able to glimpse an inverted triangular space which was lit more brightly than this cavern. And in that brightly lit space she glimpsed a blurring rush, as of hordes of armoured heads and backs moving at a frenetic pace. Line upon line running in perfect formation.

And now that she was focused at last, her waning, depleted energies drawn to the maximum alertness she was able to summon up, she could hear clearly – too clearly almost – the thunderous roar of those cloven hoofs pounding the solid rock floor of the caverns. And the grunting and chuffing of tens of thousands – or perhaps it was lakhs – of those devilishly bred rakshasas. They were on the move. And that could mean only one thing. That Ravana was moving them up to the surface in preparation for a battle. And that in turn meant that Rama and his forces were here at last, upon the island, and that they would soon join weapons with the army of Lanka.

The pounding rhythm of the rakshasas vibrated through the ground, through the rock upon which she stood, through her weary bones, up to her skull, where it joined the throbbing of her head and the drained emptiness that her consciousness had become. She felt herself mesmerised by the rhythm for several moments, the constant pounding acting like the beat of a dhol-drum, lulling her already battered and beleaguered senses . . .

Then it came to her with a shock like cold water splashed upon her face: all those vicious beasts racing through the cavern were going to do battle against Rama, her Rama. Very shortly, her beloved would face these beasts, and perhaps be wounded by them, possibly even killed. The father of her unborn child. She pressed her palm against her belly, and thought she felt the embryo within her stir and then thrash with great force, anguished by the sound of the bestial hordes going to war against its father. She experienced a moment of dizziness and nausea as the thrashing continued, and stumbled over to the nearest support, a large black boulder shot through with ugly red veins, where she sat a moment to regain her equilibrium.

She caressed her belly soothingly, trying to calm the unborn life – or was it *lives*? Lately she had begun to sense more move-ment within her womb than could be caused by a single embryo – while empathising with their anguish. *Their* anguish? Yes, now that she thought on it, she grew certain that she bore more than one life within her womb. *Two*, came the answer from her inner being, the voice of her blood, her life-force, her in-tuition, given substance by the sparking flame of brahman within herself. Yes, *two*. She was certain of it now. And at this moment, as events in her life, and therefore *their* lives as well, reached an epic pinnacle, she could guess how they must feel, blind and helpless and imprisoned though they were – even as she herself was blind and helpless and imprisoned in this subterranean sorcerous cage. In their captivity and inability to act, she and her unborn children were as one at this moment.

She pressed her hand to her swollen belly, longing for the power to *act*, to join her karma to that of Rama, to do more than simply await the outcome of a war that would surely change her life, and the future history of the world itself. Had she but a sword, or a bow and a quiver, or even just her freedom and her bare hands, she would not hesitate to add her strength to Rama's forces and wage battle against the armies of Lanka. Women warriors before her had fought in her condition; some of the greatest warriors had been birthed – nay, simply dropped – upon blood-spattered battlefields. *Born into blood, sworn into blood*, as the old Arya legend went. Neither her condition nor her present state of extreme weakness would have stayed her from joining the war against Lanka.

But since she could not do so, all she could do was wait. And her unborn offspring must wait with her. She felt a stirring within, as if they sensed her thoughts, and knew exactly what she felt, and had they but the power to voice their own thoughts, she was sure they would have argued hotly and fiercely with her.

She smiled indulgently. Not yet born, and already ready to fight? What else could she expect of the children of two kshatriyas who had spent the better part of their lives fighting for dharma?

'Fear not,' she said softly, stroking her belly gently, 'some day, when you are a wee bit older and able to at least hold a sword in your hand, you will get your chance. Until then, both you and I must wait patiently, no matter how difficult it may be.' She listened to the sounds of Ravana's sorcerously created warriors pounding through the labyrinthine caverns around, below and above her, racing even now to attempt to end the life of her beloved, the father of her unborn children. She added grimly, 'And until you are ready to fight for yourselves, your father will fight fiercely enough for all three of us.'

So may it be, Devi, she prayed. *Make his strength threefold. For he now fights for three lives, not one.*

It was a grim assembly that gathered once again in the clearing at the heart of the valley. Gone were the eager comments and sharp observations. Not one of Rama's generals and advisers was spared of cuts, scratches or lacerations. All were coated with a fine layer of dust and grime, and tear streaks marked many snouted visages. The sound of wounded vanars and bears was all around, made the more heart-tugging because those wounded or dying struggled pitifully to restrain themselves from crying out openly, and only exhibited their agony in helpless coughing or fits of delirious moaning. In the dim, dusty air of the plateau, the bear lords looked no less menacing to Hanuman's eyes than kumbha-rakshasas. Jambavan's ruby-red pupils smouldered with a fury that sent a trickle of unease down the vanar's curved spine; the king of bears looked as if he would eat the first rakshasa he met alive, horns and hoofs and all. Every one of those gathered here had lost one or more blood-kin or friend. The dead still lay in great heaps, awaiting cremation later that evening, after the day's fighting was done, for even vanars and bears were aware of the edicts of Manu Lawmaker and the ancient sages regarding the rules of combat, and Rama's army would follow them scrupulously, whether or not the enemy chose to do so. It was testimony to Rama's leadership and the respect all had for him that they were not shrieking and raging with fury at the treachery of the king of rakshasas. Nor were they incapacitated by grief and fear at what new terrors the Lord of Lanka might have in store for them.

If anything, despite the tragic gloom that hung about them, despite the atmosphere of uncertainty and unease, despite the grief at the bitterly unfair slaughter and massacre, there was still an air of dignity in the face and bearing of each and every one. Even King Sugreeva, the oldest and weakest, bore himself with stubborn pride, although he had lost a son, Angad's smallest brother, no older than little Sakra, to the terrible 'killing stones', as the vanars now called the sorcerously motivated rocks and pillars. After all, they were still Rama's soldiers, and there was still a war to be fought. A war for dharma.

Rama spoke in a quiet yet clear voice appropriate to the occasion, briefing them on all that he had observed and studied during the long night of the killing stones. Sugreeva nodded from time to time, Angad interjected a comment or two, and others added their own contributions to the gathering of intelligence on what the enemy's plan might entail next. Hanuman described to them all how, when seen from high above, Ravana's scheme seemed quite clear. By raising the sorcerously constructed fortress, he had ringed all of Rama's forces into a central walled-in area, some several yojanas wide and long. Unable to retreat back to the sea, vulnerable if they attempted to scale the towering smooth-faced stone ramparts, the vanar and bear senas were left with only one choice: to proceed southwards towards the capital city.

'Then that is what we shall *not* do,' Angad said angrily, almost spitting with vehemence. 'We shall not fall into his trap.'

'Aye,' said General Susena, whose left paw had been nearly severed by a descending block. He held the disabled limb against his chest, face pale from blood loss but no less fierce with war lust. 'My Mandaras will take the front line and mine their rakshasa bellies the way we mine silver!'

Several grunts and noises of agreement echoed this sentiment. Rama waited for them to finish, then shook his head decisively, once. 'No. We shall do exactly as they wish. We shall march south and besiege the capital.'

General Vinata of the Mandeha vanars frowned. 'But my lord Rama, we may be marching into a trap.'

General Satabali, who had lost two brothers and a wife to the killing stones, grunted in agreement. 'Most certainly. They wish to shepherd us into an ambush like sheep. It is evident from the lie of the land as Hanuman described it. I could even point out the likely spot where the ambush will take place.' He indicated a spot on the dirt map that Nala had sketched quickly but expertly as Hanuman had described his sky view of Lanka. 'Here, here, and here. They will strike us from the flanks and behind, using the natural cover of the terrain and these thickets to conceal their approach until the very last minute. Then they will no doubt throw open the city gates and sally forth to catch us in a pincer and crush us.'

'My vanars are well versed in the art of war, Rama,' King Sugreeva said. 'Heed their advice well, my friend.'

'I respect their knowledge of warcraft and do indeed heed their advice, King Sugreeva. But when the enemy makes his plan known, he also makes his weaknesses known.'

Several furred faces frowned. 'What do you mean, Lord Rama?' General Nila asked, his dark fur still matted in places by the blood of comrades and loved ones he had tried to save.

Rama looked at each of them in turn. 'In my father's court at Ayodhya, as a boy, I saw many emissaries from far-flung lands arrive and speak at length about their peoples, cultures, social customs, and other matters. Among these nations was a land far beyond the red-mist ranges, a great nation spread across an archipelago of islands. It is said to be a beautiful land, a veritable heaven on earth, and its people are as beautiful as the land they live upon. We Aryas have many things in common with them, including our adherence to morality and the strict tenets of law and custom. Yet there is a great deal of difference between us, and it is in these differences that we can learn so much. For instance, among their warriors there is a principle of war termed shima.'

'Shima?' Angad repeated with not a little trace of puzzlement. 'I have never heard of such a thing before. Is it a siege machine? For that is one thing we do not have. We will need siege machines to breach the walls of Lanka.'

'The walls of Lanka,' Lakshman said curtly, without preamble or any attempt at diplomacy, 'are made of the same stone blocks as those walls that skirt the plateau.' He inclined his head in the direction of the walls that, while not visible here, miles from the rim of the cliffs, still loomed large in everyone's mind's eye. 'A siege machine that can breach three-yard-thick stone walls has not yet been invented, to the best of my knowledge.'

Angad looked as if he was about to retort sharply to that but restrained himself. He nodded, understanding both Lakshman's response and his directness. In a sense, Hanuman thought, the young Prince of Kiskindha and the Second Prince of Ayodhya had many qualities in common.

The bear king's baritone rumbled like thunder.

'Go on, Rama,' Jambavan growled. 'Tell them about shima. Tell them about how, at times, letting the enemy know your plans is an effective strategy. For he then believes that he knows your plan of attack and defence and arranges his forces accordingly. So he is already *reacting* to you instead of *acting*. While you, knowing that he knows your every move, are free to change your plans at any moment, thereby surprising him and forcing him to continue *reacting*, except that now he knows not what you will do next, and because his forces are deployed to deflect your alleged plans, he is unable to reposition them quickly enough to respond to your new movements.'

Jambavan's eyes bored into each one in turn as he looked around at the war council. 'Rama means to use the precept of shima to feed Ravana information regarding our war plans, giving out all our military secrets to the lord of rakshasas and setting us up for an even greater massacre than the one we suffered last night.'

8

There was silence for a long moment as everyone absorbed the bear king's words.

Finally Sugreeva spoke. 'A remarkable strategic manoeuvre. I have never heard of such a tactic in all my years. Is that what you intend, Rama?'

'It is, my lord Sugreeva.'

Angad frowned and scratched his head unabashedly. 'It sounds . . . complicated. Will it work?'

Lakshman gave him a withering look but refrained from answering that rhetorical query directly. Angad shrugged as if to say, *Well, I didn't want to admit that I don't really understand a word of it.*

General Satabali spoke, his age-ripened features cast in deep contemplation. 'That is not the question to ask, Prince Angad. The questions to ask are, "How may this be accomplished?", by which I mean how may we pass on our plans to Ravana, and more pertinently, "What are those plans to be?"'

Rama said quietly, 'The plans are the same ones we discussed yesterday evening at our war conference. They were designed for a direct siege-assault on Lanka's forces at the gates of the city. The triple formation, the order of attack, the flank troop movements, the counter-circling . . . we shall let Ravana believe that that information is the sum total of all we have planned for the forthcoming battle today.'

General Satabali stared in dismay. 'Our entire battle plan? But Rama—'

Rama held up a hand, palm outwards. 'Before you say anything further, my good general, you should know that the plan we are speaking of – yes, our entire battle plan – is already in the enemy's possession. It has been delivered to Ravana, and even now, the spies who transported that information are back amongst us, sniffing out more intelligence.'

He gestured at the open clearing in which they stood, bordered on all sides by a dense thicket of a mixture of trees and foliage. Their gathering stood in the very centre of the open area, several dozen yards from the nearest tree or rock. Hanuman knew why, as Rama had asked him to scout out and find a place meeting these requirements before summoning the war council to this spot.

'Why do you think I chose this location for our conference? Even now, eager eyes watch us.'

Angad started, twisting around, his eyes popping. 'Spasas! Among us? Impossible! My angadiyas would sniff out a rakshasa a mile away, even before it approached our ranks. So would any vanar for that matter.' At a growl from Kambunara, he added hastily, 'And any bear too, I have no doubt!'

Rama met Hanuman's eyes. 'But what if they do not smell, or look, or act like rakshasas? What if they appear to be, to all intents and purposes, vanars, no different from your own people?'

'Vanars?' Sugreeva asked, then sighed plaintively. 'Yes, I have heard of this from the olduns. There is a line of rakshasas capable of altering their shape and outward appearance. But what of the smell, Rama? How can they make themselves *smell* like us?'

'Why don't we ask them how, my lord Sugreeva?' Rama said simply. He nodded at Hanuman. 'Flush out our rakshasa spies.'

Hanuman rose into the air, hovering a couple of yards above the others. Suspended in the air, visible to anyone watching

from the thicket around them, he issued a sharp, piercing whistle.
It was the prearranged signal.

At once, a flurry of movement exploded in the trees to the
south-west of the clearing. Leaves and twigs flew and fell to
the ground, as a brief, violent struggle broke out in the upper
branches of the trees bordering the clearing. The shrieking of
outraged vanars carried all the way to the council. The struggle
did not last long, because, Hanuman knew, the trap had been
laid carefully and shrewdly. The one thing the spies had not
been expecting was to be spied on themselves! Yet again he
admired Rama's ingenuity as a warrior as well as a master
strategist of warcraft. When he had carried his lord down from
the ramparts, Rama had done more than restore strength and
courage to his tortured soul; he had given him simple, explicit
instructions about a dozen chores to be carried out at once.
The work had cleared his addled brain more effectively than
any hours-long pravachan.

He marvelled once more at Rama's sharpness. Even his own
preternatural powers of perception had not sensed the presence
of the spasas. Yet Rama had, and had devised a plan even while
dealing with a hundred other details as well as the terrible tragedy
of the night before. That itself infused Hanuman with new strength:
to be guided by such a leader was sufficient to instil shakti in
the weakest warrior.

A few moments later, a group of figures dropped from the
trees to the ground below. One of them rolled and leaped up
and attempted to flee, but was quickly caught once again, subdued,
and bound tightly. From this distance, all the parties involved
looked exactly like vanars. And even as the captors forced their
struggling, *cheeka*-ing prisoners to march towards the war council
in the clearing, there was no way to tell them apart. Hanuman
sniffed the air carefully, but all he scented was indication that
the prisoners had been consuming a diet that would be considered unorthodox, even repulsive, to a Kiskindha vanar. Which
could be said of almost any of the variegated tribes of

vanars that were part of the great collective of Rama's patch-work army.

As the group of vanar captors and prisoners came closer, he heard the other generals exclaim. He knew what they were wondering at: the three vanars who were herding the two captives were none other than the same Kiskindha spies whose lives King Sugreeva had spared after their assassination attempt on his life, at Rama's request. They had cowered, fearful for their lives, that day on Mount Rishimukha. Today they strutted boldly, their faces bright with pride at having accomplished their given task. They stopped within a few yards of Rama and the war council, forcing the two captive vanars to their feet. The pris-oners bared their teeth and issued low growls but complied. One of them, a mangy-looking vanar with buck teeth and a chewed-up tail, glanced fearfully at Hanuman. Evidently they feared him the most of this assemblage. That was to be expected, for if they were rakshasas they certainly knew of his rampage in Lanka just two days ago. And after the night of the killing stones, not just they, but any rakshasa in Lanka had good reason to fear Hanuman's wrath. He could feel his body expanding involuntarily as his pulse raced. It would bring him great satisfaction to grow to giant size, take these two wretched infiltrators in his fists and pound them on the stone ramparts that had slaughtered so many of his compatriots, staining that sorcerous stone with their cursed blood. But Rama's orders had been quiet yet clear: the spies were not to be harmed in any way.

Their captives pinned to the ground, and placed under the baleful eye of Hanuman himself, the three vanars who had not long ago sought to take King Sugreeva's life now came forward and prostrated themselves before him. 'My lord,' said the spokesman for the trio, a heavy-shouldered vanar with a dark blackish-brown pelt. 'As you instructed, we watched them through the night.'

Angad stepped forward incredulously, sniffing curiously at

the captives. 'You watched these spasas through the night of killing stones?'

The leader nodded. 'Such were Lord Rama's instructions. *No matter what happens*, keep the spasas in our sight always.'

Lakshman nodded. 'Rama told me to pass on those instructions last evening before we assembled for the war council.'

Hanuman spoke up. 'And I was the one who flew and found our own Kiskindha spasas and passed on the instructions.'

King Sugreeva stroked his white beard bemusedly. 'These three are familiar. Are they not . . . ?'

Rama nodded. 'The same three men that Vali sent to assassinate you on Rishimukha, clawtips stained with blackjuice poison.'

'The vanars you pardoned,' said the old vanar Plaksa, who was leaning on a hickory staff, his ancient face lined with age and pain, for he suffered greatly from the ailments of age – his companion, Sugreeva's other adviser Prabhava, had perished in the night, crushed between two piles of fusing rock. '"If an enemy respects you more than he respects his own cause or leader, make of him an ally, not an enemy." Those were the words of the ancient vanar Manasi from the Satya-Yuga. Today, Rama has proved them true.' Despite his shaky voice and weakness of lung, the old vanar's words still carried a great reverence, as did his rheumy eyes, which fixed adoringly upon Rama. Hanuman felt a surge through his heart and veins at hearing Rama praised by Kiskindha's greatest ancient tutor of artha and dharma.

Rama inclined his head, acknowledging the tribute. 'Guru-dev,' he said, using the highest tribute a mortal Arya could address to a learned one, 'you honour me by comparing my expedient battlefield decision to the wisdom of your ancient forebear.' He performed a perfect namaskaram to the ancient vanar. 'With your blessings, may the rest of my hastily devised plan prove as fruitful.'

Plaksa's wizened features contorted. It took Hanuman a

moment to understand that the ancient tutor and adviser was attempting a rare smile! 'My lord Rama, even Skanda and Ganesa commanding the armies of the devas, with Indra riding Airavata in the first rank, would be hard pressed to oppose you on this battlefield or any other. It is your ka to wage this battle of dharma.'

Rama did not question or spend more time on this cryptic response. Instead, he instructed the leader of the Kiskindha spasas to continue his debriefing. He asked him to be quick and to the point, for already the first rays of daylight were showing over the peaks of the rolling hill ranges of Lanka.

The heavy-shouldered vanar explained, 'Our great brother Hanuman told us that Lord Rama had scented spasas in our midst, disguised as vanars. We were to scent them out and keep a close watch on them night and day, no matter what happened, until Rama called for us to apprehend them and bring them to him. We found them easily, for their scent was unusual, as if,' he paused briefly to sniff loudly, seeking words to describe the scent in question, 'they had been feeding on spoilt berries and grapes that even Dadimukha, master of the gardens of Vrindavan, would not have used to make his honey-wine.'

Vibhisena spoke up. 'They are the result of an old breeding experiment by Ravana in the Bhayanak-van. A crossbreed between rakshasa and vanar that turned out to be more vanar than rakshasa. Even their brood-mother Tataka scorned them and they would have become food for their other hybrid siblings, as happened with so many other unsuccessful crossbreeds. But Ravana found them "interesting", he said, and ordered them brought to Lanka. Even then he knew that some day he would find a use for them as spies, no doubt.' Vibhisena shook his head in wonderment at his brother's great strategic mind. 'They are vanars in every outward sense, but their inner organs resemble those of rakshasas more, and so do their feeding and mating habits.' He paused, sniffing disdainfully. 'That is the reason for their off-putting scent.' He added uncomfortably,

'Ravana determined these things by dissecting several of them and studying them closely. These two must be among the last who remain of the original litter.' He gestured to the vanar who had been speaking. 'Pray, continue.'

The Kiskindha vanar went on with his tale. Rama's three spies had watched the two Lankan spies closely. The Lankans had spied on the war council, noting every detail of strategy with avid hunger. Later, when the killing stones began their terrible slaughter, the Lankans had scampered in the direction of the capital city, and the Kiskindha vanars had followed. A pause and an inflection in the spy's voice revealed his emotional reaction to the massacre of the night before, and Hanuman could imagine how hard it must have been for the trio to stick to their appointed task in the face of such unexpected horrors. The spy continued, explaining how the two Lankans had led them back to the city of Lanka and had been permitted to pass through. Determined to fulfil their orders to the letter, the three Kishindhan vanars had managed to breach the Lankan defences and enter the city as well, though the vanar did not explain in detail how they accomplished this task. 'The guards were overconfident, the walls were high,' he said scornfully, 'but the ground was soft and it was easy to dig beneath the walls.'

Once inside Lanka, it was not hard to pick up the scent of the two Lankan spies, although it was terrifying to be within the city of their most feared enemies, alone and unarmed. But by hiding in plain sight – pretending to be Lankan spies themselves – they had simply strutted through the other barricades and guards and followed their targets right into the heart of the capital. There they had managed to conceal themselves in the high branches of a great banyan tree and watched as the two Lankans passed on their vital information to a rakshasa general with the most magnificent teeth they had ever seen on a living creature.

'General Vajradanta,' Vibhisena said, on hearing this description. 'He can bite through the blades of three swords at once, leaving perfect indentations of his teeth on all. He is blessed with a boon that enables him to bite through anything he chooses.'

After being debriefed by their general, the two spies had wined and supped and been allowed to indulge in Lankan hedonism most of the night, until they fell into a drunken, satiated stupor. Early this morning, they had staggered awake and made their way blearily back to Rama's army before dawn. On Hanuman's instructions, the three Kiskindha vanars had stayed close by the two Lankans in the trees, falling upon them when Hanuman gave the prearranged signal. And here they were.

Satabali nodded at Rama, Lakshman and Hanuman, including them all in his gruffly spoken congratulations. 'Smartly scented, shrewdly devised, brilliantly executed. But what would you do now, Lord Rama? Your Lankan spies must be killed, or they will go back and tell their masters all your *real* plans.' He added with a chortle, 'Unless you think that *these* spasas can be made allies as well!'

Rama studied the two rakshasas crouched on the ground. They looked amazingly like vanars. Hanuman sniffed. Their baleful eyes glared angrily up at the mortal yodha, as if they desired nothing more than to tear out his throat. He resisted the urge to cuff them for their insolence, knowing that if he did, he might wish to hit them harder than living bone could endure.

'No,' he said quietly. 'They can never be our allies. But we shall not kill them either.'

Angad asked with his customary impatience, tinged with genuine curiosity, 'Then what do you wish done with them?'

Rama's lips curled in a semblance of a smile. 'They shall be escorted to the gates of Lanka and handed over to the sentries there. Hanuman, you shall do this, fly them there and return as swiftly as possible. Dawn is upon us, sunrise is nigh, and we have many preparations yet to make. Go, my friend. Do as I have instructed.'

Hanuman needed no second bidding. He moved forward, bending down and scooping up the two rakshasa-vanars in both arms, then took to the skies with a swiftness that brought startled, choked gasps and a *cheeka* of outrage from the two Lankan spies. In moments he was cutting through the sky like a falcon pouncing on its prey.

'I don't understand, Rama,' Lakshman said. 'Doesn't this defeat the plan of shima you described earlier? Won't the Lankan spies now go back and tell Ravana everything you outlined this morning as well? If what our Kiskindhan spies told us is true, the Lankans were able to read our lips and so deduce everything we discussed here at this war council as well. Now both our original plan and our counter-plan are in Lankan hands!'

Rama smiled. 'What makes you think that either of those were our real plans?'

Lakshman looked at him, dumbfounded for once. So did everyone else.

Rama said quietly, 'Now, if you will listen closely, I will tell you what we must do today to turn the tide in our favour and show the Lord of Lanka that we are not an enemy to be dismissed lightly. It is time that we showed him that rakshasas can be slaughtered and massacred too.'

9

Hanuman flew up several hundred yards, high enough to view the lie of the land, yet not so high that he could not be seen easily by Angad and the other generals and captains and chiefs of the armies. He floated in mid-air, examining the scene below with great curiosity.

He had deposited the Lankan spies at the gates of Lanka, dropping them from a height of several yards right at the feet of the startled gate-watch kumbha guards – high enough to injure and cause pain, but not kill – and before the kumbhas could so much as raise their spears and howl a warning, he was speeding back to Rama. He had rejoined the council barely a moment after Rama had begun outlining his *real* plan. And now, only a short while after the council had ended, here he was, in the sky again, preparing for the first battle against Lanka.

He hovered in the air and examined the lie of the land below. To the north-east, the sun had risen above the rim of the ocean horizon and cast its golden light upon the world. Seen from this height, the ocean glinted and glistened, encapsulating Lanka as the waters of a pond encircled a lotus.

Only now, in the clear light of day, could he truly see the results of Ravana's sorcery of the night before and compare the land that lay below him now to the Lanka he had seen only a day or two earlier on his previous visit.

What had been a lush, fecund plateau sloping down on the

south side into a valley which then rose again to the foothills of mountains had been transformed into a vast pen bounded on all sides by the towering fortress wall. In a sense, Rama's forces were now contained within the walls of Lanka. But this was illusory, for these walls were intended to imprison not to include. Lanka's true walls of defence were much farther south, where the inner fortress city now lay, resurrected in all its former blackstone rakshasa glory, the volcano beyond it spewing red-hot hellish rage. This was the Lanka they all knew from fables and legends, the land of rakshasas and Asuras and unspeakable things.

What Ravana's sorcery had achieved the night before, apart from killing almost a tenth of Rama's forces – decimating them in the most literal sense – was to imprison them in this part of the island, the northern end. Hanuman could see for a good yojana in every direction from his current vantage point: the armies of vanars and bears were spread thickly across the landscape, fenced in by those menacing blackstone walls with their cruel spiked spears that protruded several yards.

After the council had ended, the first thing Rama had done was offer a prayer for those who had fallen during the night of the killing stones, followed by a second prayer for those who had been spared. Speaking briefly to the commanders, captains and tribe chiefs of both the vanar and bear forces, his words passed on through word of mouth to the assembled warriors, Rama had declared it a sign of their good fortune that although they had suffered great losses during their first night in Lanka, almost all their commanders and leaders had lived to see daylight. That surely indicated that they were meant to live and to extract reprisal for their fallen soldiers. The next thing he did was quickly sketch out his analysis of Ravana's strategy, based on his observations of the manner in which the fortress had been raised, and the design of its fortifications. He pointed out what they had all observed by then in the slanting light of sunrise: 'These fortifications are designed

to contain us within, not keep us out. That itself tells us everything we need to know about their next plan of attack.'

Hanuman watched now as the lakhs of vanars and bears
carpeting the landscape below milled about in confusion, seemingly still fearful and disoriented after the night's traumatic
events. Slowly, with apparent difficulty, the troops to the south
began to organise themselves into battle formations, lining up
in typical fashion. Farther south, he could see the clouds of
dust raised by the approaching armies of Lanka. To all appearances, Lanka's armies had come from the city and were attacking
from the south, as was logical, and Rama's forces were responding
by forming up to face the defenders.

But appearances could be deceptive.

The troops were doing as Rama had ordered, playing their
part exceedingly well. Slowly, in apparent confusion and with
visible reluctance, the vanar and bear lines began to form, facing
southwards. This left a great patch at the northern tip of the
plateau completely deserted. Not a single vanar or bear was
visible for several miles at that end.

A movement by the wall at the northern tip of the plateau
caught his eye and he shifted his attention to that spot. That
was the farthest point north, literally the place where he had
pressed the cliff face to provide a more negotiable slope for
Rama's armies to climb from the beach. Now it was bounded
by the rampart wall. It was at that very point that he had
found Rama an hour or so earlier, and carried him down to
the ground below. Rama had spoken to the council about his
search for a stairway down from the top of the rampart to the
ground, and how he had found no such thing. Which defied
all logic. What good was a rampart wall without steps for
soldiers to climb to the top to defend the wall? There was only
one answer to that, Rama said: the wall was never meant to
be climbed, either by the defenders or the attackers. It was
merely intended to fence them in.

Which raised the next, most vital question: now that Ravana

had Rama's army fenced in upon this part of his kingdom, imprisoned by those unclimbable walls on every side, how would he launch his first attack? The logical choice would be from the south, from the direction of the city of Lanka itself. But that would be too simple, too obvious. And Ravana was not given to simple strategies, as the sorcerous display of the night had itself proven.

No, Rama had said, had Ravana desired to attack them in the usual fashion, sending his armies across the mountain ranges to engage Rama's forces in face-to-face confrontation, he would not have designed the walls as he had. It was no mere coincidence that Rama had been raised up by the rising wall, for by that happenstance he had been able to discover the lack of an ingress for Ravana's soldiers in the rampart walls, and from that lack he had been able to deduce Ravana's entire battle strategy – and prepare a counter-strategy of his own.

And that was what was being put into action right now. From the moment Nala's messengers had brought word of the event that Rama had told them to look out for, the die had been cast. Just as Rama had predicted, the scouts posted as close to the walls as they could possibly get had felt tremors from deep within the ground. Anybody else would have thought that this was evidence of some new phase in Ravana's sorcerous redesign, but Rama was confident that it meant his analysis was right, and had immediately given the word to move to the next phase of their counter-strategy.

Hanuman watched with bated breath as the troops below moved farther south, as if they only had a mind to engage Ravana's troops arriving from that direction, with no awareness of any other threat. As they moved, they left the entire plateau apparently empty.

Back on the ground, he had watched along with everyone else as Rama had pointed out the crevices and crenellations carved into the foot of the wall at regular intervals. In normal fortifications, Rama had explained for the benefit of the two species, who had no previous knowledge of such things, those apertures would lead to stairwells and tunnels providing passage-ways for troops defending the wall to travel along its length and to the top of the ramparts to reinforce the defences. But as he had already discovered, there were no such stairwells leading to the top of the walls, which left only the other possi-bility – passages. It had taken only a few moments of quick scouting by a handful of bold vanars to report that, indeed, the crevices and crenellations led to passageways within the walls, and that these passageways led not upwards, as would have been usual for a fortification of this type, but *down*. Once Rama heard this, he had smiled a smile such as Hanuman had never seen before. And then he had outlined the strategy they were now putting into effect.

Hanuman focused his gaze on the dark shadows gathering at the foot of the walls. At first it would seem that that was all they appeared to be, shadows. But in many places they fell the wrong way, aslant to the angle of the sunlight streaming down from the eastern sky. And they moved as no shadows could possibly move. As he watched, they grew bolder, emerging into the light as they saw that Rama's troops had abandoned this region to march south, just as their master had intended.

Now he saw the flash of a rakshasa's tusked snout, now the gleam of a horned head, now the silvery flash of a steel weapon being unsheathed. Ravana's troops were coming up through the secret passageways inside the wall, just as Rama had predicted, and were now waiting until sufficient of their number had accu-mulated to launch the first attack. He smiled grimly. So this was Ravana's plan, just as Rama had expected: the Lord of Lanka intended to catch them between a rock and a hard place – or to be more accurate, between a rock *wall* and a charging army. He was launching his forces from the south, duping Rama into moving his troops to fight there, and when the battle was fully underway, with all of Rama's troops committed, he would order these rakshasas creeping up through the secret passageways to strike at Rama's armies from the flanks. Rama's forces would be bound on all sides, hemmed in, and it would be easy for the rakshasa hordes to press them inwards until they had nowhere to turn or retreat. It was a brutal, cruel plan, and a brilliant one.

He watched as the rakshasas emerged more boldly now from the walls, like cockroaches swarming out in the absence of the occupants of a house, and lined up in preparation for their devious assault. There was nothing between them and Rama's unsuspecting troops to the south except a few empty miles of dense thickets. They would wait for the battle to begin before launching their assault.

He flew a yojana or so in a southwards direction, until he was floating over the approaching armies of Lanka. They looked formidable in the early sunlight, endless lines of rakshasas racing in the familiar thumping marching style that he had seen before during Rama's battles in Janasthana. There were legions of kumbha-rakshasas among them too, dwarfing their fellow rakshasas and wielding great wooden hammers with iron heads. Even though they were far fewer in number than the other rakshasas, the cloud of dust spiralling up from their battalion was denser and greater than that rising in the wake of the whole of the rest of army.

He watched as the rakshasa army came within a mile of his own forces and slowed to a halt, the two armies arrayed across the width of this end of the island, spread thickly across some two and a half yojanas. Even now, Rama's forces were much more numerous than those of Ravana, but in this too, Hanuman knew, appearances were deceptive. Ravana had many tricks up his sleeve, and even Rama could not second-guess every one of them; while all the troops that Rama commanded were there to be seen and counted.

He grinned slyly. Well, perhaps not *all*.

He flexed his body and prepared to carry out the next stage of Rama's plan.

*   *   *

General Vajradanta watched from a promontory atop Mount Nikumbhila as the Lankan forces reached their appointed places in the valley below. A glint of movement in the sky above caught his attention and he peered up to see a tiny speck flying high overhead. He scowled. That was the vanar champion, Hanuman. He could not tell whether the flying vanar seemed so tiny because he was so very high, or because he was merely his normal vanar size, but in either case, he knew that the simian was doing exactly the same thing as he was: spying out the lie of the land before the battle commenced. He watched as the speck sped northwards, back to the enemy ranks, and briefly contemplated calling for a regiment of archers to loose. He dismissed the idea almost at once: the vanar was flying too high and too swiftly for even the most accurately aimed missiles to catch.

He returned his attention to examining the troops below. From this projecting ledge of stone, jutting out several yards from the promontory of the fortress ramparts and enhanced by the considerable height of Nikumbhila itself, he had an excellent view of the valley below as well as a clear sight of the landscape for several miles in every direction.

Even from this height, the reverberating sound of the bone-horns of the heralds was faintly but distinctly audible, as the rakshasa leaders far below ordered their hordes to halt. The densely packed rakshasa lines slowed from a canter to a trot, and finally came to a trundling stop, the dust cloud created by their movements slowly carried away by the strong early-morning winds. At once, the inevitable fights and arguments broke out between the more belligerent tribes over stopping too soon or too slowly, and were suppressed as quickly by the barbed metal-rope lashes of the kumbha herding officers.

Vajradanta examined the formations carefully, turned to issue a few crisp orders regarding troop adjustments for his lieutenants to courier down through the trained vultures used for this purpose, then decided that the ragged formations were about as close to orderliness as any rakshasa army was ever likely to achieve. With a grunt of satisfaction, he turned and strode back along the jetty, walking across the promontory to the spot where the rest of the Lankan command stood. As he approached, he could see the black fortress walls undulating in both directions, running along Lanka's coastline for as far as the eye could see, an impenetrable defence that no army could possibly breach. It made him want to roar with exultation at the sheer power and might of his leader and his race.

Generals Mahaparsva, Mahodara and Virupaksa stood watching the battlefield with glowering eyes. They were naturally resentful at Vajradanta being chosen over them to command the army, after that wretched vanar's rampage in the tower three days earlier. The looks of malevolence they shot his way didn't bother him one whit. He could bite through any of their limbs without even straining his jaw muscles. The only one who did inspire some slight unease was the veteran Prahasta, who had wisely suggested that he maintain his position of city commander and manage the defences against any possible intrusion or siege. Siege! Intrusion! Ludicrous, given the formidable new defences that Ravana's sorcery had wrought. But he was still glad that Prahasta was not among the rivals who stood glaring at him from the rampart circle.

A little apart from them stood the sorcerers Vidhujjivha and Malyavan, looking even more smug than usual after the display of their Asura maya the night before – even though they were barely apprentices to Ravana's mastery of the dark arts. Several other lesser officers of the Lankan hordes stood about, debating battle strategy, the weather, omens and portents, and even, in at least one case, whether bears were worth ravishing sexually. He allowed himself a smirk at that last query. Rakshasas would be rakshasas, after all. A flash of movement told him that Ravana's cousin Supanakha was watching covertly, which was her usual style. Vajradanta bared his teeth, tilting his face to catch the slanting sunlight and send shards of reflections dancing across the faces of his fellow rakshasas.

It was more effective than bellowing for their attention. At once, they all grimaced and cringed as one, shielding their light-sensitive rakshasa eyes from the splinters of reflected light with paws, helms, weapons. All conversations died out, and he saw a flash of tawny fur not far behind the sorcerers as the shape-shifting yaksi came closer to eavesdrop more effectively.

He grunted and began without preamble.

'While we await our lord, let's appraise you of developments. As you must know already, if you aren't deaf or senile yet, the night's sorcery was smartly done. Our spies tell us casualties on the enemy's side were large, as many as two out of every five of their warriors were killed by the shifting stones. And the rest of the vanars are demoralised and terrified of more sorcery, which makes them weak and nervous to fight. So the vanars are as good as minced, take it from me.' He flashed his teeth again. 'I'm looking forward to seeing if their marrow's as tasty as they say it is. I wager they'll gibber and flee at the sight of our kumbhas alone, which I propose to send in the front line of the first wave.'

'Maybe they will, and maybe they won't. But you can wager yourself back that the bears won't be that much of a pushover.' The speaker was Mahaparsva, the general who had been next in line for promotion until Vajradanta got bumped up the line by Ravana. His triple-hinged mouth flapped and unflapped, revealing the sucking maw within. His tall, slender frame belied his ramrod strength and speed in combat. He sneered disparagingly at Vajradanta. 'And you don't have enough kumbhas to throw at the bears as well, do you, Jaws?'

Vajradanta bristled at the use of his most disliked nickname, but knew better than to draw attention to that deliberate provocation. Returning Mahaparsva's sneer with a scornful gesture of his own, he retorted: 'We have something extra tasty planned for the bears, Purse. Why, would you like to go give them all bear hugs before we slaughter them?'

It was Mahaparsva's turn to bristle at the use of *his* nickname, a reference to the folding flaps of his oral orifice. He scowled sullenly.

Virupaksa snarled and pounded his chest, issuing a subvocal roar that Vajradanta could feel vibrating in his teeth and inner ears. The warrior almost never spoke, but he hardly needed words to express his impatience to delve into the fray and perform his usual grisly routine of separating enemy torsos from limbs with the efficiency and speed of a butcher on a feast day. His muscles – indeed, his muscles upon muscles – bulged and flexed and he gripped the edge of the rampart wall nearest to him. The yard-thick block of stone actually began to crumble at the edges under his crushing grip. The sorcerers Vidyujjivha and Malyavan sidled away from this unseemly display of brute strength, their frail, pot-bellied bodies wasted away by years of poring over forbidden texts lettered with mortal blood on endless scrolls of parchment made of mortal skin in the deep, fetid dungeons of Lanka. Their eyes shone with a rheumy, cataract-obscured light that unnerved Vajradanta far more than Virupaksa's impressive show of strength.

'We shall leave the breaking of our walls for our enemies to attempt, shall we, Viru?' said a clear, calm voice from above them all. Vajradanta looked up with a start to see Ravana himself, standing at the golden railing of his pushpak chariot, his ten heads seeming to stare in ten directions at once. Immediately, Virupaksa released the rampart wall. Everyone else stiffened in mute attention. Ravana smiled down at Vajradanta. 'And my dear general, before you proceed with today's scheduled programme of slaughter, there are two useful pieces of information I think you might like to gain possession of.'

Reaching down with two hands, Ravana brought up two vanars, their terrified furred faces dwarfed by the rakshasa lord's immense handspans as he gripped them by the backs of their heads and raised them squirming for all to see. He tossed them contemptuously down to the rampart platform, where they fell in two ragged heaps, moaning and crying out shrilly. Then he descended and alighted on to the rampart himself, like a lion among his pride.

The two hybrid spies writhed on the stone slabs of the rampart, prostrating themselves before Ravana. 'Mercy, O Lord of Lanka, we are your humble servants.'

Ravana kicked them hard enough to draw the sharp crack of bone splintering, and one of the two turned pale with shock and pain. He ignored them both as he addressed the assembled commanders. 'To put it briefly, it would appear that Rama's army is falling into the very trap I had devised. At least that's what these two buffoons learned this morning before they were exposed and sent back to us like simpering whores.'

Nobody sought to correct the King of Lanka by pointing out that the trap in question had been thought up by General Prahasta in collusion with Ravana's own elder son, Indrajit. If Ravana chose to call it his trap, it *was* his trap. He strode to the edge of the rampart, gazing out across the assembled army in the valley below. 'I see that you have aligned our hordes according to the plan, Vajradanta.'

'Just as you ordered at our earlier conference at dawn, my lord,' Vajradanta said obsequiously, trying with some difficulty to bow his thick, overdeveloped torso. 'Everything is precisely as you instructed.'

Ravana was silent for a moment, seeming distracted now. Several of his heads were murmuring, one snarling, and at least three seemed to be meditating – at least, their eyes were rolled up in their sockets. Vajradanta tried unsuccessfully to avoid staring at them out of sheer curiosity. Finally Ravana nodded curtly. 'Well done. And speedily too.'

Vajradanta blinked, surprised at the unexpected praise. He glanced around, licking his lips excitedly, to see if the others had noted this uncharacteristic compliment paid to his generalship. Judging from their dark, scowling expressions, they had. He almost grinned, but checked himself. It would not do to bare his teeth to his master and commander; among rakshasas, it was a sign of challenge. To Ravana, it would be a sign of defiance and insubordination, punishable with instant death. Nobody grinned at Ravana and lived to grin a second time. He kept his lips sealed.

Ravana strode out on to the ledge where Vajradanta himself had stood not long before, gazing this way and that, examining the troop positions and land layout with closer attention. Finally, satisfied, he nodded again, and turned back to Vajradanta. 'Yes, well done indeed. I could not have aligned them better myself. Now we shall rearrange them all anew.'

Vajradanta blinked rapidly. Had he misheard his commander? 'My lord?'

Ravana gestured casually with a hand whose wrist alone was as thick as Vajradanta's shoulder. 'I shall give you the codes for a new formation. It must be done within the hour-watch.' He paused, reflecting, squinting at the rising sun. 'Nay, within the half-hour. Time is of the essence. This battle should be over and done with long before noon.'

Vajradanta stared in numb confusion. 'Within the half-hour? New formation? My lord . . .'

Suddenly Ravana was all too close to him, his powerful arms within easy striking distance, his breath hot and scented with a dozen different odours – actually, ten, to be exact. He placed one palm upon Vajradanta's shoulder; it felt as heavy as a bag full of iron ingots. One squeeze and the general's shoulder would be . . . no longer a shoulder, merely fragmented chips of bone and gristle and cartilage. He swallowed nervously, carefully keeping his lips pressed together to avoid showing his famous teeth.

'Vajra,' Ravana said quietly, with breath that was redolent of scented paan, supari nut, and something else that the general could not identify – it could not possibly be roasted mortal flesh, could it? 'You are named for your lightning-sharp teeth. Surely your intellect is not as slow as molasses?'

Vajradanta swallowed a gob of blood, only then realising that he had bitten the inside of his own cheek when Ravana's hand had descended on his shoulder. 'Nay, sire. I understand perfectly. The new formation shall be aligned as you desire within the half-hour. You have but to provide me with the codes.'

Ravana's heads peered at him. It was unsettling to be gazed on from this close by that entire formidable rack of heads, their moustached, grinning, leering, scowling, chewing, abusing, suckling faces within spitting distance of his own. When one chuckled softly at last, he hardly knew which one.

'Excellent.' The hand on his shoulder patted him heavily, then, mercifully, was removed. 'I knew I could count on you to be a good trooper, my toothsome friend. Here are the codes. See that they are carried out at once.'

He gestured, and a scroll held by one of the waiting vulture-handlers nearby was plucked clean out of the rakshasa's hands and wafted in the air. In a trice, lines of instructions coded in the Lankan secret communication shorthand appeared on it magically. Vajradanta caught the scroll as it fell out of the air, and rolled it up neatly, gesturing to the same handler to come forward and take it. The rakshasa approached fearfully, all but crawling across the rampart to avoid raising his head in Ravana's presence, and in another moment the precious instructions were being tied to the foot of a reluctant vulture. The bird bit hard at his handler's gloved arm, squawked an ugly, resentful cry, then took off with a fluttering of its ragged wings, soaring on an air current down to the valley below.

Vajradanta gestured to another pair of handlers and quickly

dictated a series of follow-up codes to his hand-picked lieu-tenants below that would ensure the new instructions were carried out with the lightning speed for which he had been named.

That done, he turned smartly to his master. 'My lord, I myself ought to descend to the valley in order to see that the instructions are carried out with the efficiency you desire.'

Ravana nodded obscurely. 'In a moment, my lightning-toothed one. I understand. You will need to crack a barbed whip, bust a few skulls, and generally use a combination of bullying and brute force to ensure that the re-formation is carried out in time. I was once a lowly lieutenant in the rakshasa ranks too, you know. I recall how hard it can be to keep a horde in order – sometimes even to keep them heading in the right direction in a battle! But wait a moment longer. I have one last jewel of information to impart.'

Vajradanta bowed his head, straining his thick neck to do so. He waited patiently as the sun inched higher in the eastern sky, already casting its gaudy light across this entire part of the world.

'Yes,' Ravana said, his central head gazing dreamily into the distance, visualising something none of them could see. 'You see, sometimes the prey that has eluded the predator long enough begins to believe that it *is* the predator.'

He grinned with four heads simultaneously at the commanders of his armies gathered on the rampart top. 'It is then necessary to remind him that just because the predator chooses to prolong the hunt, that is not proof of the predator's weakness, but of his superior skill and self-confidence. For what fun is a hunt that is ended in a flash? The true test of skill comes only in contests of endurance.'

He effected a gesture that Vajradanta thought was directed at him. It took the general a moment to realise that Ravana was gesturing at the rakshasas standing directly behind him, the two sorcerers Vidyujjivha and Malyavan.

'Fellow misappropriators of brahman shakti,' Ravana said, one head chuckling at his own wit, 'it is about time you earned the right to the considerable fee I pay to keep you in my employ. I have a task for you to perform. Do you see these two wretches here?' He gestured at the still prostrated vanar-rakshasa hybrids. 'What are your names, wretches?'

The two broken-spirited creatures stared up in abject terror. 'S . . . S . . . Suka and Sarama,' said one, answering for both. The other merely gibbered wordlessly, spittle oozing from his mouth.

'Suka and Sarama,' Ravana said thoughtfully.

Suddenly he bent, gripped the two vanar-rakshasas by the skin of their necks, and with one casual flick of his powerful arms flung them over the ledge and into the valley below. Simultaneously astonished and delighted, the two sorcerers rushed to the edge of the rampart and followed the flight of the vanars as they hurtled to certain death, too shocked even to emit screams. 'You see,' Ravana said, sounding disappointed. 'They cannot fly. I must have pigs with wings for the crucial phase of today's plan. That is the task I entrust you with, sorcerers: grow me enough wings to make an entire battalion fly.'

He chuckled at their stunned expressions. 'Fear not. I will provide you with the means to accomplish it. And the mantras. It's just that I need you to do it yourselves, as I have other business to attend to meanwhile.' He gestured below. 'A little matter of a battle to be won.'

Then he clapped a hand on Vajradanta's shoulder again, almost crushing it to shards. 'Now, my sharp-toothed friend, take my pushpak, race down to the valley, and carry out my instructions to the letter. It's time to show Rama and his furry companions that vanars can fly too. They just have a little trouble landing in one piece!'

*   *   *

Rama and Lakshman reached the top of the rise. Mount Suvela, as Vibhisena had called this peak, was barely worthy of the title of mountain, but it afforded the best view for yojanas around. From here, the two brothers could see the towering eminence of Mount Nikumbhila, perhaps a yojana and a half farther south, with its massive fortifications. Lakshman said he thought he could spy figures atop the fortifications, and as he watched, Rama distinctly saw an object rise and fly up into the air before dropping slowly into the valley below. From the manner in which the sunlight caught the object and reflected gaudily off it, like a lamp's light off the jewellery of a queen, he had no doubt it was Ravana's pushpak chariot. And where Pushpak was, Ravana was too, most certainly.

From this vantage point, they could just glimpse the endless lines of the rakshasa forces, still tramping this way and that in complex formations, raising new clouds of dust that were quickly carried away by the unusually strong sea wind.

'What are they doing?' Lakshman asked, frowning. 'They seem to be rearranging their lines. Why would they do that now?'

Rama watched the swirling dust-haze of the rakshasa army movements for several moments. 'We must not make the mistake of underestimating Ravana. He is too shrewd to be easily duped. I wish there were some way we could know if he has swallowed the story the spies carried back to Lanka.'

Lakshman shrugged philosophically. 'Well, it is too late to do anything now. Our forces are committed. They only await our order to cover the last mile or two before engaging the Lankans.'

He gestured to the left. 'They look quite professional now, don't they?' he said with more than a trace of pride. The days of hard drilling and disciplining had borne fruit, the more so after the bitter losses suffered by the armies, for nothing toughened soldiers more effectively than sudden death.

Rama turned his attention to the armies of vanars massed

in the declivity to the left of Mount Suvela. While nowhere near as organised and neatly arrayed as the armies of Ayodhya or other Arya nations, and lacking any uniform – lacking even a uniformity of pelt colouring, shape or size – the vanar forces were nevertheless impressive when he recalled the ragtag swarms he had first set eyes on when Hanuman arrived at the southern shore. They had been akin to wild monkeys then and anyone could have been forgiven for mistaking them for their simian cousins. But now they were vanars, bearing themselves as proudly as was possible with their curved spines, their tails all held upright to avoid bothering those behind and beside them, and attempting manfully to move as units, instead of scampering individually with the abandon they were so accustomed to in their native lands. Yes, Lakshman's training had borne fruit indeed. It was testimony to the commitment and devotion of those brave little warriors that he could actually count the number of lines in which they were arranged.

He smiled. Despite the apparent enormity of their numbers, he knew that those were barely half the number of vanars under his command. He exchanged a glance with Lakshman and saw the glint in his brother's eye as he acknowledged the same observation. There was neither sign nor sight of the rest of the forces, and that was most impressive of all. Yes, they were ready now for battle, or as ready as they were ever going to be.

A *cheeka* from behind alerted them to the arrival of Nala. Rama turned to see the spry little vanar racing up the grassy hillside. 'Rama!' He was glad that the bridge-builder had not been one of those who perished in the night of the killing stones: Nala was an ingenious engineer and was invaluable in calculations and plotting, as well as map-making. It was he who had translated several of Rama's and Lakshman's troop movements into practical deployments, and of course, without him the whole backbone of their main plan would be worthless. If they succeeded in pulling off this bold and desperate plan today, a portion of the credit would belong to Nala.

But more than his ingenuity and skill, it was his passion that Rama loved about Nala. Witness the way he had come bounding across the miles when he could as easily have sent one of Angad's couriers – artfully arranged at intervals across the battle theatre for that very purpose. Like Rama himself, he swore by the maxim that if it was worth doing, it was worth doing yourself.

'Rama,' he said, chopping his sentences up to gasp for breath. 'All goes just as you said. The angadiyas just brought word. Tremors from beneath the northernmost walls! Just as you predicted. And our lookouts have spotted them emerging.' He sucked in a longer breath. 'They are ugly brutes, Rama, larger than normal rakshasas and oddly made, with some kind of armoured hide growing on their backs and chests.' He touched himself on the aforementioned places and grimaced. 'I do not know how we will be able to bring them down, but Angad and Kambunara say they will find a weakness, everyone has a weakness.'

'That they do,' Rama agreed grimly. 'Including us. What of the other lieutenants? Have they been deployed as instructed?'

Nala nodded vigorously, pointing as he described each one's position. 'Under the command of General Nila, Mainda and Dvivida man the eastern flank. Under Prince Angad, Rsabha, Gavaksa, Gaja and Gavya to the south. Susena commands Pramathi, Praghasa and the twins in the west. And King Sugreeva himself mans the centre with the main Kiskindha fighting force.'

Rama glanced at Lakshman. They had both urged Sugreeva not to enter the fray himself, given his ailing condition and the injuries he had sustained the night before. But the vanar king would not hear of it. 'If not for you, Rama, I would have no army to command. If my life is forfeit in your cause, it is forfeit. Say not another word.' And he had bounded off southwards with a strong, proud gait that all knew was costing him a great price to maintain.

Rama nodded. 'It is time then. Summon Anjaneya.'

'Here, my lord.' Hanuman descended from the sky with the suddenness of a bar of light emerging suddenly from behind a passing cloud.

Rama looked the vanar in the eye. 'My friend, my brother in blood and destiny. Do exactly as we planned and leave the rest to the devas. If we are meant to succeed, then they will fight side by side with us today. Go now. Give the word to begin the march. Make sure every contingent executes their orders exactly as planned unless they hear otherwise from me. And remember, you are to watch everyone and everything and report back to me constantly, but above all you are to watch me for further instructions and any alterations in the plan that I may issue. For only you can reach our far-flung legions in time to convey my words. I know it will seem strange and frustrating, to only watch without entering the fray yourself, but you must do this for me. You will have your chance to kill rakshasas very shortly. Only do as I ask for this first phase of the battle.'

Hanuman bowed and touched Rama's feet, then Lakshman's. When he rose again, his eyes were shining wet. 'By your grace, my lord,' he said, 'I pray I do not let you down today.'

Rama placed a hand upon Hanuman's shoulder, and from the vanar's response it was evident that Hanuman was overjoyed at this rare show of warm affection. 'You will never let me down, my brother. Go now and add your name to the shining annals of the greatest yodhas of the Treta-Yuga. Today you will do us all proud. I know this to be true.'

Hanuman stared mutely at Rama, then blinked away sudden tears. Before anyone could say another word, the vanar raised his chin and flew straight up with astonishing speed, gone in a blink.

Rama turned back to Nala. 'Go now, my young architect. Send back word to all through the angadiyas to start the movements I outlined earlier.'

Nala nodded vigorously. 'They will do exactly as you desire,

Rama. There is scarcely a vanar or a bear on this field that does not have a fallen friend or blood-kin to avenge today in Lanka.'

'Even so,' Rama said, 'remind them that while the desire for vengeance is a good servant to a soldier, it is a bad master. Let them curb their anger and unleash it only when permitted to do so by my order. And remember that the signal to change the formation will come from above, from Maruti, not from me or you or the angadiyas. Is that clear?'

Nala nodded, sombre now. 'All shall be well, by your grace,' he said. He dipped his snout to kiss Rama's feet, then Lakshman's, before they could protest – for neither approved of this particular vanar custom – then in a trice was bounding back downhill, already yelling out instructions to the nearest angadiyas. Before Rama could draw his next breath, the words he had spoken were being passed on through the ingenious and wildfire-quick network that was one of the great strengths of the vanar armies.

He turned back to see Lakshman scouring the lands below, to the south, then the east, then the west, and finally the valley before them and behind them.

'What are you looking for, Sumitra-putra?' Rama asked, although he could guess.

'Bears,' Lakshman said, then flashed a wolfish grin at his brother. 'I am looking for any sign of bears, Kausalya-putra.'

Rama inclined his head slyly. 'And did you find any?'

Lakshman held out his hands, palms upwards. 'Not a one. It is as if they have all vanished off the face of Lanka.'

Rama nodded slowly. 'Good. Then we are truly ready to begin.' He picked up his bow in one hand and his sword in the other, preparing to give the final signal to the vanar armies. He paused, then glanced at Lakshman again. 'Son of Dasaratha, you have not spoken a word concerning my battle plan since our first war council this morning. Even now, you speak of everything but the plan. Will you not offer me one argument or correction?'

Lakshman looked back at him with a tight smile, his own bow off his shoulder and in his hands now, an arrow already on the string. 'Is that not enough to tell you what I think of it, Dasaratha-putra?'

Rama smiled back. 'I am blessed to have you by my side today.'

He raised both the bow in his left hand and the sword in his right, kept them aloft long enough for Hanuman to note, then dropped them to his sides in the pre-agreed signal to start the battle.

Then, as one being with two hearts, the brothers surged forward, sprinting down the southern slope of Mount Suvela, towards the field of battle.

KAAND 3

THE BOOK OF SKULLS

A horn carved from the tusk of a mahish-asura, an extinct species, sounded across the Lankan side of the battleground, calling the rakshasa armies to order. Its grating, low-pitched trumpeting, resembling a bull elephant's mating call, nevertheless carried far enough to reach Vajradanta's ears.

The general, seated atop a kumbha-sur, one of a small number of hybrid broken-surs crossbred with kumbha-rakshasas, pointed the leaf-shaped head of his lance at his herald. The nervous albino rakshasa, colourless eyes covered to protect them from the blinding sunlight, raised his own horn to his maw, inserted his oral orifice entirely into the opening of his mahish-asura trumpet, unusually large as befitted the army's main herald, and issued a call both higher-pitched and more threatening than any of the earlier ones.

It was echoed by identically high-pitched trumpeting from the far corners of the battleground, some from so far away that even Vajradanta, mounted four whole yards above high ground, could not see the flanks and rear formations. The trumpeting was echoed as well by the enraged lowing of bull elephants in the prime of masth, the mating frenzy that drove them to battle one another and tear up the countryside in search of mates. The masth tuskers had been corralled and harnessed specially for this battle, and it took a score of rakshasas controlled by kumbhas to hold each one down with ropes. At the sound of the high-pitched horns, laced with notes that were designed to enrage them, they renewed their frantic efforts to free themselves.

Elsewhere, kumbha sergeants lashed their troops one last time, bellowing orders that had been repeated so often that some of their command actually moved their lips in time with their sergeants' words, repeating by rote.

There were a variety of species of rakshasa on display. The kumbhas were a familiar sight, their numbers woefully depleted, yet the two hordes that stood today on the grounds of Lanka still made for a formidable sight. Their hulking shapes bristled with horned armour, their fists clenching mostly the blunt-edged mace-like pounders they preferred in battle.

The wagh-rakshasas were distant kin to Supanakha, though she was a yaksi-rakshasa crossbred and unique, and resembled various sub-species of felines: some with thick yellow-and-black-striped bodies, some sleek, jet black and muscular like bagheera panthers, others spotted like leopards crouched on their hind legs, yet others sporting the pair of large fore-fangs and white fur of the Siberian cats, and even a platoon's worth of leonine rakshasas, mangy manes and roar and all. The rest were an amalgam of various lesser breeds, an odd admixture of rakshasa and clouded leopard, golden cat, jungle cat, marble cat, fishing cat, lynx, caracal, cheetah, pallas cat, desert cat, civet, toddy tiger, marbled polecat, palm civet and binturong.

The lupine sub-species were collectively known in Lankan commonspeak as the 'dog fighters'. Their hierarchy – for all rakshasa sub-species were decided by strength and viciousness bred over generations to determine the order of their varnas, in a mocking imitation of the castes that mortals followed – was headed by the wolf variants with their sleek grey fur and great slobbering jaws. These were followed by the jackal-rakshasas, then, in successively descending order of varna, the red foxes, the desi foxes, the dholes, hyenas, coyotes, and the various mangy pariah cross-mutations.

Farther outfield, though he could not see them, Vajradanta

visualised the ranks of the mahish-rakshasas, claiming descent directly from the legendary Mahish-asura himself, he who had compelled the ur-Mother Goddess, Devi, to take a rebirth in order to rid the world of his menace. They were less respect-fully known as the 'buffalo buffoons', on account of their rela-tively underdeveloped intellect – no rakshasa sub-species actually took pride in calling itself *intelligent* – and obvious physical characteristics. Here one found the gaurs, the bantengs, the yaks, the mithuns, oxen, bison and tsaine rakshasas.

Bearing a biological similarity to the mahish-rakshasas, but no obvious physical resemblances apart from similarly cloven or hooved feet, were the antlered families, as they preferred to be called, or ghaass-phuss eaters as they were more often known, for their digestive systems were better suited to vegetaria-nism, despite being rakshasas. It often made them the fiercest fighters, perhaps to redress any misconceptions about their eating habits reflecting their capacity for inflicting violence upon fleshly creatures. These came in an astonishing number of variants: the most recognisable were the shapus, marcos, nayans, bharals, ibex, leapers, markhors, nilgiri tahrs, hightars, nilgai, fourhorns, chinkaras, blackbucks, sambhars, kashmiras, thamin, swampers, chitals, chevrotains, hoggers, muskers, munt-jacs, wildtusks and barkers. Seen from a distance, their torsos and lower bodies concealed by high grass, one could be forgiven for mistaking them at first sight for a herd of unusually diverse deer-like creatures. Closer up, one would be left in no doubt at all that they were savage rakshasas.

And finally there were the few exceptions that were not enough to make up a tribe, let alone a horde, but were invalu-able as wild cards in a battle. These were the one-horns, strik-ingly similar to the near-sighted armour-plated animals on the mainland, except that they could stand briefly on their hind legs at times, and were rakshasas through and through; the elephants, differing only from their normal counterparts in that they had been raised by and with rakshasas for generations and taught to fear and hate the scent of mortals and other enemies of the Asura races; and the broken-surs, once perhaps related to the desert horses with their water-carrying humps that mortals sometimes harnessed to cross the vast desolate Sahara and Gobi aranyas, but with that unique cloven skull from which their name derived, meaning literally 'broken-headed', and their squatter, speedier, more horse-like skeletal structure.

All in all, it was a formidable line-up, enough to strike terror into the heart of any army in the three worlds. Indeed, it was the rakshasas that had formed the vanguard during Ravana's legendary invasion of Swarga-lok, the heavenly realm of the devas, when the other Asura races had displayed typical last-minute jitters at warring with the very gods themselves. And it was the rakshasas that had had first spoils of conquest in those divine realms.

Vajradanta licked his chops as he recalled the hedonistic glories he had enjoyed on that campaign. His nether organs stirred at the recollection too. He grinned, baring his famous teeth at last as he urged his kumbha-sur forward, raising his ten-yard-long lance high into the morning air, catching the sunlight, and roared: 'Ra-van-a!'

For that was the war cry of the united rakshasas of Lanka now, agreed upon after some cajoling – and cudgelling – on the part of their lord and master after his reawakening, replacing the dozens of separate tribe and horde cries that had been customary before. *Ra-van-a*. He Who Makes The Universe Scream. Vajradanta personally thought it was a splendid war cry. And what could strike fear into the hearts of the enemy more effectively than the name of the most dreaded creature in all existence?

As he spurred his mount into a trot, then a canter, taking it slowly only in order to let the other commanders follow apace, he heard the cry resound across the massed ranks of the Lankan army, echoed in a hundred different animalistic accents and variations, until it coordinated roughly into a deafening, bone-shuddering boom of a sound.

'RA-VAN-A!'

Vibhisena reached the top of Mount Suvela just in time to hear the Lankan war cry resound from the foothills of Mount Nikumbhila. That the engorged exultation carried all the way to this spot, miles from the actual battlefield, reflected the mood of the rakshasa hordes. They did not merely intend to win; they *were* winning. Their palpable sense of victory rolled across the valleys and low hills that separated him from the place where so many lives would engage in a struggle to the death only moments from now. He bowed his head and mouthed a prayer for Rama's forces as well as for Lanka itself, not the Lanka of Ravana and his bestial hordes, but the gentle, pure Lanka that had existed long before the Lord of Asuras had wrested this pristine island away from his brother Kuber, and that would, he believed, survive long after Ravana's evil reign ended. For it would end, he believed. He might not have the unshakeable faith that Hanuman had in his lord and master, but he believed in Rama too in his own way, or he would not be standing here today, on the wrong side of a theatre of war wherein the fate of his own land, his own people, was being decided.

He caught a flicker of movement in the sky and glanced up to see Hanuman flying overhead. The vanar was crisscrossing this section of the island-kingdom incessantly now, checking and rechecking troop formations and movements, for in this first phase of the battle, Vibhisena understood, manoeuvres would be crucial to gaining the upper hand. He prayed that Rama's armies, numerous though they were in sheer head count, would be able to withstand the far greater strength and skill of Ravana's hordes – not to mention the fact that the armoured, armed and battle-hardened rakshasas had enormous natural advantages over the naked, mostly unarmed and completely unblooded vanars. At least the bears possessed bulk and size in this otherwise woefully unequal clash.

As the last of the vanar troops in the declivity to the left disappeared over the top of a rise, going out of sight for a moment – they would appear again once they crossed the ghats and arrived in sight of the main fighting plain – he wished, not for the first time, that he was a warrior too, if only so that he could pit his own strength in Rama's favour. But that was wishing for too much. A rakshasa he might be, but a life-time of hard penance – bhor tapasya – and the fasting, self-deprivation and sacrifice necessary to pursue his brahmanical goals had depleted him of the savage energy of his race. Yet he knew he was stronger than an entire regiment of rakshasas in the one thing that mattered most to him – spiritual strength – and it was that which enabled him to stand tall now on the peak of Mount Suvela, where Rama and Lakshman had stood only a little while ago, and gaze out at the impending battle.

As the horns of Lanka sounded the final command to charge at full galloping speed, and the war cries echoed from the walls of the stone ramparts that now fenced in the land on every sea front, Vibhisena released a great pent-up sigh and lowered his weary body to the grassy mound. He sat cross-legged and focused his mind on the perfect incantation of slokas to help ensure the fruition of Rama's just cause, and the downfall of his own brother Ravana's empire.

So engrossed was he in his meditation that he did not see the vanar Hanuman whoosh by only a hundred yards over-head, on his way to carry out yet another overlook of the enemy forces.

Hanuman slowed his flight until he was hovering directly over the rakshasa army. The hordes were moving at canter speed now, and were building up momentum to reach a full-out charge. Already the dust cloud raised in their wake was half the height of Nikumbhila itself, and growing steadily. It provoked his senses to see the army of rakshasas charging headlong in the direction of his comrades, but his orders were explicit and undeniable: he was to stay aloft until Rama called upon him. His surveys completed now, he was only to wait and watch. The hardest task of all, for a warrior. He hovered above the theatre of war. For a moment, he was overwhelmed by the urge to expand himself and simply drop down like a hammer from the sky, pounding the rakshasas into the dust of their own homeland, but his devotion to Rama overcame this urge, and he subsided, forcing himself to remain a calm and detached observer as his mission required him to be.

A reflection off a bright burnished object distracted him and he glanced in the direction of the mountain that towered above the valley in time to see the celestial vehicle of Ravana rising swiftly to the top of the highest ramparts. He scanned the ramparts suspiciously, alert for any sign of mischief, but that was clearly unlikely: the forces of Rama were yet miles away, too far for any flung missile to reach. Correction: too far for any physically flung missile to reach. He could not vouch for sorcery's tricks.

He vowed to himself silently that were Ravana or his minions to use sorcery to strike at Rama from that high rampart, he would not stand by and let it happen unchallenged: for anything that came from the sky was in his domain, and he could not be expected to stand by and let death rain down around him. The ground war was off limits, but surely not the skies where he roamed. Even Rama could not find fault with that simple logic.

At present, there was no visible sign of threat from the high place. Pushpak, gleaming and resplendent in the morning sunlight, like the divine machine it was, reached the highest point of the ramparts and landed as gently as a feather alighting, vanishing beyond the crenellations that bordered the top of the fortress wall. From his present spot, he could not see beyond that point – not without flying up there and peering down, which his orders did not permit him to do. He sighed in frustration and returned his attention to his given task, watching the battle below.

General Vajradanta's kumbha-sur was flying across the valley floor now at full gallop. Grinning with exultation at the sheer joy of anticipation, the general whipped his head from side to side, checking his flanks. For as far as he could see to east and west, the ground was being churned and pounded by the front lines of the rakshasa hordes. After the last trumpet call announcing the full charge, the war cries had fallen briefly silent. Now the thunder of hoofs and footfalls alone filled the air for miles around. A rakshasa army charging at full speed was a terrible, awe-inspiring sight to behold, and he was proud to be leading this one. All the brutality, abuse and humiliation he had suffered in his centuries-long rise to this rank felt well worth it now. He commanded the greatest rakshasa army in the three worlds, the last Asura fighting force left in existence, and only Ravana himself stood above him in the military hierarchy. He felt the power of his position with every bone-shuddering step, felt the exhilaration of impending combat fill his veins and organs, felt the certainty of victory over the enemy on this glorious Lankan autumn day, and urged his mount to go faster, faster.

Finally the enemy ranks grew closer. No doubt the monkey army was loath even to attempt to match the Lankan charge; that was why they had hung back so far, compelling the rakshasa hordes to come to them. He could see them now, at the far end of a canyon that rose up to either side. Somewhere only a few miles to the west was Mount Suvela, the tallest peak in these parts after Nikumbhila. That was where he would have stationed himself and his most trusted commanders if he were the mortal Rama. He felt certain that Rama was there now, on the peak of Suvela, watching with growing horror as he witnessed this merciless charge of the rakshasas towards his pathetic forces. Vanars? Hah! What was a vanar before a rakshasa? No more than a pile of fur-clad bones to be easily crushed with a single blow, barely a mouthful's worth of feeding. The spies Ravana had sent into the enemy camp – and who were now lying in blood-spattered pieces at the foot of Mount Nikumbhila – had brought back impossible counts of the enemy. A million vanars, perhaps over a million! Faugh! A quarter of a million bears! Juaaagh! There could be no more than a quarter of those numbers. At best, surely no more than five lakh vanars and a lakh of bears. And even those unlikely figures would have been greatly depleted by Ravana's magnificent wielding of Asura maya the night before. Even he, Vajradanta, had harboured great anxiety and doubts when Ravana had made vague boastful claims about how the enemy would be dealt with in the night itself, without deploying a single regiment of rakshasas! But the morning had shown Ravana's words to be not just true, but awe-inspiring. If Asura maya did not require such immense amounts of sacrifice and penitential preparation beforehand, he had no doubt that Ravana could have eliminated Rama's forces entirely and won this war through the use of his sorcery alone.

The entrance to the canyon loomed before him. He barely had to nudge his mount to steer it into the opening. He frowned as his kumbha-sur pounded its way into the canyon's mouth, barely a kilometre wide. There would not be room enough for the hordes to ride abreast, but that would not be a great hindrance. He had given instructions beforehand for them to fan out and ride around the canyon on either side, meeting up on the far side of these ghats and rises. He would have preferred to halt well before this spot and wait for the enemy to come forward to engage them, but Ravana's orders had been explicit: engage the enemy wherever you find them, do not wait a moment longer. For some reason, the Lord of Lanka wished to take decisive action well before noon, although Vajradanta could not understand what the time of day had to do with anything. In any case, the enemy was not coming forward to meet them, so they had no choice but to go to them.

He led his own vanguard into the canyon, the sounds of their feet and hoofs echoing deafeningly off the canyon walls. He could see the vanar forces huddled at the far end of the canyon, bunched together in a kilometre-wide mass like a herd of sheep unaware of the slaughterer's axe approaching. He flashed a brilliant grin. This would be a massacre of epic proportions. His enthusiasm did not flag even when he rode closer and saw the masses of brown- and black- and red- and silver-furred creatures extending far back, for miles it seemed. Yes, there certainly were a great number of them. Easily as many as the Lankan army's own numbers. But even a vanar or bear for every rakshasa was hardly fair. They would ride those foolish monkey kin into the dust of this canyon if they simply stood there like that, no doubt stunned into immobility by the sight of the oncoming rakshasa onslaught.

Speaking of bears . . . He scanned the great mass up ahead, exerting his excellent vision to see where the bear troops were stationed. But to his surprise, he could see only those yard-tall furry creatures with their long looped tails – all held up stiffly behind them for some laughable reason – standing in surprisingly neat rows. No sign of any taller beasts. He was not pleased at that observation, and his grin faltered briefly, for it meant that the bears were elsewhere, perhaps on the flanks beyond this canyon, and that meant that the other hordes, rather than his vanguard, would engage them first. But there was nothing to be done about it now. He would smash into the vanar lines at this furious headlong pace, cut through them like a sharpened talon through yielding flesh, and then emerge at the far end to rejoin the rest of the regiments and engage the bear troops; perhaps even outflank them and catch them in a palm-meeting-palm slap, like a fly smashed between two rakshasa paws. Yes, that would work.

He regained his grin and rode down on the vanar ranks. Still standing in immobile rows, the poor pathetic, inexperienced fools. Did they think those neat lines would make any difference to the oncoming hordes? Did they think they could withstand the juggernaut of an all-out rakshasa charge that way? What a novice this Rama Chandra must be, to order his soldiers thus! And what a coward, to stay high upon a mountain watching anxiously, as his forces did the real fighting down below.

Well, Vajradanta would show him a sight he would not forget for the rest of his all-too-brief life.

The general spurred his mount, which was already frothing madly at the mouth and chugging breath frantically as it rode at breakneck speed. The perfect vanar lines, looking like nothing so much as a welcoming carpet of fur laid down for him and his vanguard to ride over in their certain victory, loomed as he crossed the last few hundred yards that separated them.

'Ra-van-a!' he roared again, raising his twin weapons, lance in one hand, the great hacking blade in the other. The canyon walls exploded with the echo of his vanguard's responding cry:

'*RA-VAN-A!*'

2

Five hundred yards or less. And closing fast.

Sugreeva squinted to see through the rising wall of dust that came thundering down the length of the canyon towards his position. He resisted the urge to grimace or reveal his discomfort in any way as he realised how close the Lankan front line was now, and the fact that they were coming on with no sign of slowing or stopping. Which was all to the good, for that was how Rama had wished it to happen, and it was a happy omen that Rama's prediction had been proved right.

He drew a slow, easy breath, not too deep or fast, for he would need every breath, every ounce of energy for the battle ahead. The Lankans were approaching at a frightening pace; and if bestial rakshasas, armed and armoured to the snouts, were not enough to instil terror into the stoutest heart, a large number of these were mounted as well. He had never seen such mounts before: they vaguely resembled the desert 'ships' that he had heard tell of from distant travellers, the hump-backed creatures that were said to have awful dispositions and that could survive days in the arid sands without a drop of water. But these looked like deformed mutations of those beasts, their heads split into two unnaturally jutting out sections, each section with its own set of enormous squarish yellow teeth, as if someone had cleaved their heads down the centre of the scalp with an axe. What were they called, these broken-headed creatures? He didn't know, but they looked every bit as dangerous as the snarling rakshasas that rode them. Right now, every one of them was slobbering wildly, mouth foaming liberally as they bore down on him and his vanars. And these were only the front lines. Behind them, stretching up the length of the canyon and far beyond it, were thousands upon thousands of roaring rakshasas of every description. He had never heard of most of the sub-species he saw now, let alone seen them in the flesh. He wondered which of them would be the one to strike the blow that would send him to his ancestors. The one in front, leading the charging horde, seemed the most eager: a stocky rakshasa with blinding razor teeth that caught the sunlight and shone as brightly as a shard of volcanic glass.

Three hundred yards or less, and growing larger every moment.

As he prepared himself to die with honour for Rama's cause, he glanced briefly to either side. From his peripheral vision, he could tell that not one of his brave warriors had budged an inch since he had given the order to halt and stand at atten-tion. He had no doubt that their fur was as damp with sweat as his own, their hearts pounding as loudly in their bony vanar chests, their blood roaring in their veins almost as loudly as the oncoming rakshasa hordes. But they were the pride of Kiskindha, warriors tracing their ancestry back to the earliest age. They had followed him out of Kiskindha when Vali the Usurper had wrested control of the kingdom, had lived on berries and bitter gourds in his years of exile, and had marched behind him when he returned to the city to reclaim his throne. More importantly, they had drilled on the coast of the mainland under the tutel-age of Lakshman for long hours before and after the arduous bridge-building, had disciplined themselves to acquire skills that no vanar in history had ever been able to master. And master them they had; for even difficult-to-please Lakshman had finally raised his eyebrows in surprised admiration and acknowledged their progress, the very day before the passage to Lanka.

Now they stood by Sugreeva in the face of this horde from

Narak, the worst of the hellish realms. Preparing to meet near-certain death. Because it was essential to Rama's plan. That was the reason why Sugreeva had decided that he would stay with his men to the last; if the Kiskindha vanars had been chosen to shed first blood in this war – he did not count the treacherous murders caused by Ravana's sorcery on the night of the killing stones as blood honestly shed – then he would stand with them to the end. His resoluteness had overpowered even Angad's incredulous arguments; if anything, when he commanded his son to cease arguing and declared himself committed beyond debate, he had seen a surprised glow of pride and tearful joy in the young prince's eyes. It had been a long time since Sugreeva had done anything to earn that look, and now, as he faced the thundering whirlwind that approached at the speed of death, he cherished its memory and the memory of the tight hug Angad had given him before parting wordlessly.

Two hundred yards or less, and now picking out their targets and aligning themselves accordingly.

And as if proving the very rightness of his choice, he had felt the years of self-pity, misery and frustration melt away like the frost on the firs in the northern ranges when the first thaw came. He had experienced a straightening of his age-bent spine, a quickening of his snail-slow pulse, a tightening of his sagging muscles, and most of all, a resoluteness that was as solid as iron forged and smelted and beaten in the furnace, as the mortal blacksmiths did to shape their sword weapons. As a king, he had done many things that could be termed morally ambiguous. His rivalry with his late brother Vali was the most questionable of all, morally speaking; he had, in a sense, been the first to usurp Vali's throne, and the guilt of that had weighed heavily on him, even though he had known he was doing the right thing in law and the people themselves needed him to be their king. He had never thrown off that guilt entirely, and it had aged him greatly, as had the long, bitter struggle that had followed, ending only in the death of his brother at Rama's hands. A part of him had been lost as a result of that bitter conflict, for no fight was as debilitating as a fight against your own kith or kin. Emotionally and morally speaking there was no winning that struggle, not for him personally.

But *this*, what he was doing now, was righteous and right in every sense. He was standing on the floor of a great canyon in the feared land of rakshasas, heading the entire contingent of Kiskindha vanar warriors against the vanguard of Ravana's army. It was an act to be proud of, that his grandchildren would speak about reverentially to their own grandchildren some day. It was the stuff of which legends were born, and about which histories were penned. And it was right in every way, unassailable morally. In the end, he realised, as an errant tear escaped his left eye unexpectedly and rolled down his age-lined snout, a king's job was so fraught with compromise and moral ambiguity that there was only this one thing he could do without compromise or self-doubt or debate: he could stand with his people and die with them.

Less than a hundred yards, and now looming as large as nightmares viewed under the influence of an excess of honey-wine.

'Time,' he said softly, then repeated it louder. 'TIME!' he said as forcefully as possible, and was surprised to hear that it was far louder and far more commanding than he had thought he could sound any more, as inspiring an order as he had ever given, audible and rigid as smelted iron even above the drumming madness of the oncoming rakshasa hordes.

At once, his loyal, disciplined vanars did as they had been instructed. Every second warrior in each line leaped upon the shoulders of the warrior in front. The warrior in front crouched slightly, to balance himself, and then braced his body by reaching out with both paws to grasp the shoulders of the vanars to either side. The vanars on the outermost lines, near the canyon walls, braced themselves by reaching forward and gripping the shoulders of those before them. Forming a simple but effective two-layered grid. The vanars poised on top of their fellows crouched low, baring their teeth and tensing their lithe muscles in preparation for their next move. The entire process was accomplished in a fraction of a moment; leaping up was to a vanar what taking a step was to a mortal. Once aligned, they let go of one another's shoulders and prepared to leap literally into the jaws of death.

Forty yards . . . thirty-five . . . thirty . . .

And now there was no time left to reflect any further, no time for regrets, sorrows, memories, guilt or forgiveness, no time for tears even. Sugreeva dabbed his left cheek fiercely with the back of one hirsute paw and braced himself. The vanar beside him, his general Sarabha, said urgently, 'My lord . . . if you will.' Meaning that he should leap upon Sarabha's back. For in the plan they had developed, the vanars in the top layer would almost certainly have a substantial advantage over those on the bottom. They would at least have an opportunity of dying fighting, while those on the ground were unlikely to even survive the first impact – especially those in the front rows. But he shook his head fiercely, disdaining the offer, and stood his ground resolutely, paws held ready by his sides, claws arched to strike, teeth bared. A snarl rose from his throat and he felt that old friend of all warriors, regardless of race, species, skill or age, arrive to take over command of his faculties: battle rage was coursing through his veins now. He felt the same rage ripple through the massed ranks behind him, felt their readiness to die – but to die killing rakshasas – and suddenly he was a young vanar once more, barely a few summers of age, facing his first battle, a clash with vetaals in a dark forest clearing just before dawn.

Fifteen . . . ten . . . nine . . . eight . . .

He raised his voice one last time in a battle cry that was the only departure he had ever made from the Kiskindha screech.

'*For Rama!*' he shrieked.

The cry was all but lost in the terrible, unspeakable impact as the two armies collided.

Hanuman cried out in outrage.

Suspended directly above the canyon, barely three hundred yards overhead, he was low enough to smell the sweat and rancour of the rakshasa hordes and their vile mounts, as well as the familiar musky blood odours of his Kiskindha comrades. He saw the pre-planned manoeuvre executed with astonishing perfection mere moments before the Lankan front lines struck, the vanars leaping upon one another's shoulders too late for the rakshasa general to slow or halt his army's onslaught – not that the shiny-toothed fool would deem vanars leaping on one another's shoulders to be any kind of threat – and heard the last cry of King Sugreeva, shrieked a fraction of a second before the first mounted rakshasas struck the vanar lines. With his preternaturally enhanced senses, Hanuman could see clearly every detail of his king's snout, even the track of the single tear that had escaped his rheumy eye and travelled through the dust that had settled there. His heart swelled with pride. He had never in his own lifetime seen King Sugreeva stand so tall, look so strong, so resolute, so invincible . . .

Then the Lankan vanguard struck the vanar front line.

The sound that resulted from the impact of the two armies colliding – or more accurately of the rakshasa army colliding with the vanar army, for only the former had been moving – was a sound like nothing Hanuman had ever heard before. As soon as it entered his ears, he wished he could dispel it for ever; wished he had never heard it before, and would never hear it again.

It was the sound of metal crunching bone, of steel smashing flesh to pulp, of blood exploding out of living bodies as a bladder-balloon filled with wine bursts when stomped by an angry elephant's foot.

It was the sound of vanar skulls striking solid rock after a fall from a height of several hundred yards – a sound he had heard once too often during the bridge-building. Of fragile vanar bodies crushed by hurtling rakshasas with a velocity great enough to shatter bone to the texture of squeezed marrow, skulls to the consistency of squashed brain, organs to paste. It was the sound of a thousand mounted rakshasas, each mount and rider's combined weight easily close to half a ton, striking the bodies of ten thousand vanars each weighing no more than a few dozen kilos. It was the sound of hammerheads as big as vanars themselves, falling like the wrath of cruel devas upon his comrades. It was a thousand sounds like these, each one as terrible and gut-wrenching, all issued at the exact same moment, until the total din of their emission was like a thunderclap on a sunny day.

The cloud of dust that had followed close on the heels of the charging rakshasas rolled over the canyon, boiling and seething as the front lines struck their target and inevitably slowed, and the hordes following behind spread out, milling about, roaring and striking and chopping and gashing and hammering, each rakshasa seeking its own victim – or dozen victims, if they could be had – with great gusto.

The cloud enveloped the ensuing battle, wrapping both armies in its thick embrace, mercifully concealing unspeakable death, unwatchable slaughter, unbearable butchery. Only the sounds of battle escaped its clutches, the roaring exultation of rakshasas engaged in mindless slaughter, of kumbha-surs, broken-surs and masth elephants trumpeting and calling out in dazed madness, of vanars shrieking their death cries as they sacrificed their brave little souls.

Out of the fog of the dust cloud a hearty roar was recognisable above the others. Hanuman distinguished it from the rest, knowing it came from the throat of the general of the Lankan vanguard, the one with the fearsome teeth. The strong wind that had blown at unpredictable intervals all morning, near tempest-like at times, then falling to complete stillness for long moments, suddenly swept down into the valley, bringing the unlikely odour of the deep oceans, brine, the scent of fish, cloying and sweet and salty at once.

The wind parted the dense cloud of dust in patches and strips, affording the flying observer overhead scant tantalising glimpses of the battle raging below.

He saw the rakshasa general, still astride his ungainly mount, laying his bladed weapon left and right, slaying vanars before they could come within striking distance of him. He had lost his lance somewhere, but the great blade was enough to cut a swathe of bloody slaughter through the vanar ranks. He urged his mount on with his knees, kicking his barbed heels into its bleeding flanks, and with a squealing protest the beast lurched forward, gnashing and snapping at vanars as it moved through the mass of Kiskindha warriors like a boat through swampy marsh water. Many unfortunate vanars came underfoot and were crushed beneath its lumbering hoofs, their bodies smashed like those of rodents, leaving blood-spattered furry corpses in its wake. The rakshasa general's bladed weapon likewise sent arcs of vanar blood flying each time it swung through the air, leaving an assortment of chopped and severed limbs and shrieking, dying vanars.

The wind puffed again, and the dust rolled over once more. The general laughed a great rakshasa laugh, his gleaming teeth stained with the blood of his enemy, and then was lost to sight again, concealed by the rolling dust.

Hanuman gnashed his own teeth in frustration. He longed to plunge down, like an arrow aimed at the heart of that rakshasa general, and slice him in two like a ripe fruit. It took every bit of his self-control to remain floating here, watching this most heart-rending scene. What did Rama expect of him? To simply watch his fellows being cut down like lambs before a butcher's blade? To hover like a dragonfly when his tribe-kith and clan-kin were being slaughtered mercilessly? When his own king, so

brave and proud despite his years and ailing health, was undoubtedly breathing his last only a few dozen yards below?

But Rama's orders had been undeniable. 'Watch. Nothing
more. Until I give the word.'

And so, gnashing his teeth and beating his chest with impotent fury, he watched and waited for Rama's word, as the
unequal battle raged on below.

3

Around the time that General Vajradanta was leading the first charge into the canyon, and King Sugreeva and his Kiskindha vanars were preparing to meet the vanguard of the Lankan army in that first terrible clash, the site of another battle, only a few miles south of that canyon, was deceptively tranquil and calm.

In the shade of the densely wooded valley, bounded on all sides by rolling hills, the slanting rays of morning sunlight could barely touch the bottom of the vale. In the few places where they succeeded, the pure golden light of morning leaked through the closely interwoven branches of the trees, seeping through sluggishly to fall upon the leaf-strewn forest floor in ripples, slats and dappled patterns. Occasional beams of sunlight broke the greenish dimness, dust motes and insects swirling in them lazily. Birdsong still filled the air sporadically, and the chirring and whirring of insects and clicking and hissing of smaller creatures in the undergrowth only added to the sense of tranquillity.

Seated atop a latsyoa tree's upper branches, the vanar leader Mandara-devi was reminded of her home in the Vidarbha ranges where she had spent much of her childhood. She had sat in trees much like this in valleys almost identical to this one during her childhood years, except perhaps for the eastern wind that blew softly through the woods now, carrying the faint salty odour of the sea, and the fact that an army of rakshasas hellbent on killing her and her companions lay over that hill.

She glanced back, parting a branch to see northwards, and peered at the southern face of Mount Suvela. That was where Rama and Lakshman were to station themselves to watch the progress of the first part of the battle today. She could glimpse no sign of them, though it should have been easy enough for vanar eyes to spot a mortal's form against the lush grass of the mountainside, even at this distance. Instead, she found, on the rim of the eastern edge of the peak, a solitary figure that looked like . . . *a rakshasa!*

For one heart-stopping instant she almost panicked and issued an alarm, thinking that the worst had happened, Ravana's devious plan had succeeded and Rama's armies had been outflanked.

Then she saw the wind billow the solitary figure's garment, and recognised belatedly the white garb of Rama's ally Vibhisena. She breathed more easily, slowing her heartbeat. A rakshasa, true, but the one rakshasa in Lanka that could be trusted by vanars. There had been some muttered grumbling when Rama had taken the ocean-sodden rakshasa into his protection, trusting him on first sight and word, but Mandara-devi preferred to leave such decisions to those best suited to make them. The idea that Vibhisena could be a spy who would dupe them was too sickening to contemplate: better to be just a soldier and fight than to let one's mind rest on such befuddling thoughts. And while she had been a tribe-goddess to the Mandaras for a third of her natural span, she had been a soldier for almost all her life. It was her varna.

She let the branch fall back into place and returned her attention to the way she had been facing. That was where the rakshasa hordes would come from, and the last word from the angadiyas had been that they were no more than a half-watch away, and approaching with great speed. She wondered how King Sugreeva's Kiskindha contingent was faring, in the canyon a few miles farther north. It was too far for her to see or hear anything, but in a more silent moment, when the birds and insects fell still, as they would sometimes do in such tranquil forests, she thought she could hear, faintly, a distant roaring and gnashing, as of armies clashing somewhere. She could not tell if she was imagining it because she knew to expect it, or if she was truly hearing it. But there was a faint sound coming to her ears from somewhere, something that didn't seem to fit into the natural pattern of things. It was a terrible ghost of a sound, like the sound of ten thousand vanars dying unspeakably horrible deaths all at once, and she shivered despite the warmth of the day.

She sent up a silent prayer for King Sugreeva and her fellow vanars, may they fare well. She had two sons-in-law and one daughter in the Kiskindha contingent, and seven of their children, her grandchildren, as well. For that matter, she had kith or kin in all the various vanar armies fighting here today, but for some reason the little anxiety she felt was focused only on those in the Kiskindha army. For as the vanguard, they would be bearing the full-frontal assault of the rakshasa charge, and she had heard enough of Rama's plan to first lure and then entrap the rakshasas in that narrow canyon to not want to know anything more. The thought that her grandchildren or her sons-in-law or even her daughter might already be lying dead only a few miles distant was one she did not wish to dwell on. She wiped such thoughts clean from her mind, but with a small effort.

'Mandara-devi.'

The voice was urgent and excited. She recognised the gruff tone as belonging to Dvivida, one of General Nila's two chief lieutenants. While Nila had nominally been given charge of the Mandara contingent after her kinsman Vinata was injured in the night of the killing stones, Dvivida was one of her own. In fact, if she didn't know better, she would have thought him of her own line, so similar was his glossy jet-black pelt and burly, muscled physique to her own stocky shape. Perhaps she had in fact begat this handsome young beast through one of the many, many lovers she had taken in her younger years . . . Sometimes, among vanars, it was difficult to tell for sure.

Dvivida squatted on a branch nearby, his beautiful burnished pelt almost denuded of fur, testifying to the numerous wrestling bouts he had participated in – and won, mostly – over the years, making him one of the most lauded wrestling champions in vanar history. His jewellery – for all her Mandara vanars wore silver jewellery from their own mines – was sparse and close-hanging, but his earlobe piercings were profuse, marking the many victories he had achieved in single combat. She saw a flash of white teeth in the gloamy shaded darkness. 'They come.'

Those two simple words caused a thrill to race down her spine. Veteran of so many wars as she was, she nevertheless felt a thrill that was wholly new and unfamiliar. 'Are we all ready? Tell them to make sure that nobody makes a move until I give the signal. Understood?'

Dvivida's teeth flashed again. 'Not a tick will twitch on anyone's pelt until you give the signal, my lady. They know that anyone who dares panic and moves too early will have to answer to me, even if he or she survives the rakshasas.'

Mandara-devi resisted the impulse to smile back in response to Dvivida's smug grin. Her vanars might not have been as well trained and drilled in the mortal ways of battle as the Kiskindha army, but they were good, honest vanars, mischievous at play and obedient to a fault in a crisis. She doubted that Dvivida would need to wrestle any soldier after this battle to discipline him, but if he did . . . well, then she pitied the poor bugger. She had wrestled Dvivida himself only twice, and although she had won the second bout by the hair on the tip of her tail, she would not wish to repeat that experience any time soon. 'Are General Nila and his vanars in position?'

'Ready and waiting as well, devi. They will not enter the fray until you give the word, or . . .'

Or until they receive word of your demise . . . That was the pre-agreed arrangement. She clicked her tongue softly, approvingly. 'How many, how far, and how fast?' she asked.

Dvivida's grin faltered ever so slightly, then was back again as bright and insolent as before, but she had caught that brief hesitation and it spoke more eloquently to her than any dry narration of figures and estimates. 'Never mind,' she corrected herself quickly. 'Go on, back to your position. We leaders must be spread as far as possible, as we agreed.'

Dvivida nodded and was about to turn away when Mandara-devi hissed, 'Dvivida.'

The burly vanar turned back, curious. 'My lady?'

'May you fight with the strength of our brother Hanuman and the will of our lord Rama.'

Dvivida looked at her a long moment, his small bright eyes gleaming in the darkness. Then, without a word, for among Mandaras deeds spoke louder than words, he vanished back whence he had come.

She stilled the pounding of her heart and sought to remain calm. She slowly became aware of the silence that had fallen upon the forest in the valley. No birdsong or insect call broke the stillness now; even the sea wind that had blown this past watch, sometimes as fiercely as a gale in the making, had died out. She sensed the same disturbance that the wild creatures and birds and insects of the forest had sensed, and focused her attention on its source, just over the rise of the ghats up ahead to the north. It was a mild vibration in the ground, transmitted through the trunk of the latsyoa tree, all the way up to the high branch where she squatted. She arched her tail, touching the tip to the branch, and felt the unmistakable trembling of the oncoming horde. She sighed. It seemed such a beautiful, idyllic day . . . too beautiful for the carnage and slaughter of battle. Yet such was the tragic irony of war: instead of enjoying nature's beauty and fruits, we foolish creatures squander our lives and seed the earth with our wasted blood. She prayed once more for all her vanars, for Rama's cause — and yes, even for the rakshasas of Lanka, that they might some day learn the meaning and value of peace. Perhaps even today.

Then she focused her attention fully on the direction from which she knew the enemy would come, the slight depression in the lowest hillock of the ghat to the north, barely a quarter of a mile from the tree on which she sat. The morning sun was just high enough to touch the tips of the grass on the peak of the rise, turning them into an army of gleaming blades, waving gently like a benevolent gathering. As she watched, the trembling turned into a shuddering. And then the shuddering grew into a palpable, audible sound. A thundering reverberation that sent squirrels and other small denizens of the forest scurrying for cover, a few smaller birds fluttering away in panic. The stillness around her grew grim, as if the forest itself knew what that sound portended. And perhaps it did. For nature's creatures were the first to know of oncoming disaster.

She could feel the hackles on her own body rising, a part of her mind, that primitive simian part that linked her and all vanars to their monkey and ape forebears, as it linked mortals too, screaming, '*Run, flee, fly!*' and she used that impulse, turned it into fuel to feed the fire of outrage that had been sparked when she saw her son and his entire family crushed to death on the night of the killing stones, her brother fall in the bridge-building, her cousin drowned by the tsunami, and the almost certain deaths that lay ahead for so many of her beloved kith and kin.

Who were these rakshasas then, to travel to foreign lands and wreak havoc and destruction? Did they think they could continue unchallenged for ever? Well, they had erred in kidnapping Rama's beloved. For at last here was one who would not brook their transgressions. And her love of Rama and her anguish at his suffering fuelled her anger as well, and the fire within her grew and grew, until the thundering of her own mighty matriarchal heart was no less than the pounding of the ground just over that rise . . .

The first figures appeared, lining up along the top of the rise from end to end. Ragged, horned, sharp-cornered silhouettes, limned by the light of the risen sun, half cast in golden burnished light, half shadowed. She caught her breath as their numbers grew, and grew ... hundreds, then thousands, then, as they began to roll down the sloping incline, tens of thousands. How many were there? At least they were all on foot, she saw. Her vanars feared the rakshasa mounts more than the rakshasa themselves. She was also relieved to see none of the kumbha-rakshasas that General Nila had warned them about; these were only the standard breed that she and her vanars had fought before – not often, not always victoriously, but at least they had had some brushes with this kind.

But never in such vast numbers.

She shuddered briefly as the rakshasa army began rolling down the slope of the ghat like a juggernaut, its thundering tearing up the grass and churning up the fertile soil to sods and clumps. And still they came on, lines upon lines of the blade-armed, horned and tusked, taloned, armoured and shaggy furred beasts.

The birds of the forest, keenly aware of the destruction that would soon follow, called to one another and rose as one enormous mass, filling the sky above with their cries and the flapping of their wings.

For a moment the sky was shrouded by the cloud of fleeing avians, and the already dim forest in which Mandara-devi waited turned even darker as if foreshadowing the dark deeds that would be accomplished in its idyllic shade.

4

Inside the cloud of dust and blood and madness, King Sugreeva grew slowly, gradually aware of the impossible: he lived yet. Somehow he had survived the first collision of the rakshasa hordes with his vanars. Because the oncoming mounts were riding too swiftly and were too large to swerve or correct their course, and because the vanars were so small, many of those in the front lines were literally bypassed without a hoof or a spear or a blade so much as touching them. Not all, of course: for every vanar like Sugreeva who came between those thundering beasts, at least two other unfortunate vanars fell beneath their crushing hoofs. The front line that had stood so bravely with their king, facing the oncoming rakshasa vanguard with the perfect courage of soldiers confronting certain death, was wiped out in a flash, like a line drawn with powdered ash erased instantly by a splash of water. The ferocious charge of the rakshasa vanguard, led by the cavalry, crashed into the vanar ranks like an elephant into a bamboo thicket. Some seven thousand vanars, brave Kiskindha warriors all, the majority with some prior battle experience, but far too many facing combat for the first time in their very young lives, were killed on impact, their mashed bodies driven together into piles of mangled flesh and splintered bone. So much blood was released in that terrible clash of Rama's armies and Lanka's hordes that the dust of the floor of the canyon was stained red ochre, a deep, dull, almost brownish shade that fittingly approximated the colour of the rough cloth worn by Arya sages since the beginning of time, for it was the colour of transcendence. The front lines of the rakshasa charge were splattered with vanar blood, gristle, pieces of flesh and splinters of bone so that in an instant they resembled butchers after a long day's work.

And yet, those front-line vanars were the lucky ones.

A few thousand more of their equally brave comrades, in the lines behind them, provided the soft obstruction that slowed the charge, their shrieking, mangled bodies forcing the mounts as well as the foot soldiers to reluctantly come to a halt. Vanars were squashed under the thundering hoofs, pushed along brutally, and piled upon and over and under – and *through* – the bodies of their comrades behind them, until the mass of piled bodies that resulted was yards high in places, with several hundred wounded or incapacitated vanars caught in the morass, most doomed to slow, tortuous deaths but several simply stuck and unable to break free of the twisted, writhing knot of piled bodies. A few dozen rakshasas and their mounts broke their legs or slipped and fell and were hard pressed to regain their footing, so gory was the canyon floor, with so much flesh and gristle and blood underfoot. The masth elephants that had been thought to be of such obvious value in this charge proved to be a mistake, perhaps the only one the rakshasas made in that first clash, for they could not be stopped, and simply barrelled onwards, ramming through the growing pile of bodies and shoving them forward, crushing the press like piled grapes, until they collapsed as well, and were struck by the tuskers following them in turn, which infuriated them further and led to spontaneous fights among the beasts, all piled up together and squealing and screaming horribly, for the assortment of jagged weapons in the press was sufficient to inflict mortal wounds on the maddened elephants. And thus they added their own tormented corpses to the great wall of carnage that rose in the centre of the canyon.

And that was all in the first impact.

The vanars who had crouched on the shoulders of their comrades in the moment before the rakshasa vanguard struck their lines leaped high into the air, just as they had been instructed. Their timing was perfectly planned and executed, so that at the exact instant when the rakshasa charge smashed into their ranks, they were in the air, suspended several feet, or even yards in some agile cases, above the fray. In the moments it took them to succumb once more to Prithvi ki dor – the invisible thread of gravity that tied every creature on earth to its planet-mother – the rakshasa charge had struck the Kiskindha lines, ploughed through them like a threshing blade drawn by rampaging oxen, and passed twenty yards or more beyond them, so that when they descended, it was upon rakshasa helms, heads, shoulders, chests, backs, or mounts. In a few unfortunate but inevitable cases, some of the leapers came down only to be impaled upon rakshasa spears or horns. But most were shrewd and agile enough to avoid such pitfalls and fell upon the foe, going to work at once as they had been trained.

The rakshasas were thick-skinned, often scaled or armoured, with spiked cladding or sharp horns or tusks. But they were designed for attack, not defence. Rakshasas had no natural predators or enemies, except maybe mortals. And their armour as well as their natural defences had evolved to injure, maim and kill, not to ward off enemies who attacked them, certainly not lithe, limber little vanars who leaped twenty feet into the air and then landed upon their backs or necks, while they were still engaged in a headlong forward charge and crushing or hacking down other vanars.

So perfectly had the leaping been timed that it spelled certain death for the vanars who had borne their fellows on their shoulders. But they had known the inevitability of their fate: had they not undertaken this manoeuvre, all of them would have died. This way, the leaping vanars got a fighting chance, and the element of complete surprise. For in all the millennia that the rakshasa races had been battling – and they had been warring ever since the beginning of creation; it was what they did – no enemy had ever sprung such a tactic, and timed and executed it so brilliantly. This was the very thing that Lakshman, for this was his brainchild, had counted on.

Even as the mounts and hoofs and flying blades and spear-points of the rakshasas crushed and maimed and slaughtered the vanars on the ground, the flying vanars laid into the enemy with a ferocity that could not be compared to anything else. They bit at the ring of neck that was exposed between helms and breastplates, ripped out unprotected bellies, tore into the soft fleshy portions on either side of the rakshasa spines, where the liver and organs of liquid purification were housed, their sharpened talons and teeth working damage in small areas in a fashion calculated to cause irreparable damage. Livers were torn out, throats ripped open, bellies slashed and entrails removed in a blood-spraying flash, eyes gouged and turned to useless lumps of fleshy pulp. Some vanars were given the gift of landing on the mounts themselves, and it was short work to do their deadly damage to the startled kumbha-surs and broken-surs. That was even more effective than killing their riders, for the already crazed beasts barely realised that they had been dealt fatal blows, and rode on mindlessly for several dozen yards, until they shuddered and tumbled head over heels, tossing their rakshasa riders like clay dolls to smash into other rakshasas ahead of them, or into the rocky canyon walls, joining the growing pile of corpses in the enclosed mortuary that the place was fast becoming.

Almost none of the rakshasas or mounts was able to resist even a single flying vanar. Apart from those few unfortunates who landed on open blades or points, the rest of the contingent did their bloody work, then leaped again, landing on new victims farther back in the rakshasa lines – for the sheer momentum of the charge kept the whole vanguard moving, even after it had ploughed into the rising heap of vanar dead – and repeating their killing. By the third or fourth leap, the rakshasa onslaught had slowed sufficiently for the Lankans coming up, mostly on foot by this point, to see the danger and take action. But almost at once, as if aided by the very Prithvi herself, the dust cloud thrown up by the charge as well as the impact obscured the air for yards ahead, blinding the rakshasa hordes. And since they were still expecting to see the enemy ahead of them, and a much shorter enemy at that, barely one-third their size, the last thing they were expecting was for bloody murder to come dropping down out of the skies.

By the time the rakshasas had cottoned on to the strategem of the flying vanars and begun to roar warnings to their fellows in the lines behind, the Kiskindhans had taken an impressive toll. Nowhere near as many rakshasas as vanars died in that first wave of assaults, nay. The vanar casualties in that first rakshasa charge must have numbered well over ten thousand, whereas barely a couple of thousand rakshasas were slain. But by this time, the vanars lined up beyond the end of the trough created by the ploughing slowdown of the rakshasa charge had begun leaping over the corpses of their fallen comrades and entered the fray too. They sprang on to those enraged rakshasas who had escaped their flying fellows, landing upon them two or three at a time. In some cases, half a dozen vanars landed upon a single rakshasa, and the sheer viciousness of their attack almost equalled the brutality of the rakshasas themselves. Some rakshasas, blinded by the swirling dust and blood splattered into their eyes by the collision, saw only nightmarish glimpses of flying vanars leaping on to their fellow rakshasas and tearing them open. To their startled minds, deluded by their over-confident generals into expecting a puny, monkey-like enemy, it was as if the vanars had been empowered by some sorcerous means. Not particularly gifted with intelligence, their rakshasa brains were too slow-witted to think of looking up. What the vanars lacked in size and strength and weaponry and armour, they valiantly made up for by sheer courage, speed and ferocity.

Sugreeva knew and sensed and saw and heard and scented all this without actually needing to pause and look. He himself awakened as if from a long, dreamless stupor to find that he was crouched atop a dead rakshasa and his maimed, howling mount – the foolish creatures the enemy rode seemed to make more noise than a hundred vanars – wielding a length of hardwood almost as thick as the trunk of a young tree. He could not recall how he had come by the weapon – probably it was the pole of a spear and the bladed metal point had broken off somewhere – but to his vanar touch, its rough, unpolished length felt exactly like a young sala trunk that he had once wielded in a battle. He was flailing the weapon around, hefting it overhead and swinging it wildly. The bodies of two rakshasas lay nearby with their heads and shoulders smashed, and naked white bone exposed through their torn muscles, and it took him a moment to accept that he had slain those two as well as the one on whose body he now stood – and at least three more lying farther behind him in the ugly press of bodies dead or dying.

The rakshasa charge had finally been shattered, and now warriors of both forces milled about in the dense fog that covered everyone, turning rakshasa and vanar alike into dust-coated demons roaring and shrieking and swinging and leaping and fighting to the death. A rakshasa with a lupine gait came loping straight at Sugreeva, its red eyes glowing in the dust like a timberwolf he had once faced in the Nilgiri ranges, then leaped, snarling, in a high arc that would bring its weight down upon him with crushing finality, and he swung the tree trunk with a deftness that surprised even him, catching the oncoming rakshasa at the highest point of its leap, in the soft, vulnerable flesh of its throat, cutting off its lupine howl and nearly severing its spine at the neck. The corpse of the beast, head hanging backwards now, open throat wound gushing arterial blood, collapsed in a heap on the canyon floor, raising the dry dust that lay there and adding to the opacity of the air. Sugreeva issued a *cheeka* of triumph, then turned his attention to a trio of feral catlike rakshasas that crept out of the dust fog. He kept them at bay for a moment by some deft swinging of the pole, a distant corner of his mind thinking, you will pay dearly for this vigour, Sugreeva; you are too old and weak to fight like this for long, your muscles will not support your defiant will much longer.

Then, just as two of them were about to outflank him and the third was crouching to leap from behind him, a blur of vanar fur streaked out of the dust haze and leaped at the cat rakshasas. Two vanars and the leaping cat rakshasa met in mid-air, all three tearing and scratching and ripping viciously on impact. Two, a vanar and the rakshasa, fell like stones to the ground, badly mauled and bleeding to death; the other vanar leaped back into the attack against another rakshasa and was lost again in the haze. From the other side, with feral roars of fury, the other two cat rakshasas prepared to attack. Sugreeva turned his pole, gripped it with both hands and slammed it into the chests of the leaping enemies, stopping them in mid-leap but also driving himself backwards beneath their considerably greater weight. For a heart-stopping moment, he thought he would be pinned down beneath them, but then he shoved forward with a snarl and was shocked to feel *them* yielding and falling back. Without thinking about it, he turned the pole and impaled one of the rakshasas on its jagged point, then slammed the side of the polehead into the skull of the other one, feeling more than hearing the cranial bone crack with a nauseating impact. What invisible god had granted him the strength to push back *two* rakshasas, each weighing several times his own weight? '*For Rama!*' he shrieked, and fought on.

It went on like this for a while. Attacking, killing, being attacked, fending off, vanars joining him in the fray, him coming to the aid of vanars, making stands against oncoming rakshasas, taking advantage of the few blessed instants of dust-shrouded obscurity to finish off the crippled rakshasas lest they rise again and attack from behind: all the grisly grind and clatter and grimy glamour of the battlefield.

Somewhere in the midst of all the carnage and the gore and the slaughter, two realisations came to Sugreeva simultaneously: one, that he was stronger than he had ever been before, faster and with more stamina than he ever knew he possessed. Even after what seemed like an hour-watch of brutal, punishing combat, he was still on his feet, still wielding the yards-long spear pole, still slaying rakshasas before they could come within killing distance of him. Never before, not even in his younger, more virile years, had he experienced such a sensation of power and strength and resoluteness.

The second realisation was that it was time to move to the next phase of Rama's plan.

He drove the end of the pole into the face of a charging bear-like rakshasa, shattering the beast's jaw, sending slimy yellow tooth fragments flying in all directions, watched the beast fall in a thrashing heap upon the bodies of other rakshasas he had slain, then, with great reluctance, almost regret, turned and began issuing the ululating call for retreat. It took several moments before his message penetrated through the fog of warlust that had gripped his Kiskindha warriors. And several moments more before they were able to disengage themselves from the enemy and fall back. Once in effect, the retreat was also hard, for it was painful to clamber over the veritable hillock of dead or dying creatures, including so many of their own fallen comrades. But there was nothing to be done for them, and his orders were clear: stand and hold the first charge, take as many rakshasa lives as possible, then retreat so swiftly the enemy should be bewildered by your disappearance. He barked orders to his vanars, painful orders compelling them to leave the wounded and near-dead and fall back at once. It pained him to turn his back on the enemy as well, when he could have taken more rakshasa lives and helped alleviate the unequal balance, for he knew in his heart that their losses were nowhere near his, but Rama's orders were Rama's orders, and the vanars fell back, leaving the rakshasas in the canyon milling about in utter confusion, unable to understand where the little monkey beasts had disappeared to all of a sudden. Their valiant work done, the vanars of Kiskindha retreated under cover of the dust cloud to permit the next phase of Rama's plan to be put into effect.

5

They came boldly, arrogantly even, knowing the enemy was here somewhere, smelling the unmistakable scent of vanar in the forest. Mandara-devi had watched as their leaders had ordered them to proceed with care and be prepared. But the troops had grunted derisively and shrugged off the cautions. What had they to fear from naked, unarmed little monkeymen? This would be like a pack of tigers on a rabbit hunt, they snarled.

They were right. Except that this time they were the rabbits.

The plan called for her to wait until the entire rakshasa horde was inside the confines of the forest before ordering the attack. But the rakshasa general leading this contingent was wiser than most. He ordered a third of the troops to fan out through the woods, sweeping it from the south end up to the north, while the remaining rakshasas waited outside. The troops ordered to hold back squatted on their haunches grumpily, peeved at being denied the chance to snack on hot squealing vanar flesh. She eyed them uneasily, trying to decide what to do next. Finally she came to the conclusion that there was nothing else for it. She would simply have to go ahead as planned, and hope for the best. Too much depended on them coordinating this battle with the others for her to wait much longer. As it was, she was certain that the other vanar contingents would have engaged the enemy by now. Any moment now, Hanuman would appear overhead, expecting to see the battle in the valley over, or in its final phases.

She watched as a pair of lumbering rakshasa brutes passed

directly beneath the tree in which she was ensconced. She decided that they would do as well as any, and raised her head, arching her throat to cry out an ululating call that was instantly taken up and answered by hundreds, then thousands, then tens of thousands of vanar throats across the valley – and beyond it as well. The rakshasas below jerked their heads upwards with a start, then howled their fury as well as communicating to their fellows that the enemy had been sighted. One of them began hacking at the tree with his enormous-bladed weapon, as if he would chop it down to get to her. She was glad rakshasas could not climb trees; then she wondered mischievously if that was such a bad thing – perhaps a tree battle would be better than this uneven fight.

She *cheeka*-ed, leaping to a lower branch, then still lower, to afford the blundering beasts below a better sight of her. She hung from a branch, using her tail to suspend herself upside down, bringing her within a few yards of the ground. They howled and waved their stubby rakshasa arms – these were some kind of bull breed, with short, thick, menacing horns, stocky upper bodies, and massively overdeveloped lower bodies, with haunches that looked powerful enough to kick an elephant to death. As if reading her mind, the stupid beast who had been hacking at the latsyoa's trunk turned around, dropped his weapon, braced himself with his stubby arms flat on the ground, and released a powerful kick. He misjudged the distance and only landed one rear hoof on the trunk, but the impact was enough to jar her bones. The trunk cracked, protesting loudly, and the other rakshasa roared to his companion, who glanced behind, corrected his angle and prepared to deliver another mighty back-kick, this one aimed to—

She leaped off the tree and on to the next, just as the rakshasa's kick shattered the latsyoa's trunk, sending splinters flying. Even as the tree began to fall, creaking loudly in protest, she leaped to a third and then a fourth tree. The rakshasa who had been watching her howled to his companion, who grabbed his weapon and shot to his feet. Both trundled after her, bellowing loudly. Other rakshasas were running towards them now, thrashing noisily through the dense undergrowth, roaring to one another. So far, so good, but how were the other vanars—

She heard a commotion explode to her right, then another farther away to her left, then the whole forest erupted with the sound of teasing vanars *cheeka*-ing and angry rakshasas bellowing as they gave chase. She swung from tree to tree, going as fast as she could without actually leaving her pursuers behind. She was in no danger of being caught, and she didn't want to lose them. The whole point of this tactic was to make them follow. She wished more of the enemy had entered the forest. The plan depended on them all being within the woods, not outside it. But there was nothing to be done about that, so she raced along, and hoped that the commotion she and the other teasers were causing would bring more pursuers. She caught occasional glimpses of silver jewellery reflecting a beam of sunlight, or a flash of white vanar teeth against glossy jet-black fur, and knew that all were doing their job as planned.

But theirs was the easy part.

She heard a sudden surprised grunt from one of the rakshasas chasing her, followed by a disgusting squelching sound, and paused, clinging to a branch of one tree with her tail and a branch of the next with one paw. She hung suspended momentarily, listening and scenting. The undeniable odour of freshly spilled blood filled the air, and was followed by a rakshasa howl of outrage. She grinned and turned to watch as the battle began in earnest.

Kambunara stepped out from behind his tree with a paw outstretched, claws extruded fully. The trundling rakshasa in the fore of the group chasing Mandara-devi was too intent on the pursuit, and on keeping sight of the fleeing vanar, to even notice him until the very last instant. The rakshasa sensed something and lowered his sights just in time to see the brown-furred Himalayan bear, as tall as himself and as wide in girth, appear from behind the trunk of the tree that had concealed him. Kambunara saw the Lankan's foaming mouth open as he tried to bellow a warning to his fellow rakshasas, and twisted his torso with the powerful side-swiping movement that his kind were masters of. His outstretched claws caught the oncoming rakshasa right in his throat, slashing it to raw, ragged ruin, and the warning died a squelching death before it had begun.

Kambunara followed through with a swipe in the opposite direction, using his left claws this time to finish off the rakshasa. The bull-headed beast collapsed to the leafy ground, heaving and thrashing in his last throes.

He heard a roar of outrage explode and looked up in time to see several more rakshasas approaching at a run. Even as he stepped forward to greet them with the appropriate bear welcome, he saw several other dark-furred shapes step out from behind their trees to deal sudden death blows to racing rakshasas as well. Across the length and breadth of the forest, the sounds and scents of bears felling rakshasas rang out like a brutal symphony. Two of the rakshasas in his path made it past the other bears and one swung an enormous-bladed weapon similar to the battle axe he had seen mortals use in their wars. Bears were not limber enough to dodge like vanars, or to simply leap out of the way, so he shot out a paw and grasped the wooden shaft of the weapon in mid-air. The rakshasa grunted, startled, then died with the same startled expression on its mottled mongrel-breed snout as Kambunara twisted its own weapon to drive it home into the rakshasa's midriff. Even before that enemy fell to its knees, its steaming guts pouring out on to the leaf-strewn forest floor, Kambunara swiped backhanded at the second oncoming foe with a snarl of effort. The rakshasa, in the process of raising his own sling-blade weapon, was too slow to dodge the unexpected move and took the full brunt of the blow on his – or her? – face, screaming in outrage as the deadly claws ripped open skin and flesh and destroyed its eyes. It turned, dropping its weapon to clutch at its blinded organs, and, still running, crashed headlong into the trunk of the tree Kambunara had been lurking behind. A sickening crunch suggested that it had cracked its skull on the hardwood trunk, and Kambunara had only to slash again at its lower back, severing the spine in at least three separate places, and it was done.

The forest was ringing out with the sounds of bears killing rakshasas, but in only moments, as the pursuing Lankans became aware that they had been lured into a trap by the vanars, the oncoming rakshasas slowed, waited for their companions, and then roared to one another across the forest, organising a more efficient advance and attack. Kambunara had expected that, although he had hoped for more to fall prey to bear claws before they wised up to the ambush. He waited for the rakshasas to regroup and then advance – even as his bears closed their ranks and prepared to meet the next onslaught.

During the brief hiatus, Kambunara cleaned his claws on the bark of a tree. As he did so, a sound alerted him, and when he glanced up he saw Mandara-devi herself seated on a lower branch. She looked as matriarchal as ever, her white-streaked fur and her jewellery belying her willingness to risk her own life like any of her soldier vanars.

'Is that all you could bring us today?' he asked.

She grinned at his impudence. 'Only about twenty-thousand-odd followed me and my teasers into the woods . . .'

He shrugged, showing no sign that the number was either greater or smaller than what he had been expecting. 'We'll try to make do. Is that all of them?'

She sighed, losing her grin. 'They have a smart general. He stationed two thirds of them outside the forest.'

He nodded. They had hoped for the whole horde to come crashing in but had not truly expected that; it would have been too easy. 'Then we shall have to go to them.'

The sound of bellowing rakshasas caused him to look down

again. The rakshasas were advancing now, approaching at a slow, sensible pace as befitted the dim, close confines of forest fighting. He could see at least half a dozen advancing on his position alone.

'After we deal with this bunch, that is,' he said.

'Actually,' Mandara-devi said from the tree, clambering up to a higher branch as she spoke, 'I thought I might do something about that. Perhaps see if they're able to ignore an outright challenge from a vanar. That would make your job much easier, would it not, my rksa friend?'

Kambunara grunted approvingly. 'You do that, my lady, and I shall personally kiss your furry behind in gratitude.'

She chittered in amusement at his comment. 'Well, just for your information, that particular part of me is *not* furry.' And with a flash of that same anatomical part, she leaped up and away, racing back the way she had come, to the north end of the valley.

Kambunara grinned and turned his attention to his approaching rakshasa visitors. 'Come on then, you slow-witted, illegimate spawn of Ravana. Let me show you how we bears gut our fish before we eat them.'

That got him a satisfying roar of outrage in response, and a more reckless charge from the oncoming rakshasas. He growled in reply, his claws slashing and flashing in the bars of morning sunlight that seeped through the close-growing foliage overhead.

Mandara-devi raced back through the trees. At first she passed steadily increasing numbers of rakshasas going the other way; then, as she approached the northern end of the forest where she had begun her tease-run, the numbers dwindled until, reaching the place where she had waited before, she found virtually none of the enemy. Her fears were confirmed when she peered out through the branches of a diarasaqa tree.

Some forty or fifty thousand rakshasas squatted in roughly regular lines on the northern side of the valley. Kumbha lieutenants patrolled the lines, their long barbed whips keeping the troops in check. The general of the horde stood with his back to her, peering up at the sky to the north, as if seeking out something. She caught a glimpse of sunlight reflecting off some golden or gilded object in the distance, and assumed that was the fabled flying chariot that Ravana was rumoured to travel in. She would have been happier to see Hanuman instead, but supposed that he was watching over the battle of the Kiskindha vanars, as that had been his first order.

She scented Dvivida an instant before he appeared by her side. Another vanar was with him, almost as burly and well built as he, but far less attractive. This was Mainda, the other champion lieutenant, older and past his prime, but a formidable figure among the Mandaras nevertheless. He was also notorious for his predilection for honey wine. He gave her the tribe greeting, paw touching skull, even though she had specifically ordered all her vanars to abjure formal greetings during battle. She ignored the gesture, but he did not seem to mind.

Dvivida grinned at her curiously. 'Does my lady intend something?'

'If those ugly beasts don't enter the forest, the whole plan will be for naught,' she said. 'We must lure them in somehow before I give the order for the second wave.'

Mainda looked at her, his face twisted from an old injury that had left the right side unable to respond or move. It gave him a sad, perpetually snarling expression. 'The bears in the woods are greatly outnumbered. Can they even hold the rakshasas already in there, my lady? Perhaps you should give the second order and see how things turn out.'

She looked at the ageing champion. 'If I give the second order, then the rest of the bears and all of our Mandaras will come pouring down the valley from all sides.' She gestured ahead at the rakshasa horde in the valley. 'With the bulk of the enemy still out in the open and easily able to see the attack coming, what good will that do? The point of getting them into the woods is so they believe we are all hiding in here, while in fact we mount our main attack from outside, encircling them inside the forest. Then the bears battle them on the ground while we Mandaras pounce on them from the trees. It is a simple yet brilliant plan devised by Rama and his advisers and it is our job to follow it through.'

Mainda glanced at her craftily – or perhaps it was only his damaged nerves that made him seem crafty. 'True, my lady. But the plan is no longer valid, since the rakshasas failed to react as our lord Rama expected. It may be best for us to go ahead with the attack and leave the decision-making to the leaders. General Nila will surely adapt to the changed circumstances.'

She looked at him. A part of her understood what he meant – and felt. Only a little while ago she had thought and felt the same thing: leave the thinking to the leaders; a soldier's only task was to follow orders. But by that same logic . . .

'By that same logic,' she said aloud, 'we follow the orders we were given. Rama's instructions were clear. All the rakshasas must be lured into the woods, and only then will the second order be given. I intend to fulfil that order now, at any cost. Will you aid me or hang around here arguing?'

Dvivida shot Mainda a quick stern glance. 'Where you go, we follow, my lady,' said the young champion.

Mainda lowered his brow, in the vanar equivalent of a nod. 'Always.'

She breathed more easily. She had no stomach for wrestling her oldest and most experienced lieutenant into submitting to her orders, not when tens of thousands of lives hung in the balance. 'Good. Then follow my example and do as I do.'

She leaped off the tree, rolled through the kusa grass and began loping across the open grassland, towards the rakshasa horde.

6

Hanuman roared with fury as the dust cloud finally began to dissipate in a new gust of oceanic wind that blew from the east. The canyon floor below was heaped with thousands upon thousands of his fallen vanar comrades, crushed beyond recognition into piles of bleeding furry flesh. Where so many brave Kiskindha warriors had stood and faced the first of the Lankan attacks, now only corpses and body parts littered the place. His anger was somewhat alleviated by the sight of some few thousand rakshasa corpses lying intermingled as well, more than he would have expected. It filled him with pride to see how many of the enemy the Kiskindhans had felled, but did not negate his great sorrow. He clenched his fists, his body expanding with anger without his even being aware of it, and vowed that every one of those vanar lives would be paid for in full, even if he had to kill that many rakshasas himself, bare-handed.

He saw King Sugreeva leading the vanars that survived back in the retreat as planned. As the last of them reached the end of the canyon, they turned and *cheeka*-ed insolently at the rakshasas behind. King Sugreeva himself, carrying what looked like a spear pole, also turned and added his own taunt to the shrieks of his warriors.

The rakshasas, milling about in confusion after the abrupt disappearance of their foe, responded to the sound of the taunting vanars with outrage. Pointing their weapons, they roared and chuffed and spewed their fury, then lurched forward clumsily, for their bulk and weight, while a great advantage in a head-long charge, was cumbersome to them when starting from a standstill. As the ones milling about behind came far enough forward into the canyon to see their fallen comrades, they howled and roared, unable to believe that so many of their own could have been felled by these puny, impudent creatures. That incensed them all the more and they began to run in their clumsy, lumbering fashion – although, to be fair, there were some sleeker, more elegantly muscled ones that moved with considerable grace as well, for like vanars or mortals or any other creatures, not all rakshasas were alike. He watched as their run grew effectively into another charge, albeit a much less thundering and swift one than their first, for by now a great many of the mounted rakshasas in the front lines lay dead or maimed.

Hanuman watched with narrowed eyes as the general he had seen before, the one with the diamantine teeth, climbed to the top of the mound of bodies piled in the middle of the canyon, avoiding the squealing maw and tusks of a horribly wounded and trapped masth elephant. The general found his footing with difficulty, and with the advantage of the high ground now, shouted something to his hordes, gesticulating with his bladed weapon in the direction of the retreating vanars, egging them on to give chase and finish the slaughter they had begun so well.

Again Hanuman longed to plunge down and smash those bestial beings into so much bloody pulp, but restrained himself. He settled for snarling viciously, loud enough that the sound carried down and echoed off the canyon walls, resounding. The diamantine-toothed general looked up at once, and peered narrowly at the vanar flying above. He raised his blade in an unmistakably threatening gesture, baring his teeth in a menacing snarl. When Hanuman refused to respond or react, he shook his head in disgust, turned away and resumed ordering his troops in the chase.

*   *   *

Vajradanta was furious at the number of the fallen. The whole point of that thundering charge had been to crush the little monkeys into the dust. How dare they presume to stand before the might of a rakshasa cavalry attack! The piled corpses of vanars gave him cause for satisfaction, although he had expected many more to be lying there lifeless. That last-minute ruse they had sprung on him unexpectedly, leaping on one another's shoulders to fly up into the air and land on their attackers – the military mind in his head admired the sheer audacity and expertly timed execution of that tactic – had cost him the majority of his mounted troops. The few hundred broken-surs and kumbha-surs that had not broken a leg, been caught in the crush of piled corpses, or been slain by the leaping vanars were being caught and mounted again by the survivors of his cavalry unit. But he was shocked to see how few remained. Especially the elephants, who all lay dead, except for a handful that had turned and fled at the mouth of the canyon itself, perhaps sensing the carnage that lay ahead and tearing loose of their ropes, ripping out their own flesh in the process, to run wild across the valley behind. On open ground, these same masth elephants would have caused havoc among any army's massed troops, the casualties they caused cancelling out the threat they posed to one's own troops – for mad elephants could hardly be bothered to distinguish between friend and foe. But here, in this enclosed space, with nowhere to go but straight ahead, they had been befuddled and maddened further by the stench of sudden violent death and corpses, and their own lumbering weight had been their downfall, crushing them as well as those unfortunate enough to come in their path. Still, at least they had wreaked great damage in their dying. What he could not brook were the losses suffered by his rakshasa ranks – for those were not accidental but wholly caused by the vanars themselves. The little bundles of fur, unarmed and untrained in battle – for who had ever heard of vanars mounting an army? – had proved surprisingly resilent and resourceful antagonists.

Filled with chagrin, and astonished that little monkey-like creatures could inflict such damage on heavily armoured, armed, and mounted rakshasas, he determined that in this next charge he would not only break their resolve and spirits, but shatter the backbone of their forces as well. They were already on the run, no doubt horrified by the superior power and strength, not to mention fighting skill, of the Lankans, and all his troops needed to do was run them down and finish them off. There could be no more than another ten thousand or so, and he had twice as many troops still on their feet and fighting mad. He himself had already slain several dozen vanars, the foolish beasts leaping at him from all directions at once, but none quick enough to dodge his flashing blade, and those who came too close falling prey to his lightning-sharp teeth. His mouth was filled with the taste of vanar blood and flesh and fur, and he spat several times to remove it. Now, if he could only get a bite or two of mortal flesh, fresh and bloody, while the heart was still pumping, that would remove this taste. He grinned. Perhaps he would get his wish before the day was through.

'Ra-van-a!' he roared, pointing his blade at the end of the canyon. The foolish vanars still milled about there, making insulting noises and lewd gestures with their mouths – and other parts of their fur-covered anatomy as well – as if such childish behaviour would dissuade his stout rakshasas. He frowned as he saw that even their leader, an ageing vanar who had appropriated a broken spear rod from some fallen rakshasa and wielded it like a monkey waving a tree branch, was joining in the taunting. As he watched with narrowed eyes from his vantage point, gazing above the heads of his lumbering rakshasas, he saw one vanar, either the leader or someone close by, turn around and flash his brightly coloured rear end at the oncoming enemy. In quick succession, several dozen other vanars did the exact same thing, and for a moment, gaily coloured vanar bottoms flashed insultingly at the charging rakshasas, drawing new roars of outrage and fury from the racing Lankans.

Vajradanta frowned. That was no mere fright-response. He could see now that despite the approaching rakshasas being no more than a few dozen yards from their position, the vanars were still holding fast, neither continuing their retreat, nor gibbering, nor leaping away in terror. If anything, they were snarling and leering with a savage humour that he knew well from his years on the battlefield. These were warriors in full spate, taunting their enemy to come on fast and furious . . . encouraging them to race into—

'A trap!' he shouted. 'It's a trap! Desist! Fall back!' He repeated the words in several rakshasa dialects, and his lieutenants passed the order on as well.

But his words were barely heeded by the infuriated rakshasas, now a good two hundred yards ahead of him at the narrowest point of the canyon, too far away and out of earshot due to the peculiar acoustics of the place. The rakshasas charged onwards toward the leering, mocking, taunting vanars who awaited them below an overhang that arched over the narrow exit of the canyon. As Vajradanta raised his head and waved his weapon to draw the attention of his troops, bellowing at the top of his voice, he saw movement atop that overhang. Glancing up, his shouts died away, cut off in mid-command, as his military mind instantly grasped the enemy's scheme. A trap it was indeed, neatly sprung, and seeded with the lives of more enemy vanars than he would have thought it possible for any commander to sacrifice. Yet the very scale of that bloody sacrifice had been the reason why he had failed to see the trap until it was too late.

He raised his head, scouring the top of the canyon walls to left and right, and suddenly, with a sinking heart, Vajradanta knew that he had sadly, tragically, dangerously underestimated the enemy numbers, by a factor of five or ten, perhaps more.

Sugreeva felt a surge of joy akin to nothing he had felt before as he raised his eyes and saw the top of the canyon bristling with countless scampering shapes. The walls on the eastern side were lined with scores of silhouetted vanars climbing up from the far sides where they had lain hidden on Rama's orders in the dense shrubbery. As each wave climbed into view, was caught by the garish light of the morning sun's rays, and then clambered down lithely into the canyon, he was filled with pride and a sense of honour. It was worth it now to have seen so many of his fine Kiskindha vanars sacrificed in that terrible first charge of the Lankans. Worth it to see the trap in which the rest of the Lankan vanguard was now caught, encaged on two sides by the canyon, and on this front by his Kiskindha vanars, and left with only one route open – back to Lanka. His knowledge of war strategy told him that if the rakshasas were wise, they would elect to retreat at once, while they still could. His knowledge of rakshasas, gained in large part from Rama himself, told him they would rather die than retreat.

He could see the general with the flashing teeth, standing in the centre of the canyon atop a veritable hillock of corpses, staring up at the waves upon waves of vanars coming down the steep slopes of the canyon sides, raising new clouds of dust as they slid, leaped, rolled the three hundred yards towards their quarry. Already, some fifty or sixty thousand vanars were in view, with more arriving every instant in endless profusion, streaming over the tops of the canyon sides and carpeting the sand-coloured dust of the terrain until the canyon itself seemed to grow dark on account of the sheer quantity of fur coating its walls. Rama and Lakshman had debated how many of the vanars to deploy in this particular action and the decision had been unanimous: enough to not only crush the Lankans, but to wipe them out.

'To the last beast,' Lakshman had said fiercely.

'Or till they retreat,' Rama had added.

Sugreeva bared his own teeth now at the rakshasa general, in mock imitation of his toothy grin. But the rakshasa commander's attention was still turned upwards, staring in mute horror at the enemy pouring down towards his position. Already, the charging rakshasas had almost reached the spot where Sugreeva and his warriors had halted to lure them on with jeers and taunts and that classic vanar gesture, bottom-flashing. Now, as the sound and smell and sight of the new threat penetrated their thick rakshasa skulls, they slowed their charge, coming to a lumbering, puzzled halt. They began raising their snouts and muzzles and horns and tusks and gazing in all directions, scenting the change in the atmosphere before they saw or heard anything amiss. Even Sugreeva could scent the massive increase in vanar odour, for the wind was blowing down from the east. At first the stunned rakshasas seemed unable to comprehend what was happening – or more likely were unable to believe the sheer numbers of the enemy pouring down towards them. Then, one by one, they began grunting, squealing, howling, roaring, raising their rakshasa voices in outrage and protest. There was nothing a rakshasa hated more than to be outfoxed, for their advantage lay in brute strength, not wits.

The ones closest to Sugreeva, barely a few dozen yards away, stared up directly at the overhang beneath which he stood, the exact position prescribed for him by Lakshman. He glanced up as well. The overhang was barely three yards in thickness and curved across this narrow part of the canyon from side to side, like an arch designed by a builder in a hurry. It was thick with vanars, crowding it, hanging from it, tails coiled around the narrow fingers of protruding rock that stuck out at all angles, a massed group of several hundred of his kind staring down with glinting, hungry eyes, claws and teeth flashing angrily at the sight of so many of their fellows lying dead on the canyon floor. They issued a sound not unlike a clutch of snakes hissing angrily, the sound that vanars made when gathered in great numbers and confronted with a natural predatory enemy.

As more and more waves continued to roll down the sides of the canyon, the walls grew thick with gathered vanars, all issuing the same deathly sound. Sugreeva saw more rakshasas gaze up in bewilderment, and guessed that the Lankans had never seen such a sight nor heard such a sound before. He knew that this too would become part of rakshasa lore and vanar legend for ever more. The hissing grew to a climax, then faded away slowly. In the utter silence that followed, he heard a wounded vanar somewhere in the awful pile in the middle of the canyon cry out Hanuman's name, then Rama's, then fall silent.

Sugreeva drew himself up as tall as possible, preparing to fall upon the prey. For this time, it was the vanar who was the predator, making up in sheer weight of numbers and an ingeniously chosen geographical position for what he lacked in strength and size and weaponry.

He raised his wooden pole, which he preferred to think of as his tree now. The eyes of nearly a lakh of vanar warriors turned to look at him, waiting for his command. And still the numbers continued to swell as more waves rolled down the canyon sides.

With a sharp ferociousness, he stabbed the pole in the direction of the surrounded Lankan army. '*For Rama!*' he shrieked.

This time the response was loud enough to fill the entire canyon, echoing like booming thunder.

'*FOR RAMA!*'

Like dark honey wine freshly brewed from the choicest grapes of the Madhuban gardens, the vanar forces poured down the walls of the canyon. As they reached the end of the slope, they paused to brace themselves briefly against the knobbly edge of rock, then, using it to give themselves greater momentum, they leaped, hurling themselves with frenzied, ferocious energy at their foes. The air was so thick with flying, leaping vanars that for a moment Sugreeva's view of the sky and the sun, just emerging over the eastern wall of the canyon, was almost completely obscured. Denser than the dust cloud which had obscured them all during the first battle, the vanar cloud filled the air for long moments. Then, as the first vanars landed on their enemies, and on the canyon floor, the sound of slaughter began anew.

For the first time since the onset of the battle, Hanuman opened his mouth and roared with delight. He watched as the rain of vanars poured down relentlessly upon the surrounded and outnumbered rakshasas trapped in the canyon. He saw a rakshasa female, bearing two young – for many a rakshasi carried her young into battle, just as a lioness would take her cubs on a hunt to train them in the art of killing – screech with outrage and fling her young up in the air. No helpless babes, the two young Lankans met their vanar foe in mid-air and gnashed and bit and tore with great fury. Their mother grappled a half-dozen vanars at once, ripping one into two bloody halves, crushing another's head, and almost decapitating yet another, while jabbing and clawing and kicking wildly to keep the others at bay. But more and more vanars kept leaping upon her, and upon her young, and in moments the three of them were overwhelmed, more than two dozen vanars swarming over the three of them, ululating in triumph. He did not permit himself to feel any remorse for even the young rakshasas: if they were old enough to take lives, they were old enough to die. Such was the harsh reality of war. Still, he could not help wishing the mother rakshasi had left her younguns at home.

Other fights were much less ambiguous. Great hulking rakshasas with tusked mouths and horned heads or grotesquely malformed orifices went down fighting like mad elephants in masth, taking half a dozen or more vanar lives apiece before they succumbed. Others fought on bitterly, remaining on their feet, or hindlegs, or nether limbs and tail, bodies streaming from dozens of terrible wounds – for vanars did not just bite or claw, they tore out flesh and pieces of organs – battling on in the face of impossible odds, refusing to surrender or show quarter. These courageous rakshasas – and he admired their courage without hesitation, for a true warrior always respected a brave enemy – were treated with different tactics by the vanars.

In one instance, he saw at least two dozen vanars surround one adamant bull-headed rakshasa in a ragged circle, taunting and mocking it, while the ones at its rear nipped in to bite or slash and then leap back before the slow, wounded Lankan could turn around and hack at it with its enormous battle blade. The rakshasa turned and swung, turned and swung, until it was dizzy-headed and in mortal pain from countless wounds and nips and bites, and the instant it showed a fraction of weakness, vanars leaped upon its back, slashing and tearing it open like a sack of grain, clinging to its belly and lower limbs with claws and teeth working viciously, spilling its innards and organs, until by the time the bull rakshasa fell, bellowing in agony and disbelief, it was little more than a butcher's pile of body parts. It was this same tactic that vanars used to fight and kill natural predators like lions or tigers or leopards in their natural habitats, and it worked just as well on solitary rakshasas, isolated from their comrades.

The wiser of the Lankans, perhaps aware of this fact, banded together and fought back to back and shoulder to shoulder. But the vanars were wiser and had more warriors to spare and speed to offer. They penned these teams of rakshasas until they were too close to swing out wildly without injuring one another, which a couple did do from time to time, drawing furious protests and retaliatory blows from their own stricken comrades, for in the heat of battle, rakshasas were as wont to strike out at one another as at the enemy. And then, when they were virtually huddled together, jostling each other and on the verge of desperation, the vanars darted in underfoot, slipping easily beneath and between the rakshasa's lower limbs to strike telling blows. The vanars who did this were mostly killed in the press or chopped down, or simply crushed between massive thighs or beneath pounding hoofs and reptilian tails, but the instant a rakshasa turned its attention downward to kill the intruding vanar, the other vanars waiting and watching took that opportunity to leap upon it and tear into it savagely.

The battle raged on for another half-watch, and Hanuman's anger slowly began to ebb as he watched the pride and glory of Ravana's vanguard systematically decimated, then quartered, then halved, whittled down in a thousand smaller fights and sub-fights, until those rakshasas left standing, or lurching really, could barely keep their wits about them, let alone offer real resistance. The vanars were gibbering and chattering by now, as vanars did when gathered in huge numbers and confident of superiority over a larger, greater predator. The sound of their victorious cheering and taunting rose into the air to reach Hanuman, and he laughed, filling the sky with his booming glee. As more rakshasas continued to fall, he saw a few sorry Lankans nearest to their own side of the canyon lose heart and attempt to race for their lines. With that, the stubborn pride that had cost the rakshasas so dearly finally broke, and the battle turned as all battles do eventually.

In moments a handful of rakshasas, no more than one quarter of the horde that had ridden and raced into the canyon not long before, so proud and arrogant and confident of victory, were stumbling and running back towards their capital city, crying tears of rage and frustration as they went. Hanuman watched as Sugreeva noted the Lankan retreat and called a halt to the vanars seeking to pursue and kill the fleeing enemy. The vanars shrieked and screeched and showed their colourful bottoms to the retreating rakshasas, then danced cartwheels and somersaults and held hands and jigged.

Sugreeva climbed to the top of the piled dead, reaching the very spot where the rakshasa general with the flashing teeth had stood not long before. Standing atop that heap of his own beloved dead as well as enemy corpses that now outnumbered their own by a factor of two or more, he paused and stood proudly, scanning the great army of vanars that thronged the canyon, dancing and calling out with unbridled delight.

He raised the pole that had served him so well in the battle. And the vanars ceased their dancing and antics and looked up at him reverentially. No longer Sugreeva the Exiled One, or Sugreeva the Lost, but Sugreeva the Victor of Lanka, commander of the soon-to-be-legendary flying vanars who had faced down a horde of the greatest fighting rakshasa warriors in all existence and beaten them into bloody pulp.

'Jai Shri Rama,' he called. *Praised be Rama.*

The response was deafening, audible even to Hanuman floating three hundred yards above, amplified by the canyon walls to resound for miles around, heard even by the fleeing rakshasa survivors, if not by Rama himself.

'JAI SHRI RAMA!'

Hanuman smiled. 'Jai Shri Rama,' he said softly, then flew north to carry word of the victory to Rama himself. He would check on the progress of other battles en route.

7

Hanuman arrived at the valley where the Mandaras and the bears were to confront the enemy just as Mandara-devi emerged from the darkling shade of the forest. He slowed to a halt, staying well above the line of sight of those on the ground below, and watched as the tribe-goddess of the silver-miners loped toward what seemed to be a sizeable army of rakshasas. Following her closely were two black-pelted Mandaras that he recognised instantly as the lieutenants and champions Mainda and Dvivida.

He frowned as he watched the three vanars run towards the rakshasas. The battle plan called for Mandara-devi and her vanars to tease and lure the enemy into the forest where Kambunara's bears would keep them busy, while General Nila and his troops, along with the rest of the bear contingent, rode down into the valley from all sides, encircling and trapping the rakshasas in the woods in much the same way that the Kiskindha vanars had fallen upon the rakshasas in the canyon. Glancing northwards, he could see and scent fighting in that part of the wooded valley. Using his preternaturally enhanced senses, he could make out bears fighting rakshasas, the bears badly outnumbered but fighting with their customary laconic brutality. At once he grasped the situation. The rakshasas had proved cleverer than expected, leaving the bulk of their force outside the woods, and now Mandara-devi was attempting to finish her given task of bringing them into the forest so that the rest of the battle could be played out as planned.

But the plan had not required that she personally endanger her own pelt by going out alone to face forty thousand rakshasas! Again he felt chagrin and frustration at being able to do nothing but watch. He did not know how much longer he would be able to keep this up. He seethed silently, waiting to see how Mandara-devi and her two champions fared.

Mandara-devi knew that what she was doing was foolish, even suicidal. But there was no alternative. There was not time enough to think up another plan, and she was no thinker or planner anyway. This was all she could come up with given the circumstances and limited time and resources. Perhaps she could have sent Mainda and Dvivida out instead of going herself, but she would sooner throw off her jewellery and disdain her calling as tribe-goddess than do such a thing.

The sunlight was warm and pleasing on the back of her pelt. She wished she could spend a little time, rolling in this high grass, sunning herself. How could a land as beautiful as Lanka harbour such demonic species? But then, that was what this war was about, in a sense. After Rama won, Lanka would no longer be a lair of rakshasas. It would be a land of peace and freedom, where even those rakshasas who survived would live in harmony with other neighbouring nations. Or so it was to be hoped.

She emerged from the shelter of the high grass all too quickly, and into the scrubby area just before the rise of the ghats. At some point, a rivulet or stream had run through this part of the valley and had dried up, leaving behind a dirt bed, like one of the raj-margs that mortals built to carry their carts and horse-mounted armies across their kingdoms back home. Nothing much grew here, except some weeds and wild flowers. She stopped upon this dry patch, within sight of the horde.

A chorus of howls and growls and roars rose from the rakshasa troops. Several hundred stood up and hefted their weapons, their ugly orifices and snouts and jaws slobbering disgustingly as they called out. Their general was less impulsive and much shrewder. He turned and eyed her with interest, noting Mainda and Dvivida at each of her shoulders, flanking her. He issued a terse command to a kumbha lieutenant, who immediately began barking hoarse commands to the other kumbhas. Whips lashed out, containing the agitated troops even as they sought to surge forward and attack the insolent vanars who dared approach them so boldly.

She sighed inwardly. It had been too much to hope that they would all simply roar with outrage and come running at her, so she could lead them on another merry chase through the woods as she had the first bunch. This general would take some amount of finessing.

She called out to him now. 'Rakshasa! Will you not fight us? Are you too cowardly to come and face the vanar sena of Lord Rama Chandra of Ayodhya? It would seem that his very name strikes fear into your craven rakshasa hearts, does it not?'

Howls of protest rose from across the massed ranks. For a moment, even she was awed by the sheer brute muscle power collected on the slopes. Even though her Mandaras and the bear contingent outnumbered this horde, she wondered if they could truly match them in strength and fighting power. She pushed away that errant thought, keeping her energy concentrated on the task at hand.

The general smiled at her, his bullish face beaming with jagged yellow teeth. 'Fear? Your leader's name brings nothing but contempt to my warriors. See even now how he sends a female vanar to do his parleying for him! He is the coward! Too craven to come himself to beg for peace and mercy.'

This time the horde roared with delight, while she sensed Dvivida step forward beside her, his muscles rippling with anger. 'Back,' she commanded in a low tone. 'Let me handle this.'

He did as she ordered, but she could sense his fury at having to listen to Rama being insulted thus. She shared his anger and let her own show in her reply. 'My lord Rama asks for no mercy or parley. He is wise enough to trust his generals and lieutenants to make his battlefield decisions for themselves. I am Mandara-devi, guardian goddess of the Mandara vanars. I speak for myself and myself alone. Does your vile leader Ravana permit you such latitude and independent volition?'

The rakshasa general scowled. 'Lanka-naresh Ravana is the supreme commander of all the worlds. None can rival his acumen in war. If he wills it, a war is already won. Such as this one. You call yourself a guardian? Then go, take your vanars home while you still can. Or my warriors will use your bones to pick their teeth.'

She feigned a snicker. 'You wish. But we shall not let you off that easily. First, I challenge your greatest champion to single, mortal combat.'

The general of the horde stared at her for a moment, silent, nonplussed.

Beside her she heard a shocked intake of breath from both her lieutenants. Even the laconic Mainda seemed taken aback. 'My lady,' his voice murmured in her left ear. 'Are you sure you know what you are doing?'

'We shall find out soon enough, Mainda,' she said quietly.

Aloud she challenged again: 'Why are you silent, rakshasa? Are you afraid that I will defeat even your greatest champion and humiliate you before your own horde?'

The volume of the roar of protest that met this remark made even the general of the horde scowl. He looked around, issued a terse instruction to the two kumbha lieutenants nearest to him, and then came forward. A gruff cheer rose from the rakshasa ranks. Several slammed their bladed weapons against their helms or armour to show their approval for their leader's move.

Mandara-devi slowly released the pent-up breath she had been holding back. For a moment she had feared that the rakshasa general might send someone else to fight her. But she knew from

Rama's briefings that rakshasas accepted only the strongest and fiercest fighter as their overlord. This general would have proved himself beyond dispute several times before, making him the horde's acknowledged champion. She had counted on that fact, and on his ego preventing him from applying his leaderly wisdom in this one instance. To have denied her satisfaction – a solitary, ageing female vanar – would have been humiliating before his horde. He had no choice but to accept her challenge, no matter how much he resented it or distrusted her motives for demanding this fight. She saw it in his eyes, coldly intelligent and calculating, unlike the animalistic eyes of most rakshasas. Yes, this Lankan knew something of what she intended, and that knowledge only served to make him more dangerous, not less. For it meant that apart from being the horde's fiercest fighter, he was also the most intelligent.

Starting to remove his helmet, he said coldly, 'Vanar, you should know that I would normally not fight a female or an aged one. But this being war, and your kind being the aggressor who invade our noble land, I see no loss of honour in accepting your challenge. It shall cause me no regret to tear your feeble body apart limb by limb and throw the remains to my horde to feed on afterwards.' He effected a thin smile; difficult, for his features were like those of a buffalo and it only made him look leery. 'Or perhaps I shall throw you to them *before*, to feed on you while you yet live. Perhaps if you are yet of breeding age, you shall survive to bear rakshasa offspring in a Lankan dungeon.'

She snarled softly to either side, admonishing Mainda and Dvivida, who were undoubtedly livid at this insult, and curled her lip in a sneer of her own. A single glance to each of them made it clear that she would not brook their interfering in the bout to follow, no matter what transpired. Only when they looked down, acknowledging her command, did she turn her eyes back to the enemy.

She looked at the rakshasa, who was now standing only a

few yards away upon the dried riverbed, flexing his powerful muscles. 'After I finish with *you*, rakshasa, there will not be enough of you to breed with even a scuttling insect. And the same goes for your horde, which my lord Rama will squash like a cluster of bugs underfoot.' An cacophony of roars broke out across the slope: there were few things rakshasas hated more than bugs, or being compared to them. They had hated the dreaded pisacas, a now-extinct race of Asuras who had been wiped out during the Lankan civil war fourteen years ago, largely by the rakshasas themselves.

She drew herself up and let loose with a vanar roar. 'Now stop your idle chatter and come die at the hands of a vanar old enough to be your mother's mother!'

And without further ado she charged at the rakshasa general.

8

Hanuman watched in amazement as Mandara-devi charged the rakshasa general. She wasted no time with the circling and feinting that usually preceded bouts of single combat, nor did she posture and prance around as was the custom. A glance at the northern end of the valley showed him the reason for her haste: the bear company was slowly crumbling under the sheer weight of numbers of the rakshasas in the forest. And on the high slopes bordering the valley on all sides he glimpsed tiny clues – invisible to anyone on the ground below, vanar or rakshasa – that told him that the concealed vanar and bear regiments were growing restless, wondering why their order to attack had not yet come. If she did not act quickly, it would be too late, for like a thunderbolt unleashed, an army once it began to charge could not be called back.

Again he wished he could simply dive down, like a falcon falling on a snake, and pluck the rakshasa up, crushing him like an egg. Or better yet, expand himself and land with all his might upon the entire rakshasa horde itself, crushing them all like a nest of vile cobras. But as before, Rama's orders compelled him to wait and watch.

Mandara-devi sprang at the rakshasa's face, all four paws extended and teeth bared in as vicious a snarl as she could summon. It was not hard. She had resented the rakshasa accusing her of invading his land, and calling Rama a coward and a craven. As she flew at him, completely confounding any expectation he might have had that she would circle and feint for several moments before locking blows, the element of surprise worked brilliantly in her favour. The rakshasa instinctively covered his face and ducked his head down, leaving his broad, hunched back momentarily exposed. She landed precisely as planned, upon that slab of solid muscle that filled the area between his shoulders and bulged in hard lumps and knobs. At once she tore into the back of his neck with her teeth, ripping so hard into the leathery flesh of his buffalo-like hide that she could feel a tooth crack and break off as it snagged on his collarbone. He bucked exactly as a bull would, and she half leaped and was half thrown off, landing on her hind feet but at an angle that twisted a muscle painfully. She ignored the pain and sprinted forward before he could take her measure, spitting out the mouthful of his fetid flesh and blood, spitting out her split tooth as well.

He roared, furious at the pain as well as the humiliation of losing first blood to her. But even in his anger he was shrewd enough to glean her intention and dropped at once to his front paws, kicking back with his powerful haunches and hind legs in a startling display of reflexes. His hind feet were sheathed in ingeniously designed armoured shoes that expanded their size and added jagged metallic edges and barbs to the kick.

She had intended to sprint around him and then launch herself once again, but his reaction was so quick, his judgement so true, that one of the flailing warboots struck her a glancing blow. It was only a nick really, but the barbed edge was deadly sharp and rusty as iron left on a seashore, and it tore a chunk of flesh from her sensitive behind. She faltered, fell, rolled, and then regained her feet.

To find him turned around, anticipating her, and ready to lash out. He released a second kick, this one with all his strength behind it, a mighty bull-kick even greater than the one the other rakshasa had launched back in the woods. If that had been sufficient to fell a latsyoa tree, then this kick was certainly enough to fell a vanar.

She flipped herself backwards, somersaulting over and over, and over again. The lethal edge of his warboot whistled over her head, close enough for her to feel the wind of its passing. She continued to somersault, the momentum too great to halt at once. The disadvantage of such a move was that it took her away from her combatant, whereas a vanar's advantage lay in leaping on one's opponent and getting close enough to bite and scratch and tear. When she landed on her feet, he was already up on his hind legs again and charging at her. She barely had time to collect her wits and did the only thing she could do: she leaped as high as she could manage.

He was anticipating that as well.

Instead of charging head down at her and blundering past, leaving his flank open for her to slash and tear again, he leaped too. His bulk and weight made it impossible for him to spring as high as she, but his powerful hind legs and forward momentum gave him enough push to reach her lower limbs. He slashed out viciously with a gloved arm bristling with shiny metal blade extensions to his own claws, and with a sensation like an umbilical cord being severed, she felt her tail, the pride of any vanar, cut in two, close to her rear. Another blade slashed her upper thigh, opening a wound that spurted blood. A third caught the edge of her fur on her back and tugged it hard enough to rip a patch of her pelt right off, taking skin and flesh with it as well.

Both vanar and rakshasa fell to the ground, the vanar bleeding and wounded in three separate places and having lost a part of her anatomy as essential to maintaining balance as a foot was to any biped. The rakshasa, on the other hand, had only been wounded the once, though his neck was still bleeding profusely, and, from the angle at which he held his head, hurting badly as well.

She stumbled, trying to stay upright, and fought back the impulse to simply roll over and clutch at her lost organ, for to a vanar, even losing an arm was preferable to losing its tail. She thought absurdly that her grandchildren would no longer be able to play with that slender velvety tail now, or tug on it mischievously, or entwine their own little furry tails with it while sleeping blissfully in her lap.

The thought made her grin savagely, blinking back tears of pain and determination.

Out of the corner of her field of vision, she saw Mainda and Dvivida, seething and barely able to restrain themselves. She snarled briefly in their direction, reminding them of her order not to interfere. Then she looked again at her opponent and showed him her wide-open blood-smeared mouth, for the hole left by the lost tooth was oozing blood and pain as well. She feigned a careless laugh, ignoring the agony and shame of her severed tail.

'Are you ready to yield yet, rakshasa?' she demanded.

He stared at her with cold curiosity. 'Yield? You are brave and foolish, vanar leader. You should have stayed in the forest and died along with the rest of your monkey companions.'

She laughed once more. The sound seemed to startle him. 'Actually,' she said, pausing to spit out a mouthful of blood and a tooth fragment, 'that's what I had in mind for you.'

And with a yell like a monsoon cyclone wind, she launched herself at him again.

Hanuman stared in disbelief and awe as Mandara-devi threw herself yet again at the rakshasa general. This time, she barrelled into him at ground level, the complete opposite of what he had been expecting. Prepared to meet a vanar's leap, he was met instead by a creature one third his height scurrying between his legs. He corrected himself and bent down astonishingly fast for a creature of his size and bulk, but she was faster and quicker, and his blade-tipped paws grasped only fur which came away in his hands. Mandara-devi, racing between the rakshasa's legs, slashed upwards with both paws, talons drawn and held at an angle designed to cause maximum harm. She cut into the general's most tender organs with ferocious strength, then, as he doubled over, partly to attempt to grab her again, and partly to reach for his ruined organs, she caught hold of his armour and pulled herself on to his back, spreading her limbs and clinging on with all her might.

The rakshasa howled with an anguish that was echoed by his entire horde. It was a cry of such typically masculine disbelief and agony that even Hanuman shuddered. For all his earlier bluster – for their words had been heard clearly by the flying vanar – it seemed the general would not be begetting any more offspring, whether on vanars or any other species. Hanuman admired Mandara-devi's audacity and ruthlessness.

Clinging to the enraged, agonised rakshasa's back, Mandara-devi felt a pulse of triumph. She had injured him deeply, if not mortally. He would not recover from that injury, for she had not only ruined his organs of procreation, she had effectively emasculated him. That was one rakshasa who would never boast of raping vanars. As the pain-maddened rakshasa swung round and about, attempting to dislodge her, she used one claw to slash into the tough hide of his back, seeking out his spine. He howled again, fathoming her intent, and threw himself upon his back.

The impact of a hefty rakshasa weighing some three hundred kilos landing upon her with all his force shattered every major bone in Mandara-devi's body and crushed several of her organs as well. Blacking out for a moment, she barely knew when she released her hold on her opponent. She lay on her back on the gravelly ground as the rakshasa general rose again and took a brief moment to bend over and peer down at his own severed and damaged organs, whimpering once in shock.

Lying there, the sun felt warm and comforting upon her face

and body. She had no sensation from the waist down, which was a good thing, for she was certain that her legs were horribly crushed and she would never walk again, not with all the healing in the world. She enjoyed that brief moment of respite, the sun a luxury to one who had spent almost her entire life in the silver mines of her land, taught from birth to both fear and respect that blazing orb that rode the skies by day and was swallowed by the land and the oceans by night. Rama had said there was no truth in the myth that exposure to the sun would kill her or her Mandaras, and she believed him, but now it hardly mattered. Henceforth, legend would forever record that she had exposed herself to the sun and had died that very day. For she knew that this was to be the day of her death.

As the rakshasa general roared again, unable to believe how irrevocably she had damaged him, she sensed Mainda and Dvivida bounding towards her. They knew she was mortally injured and barely able to lift a paw, let alone defend herself, but she croaked out an admonishment to them. 'No!' she said as sternly as she could manage, spitting up blood and fluids, for her ribcage was a tangled thicket of splintered bones and mashed lungs. 'Remember why . . . Finish it. *For Rama.*'

Hanuman watched with unspeakable sorrow as Mandara-devi used her rapidly ebbing strength not to curse her fate or beg for help, but to order her lieutenants to fulfil Rama's orders. After all, that was why she had sacrificed her life so bravely this morning, to ensure that Rama's orders were carried out to the letter. He watched as the two burly vanars chittered with dismay at one another, while the rakshasa general regained his senses and stumbled back to where his opponent lay dying, grimacing and grunting at the agony of his ruined manhood. Then the bull-rakshasa turned, and aimed a kick with his hind legs directly at his fallen opponent. From the anger on his bullish features, it could be seen that he intended to finish her

off with this kick. Hanuman almost wished he could avert his
eyes, but still he watched as the shockingly brief combat reached
its finale: for even they who only watched served Rama.

Mandara-devi waited until the rakshasa had turned his back
upon her completely and was engrossed in lining himself up for
the death-dealing kick. She had known he would use his hind
legs to strike at her, for as a bull-rakshasa crossbreed, that was
what came most naturally to him. He had no reason to fear
her; she was shattered and broken and lying in her own fetid
fluids and solids, with blood oozing out from a dozen different
places and every orifice as well.

What he did not know was that both her upper limbs were
still intact, for the brunt of his weight had landed on her torso
and lower limbs.

When the jagged, warbooted hoof flew towards her, she
used the last of her strength, pure will really, to grasp it and
swing herself up. Her arms, still functional, served to yank her
up his leg, dragging the rest of her body behind her, and all
the way to his exposed throat. It took an extraordinary amount
of skill and strength, but she had nothing to lose now, and she
accomplished it despite the screaming agony of her ruined
body. And then she was at his neck, clinging on like a leech
in water.

With one ferocious movement, she tore out his throat, ripping
open the major blood vessels. His life blood splashed out in a
torrent, splattering and blinding her. Her last glimpse was of
his stunned face, unable to believe the death she had brought
him to; she, a mere vanar, and a female at that.

Then she fell back and the ground claimed her. She had a
moment of perfect bliss, lying in the sunlight, recalling the
faces of her family, her children, their children, all those she
loved and had lived for and fought for, and died for now,
today, in this nameless valley in a foreign land. The sunlight

felt wonderful on her upturned face, and her lips curled in a tranquil smile.

Hanuman shut his eyes briefly as Mandara-devi died, a smile upon her blood-spattered face. Even with his eyes closed, he could hear the death throes of the rakshasa general, could hear the shock and disbelief in the Lankan's voice as he bled out the last of his life.

When he opened his eyes again, the two Mandara lieutenants, Mainda and Dvivida, were taunting the rakshasa horde on the hillside. The assembled troops, shocked at the death of their leader, had fallen silent in the last few moments of the fight. The combat itself had lasted barely a twitch of the sun's passing, so sudden, brutal and ferocious had Mandara-devi's attack been. Now, as the reality of their general's loss crept into their dense skulls, the rakshasas finally succumbed to the frustration and battle lust that had been consuming them all this while. With their general no longer there to control them, they rose as one and stormed down the hillside, roaring and waving their weapons, their order to remain at bay forgotten with the death of their leader.

With whoops of exultation, Mainda and Dvivida raced before them, leading them across the grassy outskirts, then into the forest itself. The kumbha lieutenants snapped their lashes and attempted unsuccessfuly to stem their advance, as the rakshasa horde streamed after the vanars into the forest.

Moments after the rakshasas vanished into the dim, shaded forest, the ululating call for the next phase carried across the valley. And not long after, Hanuman watched as the bulk of the bear and vanar contingents appeared on the rim of the valley on all sides, then poured down into the forest, to finish the battle whose success Mandara-devi had given her own life to ensure.

9

Rama and Lakshman watched from a rocky atoll on the slope of Mount Trikuta. One of the highest peaks on the northern side of the island-kingdom, it was almost the same height as Mount Suvela, only a short distance away. Suvela's view was blocked by the hilly ranges that undulated like ocean waves, whereas the gradual incline of Trikuta's northern face led directly down to the edge of the palisade cliffs – bordered now by the fortress wall raised by Ravana's sorcery – affording them a clear view of the entire lie of the land south of this northern tip.

They had stationed themselves here these past hour-watches, waiting patiently for the enemy to make the first move. In that time, Surya-deva had ridden his gleaming chariot up to a sharply diagonal angle in the eastern sky, and the sunlight now shone down on them, its touch warm and bracing. The cool sea breeze that continued to blow sporadically, tinged with the salty odour of the ocean, did not allow them to break out in perspiration. Rama shifted his quiver a little, then glanced at Lakshman.

'Should we?' Lakshman asked.

'No,' Rama replied. 'We wait.'

Lakshman shrugged. They had had this conversation twice already since stationing themselves here. Lakshman had favoured going to the rampart walls and provoking the rakshasas that were visible there, milling about in the shade of the high forti-fication. If the plan was for the rakshasas to attempt to attack their forces from behind, pressing them back against the armies streaming out of the Lankan capital, then they ought to have attacked long before now. Rama had already received word from the angadiyas that all the other contingents had engaged the enemy on their various fronts, and he expected Hanuman to bring word of the outcome of those battles very shortly. If these enemy forces intended to do as he expected them to, then they should have moved long before now, striking Rama's forces from behind while they were in the thick of battle. But close to two hour-watches had passed, and still they lurked in the shade of the rampart walls.

Rama insisted that they wait. And so they remained here, watching from this vantage point, concealed behind this rock, baking under the sun. Waiting was not one of Lakshman's strong points. After several moments more had passed, he shifted his bow and sword restlessly, checked his quiver for the umpteenth time, then finally could stand it no more and turned to brace his back against the rock, looking directly at Rama.

'The bears as well as the Jatarupas must be in excruciating discomfort, Rama. What good is our plan if our army is in no position to fight when the time comes? I say we go down now and roust out those beasts and lure them out into the open.'

Rama kept his eyes fixed on the distant rampart walls, while replying patiently to Lakshman. 'If we do that, and they suspect something amiss, they may not come out at all. In which case, the bears and vanars who have endured this long wait already under such suffocating circumstances will have to suffer far longer a wait, or they will have to leave their hiding places and the entire plan will be exposed.'

'First of all, Rama, why would they suspect anything? They are rakshasas – some kind of new breed, no doubt, but still great big hulking idiots with bulging muscles instead of brains. I think they would simply react to the sight of us and follow us into the open. Secondly, even if the plan is exposed, we shall come up with another one.'

Rama shook his head once, tersely. 'There will be no time

for second plans. Once Ravana realises how we have made him dance this morning, he will no longer offer us the iron fist in a velvet glove. He will unleash all his dogs of war, and when that happens, it will be too late for strategy or battle tactics. Too late for shima, or war shastras.' He paused. 'And I think you underestimate not only those creatures, but rakshasas in general. They are not lacking in intelligence; it is only that they have been culturally raised to favour the more physical and violent arts rather than the poetic and philosophical ones. Given time, opportunity, and a leader like Vibhisena, I have no doubt that they will rival even our Arya nations in the proficiency and profligacy of their arts and culture.'

Lakshman snorted in amusement. 'I can't believe we're sitting here debating the rakshasa capacity for art and culture! Rama, this is war pure and simple. We should be fighting, not talking!'

'Not talking is what leads to fighting, my brother,' Rama said calmly. 'But fret not. I think you will have your wish very shortly. I believe the fighting part of the war is about to begin, for us at least.'

And he pointed with his chin.

Lakshman swung around, clapped his palm to the rock – the shaded part, for the exposed part was already burning hot – and his lips cracked in a rare smile. 'Ah, at last. A time to slay rakshasas.'

'And be slain by them,' Rama added philosophically.

They watched as the ground below finally began displaying signs of activity.

In the shadowy depths of his hiding place, Prince Angad of Kiskindha watched as the rakshasas finally arrived at some kind of decision and began emerging into the sunlit open ground. He had been sitting here waiting so long that his backside had turned numb. He could not understand why the rakshasas had hesitated this long before making their move. His angadiyas, the agile younguns he had trained to courier messages to and fro, had brought word of fighting on all the other three main fronts – north, east and west. He had heard of his father's valiant prowess in battle in the face of incredible odds, of Mandara-devi's challenging a rakshasa champion to single combat, of the brutal battle unfolding on the western front where General Susena, Pramathi, Praghasa and the twins had met stiff resistance but were fighting furiously still. Yet he and his contingent here – mainly Jatarupas, with a small company of his own hand-picked faithfuls and the bears – had had to wait hours as the morning wore on.

He peered over the edge of his hiding place and saw that the ground below was indeed seething with the enemy. After coming up through the secret tunnels that opened in the shadowy nooks and crannies of the rampart walls, the rakshasas had not made a move all morning. Now they emerged into the sunlight, moving in eerie silence on their hind legs. They seemed to be some breed of lizard-crossed rakshasa, for their hides were yellowish-brown in colouring with a mottled dark stain pattern, their rear ends adorned with long, thick tails that were an exten-sion of their torso and comparable to those of a gharial or the river crocodile that vanars feared and hated so much. They seemed able to walk upon all fours, or only on their hind legs, but their front limbs were much smaller than the rear ones, and if not for the extruding talons would have seemed near useless to an enemy. Their heads were also quite similar to the reptilian species, with browless bright yellow nictitating eyes with lids that opened and closed sideways, set on either side of their narrow tapering heads. From time to time, some of them issued clicking sounds that he had first mistaken for exclamatory gestures, but now understood were in fact commands and communications, and that this odd ticking-clicking sound was their form of speech.

As far as he could tell, they had no leaders as such, for all moved at the same pace, exactly as land lizards would, but with a springy step that suggested the ability to move with great speed when required. Lizard-like they might be, but not the slow, waterbound crocodilian type; these were land-lizard creatures, able to dart and swoop at will to catch their prey. They moved forward en masse now, leaving the shadowy recesses of the rampart walls to cover the vast stretch of ground leading to the foothills of Mount Trikuta. This entire part of the former plateau had been eroded by the killing stones, grass and trees and the land itself uprooted and re-formed overnight by Ravana's sorcery. Now it was a large barren plain, perhaps a yojana wide at this point, the tapering tip of the northern end of Lanka. It stretched for about half that distance southwards, till it reached the grassy foothills. Angad's sharp eyes made out the large rock atoll on the northern face of Mount Trikuta. He knew that that was where Rama and Lakshman would have stationed themselves. It was too far to see them clearly, but he took comfort simply in knowing they were there, watching the battle that was about to unfold, and would join in themselves shortly. It gave him great pride to fight under Rama's command, perhaps even along-side Rama himself, if the devas willed it.

He hissed at the nearest angadiya, a bright-eyed little female with a mischievous smile on her young snouted face, and used the system of paw gestures he had devised to convey communi-cations during such times, when silence was a necessity. She nodded understanding and scampered away. She would carry his order to the lieutenants Rsabha, Gavaksa, Gaja and Gavya. As for the bears, well, with Lord Jambavan himself leading that contingent, he had no reason to worry.

As he watched from his vantage point, the lizard-like rakshasas seeped out from the shadow of the ramparts like an endless flood unleashed upon the large barren field. Thousands upon thousands . . . nay, tens of thousands upon tens of thousands . . . And still they came. It seemed there was no end to their numbers. For a heart-stopping instant he wondered if perhaps Ravana had been able to summon up infinite numbers of these strange, oddly formed warriors. How would they fight them then? It was true that Rama's sena was enormous in its multitudes, even after the losses sustained during the bridge-building, the tsunami, and the night of the killing stones, and far outnumbered Lanka's armies as described by Vibhisena. But Ravana's brother, on hearing of these yellow-hide lizard beings, had admitted that these were something entirely new, no doubt hatched by Ravana in the subterranean volcanic caverns where he worked his vile Asura maya in secret. What if Ravana had been able to summon up the multitudes of the hell realms, as he had done once before, and was bringing up all the Asuras in the three underworlds again! Both Rama and Vibhisena had insisted that such a thing was impossible, because the brahm-astra unleashed at Mithila had rendered it so, but to a vanar prince visiting this strange mythical land of demons, anything seemed possible.

Then the last of the yellow beings emerged, and he breathed a small sigh of relief. Only a small one, for the sheer size of the army gathered below was awe-inspiring. He estimated there were close to a hundred thousand of the odd beings gathered below. A lakh of rakshasas! Even given the vast numbers of the contingent he led, and the numbers of the bear warriors as well, that was still enough to instil fear and doubt in him. Then he reminded himself once more of Hanuman's words: 'Rama is the source of all strength. He is the key to unlock your own inner power. Believe in him completely, without question, and you believe in yourself. For he is within you, around you, and he is yourself in truth as well. Give your faith to Rama, and you shall not want for anything. Jai Sri Rama!'

And so, hefting his weapon, he rose from his hiding place, drew himself up to his full height, showing himself, and cried with all his strength: 'Jai Sri Rama!'

And an army of vanars echoed: 'JAI SRI RAMA!'

It had begun.

*   *   *

Rama and Lakshman were too far away to see individual details clearly, but the day was bright and the view excellent, and they did not have to be falcons to see the enormous numbers of the enemy streaming out from beneath the rampart walls like a pot of water spilled across the floor of a hut on washing day. Where there had been only a great expanse of empty barren ground, a dirt field some nine miles long and four miles wide, bordering the underhills that led gradually up in steps to this northern face of Mount Trikuta, there now stood a vast army of the strangest breed of rakshasas they had ever encountered.

Even at this distance they could tell from the way the enemy moved and held themselves that they were like no rakshasas they had ever seen. Earlier, angadiyas had brought reports of more typical rakshasas, horned and tusked beasts that were much like the rakshasas Rama had been expecting to fight today. But those initial sightings had been followed by curious dispatches reporting that the rakshasas had withdrawn. Then there had been a gap of half an hour-watch, during which time Rama had waited with ever-growing anxiety, fearing that their plan had somehow misfired and that Ravana had decided to concentrate all his forces upon the main vanguard to the south, while he and the substantial part of the bear contingent as well as an entire army of vanars waited here. But now that the rakshasas were out in the open, easily discerned, he saw that they were certainly not the kind that had been glimpsed earlier by his scouts. These were a different breed altogether.

They looked almost like great . . . lizard men, standing on their hind legs and communicating with a peculiar clicking speech that carried as far as the atoll on this placid morning. It was a relief when they finally ceased emerging and the brothers could glimpse the end of their number leaving the confines of the rampart. Even a quick guess suggested no number less than a lakh, which was formidable enough. But what was more unpredictable was the nature of these beasts. How would they fight? How could they be defeated? What were their vulnerable points? Rama sighed inwardly, thinking that it would have been good to know all these things beforehand. Not knowing them, he had only one choice: to learn them firsthand, the hard way. Or rather, for his troops to learn them firsthand, risking their own valiant lives to glean this vital knowledge.

His heart went out to those vanars and bears who would brave the first encounter with these new-breed rakshasas.

He watched as the vanar contingent led by Prince Angad rose from their hiding places and issued the agreed signal for the start of the battle. Rama had not ordered them to speak those words; that had been entirely the army's prerogative, and it cut deeply into his heart, reminding him that all that transpired here today, upon this field and across Lanka, all these many, many deaths, was on account of him, and of Sita. What was a mortal to feel, knowing that millions fought and died today to reunite him with his beloved? What was a mortal to do when faced with such epic loyalty and fealty in the face of such incredible odds? What could a mortal do, except add his own weapons and life to the count, and fight alongside the brave warriors who risked all on his account?

He exchanged a glance with Lakshman, whose objections and grumbling had, as ever, died away the instant threat showed itself, and saw that his brother shared his sentiments entirely. They nodded, agreeing silently, and started down the slope, to enter a battle on which not only their own lives but the lives of many others would depend.

10

_____

As Rama and Lakshman sprinted down the long sloping northern face of Mount Trikuta, they were afforded a clear view of the battlefield. The small dense patches of scrub that dotted the low foothills between them and the vast barren plain were not high enough to obstruct their view, nor were the foothills themselves more than gently rolling mounds, the tallest barely a hundred yards in stature. They watched as the lizard rakshasas gathered on the plain below turned en masse, staring up at the looming rampart walls from whose shadows they had only just emerged.

For it was atop those very rampart walls that Prince Angad and his contingent were stationed. The idea had been hatched by Rama during the long, lonely hours he had spent stuck up there himself. The stone-block walls were easy enough for vanars to climb quickly, and even allowed them to carry up a sufficient store of suitable weapons.

Running downhill at the steady, relentless pace that he and Lakshman could maintain for days on end if required, he watched as the vanars whose little heads broke the regularity of the stone ramparts hefted the stones of varying sizes that they had carried up to the top during the post-dawn hours after Rama outlined his plan. There had not been time enough to amass a great store of stone missiles, nor to carry up any truly large ones that would be capable of inflicting great damage. But he had counted on the height of the ramparts themselves, as well as the natural lethal aim of the vanars, to be sufficient for this phase of the attack.

Unable to make out individual vanars, he watched as a multitude of little furry paws – reduced by distance and their semi-concealment atop the ramparts – raised their fists, gripping stones, and awaited their leader's order to start the attack.

'Jai Sri Rama!' Angad roared, and launched the first missile. He had picked out a brute below clicking furiously, his tongue flickering in and out of his elongated mouth, his yellow-hide pattern distinctively marked with a purplish patch on top of his flattened reptilian head. Angad flung his stone with all his strength, and had the satisfaction of seeing it strike the chosen rakshasa on the exact spot he had aimed for – the flat part of the head between the eyes. From long experience with the large lizards that lived in some climes, as well as with the vanar's eternal enemy, snakes, he had chosen that spot as being the most effective. He was proved right: the lizard-rakshasa staggered, his tail, which he had been carrying raised a foot above the ground, flopped down, and he keeled back, tipping over to fall senseless.

Thousands of other rocks and stones, flung by the other vanars atop the ramparts, flew down. Most, if not all, were aimed just as accurately as Angad's, and struck their mark. The vanar prince issued a whooping cry of triumph as thousands of lizard-rakshasas reeled and fell and staggered to crash into their comrades. The clicking sounds from the field below increased to a cacophony, as the beasts milled about in confusion, confronted by this unexpected assault. Ravana had sent these beings through the subterranean tunnels to outflank Rama and his armies. The last thing they would be expecting was to be outflanked themselves. And what delicious irony: to be using the very ramparts raised by their master to attack his forces!

For the next several moments Angad gave himself over to

aiming, throwing and cheering his own as well as his fellow vanars' successes. Thousands of the yellow beasts below were fallen on the field. He grinned, *cheeka*-ing with the enthusiasm of a youngun himself. At this rate they would win this battle easily enough. There would not even be any need to call on the rest of the vanar contingent, let alone the bears.

Then he was out of missiles, and had no choice but to fling down verbal insults and rude noises. Soon the flurry of flung stones ceased all along the ramparts. For several moments, the huge horde of lizard-rakshasas continued to mill about on the field below. Angad frowned as he estimated that at least two in ten had been downed by the attack. That was not bad at all, for vanars flinging stones.

Then his heart skipped a beat.

The fallen lizard-rakshasas were rising up again. The one he had struck down was among the first to regain its feet, helped by its thick, ungainly tail. It stood upright again, clicking furiously to its comrades, then raised its menacing flat head to stare up directly at the place where the missile had come from: looking right into Angad's eyes. At sight of him, its nictitating eyelids closed and opened several times, that forked tongue flickering in and out its large flat mouth in evident anger.

Then it leaped.

Angad had no reason to expect the fluid, springing jump which the lizard beast executed. Having never seen this species before, nor anything like it, he stared in stunned astonishment as the creature made a jump from a standing start that carried it all the way to the spear-like extensions that grew out of the lower part of the rampart walls, on which so many unfortunate vanars and bears had died the night before. Landing on the shaft of one of these extensions, the creature paused, clicking again, then launched itself a second time. This second leap carried it, incredibly, all the way to the top of the rampart wall itself. Angad was treated to a glimpse of a dark brownish-purplish underbody, with taloned feet outstretched and looking as deadly as any river crocodile's, then the beast had passed *over* his head, and landed behind him.

He turned to see the rakshasa facing him, its long tongue flickering in and out of its reptilian mouth. Then without any further warning, it threw itself at him. Along the rampart walls, he heard the sound of thousands of its comrades leaping up to attack his vanars.

Rama watched in grim dismay as the lizard-like rakshasas leaped up to the walls, turning the ambush into a counterattack. Without further ado, he shouted a wordless instruction to the nearest angadiya – several of the little couriers were within earshot of him at all times. The order was simple enough: Start the bear attack.

As he reached the bottom of Mount Trikuta and the start of the first foothill, his view of the battlefield was obstructed briefly. For the next few moments, as he sprinted up this rise, he would not be able to see how the battle fared. He did not need to see it, though: brave as Angad's warriors might be, they were no match for those leaping lizard beasts. He had no illusions about who would emerge the victor in the struggle that had just begun.

He ran grimly on, and hoped that the bears would fare better than the first vanar attack.

Angad dodged the first leap of the lizard-rakshasa by cartwheeling sideways on the crenellations of the rampart wall. He had an impression of a deadly sharp set of talons blurring through the space where his belly had been just a fraction of an instant before, then he was out of harm's way. He landed agilely on his hind legs, tail dangling out over the edge of the drop. Had he been facing any other creature, the chances were that his sudden sideways move would have caused his attacker to leap right over the edge, falling back down where it had come from. But the lizard-rakshasa was still on the rampart wall, eyes glowing bright greenish-yellow now and clicking angrily. Its tail swished to and fro sideways, and he saw that the appendage was not only strong enough to rest its entire body weight upon – unlike vanar tails – but also thick enough to deliver a damaging blow in a fight. The creature advanced towards him, and he feinted left, then right, seeking to dodge it. But it watched his every move so closely, he knew that it would not be fooled that easily. Like a snake with its beaded eyes fixed on its enemy, it was preternaturally able to anticipate anything he did next.

He heard and scented and sensed from the periphery of his vision that his vanar troopers were not faring half as well as he was against their own lizard-rakshasa foes. He could tell from the screams alone that they were being slaughtered by the dozens. He had been shocked to see how powerfully these large beasts could leap, and how high and fast. Clearly he was dealing with a foe that should not be underestimated. But he was still alive at least. And while he lived, he could find a way to turn the tables yet again.

Right now, though, as he feinted and attempted to dodge the beast on the rampart, staying alive was all he could manage. If those long talons so much as touched his fur, he had no doubt that the wounds they would inflict would be lethal. Angad had suffered scratches and bruises galore, but he had not yet had the misfortune of actually being gashed by such talons, and he had no desire to learn what it might feel like to have one's skin parted and flesh destroyed by them. The only way to survive right now was to not let the creature touch him. And that was proving easier thought than done.

He scampered quickly in one direction, swung around in a half-circle, ran that same way again, then cut diagonally across the top of the rampart wall. The creature moved with him with blurring speed, and for a second he thought it would intersect his path and he would learn what it would feel like to have those talons in his body.

At the very last instant, he threw himself sideways in the opposite direction of where his momentum was taking him, feeling his muscles strain at the unnatural movement, feeling his spine contort and bend to snapping point, and he heard the creature click furiously as it felt him moving away from its lethal talons. Something sliced through the fur on his scalp and then he was rolling on the hard stone top of the rampart, then scampering and then leaping to land atop the crenellations yet again, his back to the ground below. He saw the creature turn and seek him out, finding him almost at once, and open its mouth to issue a horrifying sound that was part clicking and part hissing, like nothing he had ever heard before in nature. At the same time, it raised its tail and released an odour of such pungent strength that he almost gagged. The stench of hate and anger was unmistakable; he had smelled odours like that on tigers when their prey escaped them.

He heard the ululating call of vanars miles away, the clarion call for the second phase of the battle as prearranged by Rama. And suddenly he knew that he could not win this bout of single combat, that as much as his princely ego demanded he stay and fight to the bitter end, his dharma lay in surviving to lead his vanars into the battle that still lay ahead. There was a great deal more work to be done and he was needed there. Nothing would be served by his dying violently atop this rampart wall here and now.

With a *cheeka* and an ululating call of his own, summoning the surviving vanars to follow him, he turned tail and ran as fast as his lithe legs would carry him, down the length of the rampart, racing in a line that would carry him around and beyond the army of lizard-rakshasas gathered in the field below. He did not need to wait to see if his vanars followed, for he could hear their answering cries already. But behind him, outraged at being deprived of its easy prey, he heard too the same clicking-hissing sound of the creature that had almost ended his life, protesting. He did not know if it would pursue him, and if it did, whether it could run fast enough to catch him, and he did not wait to see. He simply ran pell-mell, heading for the far side of the open field, to where the next part of the battle was already unfolding.

They came over the hillock at a steady run, in time to see the vanars on the ramparts – those who had survived – racing south-wards along the wall. Rama was relieved, because there was no point in sacrificing those vanars. They had done their job already by forcing the enemy horde to turn around, breeding the first part of the confusion necessary for the successful completion of his plan.

Even so, he could see that the lizard beasts were wreaking havoc. The vanars on the ramparts had been almost completely massacred, and a pitifully small number were escaping. He did not allow himself to dwell on that, just as he had not allowed himself to be dismayed by the initial reports from the angadiyas of the carnage in the canyon, the terrible losses in the eastern army and reports of strange developments by the gates of Lanka. The war would be long and hard, he had no illusions about that, but the only way to win it was to fight it one blow at a time, one fight, one battle . . .

As he and Lakshman started down the hillock, he saw the scrubland ahead suddenly come alive with vanars, as the main force of the northern army – so designated by him to avoid confusion – showed themselves.

11

Angad finally judged it safe to glance back, and was relieved to find that the lizard beast had not given pursuit. He did not know whether the creature could have caught him – those two leaps up the rampart had been astonishing, more than most vanars could ever accomplish, and he still feared the lash of that thick scaly tail. But the rampart behind him was empty except for other scurrying vanars who raced up to him and gathered around, looking back as well as down. He was angered at how few had survived – it made him want to leap back into the fray and make the enemy pay the price for taking so many vanar lives. But a commotion from the army of lizard rakshasas on the field below helped distract him from thoughts of revenge.

The lizard beasts were turning once more to face southwards, in the direction they had been heading until Angad and his distractors had turned them around. Clicking frenetically to one another – he guessed that they communicated and passed on messages and orders in this fashion, as well as expressing their emotions, if they had any – they summoned back those of their number that had leaped up to the battlements. These beasts, a tiny fraction of the larger force, leaped down to the ground again, joining their fellow reptilians as they faced the new threat.

Angad raised his vision to view the threat they had identified. Beyond the dense expanse of the lizard army, the scrubland that skirted the foothills ahead had come alive with furry vanar shapes. The scrubby plants and bushes, while too small to conceal any larger creatures, were sufficient to hide vanars, who could double up and squat easily for hours on end. Now, as they received the order, they revealed themselves. From every tiny bush, bit of scrub, rock and depression, vanars emerged into the open. They were Jatarupas all, smaller in stature than most other vanars, and with the distinctive colouring to their head-fur, which they tinted with vegetable dyes to an assortment of colours and shades associated with their tribe, hierarchy, sex, in a complex, arcane system of colour-coding that even Angad could not claim to understand completely. The few trees that dotted the area shook violently as literally dozens of Jatarupas detached themselves from each one and bounced down to the ground. Grinning with their customary devil-may-care attitude, a stark contrast to the Kiskindha vanars' more steadfast attitude, or the Mandaras' burly laconicism, they appeared to be young mischief-makers out for a jaunt rather than a small army of vanar warriors. Yet their numbers left no room for doubt on that front: there were almost twice as many Jatarupas now revealed on the field as lizard rakshasas, forming the largest vanar army in Rama's entire force.

The lizard beings seemed far from dismayed at the appearance of this new threat. If anything, they seemed agitated but enthusiastic. Angad eyed them doubtfully as they milled about in apparent confusion – he was already able to sense that what seemed like confusion was in fact an esoteric pattern of communication and tactical rearrangement that could only be understood in their own terms. It was useless to attempt to fathom their actions, noises or gestures by comparison with those of vanars, mortals or even other rakshasa species. These were something quite different altogether, and he knew that Rama's warriors would have to understand their fighting methods quickly in order to gain the advantage in this battle. Glancing at the sheer weight-and-height disparity, and already aware of the agility, speed and shrewdness of the lizards, he did not feel very confident that the short, overly furred Jatarupas would be able to stand up against them, despite their superior numbers.

But Rama had another ace up his sleeve. A very devious and shrewd gamble that, if it came off, might turn the day yet.

Rama came over the last foothill and slowed. He and Lakshman were now overlooking the field of battle itself. Only a few hundred yards before and below the peak of the foothill on which they stood was the scrubland where the Jatarupas had now revealed themselves in full force. Farther ahead, on the barren land skirted by the curving crescent of the rampart walls that bounded the plateau, were the lizard-like rakshasas. The beasts had turned back to face the vanar army, and if he understood even a little about their stances and odd communication, they would attack soon. It was imperative to his plan that they do so, rather than wait for the vanars to come at them.

For only then could the bears emerge from their place of concealment and join the fray. And from the looks of it, the bears would be essential to winning this battle.

But long, precious moments passed and still the lizard creatures remained as they were, milling about in an odd shambling pattern, as if playing out some peculiar fireside ritual dance, moving this way and that endlessly, issuing those vexing clicking sounds all the while. It sounded like a plague of crickets!

He issued word through more angadiyas for the vanars to do as planned in such a circumstance.

As he watched, a few moments later, the Jatarupas complied.

Calling out in their cheerful childlike voices, they began rolling and tumbling to and fro, performing elaborate somersaults, then climbing atop one another's shoulders and throwing each other high in the air, to be caught by other groups then passed on yet again, until in a moment the air was filled with flying, tumbling, somersaulting, cartwheeling vanars with fur tinged all hues and colours. A fantastic carnival of acrobatic performers, and a sight that would make anyone, adult or child, clap their hands with glee and cheer happily. But there was no one to cheer or clap here. Only a horde of strange rakshasa enemies who stared with their nictitating bright yellow eyes in apparent fascination at this exotic display of acrobatic talent.

Rama noted that the clicking had ceased.

A moment later, he noticed several of the lizard beings moving forward, shambling across the dust of the open field, dragging their tails behind them like tired crocodiles emerging from a river. More and more of their number began moving as well, until soon enough the entire army was advancing, not in a head-long charge as rakshasas were wont to do in a battle, but in the deceptively slow, sluggish fashion of cold-blooded reptiles. He was not fooled by their apparent sluggishness, for he had seen how they leaped to the ramparts to deal with Angad and his small force. He hoped the Jatarupas had all been able to see that and would be sensible enough not to underestimate the enemy. From what he knew of them, the jolly, colourful vanars were not foolish at all, but they did have a tendency to over-confidence that was sometimes their undoing.

He watched as the Jatarupas continued their mad antics even as the enemy host approached in their odd, shambling fashion. The distance between the two forces closed steadily – a hundred yards now, then seventy, fifty, thirty . . . and now the first lizard beasts were barely twenty yards from the vanar army. He tried to estimate how much open field the lizards had left behind them.

'Not more than a mile,' Lakshman said grimly, voicing his own concern.

That was not enough. He needed the lizard beasts to clear at least three miles of open field, or he could not deploy the bear army. *Be patient just a little while longer*, he said silently to Jambavan. He wished he could send a spoken message via the angadiyas as he did when communicating with the vanar forces. But as soon as the thought left his mind, he felt a tingling sensation, as if the bear lord heard him and understood, and had sent back a gruff assurance.

Then he waited for the battle to begin.

Angad watched as the lizard beasts approached within striking distance of the Jatarupa army. Even now the playful vanars continued their mad antics, leaping and whooping and dancing like a tribe drunk on honey wine at moon-feast time. He shook his head, vexed. Could they not see that these beasts were not like regular rakshasas? Had they not glimpsed how fast they leaped and how high? He wished now that he had elected to lead the Jatarupas instead of manning the much smaller force on the rampart walls. Contrary to expectations, it had transpired that the larger force was facing the greater danger.

But it was too late to change the plan. All he could hope was that Rama's war strategy was astute enough to anticipate and adjust to all possibilities. And that the Jatarupas were able to stand up to this new breed of rakshasa better than his warriors had.

Too far away to participate actively in the battle, too far even to fire arrows that would be better used at closer range, Rama and Lakshman prepared to watch as the battle began.

The lizard beasts made the first move. One moment they were all still as stone statues, even their clicking communication fallen completely silent, as they stared ahead with unblinking yellow eyes, glaring with serpentine coldness at their enemy. Then, abruptly, without any warning or sign, they attacked. Not by running forward, or by charging in lines as any normal rakshasa horde would do, but by leaping high into the air, with such suddenness and force that it seemed as if they all launched themselves at once. Perhaps they had indeed done that, their uncanny clicking communication enabling them to maintain individual independence in movement and action while uniting them all mentally. One moment the field before the Jatarupa army was filled with three-yard-tall lizard creatures. The next instant it was the air above that same field that was filled with the creatures, all leaping with ferocious energy and momentum, all but flying through the air. That first launch carried them some fifteen or twenty yards up, and with enough force to propel them forward across the intervening distance between the armies.

In the late morning sunlight, their talons and fangs gleamed and glistened brightly.

Like a rainfall of snakes they landed on their vanar foe, rending and tearing, lashing and biting down. They moved like acrobats themselves, not with the tumbling grace of the Jatarupas, but with manic intensity. Their movement seemed clumsy when seen individually, but taken as a whole group it was undeniably concerted and coordinated with perfect precision. No doubt about it, these were creatures with a communication system so flawless, they did not need to line up and march or attack in rank and file; transcending those trivial disciplines altogether, they danced a deadly dance together in battle.

Both Angad from the high ramparts and Rama and Lakshman from the overlooking hillock watched with horror as the lizard rakshasas fell upon the vanars like no army they had ever seen before.

The Jatarupas were no fools. Their acrobatic antics had served a definite purpose: they had glimpsed the enemy's style of attack and had sought to confuse and diffuse it by leaping and tumbling. In this manner they hoped to dodge the beasts while flying at them themselves.

But the lizards' uncanny ability to coordinate with one another rendered this useless. Rama watched as vanars flew through the air, tumbling in trajectories that should have been impossible to predict or intersect. And yet they *were* intersected, by lizards that met them in mid-air and slashed them viciously, laying open their flesh, severing limbs, decapitating. And even before the great beasts landed again, only to leap once more with greater force, they were clicking to one another, communicating other vanar movements, and leaping precisely to intercept those vanars and cut them down with ruthless efficiency in mid-air. So huge was the army of lizards and so widespread that the vast majority had to leap several times before engaging with the enemy. They kept springing forward, tens of yards at one jump, and in mere moments the entire scrubland was awash with battling vanars and lizards, a bizarre dancing battle fought almost entirely in mid-air. For the Jatarupas could not alter their natural fighting style so quickly, and continued to leap and cavort and frolic in their acrobatic way even as they were being massacred by this strange new foe.

The vanars did fight back. Angad saw several of them inflict slashing wounds and lay open the soft underbellies of the lizard creatures. But the lizards went on to leap again, undaunted by the greenish-yellow ichor oozing from these cuts and slashes, while the vanars mostly fell dead on the spot or with mortal injuries.

Simply put, the Jatarupas, with their exotic fighting method, had met a foe whose method not only matched theirs but exceeded it. To put it bluntly, and bloodily, they had been outmatched.

And that could only mean one thing, Rama thought with the cold clarity that came to him in such moments of crisis during a battle: the enemy had anticipated his move and outwitted him. That was the danger of shima: in letting the foe know your plans, you also risked his being able to unleash new alternative counterplans of his own. Ravana had not succeeded in his attempt to outflank Rama's armies and catch them in a hand-clapping action. Rama had rendered that impossible by splitting his army into separate forces and engaging the enemy on four different fronts, each on a ground of his own choosing and his own terms. But Ravana had outmanoeuvred him by pulling back the ordinary rakshasa regulars Rama had expected to attack from this northern rear position, and deploying these strange new creatures instead.

Rama watched as his army of brave, eccentric Jatarupas was smashed to smithereens by the lizard force.

12

Angad howled with anguish as thousands upon thousands of Jatarupa vanars were cut to shreds by the leaping rakshasa army. Now the entire lizard force had covered the scrubland, and the air and ground were thick with flying bodies. He could hardly bear to watch as vanars were cut to ribbon by multiple lizards at once, body parts flung to the winds. Blood and gore filled the air like the macabre festival of colours celebrated in one of the mortal ritual holidays he had once witnessed. Instead of the powdered rang and water that the mortals threw to celebrate the colours of the coming spring and the harvest being seeded, it was vanar blood and gristle that flew through the air. The air was so densely reddened that he wondered how the warriors of both sides could even see each other. It was as if a cloud of red mist had fallen upon the battlefield, engulfing both forces.

Still, he could see, the Jatarupas were not yielding quarter. They stood their ground, leaping and calling out and chittering to the last, slashing and causing as much damage as they could inflict upon the enemy. Here and there a few lizards even fell, cut open and killed by the multitude of wounds they had received from several vanars leaping upon them at the same time. In this fashion, the battle, uneven and disproportionate as it was, did continue awhile, with perhaps five or seven vanars dying for every mortally wounded or killed lizard. But the count was increasing so rapidly that were this fray to last even a single day, every last Jatarupa on the field would be dead or mortally wounded.

But in standing their ground so bravely, and facing the enemy despite being outmatched and outmanoeuvred, the Jatarupas had achieved the fruition of the next part of Rama's plan.

They had left room for the bears to be set free.

Jambavan sensed rather than felt or heard or saw that it was time for him to emerge. The bear lord had sustained himself for the past several hours by reducing his breathing to a minimum, using a method that the mortal sages of the Arya world referred to as pranayam yoga. In fact, his method preceded the mortals' form of yoga by several millennia, deriving as it did from the original yogi himself, Lord Shiva the Destroyer. In a past life, Jambavan had served his lord personally, and in exchange for that lifetime of service diligently fulfilled he had been given knowledge of the Three-Eyed One's most personal accomplishments in the field of self-attainment. This gift he in turn had imparted to his bear fellows, and on this day in Lanka it was what had made the fulfilment of Rama's plan possible. In fact, he himself had suggested this particular concealment, when Rama had mused about how they were to hide such large, obvious creatures as bears. He and his kind could hardly crouch between scrubby bushes or cluster in trees as the Jatarupa vanars could. Nor were the trees around here sufficiently large-trunked for a bear to hide behind effectively. So he had suggested this place, and it had served its purpose beautifully, for the enemy had bypassed it without ever being aware that a whole army of bears lay concealed within its confines. But not for much longer. This Jambavan knew. For in the infinite knowledge of his deva-granted wisdom, he had indeed heard Rama's silently spoken missive, just as he was aware of the progress of the battle between the Jatarupas and the reptilian rakshasas.

With a flexing of great muscles, he raised his powerful paws and began to dig his way out of his place of concealment. It had taken almost an hour-watch to dig himself in, and for the Jatarupas, supervised by Rama himself, to cover him, along with the rest of his bears. Now it took only a few moments to dig his way out. They had been lucky in that this entire patch of some twenty or more square miles was all loose dirt with almost no stones or rock for several yards beneath the surface. Being barren, there were no weeds or roots to form sods either. So it had been relatively easy – no, perhaps not easy, but possible – for his army of bears to dig their way a yard or more into the ground, and then for the Jatarupas to shovel the dirt back over them and stamp it in energetically to create the illusion of a flattish if somewhat lumpy field once more. Any unevenness could be attributed to the night of the killing stones, which had disrupted the entire landscape of this northern tip already. No enemy would suspect that an army of bears could be buried under a yard of packed dirt. In fact, it was impossible to do such a thing, for how could any creature breathe and survive several hours in this fashion? Impossible, that is, for any army except Rama's, and any host of bears except that of Jambavan, with his mastery of the science of yoga. Even so, he knew that a few unfortunate specimens, unable to master the art, or lacking the discipline required to sustain the slowing of one's metabolism and breathing to the near-death level required to survive such a feat, had choked and suffocated to death already. They were a tiny fraction of his numbers, but if they had had to spend several more hours thus, perhaps he would have lost many more.

But now it was time. He worked his great paws furiously, digging away the dirt and then the topsoil, and finally broke free, lifting his snout to breathe in the dusty but blessed air of Prithvi once more. He gasped in great lung-filling breaths, willing his pulse to resume normal pace once again. Then, moving as quickly as was possible under the circumstances, he dragged his large, heavy bulk out of the ground and stood, examining the field around him.

Incredibly, he was not the first to emerge. He took pride in seeing several hundred bears already out of the ground, or breaking free even as he scanned around. Of course most had probably been buried a bit less deeply than himself, and so had had to dig less to get out as well, but even so, it was a mark of his achievement as a leader and as a teacher of yoga that so many were able to respond so quickly. If slowing one's bodily functions in the shav-asana state – literally 'like a corpse' – was hard, then returning those functions to normal pace, while not as hard, was arduous and demanding. Under the circumstances, it also had to be done quickly, for it was no use wasting precious moments on regaining one's senses and strength. They had to be ready to fight at once.

Which made it much like rousing oneself from a state of calm to one of full-blown fury. For nothing could raise bodily re-actions faster and more effectively than anger. But controlled anger, so that it was useful, not excessive. He willed his glands to produce the secretions that would bring him quickly to a fighting fury, while retaining control over his mental and intellectual faculties.

Around him, the bears who had emerged were doing the same thing, clenching their jaws and tensing their powerful upper limbs tightly, sheathing their claws and fisting their paws to enhance the arousal.

And all the while, more and more bears broke ground and emerged blinking and breathing into the clear bright light of day. Now there were a few thousand, then twenty thousand, then twice that number . . . Until the vast tract of barren land was covered with an army of bears the likes of which had never been gathered before on the face of the earth, nor would ever be gathered again. For in his heart, Jambavan knew that this great army was assembled only for Rama's cause, and no cause as great or as righteous could ever summon such loyalty, such sacrifice, such unity between species, for perhaps as long as the world existed and until the last day of Brahma ended to give way to the final tandav of Shiva as he danced to destroy the world and make way for a new one.

Jambavan felt the power of all his strength, all his will, and all the shakti of his yogic knowledge and mastery, as well as the fury of outrage of Rama's suffering, well up inside him, awakening every cell, every pore, every vessel of every organ in his body and mind, until he was in full battle rage, ready to unleash the power of the bear army.

He raised his snout and roared. Then lowered his head and lumbered forward to the attack.

Rama watched with pride and an unnameable emotion as the bear army stood on the plain, tens of thousands upon tens of thousands of great hulking, shaggy, furred beasts, each a formidable force unto him- or herself. A small contingent of their number had been dispatched earlier to aid the Mandaras in their forest valley battle. But the bulk of his bear army was right here, kept in abeyance until this crucial moment. And seeing them rise up out of the ground, he felt that he had done exactly the right thing. For could any force withstand that great army led by Jambavan?

As Jambavan roared and thundered forward, the bear force lumbering with him, the lizard beasts ceased in their fighting and dropped to the ground, falling still and silent once more. The Jatarupas, having the advantage of knowing about the bears, used this brief respite to hack and slash and cut the enemy, slaying several hundreds as they stood motionless, eyes opening and shutting but without moving any other muscle in their long reptilian bodies.

Then, as the bears' lumbering run accelerated into a full-blown charge, the lizards moved as one, a great swivelling and turning that brought them all face to face with this new enemy that had appeared so unexpectedly while they were busy battling the vanars, and their clicking began anew. But this time, Rama felt, there was a difference in the pattern and pitch of their communication. He could not be certain of course, but he sensed a faltering in the rhythm of their clicking, a dulling of volume, a hesitant, uncertain start-and-stop pattern that he had not heard before. If their earlier communication was a confident, aggressive, bold outburst of chatter, the equivalent of a mortal roar of 'attack and destroy', then this new sound was more akin to a curious cry of 'What is this now? What should we do next?' He had no doubt that given even a few moments longer, they would regroup and figure out some way to deal with the new threat, and their skills would be almost as devastating as against the vanars.

But they did not have the luxury of those few moments. The ploy of burying the bears and then recalling them so suddenly, and of trapping the rakshasa force between two armies – of outflanking the very force that was intended to outflank his forces – paid its dividends now. As the lizard beasts stood in stunned confusion, unable to decide how to deal with this unexpected new enemy, the Jatarupas realised what was about to happen and quickly and quietly pulled back, leaving the reptilian creatures standing alone and defenceless before the oncoming bear charge.

With a sound like a great fist driven into living flesh with the force of a hammer, the bear army slammed into the lizards.

The lizard beasts, formidable though they were when attacked, were not built for defence. Like the natural reptilian species they resembled so vividly, they possessed the same soft underbellies and under-jaw vulnerability. When attacking, their powerful leaps and slashing talons negated these disadvantages. But when standing still in stunned confusion, as they were now, they made soft, easy targets.

Jambavan rammed into a lizard headlong, ripping into its belly with his right fist, tearing open the soft flesh with such impact that a great gush of ichor spewed out like vomit. He saw the beast's enormous mouth, as flat as a crocodile's but with high fangs placed like a snake's, open as if to issue a sound of anguish, but without a word or even a click, it collapsed in a gelid heap at his feet. He was already moving on to the next, swinging his great fist to slash it viciously across its thick reptilian throat. The joining of its head to its body was too solid and fleshy for him to actually decapitate it, but he ripped it sufficiently that the head sagged limply to one side as the creature fell with a soft thud upon the ground. In the time it took it to fall, he had moved on and killed another of its fellows. Around him, bears were finding their own chosen targets just as easy to kill.

The situation changed slowly as the beasts, sluggish though they were, and clearly stunned by the sudden appearance of this unexpected foe, regained their wits and began corresponding yet again with those unnerving clicks. But their confidence was so badly eroded, and the ferocious onslaught of the bears so great, that even their rallying response was too feeble, too late. They tried leaping high and fast and in all directions, as they had done before, but whereas the vanars had been leaping as well, and had been much smaller creatures with far inferior strength, the bears were a different story altogether.

Jambavan tracked a lizard leaping elliptically, and when it came flying down at him, its talons blurring, he was already half turned away, out of the range of those slashing blade-like tips, then twisting his body around in that famous side-to-side swinging action that only bears could effect with such power and grace, cutting back at the enemy with his own formidable claws. The lizard's torso seemed to explode in a burst of green-yellow ichor as it hissed out a cry that reminded him of a giant swallowing snake he had once fought deep in a tropical jungle, ten times his length and as thick as himself. This creature was a far less competent foe than that great anaconda, and died far more easily, the light winking out of its bright eyes like a firefly slapped by an irate bear.

Jambavan slaughtered and sang his song of battle, slaying dozens of the creatures himself, until he lost count of how many he had dispatched, or of the progress of the battle as a whole. Such battle madness was unavoidable, even to a creature as enlightened and in control of its senses as he; it was a relaxation of the normal sensory awareness of time and tide and logic and sense; in its own way, this state of battle lust and killing fever was no less than a meditation itself, albeit a brutal and life-negating meditation that did not bear the fruits of a true transcendental trance. But it helped make the butcher's task that much easier – made it possible even, for killing, however necessary, however justified, if you could ever call killing justified, was no glorious deed to be sung about and praised in paeans. Jambavan, like any true warrior, fulfilled this part of his dharma, but in doing so allowed himself to be neither clouded by the illusory vainglorious pleasure of victory, nor disabled by the horror of his acts of violence.

When the fugue of bloodletting passed, he found himself standing on a place of blood and ichor, corpses and severed parts, body organs exposed and stinking fetidly, of blindly staring yellow eyes in lifeless reptilian heads, a scene of such exotic carnage as he had never witnessed in his years before, nor ever desired to set eyes on again.

Rama looked upon the battlefield with a sense of awe that he had not thought himself capable of feeling since he was a boy and still uninured to the excesses and cruelties of life. Even as a young man of fifteen years of age, the year that Brahmarishi Vishwamitra had come to Ayodhya to take him with him into the Bhayanak-van on that fateful mission, he had not experienced such a sense of utter disbelief.

The bears had wiped out the force of lizard rakshasas. Those few thousand that remained, gutted or wounded, struggling feebly to fight back, were being slaughtered even now. The bears, aided by the Jatarupas, who were more than eager to avenge their own losses, went about the field dispatching the survivors easily, with a sense of dutifulness that was almost frightening to watch. This was no longer battle lust that drove them, but a simple sense of survival. There was no point in leaving alive any of the foe, when they knew full well that those survivors would only return to hunt them once again. Even so, his time-toughened warrior's mind found it hard to stomach this necessary act. He consoled himself with the knowledge that these creatures were a sorcerously bred hybrid creation of Ravana, not a natural breed of rakshasas that lived and raised families like the other rakshasas – Vibhisena had confirmed as much when he had joined them a little while earlier. And in that case, they were only undoing the work of unnatural sorcery, not truly killing life created by the honest purity of brahmanic shakti itself.

Yet he still could not help feeling a sense of sickening unease at being the sole cause of an entire kind being wiped out so completely and finally. Thus were genocides committed. Did it matter any less if the race thus extinguished was a sorcerously created one? He was grateful that he had not the time or the luxury to dwell on the moral and ethical ramifications of such issues. His dharma only called for him to go to war, and this war required that the reptilian force be destroyed to the last member. So be it.

13

They met at the lowermost foothill: bear lord, vanar prince, mortal princes, and a solitary rakshasa brahmin, for Vibhisena had come down from Mount Suvela and joined them a short while ago. They embraced. And exchanged looks full of the undefinable emotion that passed through the hearts and minds of warriors at such a time. There was sadness there, at the losses of their fallen comrades – for despite their superiority, the bears had sustained losses too, and the Jatarupas had paid a heavy price. There was relief and even joyousness, for they had won the battle. There was guarded wonder, for it was only just approaching noon, and this was just the first day of the first real battle of the war to rival all wars to date. But above all there was love, and friendship, and camaraderie, and great, indescribable happiness at seeing one another again, and taking comfort in each other's living, breathing presence once more.

Before they could speak a single word, a great shape dropped out of the sky, landing as softly as a feather beside Rama.

'My lord,' Hanuman said, kneeling down to touch the feet of his chosen master. 'I come to bring you news of the war thus far.'

Rama blessed him without protesting overmuch. He still did not enjoy shows of obsequiousness, for he knew how easy it would be for such fealty to turn into a god-like worship, and he was still far too much a mortal creature of flesh and blood to desire to be venerated like a deva. 'Give us your report, my friend. We have had some word from the Prince of Kiskindha's fleet-footed couriers, but it is your overview that I long to hear most. Leave out no detail of significance; rather tell us all that is worth telling, but do so as briefly and efficiently as possible, with no formal embellishments or ornate phrasing, for we are still soldiers and the war is only just begun.'

Nearby, a familiar saucy *cheeka* rang out, as the small furry shape of Hanuman's half-brother Sakra bounded up the hillock. The little vanar had found employ in the company of the angadiyas and his natural exuberant energies were diverted productively in ferrying messages to and fro. But on sight of his illustrious brother, he still seemed to turn back into the childish monkey-fool vanar he was at heart.

Hanuman shot Sakra a stern look to admonish him for inter-rupting such an important convention. Undaunted, Sakra remained where he was, seated on his haunches and scratching his left ear with his left hind leg, exactly as a monkey might do, while eavesdropping blatantly upon their conversation. He was ignored by all, by unspoken mutual consent, and with Rama's indulgent blessings.

Hanuman then did as Rama had asked, and narrated the tales of the battle of the canyon and the battle of the valley. He described how, after Mandara-devi's gallant sacrifice, the rakshasa horde was encircled and entrapped within the dense woods by the waiting vanar and bear contingents and made to suffer great losses, in numbers as well as morale. 'They were like proud wolves eager for a feast when they arrived over the rise of that valley, led by one of the greatest champions of Lanka, and they fled southwards back towards their capital with the aspect of whipped curs, leaderless, and whimpering at their losses.'

'And what of the battle in the west?' Rama asked. 'For I have received fewest reports from that front, it being the farthest from us. How fared General Susena, lieutenants Pramathi and Praghasa, their champions the twins, and the rest of the Mandeha vanars?'

Hanuman lowered his snout in a vanar gesture of sadness. 'I regret to say that the general was killed, as was Praghasa, but the twins and Lieutenant Pramathi survived, and while the Mandehas sustained losses amounting to about two in ten of their original count, they held the field. The enemy was sent into retreat and was last seen by me raising a great dust cloud as it returned to the gates of Lanka.'

He paused, and Rama, who had been about to speak a few words of commiseration over the loss of the general and the others fallen on the western front, held back, sensing that the vanar was about to reveal something of great import. 'What is it, Anjaneya? Speak it aloud to me, however trivial a detail it may seem. If it troubles you thus, it is surely not too minor to recount.'

Hanuman looked at him with a puzzled expression in his reddish-brown vanar pupils. 'I do not scent the meaning of it, Rama. But perhaps you, in your infinite wisdom and your great store of knowledge of battle lore, will better comprehend its significance.'

'What is it? What did you see or hear?' Lakshman asked, with less forbearance than Rama but more gently than usual. He was as pleased by the morning's victories as any of them, his normal impatience tempered by the successes.

Hanuman looked at Rama's brother, then at Rama himself. The bear lord Jambavan and Prince Angad watched him curiously, as did the Kiskindha lieutenant Gavaksa, and the Jatarupa vanar lieutenants Rsabha and Gavya. The Jatarupa lieutenant Gaja had perished on the talons of a lizard beast on the rampart walls, while other lieutenants had died fighting the creatures on the field below. All present waited with mounting curiosity to hear what Hanuman had to say.

'It was a strange sight, my lord,' he said. 'There were survivors coming from all fronts, beaten and bedraggled and bearing wounded and hurt rakshasas, gathering before the gates of Lanka. But the gates were kept shut against them. Not a single one of them was permitted to return into the walled city. Rather, when some failed to badger and intimidate the guards into opening the gates, and attempted to enter via a sally port, while others attempted to climb the walls in sheer desperation, they were thrown off and shoved out with as much violence as might be used against a besieging enemy.' He paused, looking at each of their faces in turn to see if any of them understood this peculiar event better than he did. 'It was as if Lanka's lord and master would rather leave his armies to die than permit them to return unvictorious.'

Lakshman swore softly, using phrases Hanuman did not understand. 'Then they will attack us once again. They are left with no other alternative. They will charge our armies with greater ferocity than before, for now they know they have nothing to lose, and everything to gain. A wounded lion is more dangerous than a sleeping one.'

'A wounded lion is a wounded lion,' Rama replied softly. 'And I do not believe Ravana is so mindlessly cruel that he believes such tactics will enrage his forces into seeking victory where they failed so miserably before.'

'But they did not fail miserably, Rama,' Lakshman argued persistently. 'They failed, yes, but only because we outmanoeuvred them and outwitted them at every turn. Now they are aware of our tactics. Indeed, we have used up all our surprises, and revealed all our forces. Our armies have sustained great losses, perhaps greater than the armies of Lanka in some cases. And while we held the ground we fought on, it was not ground valuable in itself. We have yet to march on Lanka and take the city proper, for only then is our goal fully accomplished. When Lanka will not admit its own soldiers back into her fold, and the armies of Ravana remain outside its gates, how can we march on the capital and storm it?'

Jambavan spoke in his quiet, rumbling tone. The bear king had wiped off some of the ichor from his snout and features, but the stench of the substance still hung about him thickly;

yet nobody dared say so to him directly. 'We are not meant to storm the capital, Rama. That is why the king of rakshasas refuses entry to his own warriors. He is not yet prepared to let us bring the war to him. He wishes to bring the next phase of the war to us.'

The bear king paused, sniffing the air suspiciously. 'And I would warrant that he is preparing to do so at this very moment.'

Hanuman looked around, suddenly alert. 'My lord Jambavan speaks truly, Rama! I scent the odour of Asura maya in the air. The same fetid stench that issued when Ravana deployed the killing stones last night. He is about to wreak some new sorcery upon us!'

Even as he was finishing, a great *cheeka* rang out from Sakra. They turned to see the little angadiya leaping up and down in frantic excitement, his paws over his eyes. Despite covering his face, he still peered out between his furry fingers, and as the attention of the war council was directed at him, he pointed upwards with a single claw, shrieking anew.

They looked up to see what was bothering him. And stared, transfixed, as nightfall descended on them out of a clear noon sky.

On the highest rim of the canyon, King Sugreeva was seated with his lieutenants, enjoying a moment of idle indulgence, eating a little fruit to replenish his resources, while reviewing the battle's high points to glean new insights for future reference. He was in the midst of explaining the most effective method for bringing down the large broken-headed mounts that had been used by the rakshasa horde in its first headlong charge, when the day turned dark. He rose to his feet at once, scenting the stench of rakshasa sorcery at large. But his first impulse was to look down at the canyon, where his forces were resting, for fear that the rakshasa horde had somehow regrouped and gained reinforcements and was launching a fresh onslaught.

He did in fact see something to make his heart leap into his mouth. But instead of a rakshasa charge, what he saw was a dark cloud, with the texture and appearance of fog, creeping across the ground. As he watched, it entered the canyon, covering the ground with frenetic haste, like smoke billowing before a great wind. Yet he knew this was no natural fog or smoke, for the wind was still blowing from the east, whereas this bank of fog-like substance was coming from the south, from the direction of Ravana's capital city.

Then the shouts of his lieutenants caused him to look up at the sky, and what he saw there made him almost swallow his heart again out of fear and shock.

In the dense jungle of the valley, Mainda and Dvivida rested on trees, too weary to eat even though their fellows feasted and danced all around them. As inveterate fighters, both had acquired the art of resting at every given chance, and preferred a little respite for their aching bodies to filling their bellies with nourishment. Even with his eyes shut, Dvivida's mind still replayed that brutally brief combat between Mandara-devi and the rakshasa general. A whole battle had passed since, during which he had fought and killed perhaps a dozen of the enemy himself, had survived some very close scrapes and seen too many of his friends and blood-kin killed, but it was that one fight that haunted him still. He knew it would haunt him for as long as he lived, and he would tell and retell it countless times to his fellow vanars, his children and his grandchildren, and even his great-grandchildren, for it was the greatest fight he had ever witnessed in his life. That was the highest praise a fighter could pay another fighter – to tell that fighter's story instead of his own. He would honour Mandara-devi always by retelling the great fight she had fought on that dried riverbed in Lanka, for by fighting that fight she had made this battle and this victory possible.

He took the sudden commotion to be some new round of celebration. Some of the more enterprising vanars had found some fermented fruit and were pretending to get intoxicated on it. Such silliness was acceptable after a battle, more so after a victorious battle. But when the shrieking and commotion grew loud enough to compel him to rouse himself from his reverie, he opened one eye, then the other, to see what was occasioning such madness. He saw Mainda stirring drowsily on the branch of the tree beside him.

'What are they up to now?' grumbled the older vanar. He had sustained a gash beneath his ribcage that was still oozing blood, but was otherwise unharmed. He raised his snout and peered around. Being on a higher branch than Dvivida, he had a slightly better view, but at first he could see nothing that aroused his interest. Then he raised his snout to glance idly at the sky, and saw something that made him freeze.

'What is it, Mainda?' Dvivida asked, alerted more by Mainda's reaction than by the flurry in the camp. The old champion was not given to easy excitability.

'Mother of vanars,' Mainda swore, then pointed up at the sky. 'Our doom is come upon us, Dvivida. Prepare to meet the deva of all the vanar races in the afterworld.'

Dvivida looked up, parting the leaves above his head to peer at the bright blue sky. The first thing he saw was that it was turning slowly black, as if a gigantic cloud bank was creeping across it. The next thing he realised was that it was not a cloud bank at all.

'General! The sky!'

General Pramathi – for he had been promoted instantly on General Susena's death – followed his lieutenant's pointing finger. He was in the midst of taking stock of his losses, standing in the centre of the large grassy declivity where the western army had fought their battle. Tens of thousands of corpses, rakshasa as well as vanar, lay around him, reeking in the noonday sun.

He paused, and looked up.

And froze in horror.

Rama stared in grim consternation as the sky above Lanka grew dark as night. The cause was sorcery, of that he had no doubt. He could see the fog-like darkness creeping across the ground at the same time – except that creeping was too slow a word to describe the speed with which the sorcerous substance was spreading. In moments, the entire hill range, the ghats, and even the mountains that had been so clearly visible only moments ago were shrouded in darkness. And soon, he could see, the sky would be benighted too. Already the sun was covered by the advancing cloud of blackness that raced across the sky, matching the speed and denseness of the thick, oily, smoke-like substance that covered the ground below. In another few moments the whole land would be plunged into a darkness as dense as the darkest moonless night. He knew this instinctively.

But that was not the thing that gave him pause for anxiety.

What startled him was the other skyborne menace that was approaching from the south. This was much lower than the high cloud that was enveloping the world, about three or four hundred yards high, the height at which Hanuman usually flew in order to maintain a clear view of the ground below as well as spy out enough of the land ahead. The height at which a flying warrior would choose to fly.

And this dense mass moving at that height was indeed a horde of flying warriors.

Rakshasas, to be precise. Rakshasas with leathery wings on their backs, flapping with the slow, precise beats of a large foxbat or oversized condor or orc. Nowhere near as large as the vulture-beast Jatayu had been, but close enough to remind him painfully of his lost friend and ally who had died fighting Ravana in his valiant attempt to hinder Sita's kidnapping.

An army of flying rakshasas, tens of thousands of them, filled the dark sky, coming directly at him.

At the same time, from behind him came a chorus of vanar shrieks and bear howls.

He turned to look at the battlements whence the lizard beasts had emerged not long before. New enemies were emerging from those crevices now, brought up through the tunnels beneath the ground like their predecessors. They were huge, lumbering beasts, much like rakshasas in body but with a distinctive feature that he could spy even at this distance. They bore faces almost recognisably familiar, even seen from afar. As he frowned, trying to make out their faces more clearly, the darkness overhead and on the ground engulfed that entire part of the island, and all was blackness.

A deathly silence fell across the world, broken only by the sound of countless leathery wings beating the still air. And then, with a sound like thunder clapping in the distance, Ravana unleashed his war upon the forces of Rama.

KAAND 4

THE FOREVER WAR

'Anjaneya. To the skies!'

Hanuman did not need a second order from Rama. He rose like an arrow shot from Lakshman's bow, expanding his body to a size he judged optimum for fighting the winged rakshasas. Moving through absolute blackness did not worry him unduly; his vanar senses enabled him to scent his way just as effectively in pitch darkness. The air was thick with the rank odour of the flying beasts, and from the sound of their leathery wings beating the air, he knew they were only moments away from Rama's position. He set his jaw and flew to meet them, guided by his vanar senses, determined to ensure that far more of Ravana's flying warriors would die in the air than reach the ground alive.

King Sugreeva cursed aloud as the darkness enveloped him and his warriors. He knew he was fortunate to have been standing atop the rise, overlooking the canyon, well placed to see for miles around. In those last brief moments before the world went dark, he glimpsed the rumbling dust cloud raised by the horde approaching from the south, as well as the winged creatures in the sky. Then all vision was blocked out by a darkness blacker than night itself, leaving him staring in frustration.

'My lord,' someone called to him in the darkness. 'Shall we retreat?'

'Where to?' he asked rhetorically. For he knew that the other armies would be under attack as well. It would not matter whether he ran this way or that; all around was enemy territory. A stab of sadness, piercing and cold as a dagger of ice, went through his heart as he realised that all the sacrifice of the Kiskindha vanars in the first battle was in vain. Then he corrected himself: nothing was ever in vain. Every soldier's life well spent made possible a future victory.

He did the only thing he could as a good king and a general of Rama: he gave the order to prepare to repel the enemy on both fronts, ground and sky. And then he raised his battered pole, whose point he had taken a moment to taper into a spear-sharp tip, and waited for the charge of the armies of the damned.

From the dimness of the valley forest, the champions Mainda and Dvivida peered up at the sky, benighted as abruptly as if someone had thrown a rug over the world. Despite the blackness, they could still see faintly: the great volcano in the south of the island was emitting a soft glow, invisible in the bright sunlight earlier, but now sufficient to throw a candlelight's worth of illumination upwards, casting faint highlights on anything that caught the light in the sky.

They stared up in wonderment and awe at what their enemy had wrought: would that Mandara-devi had lived to see this – or then again, better that she had not.

A constellation of darkly luminescent eyes and gleaming talons glowed dully like an alien sky filled with bizarre stars and celestial orbs. It reminded Dvivida of the time he had wandered too far into the dreaded Southwoods as a youngun and glimpsed a cluster of eyes reflected back at him by starlight. He had realised at once to his undying dismay that the rumours of a horde of grotesquely malformed Asuras dwelling in those woods were not rumours but truth. He shivered and wished he could flee scampering, as he had on that long-ago occasion, back to the safety of his tribe. But on this occasion, there was nowhere to flee.

As they waited for the skyborne menace to fall upon them, they grew aware of another sound and scent. A great rumbling vibration filled the valley. They exchanged a look of bared teeth, knowing what that sound and vibration meant. Peering through the murky darkness, they made out the faint blur of movement, enough to deduce the rest.

An army of rakshasas was pouring down the ghats into the valley from all sides, encircling the contingent of Mandara vanars and Kambunara's bears within the forest valley. This time they were the ones trapped and surrounded – not just on all sides, but from above as well.

Angad stared in frustration at the dark field ahead. He could see the shadowy shapes of the creatures emerging from the battlements, could see just enough by the faint glow of the volcano's emission to make out that they were nothing like the lizard beasts; these were some wholly new breed of rakshasa. How would they fight? What were their points of vulnerability? Did they have any? And what of the creatures above? Even if Hanuman was powerful enough to fight them, there were far too many for him to deal with all at once.

He heard the code-sounds of his angadiyas ringing out across the battlefield as they communicated Rama's terse new orders. He admired Rama's ability to respond so swiftly to such a drastically altered situation, and passed on his own instructions as best as he could, ensuring that Rama's wishes were carried out efficiently, but secretly he wondered if it was possible to outmanoeuvre this move of Ravana's. For it seemed like no battle strategy that the Lord of Lanka had unleashed; this seemed like an endgame.

Jambavan's thoughts, despite the yawning disparity between him and the young vanar prince of Kiskindha, were not very different. He swore gruffly as his coal-red eyes, accustomed to seeing in the lightless depths of subterranean caverns, glimpsed the first wave of flying beasts detach themselves from their hovering mates overhead and begin a sharp plunging dive towards his position. At the same time, the rakshasas newly emerged from beneath the battlements also began striding forward, seeping across the field like viscous fluid upon a polished surface. Far in the distance, to all points of the compass, he sensed the other forces of dharma also preparing to join weapons with their nemesis in the arcane darkness. Masterfully and magnificently, Ravana had struck back at them with a war game to beat all war games. In his ancient heart, the bear lord knew that this battle just beginning would be the last battle of Lanka. Whoever stood at the end of this clash would be master of the kingdom of rakshasas henceforth.

He snarled and unsheathed his claws. At such a time there was only one thing a warrior of dharma could do. He intended to do it until the last fish-stinking breath left his burly body.

He lifted his snout and roared the challenge of the ancient ones. Around him on the benighted battlefield, the bear army raised their snouts and roared as well, defying any and all who dared to fight against them.

Across the land of rakshasas, the forces of Ravana had come into position, each poised and ready to strike at their prey, like a herd of felines marking the chital they would each pounce on in a grazing herd.

There came a pause in the tableau then, as the forces of Rama and Ravana regarded each other, able to see only briefly in the flashes of lightning-like purplish illumination that flickered in the dense black sky-fog, and in the hellish scarlet glow of the volcano at the far southern end of the island.

The creatures flying above Hanuman had slowed their progress to hover in mid-air, flapping their enormous wings slowly enough to maintain their height, without moving in any direction. Their hungry nictitating eyes were directed downwards at their enemy, and their beak-like mouths issued shrill cries from time to time, as they waited impatiently to attack. Now, as if receiving some inner command that he could neither scent nor hear nor sense, they issued a unanimous cry of triumph. This painfully ear-piercing shriek was followed by the thunderous flapping of tens of thousands of wings, as they began their murderous descent, breaking off in waves, like the one that Angad had already glimpsed, each group flying in a different tactical trajectory. Hanuman knew he would not be able to stop them all, but he intended to deflect as many as he possibly could before taking the offensive. He had placed his body in such a way that large numbers would have no choice but to attempt to bite and slash and claw their way through him in order to get at their designated targets.

From below, the roar of the bear lord was echoed by the thundering response of the bear army. The sound gave him new courage and determination.

Even as he braced himself for the pain he knew was inevitable, he heard the roars of the rakshasa hordes on the ground rend the air as they began their attack as well.

2

Hanuman roared in rage as thousands of razor-sharp beaks and claws tore into his flesh from head to toe. Sharp talons dug into the tender skin around his eyes, seeking to rip open his lids and penetrate the soft orbs of his organs of vision. He swiped backhanded, sweeping scores of the beasts from his face, some clinging on so fiercely that they tore away his skin and flesh before they were cast away. He clapped his hands together, smashing a dozen-odd to crumpled gristle. The leathery wings continued to flap even after death, as if governed by a force not of the flesh. Sharp needle-like talons pierced his chest, his arms, his taut muscled belly, his waist, his legs, even hacked at the makeshift langot, the strip of loin-cloth he had taken to wearing after the mortal fashion. They ripped away his fur in clumps, leaving pinpricks of oozing pain, tore his skin in swatches, needled into his flesh, gnawed on his bones, slashed at his tendons, attempted to tear open his blood vessels . . .

Soon his entire body was one enormous bleeding wound. This was no fight, it was a torture session. Yet he bore the agony of it without a sound of protest – not a sound after that first enraged roar of challenge – and slapped and crushed and batted the beasts, killing them upon his own body like an ordinary vanar might do to bloodsucking insects.

* * *

Angad leaped into the fray, slashing at the throat of an oncoming rakshasa. He felt his claws tear at living flesh, felt also the telling spurt of life-fluid, and heard the beast grunt angrily. As he sprang out of the way of its responding blow, dodging it with a hair's breadth of space to spare, he took comfort in the fact that these creatures bled and fought not unlike regular rakshasas. It did not make them easier to fight or kill; it merely made it possible to do so. And right now, possible was all he prayed for. The rest was ultimately up to the devas – and Rama himself.

Then all thoughts, all prayers were set aside as he gave himself over to the task of fighting for his life, as the battle disintegrated into tens of thousands of individual combats.

King Sugreeva swung his tree in a circling arc, feeling the bones of rakshasas crack and crunch and shatter as he struck them with just enough force to inflict telling damage but not so much that it would halt the swing of the weapon. He relished the feel of the supple, smooth hardwood in the palms of his unfurred fists, thanking the vanar ancestors who had brought him this weapon. He took satisfaction also, as had his son, in knowing that rakshasas were flesh and blood, just like vanars, and could be broken and beaten and killed. These new rakshasas had not the benefit of the mounts that the first attack had; they came on foot, and the same darkness that nearly blinded Sugreeva and his forces also impaired their vision, forcing them to come at the vanar army in the canyon with the customary slow, lumbering gait of rakshasas who had not built up sufficient running momentum. His vanars fought around him, a contingent of veterans from the first battle clustered around their king to offer him support and protection, and the darkness was rent with the screams of comrades and enemy alike.

There were no war cries issued in this dark and fierce battle, no howls of exultation. Only a desperate fighting that stole lives and shattered organs and bones, crippling and maiming and severing limbs from bodies. It was the brutal business of war, with the dark deva of death kept constantly busy slipping his invisible thread-noose around the souls of dying creatures and slipping them into his burgeoning sack, to be carried back to the netherworld on his black buffalo mount. Yet Yamaraj himself might have paused a moment to marvel at this strange, silent clash beneath a sorcerously benighted sky, where great armies fought one another in a strange, doomed, desperate struggle to the finish.

A trio of vanars before him succumbed to a new onslaught of arriving rakshasas, who grunted softly with effort as they dispatched one of his most beloved lieutenants – who also happened to be his sister's son – with a heartrending liquid gush of bodily fluids. His nephew Kaharimal died silently, his body torn nearly in two, only yards from Sugreeva. And the vanar king of Kiskindha grieved for his lost blood the only way a warrior could, by raising his tree and dealing a great mortal blow to the offending rakshasa. The beast collapsed beside his vanar victim, his misshapen skull shattered by the tree, brains oozing out to mingle with the rent flesh of Sugreeva's favourite nephew.

Blood and mayhem, death and destruction.

The champions Mainda and Dvivida fought on with bitter rage, both for the honour of their fallen tribe-goddess and for Rama's cause, for the two were inextricable in their minds now. The valiant vanars in the forest had a great advantage over their enemies in that they were in their natural environment, whereas rakshasas, having lived in more civilised communities and cities, were no longer as accustomed to forest-fighting as their kind had once been, millennia ago.

The bears had this advantage as well, and the darkness actually served to conceal them. Oftentimes, a rakshasa would strike out at what he perceived to be a bear, only to have his blade strike the hard bark of a tree; before he could free the stuck blade, a dark, towering shape he had mistaken for a tree would lumber forward, claws slashing from side to side, ending his confusion once and for all.

Kambunara enjoyed the business of slaughter for a while, as his dark fur disguised him well in the pitch-black forest. Rakshasas ran into trees as they attempted to charge him, and he ran into them, wreaking havoc. A butcher in a sheep pen.

But as time went by, and the battle wore on relentlessly, ever-increasing numbers of the enemy kept pouring in from over the valley's ridges to replace those who had been slaughtered. The bears and vanars began to grow weary, for how long could one fight without rest or nourishment, but they knew that retreat was not an option, and so they fought on grimly. The forest floor, dried and leaf-strewn in this autumnal season, became a morass of wet, gelid corpses and body parts and fluids. Soon the bears were standing on corpses to fight – those of their own kind as well as the enemy – while the vanars, swinging from tree to tree, began to find even the branches growing slick and sticky with blood. The forest turned into a grisly abattoir as the long night that was really a day wore on relentlessly.

Even Jambavan's great heart-stopping roar fell silent as the battle wore on. The bear king's position was inundated with the flying rakshasas. There was no longer any separation between the vanar and bear armies, as both kinds intermingled, fighting shoulder to shoulder – or bear hip to vanar shoulder, to be more exact – and combining their separate skills to maximise their killing efficiency. But the enemy had a greater advantage, dropping soldiers from the air as well as sending them sweeping across the ground. The flying rakshasas, almost as dark as the sorcerous night itself, appeared out of nowhere, snatching vanars and carrying them high, tossing them from one to another, tearing them open in mid-air. Many vanars, once tossed, twisted and turned to slash the wings of their skyborne abductors, causing the creatures to falter or fall out of the sky to crash on the ground below, often landing on warriors of both sides. The vanars in the air died one way or another, either by falling or by being torn apart by the flying beasts. And a steady spatter of blood fell from the darkness, like the ghoulish monsoon that fell year round in the hellish realms of Naraka-lok.

Jambavan fought both the ground rakshasas and the air ones, sometimes slashing upwards to tear the throats of swooping attackers, or grabbing a wingtip, ignoring the talons that dug into his already bleeding palms, then tearing the beast in two by ripping it down the middle like he might tear a palm frond. He kicked at oncoming ground attackers, using his lower claws to stab their groins and emasculate them. Those that came close enough to fall upon him, he bit at savagely, chomping through horned hide, muscle and bone in a single clean clenching of his mighty jaws. Around him the biggest and fiercest of the bears fought with similar frenzy, each one killing dozens, even scores, before ultimately succumbing to wounds too terrible to recover from and too numerous to count. He sensed rather than saw many old friends, lovers, blood-kin and tribe-kith fall one by one, until he began to realise that this was a battle that would end only with the deaths of them all, vanars and bears and rakshasas. So be it. He would be sure to tote up a butcher's bill so great that even Ravana would marvel at how a single bear's life could cost so many rakshasa ones. He bit through the throat of a rakshasa bird beast that had landed on his back, tearing into his shoulders viciously, while slashing a ground rakshasa with his lower right paw and decapitating another with his upper left paw, all in a one-two-three sequence of actions. He had long since lost count of how many of the enemy he had downed, but it would number well over a hundred. And the battle was still young.

*   *   *

The engine of war ground its minders into bone and gristle. Nothing could stay its course, no force could give it pause. The leaders of both sides fell silent, needing every ounce of their waning energies merely to survive. Many died, or were horribly wounded and struggled on pitifully till they were over-come with particularly savage ferocity, for rakshasas considered the consumption of an enemy leader's organs to be a vitaliser. And to consume them while the leader was still living was even more precious.

Thus the terrible, near-silent slaughter raged on all day and well into the evening. Above the sorcerous fog cloud that enveloped the island, the sun traversed the sky and dipped into the west, the denizens of the ocean lived and loved, mated and nursed, and wondered at the carnage that was evident even to them, for all knew of Rama's war and Ravana's reign of terror. The greybacks, who had worked so hard to bring the armies of dharma across the ocean, now immersed in the deep cold waters of the northern sea which they required in order to sustain their enormous weight and bulk, knew of the carnage that raged in Lanka, if not the specific details of each battle and fight, and wept tears that were lost in the vast teardrop of brine itself.

The birds of the land deserted the country, terrified by the slaughter that raged below, the unnatural beasts that swarmed the skies, and the dark nothingness that obscured both land and sky. They flew to other climes, cawing and honking and squawking plaintively at having lost their homes. They landed on the mainland, on the tsunami-ravaged shores, and settled in the forests bordering the ocean in great multitudes, a million squabbles breaking out with their mainland cousins, but most quickly resolved as all understood that this was a temporary migration. Or so they hoped. For who truly knew what would transpire in Lanka next? Who could say that the two great hosts warring on that darkling land would not simply massacre one another and leave the island-kingdom blood-washed and unpopulated, a ghost country haunted by the spirits of countless departed of both sides? Being birds, they did not understand the ways of mortals or Asuras, and could only wrap their wings around their trembling bodies and wait for this season of death to pass.

For the first hour-watch of the battle, Rama and Lakshman stood side by side on the hillock immediately overlooking the northern battlefield, their bows working furiously. The faint glow of the volcano from below and the occasional flickers of sorcerous purple light in the heart of the fog cloud above limned the silhouettes of the flying rakshasas sufficiently for them to shoot by. They loosed arrow upon arrow in unending succession, dropping scores of beasts from the sky. Those that came close enough to dare to lunge at Rama were dispatched with double fury by Lakshman, who shot unerringly at nictitating eyes, snarling mouths and bared throats, driving these impudent ones back. Even so, as time passed and the beasts' frenzy to kill these two warriors who were responsible for downing so many of their kind intensified, the onslaught grew to impossible proportions. At one point, the air above them was so thick with flapping wings, flashing talons and darkly gleaming eyes, they seemed shrouded in a cloud of their own. The vanars and bears on the field below glanced up at their mortal leaders and were awestruck at the number of the enemy surrounding the two Ayodhyans. But no matter how furiously the enemy tried to get at them, their fleeting arrows kept them at bay. They faced greater danger from the gore and offal splashed on their faces and bodies from the wounded and dying winged beasts. The hillock around them was littered with the corpses of the creatures, their wings continuing to stir and jerk spasmodically even after the beasts themselves were dead.

All this was possible because of the great store of arrows that they possessed, cut and shaped and polished with loving care by a special contingent of monkeys under Lakshman's super-vision back on the mainland. Yet no number, however great, could last for ever. And so, as the hour-watch passed into another hour-watch, and then yet another, and the number of their victims grew from tens to scores to hundreds and thousands, that great supply finally began to dwindle.

When Lakshman knew that they were on the last bushel, he called out to Rama above the noise of flapping wings and strangely silent attacks, only the involuntary grunts and sharp squeals of the arrow-struck breaking the deathly intensity of the scene. 'Rama, you must use your powers now.'

Still Rama continued to loose arrows and down enemies.

Lakshman called out again. 'Rama, the gifts,' he said this time, referring to the gifts of Anasuya.

Still Rama did not heed him and went on firing arrows with the same methodical precision.

Finally Lakshman dropped his bow, unsheathed his sword with one hand, and gripped Rama's shoulder with the other. The corded muscle was covered by the slimy blood of the winged beasts. 'Rama, it is time. Use your weapons,' he pleaded insistently.

As he spoke, he used his sword to continue fighting the beasts, for their onslaught had not slowed a whit even hours after the first wave. Only for brief moments did their attacks diminish as reinforcements arrived in the sky above, lined up to form a substantial new wave, and then attacked. Or at times when the giant Hanuman succeeded in flaying a greater number of the enemy, shattering their attempts at forming a wave and dissipating their numbers before they could fall on those below.

Rama reached the end of his arrows and resorted to his own sword. Blades flashing, they continued to kill as many bird rakshasas as before. Now the creatures were able to come closer to their targets, but as in any attack where a great number attack two closely clustered warriors, the space of access was limited and so only a certain number could come at the two brothers at once, and even these often got their wings tangled with another's, or clashed in their eagerness to be the one to attack the mortal yodhas. In fact, this resulted in a different challenge and possibly a somewhat reduced one, for Rama and Lakshman had now only to wait till the creatures approached within sword-range and then lash out with well-aimed sweeps, lopping off crucial parts of the beasts. The still-flapping wings, hovering in mid-air for precious moments after the death of the creatures they bore, obstructed those behind and above and reduced access to the two brothers still further.

Rama continued to ignore Lakshman's pleas.

'Bhai,' Lakshman shouted, more urgently this time. 'You must use your weapons, or our cause will be lost.'

A sudden change in the atmosphere around them distracted him. He slashed at an oncoming rakshasa, its snarling face disappearing in a small explosion of blood and shattered bone as his sword flashed in the near darkness. Then he glanced around, trying to make out the source of the odd disturbance.

3

Sugreeva thought his eyes were playing tricks on him. The rakshasas that had been attacking them so relentlessly for so many hour-watches began to recede, then faded away altogether. In moments he was standing alone in the centre of the canyon, with no foes left to fight. He lowered his tree suspiciously, looking around, then above. Surely this was some devious new strategem of the enemy. But all around him he saw vanars fall still, peering around in confusion as they found no rakshasas left alive to fight.

He sensed movement nearby and at once raised his pole, ready to strike. What he saw instead gave him pause.

He saw the mangled body of his nephew, barely recognisable now, rise up from the ground where it had fallen. The two halves of the body were barely able to cohere together, and the unfortunate young vanar's internal organs were all clearly exposed, most brutally severed. Yet this unlikely amalgam of body parts and limbs was rising to its feet and lurching forward with slow, drunken steps. As Sugreeva watched with mounting horror, all around him vanars who had fallen in battle began to rise slowly, their lifeless eyes black with a soulless light that he glimpsed by the faint glow of illumination that had expanded across the world this past hour-watch. Across the canyon, his stunned warriors stared around them in shock at this bewildering development.

The corpses of his dead vanar soldiers were coming back to life.

Except that 'coming to life' was an insufficient phrase to describe what was happening. 'Regaining the illusion of life' would be more accurate. For that was all these risen corpses were, hollow shells mimicking the actions and movements of living creatures. And to see one's comrades, fellows in arms, blood-kin, kith, rise up from the dead, mangled and horribly disfigured, was worse than seeing the most grotesque rakshasa charging on a kumbha-sur. Sugreeva swung around, staring with disbelief as the entire canyon was filled with the shakily rising and lurching figures of dead vanars revived to life. This was Ravana's sorcery at work of course, that went without saying. But to what end? What did he hope to achieve by re-animating these mangled corpses?

In a moment he had his answer. The lurching, lumbering form of Kaharimal stumbled towards him, its nearly severed head tilted at a bizarre angle, its midriff cut open to reveal every vital organ. And its arms, Kaharimal's arms, reached out towards Sugreeva as if seeking his blessing. But there was no mistaking the curled menace of those claws, nor the snarl that opened the dead vanar's mouth to reveal its fangs in a dead black maw. Still unwilling to accept this evidence of his senses, Sugreeva allowed the moving corpse to come within reach of him.

Suddenly, belying the clumsy slowness with which it had moved till now, the corpse lunged at him, the twisted head and hacked torso moving at ludicrous angles as the creature attempted to attack the King of Kiskindha.

Sugreeva recoiled in disgust as the creature's claws raked his arms, peeling off a thin strip of fur, and those snapping jaws attempted to close upon any part of his anatomy they could reach.

Moving with mechanical ease, his heart sinking with dismay, Sugreeva brought his tree-spear up with a swift, efficient action, cracking the reaching corpse's arms like sticks, then shoving it back with enough force to send it tumbling over and over, until it landed in a heap of confused limbs and spilling vitals. Yet after a moment these mangled parts began stirring relentlessly and once again the whole mass struggled to move forward, to repeat its mindless attack upon its own kith and kin.

Across the canyon, thousands of dead vanar corpses were attempting the same thing.

The onslaught of flying rakshasas died away as suddenly as it had begun.

Rama peered up suspiciously at the dark sky. He could see Hanuman's outline, writhing and twisting as he battled the beasts in the air – then he saw the giant vanar's movements slow, as even his antagonists dissipated. The few remaining winged ones flew back southwards whence they had come. In moments the sky was as empty as if they had never been there at all. Only Hanuman's hovering figure, and the mounds of corpses all around on the hillock, and the gore and gristle coating his own body were indisputable proof that the battle had occurred.

'Rama, look.'

He turned to see Lakshman peering down at the battlefield below. It was still relatively dark, but there was now sufficient faint illumination to see by, both from the volcano in the south, which appeared to be growing more agitated by the moment, and from the flashes of sorcerous purple-tinged lightning which flickered in the fog cloud above.

He stared at what seemed to be an impossible tableau.

Unable to accept the evidence of his senses, he asked Lakshman, 'What is it?'

'The dead,' Lakshman replied grimly. 'Our dead are returning to life.'

And Rama looked again, and saw that it was so.

Mainda and Dvivida wondered at the disappearance of the rakshasas. Below them on the corpse-scattered floor of the forest,

Kambunara wondered as well, sniffing a strange new scent that made no sense at all. It smelled like living dead bear, which was impossible.

Then, two tree trunks away from him, a bear he had known well and loved dearly, and whom he had seen downed after killing at least a score of rakshasas, began to regain her feet slowly. She used the the tree before her to raise herself, as a sick bear would. He could hear her talons rasping on the bark, and the sound of her heavy nether paws cracking the paw bones of a dead rakshasa underfoot, but he could not hear her breathing, even though the forest had fallen deadly silent. He could not smell her breath either, nor the odour of her effusions. What he could smell was the stench of death, but mingled with another riper, fetid odour that was like a mockery of a living bear's smell. Like flesh that was partly roasted and deliciously fragrant and partly rotted and worm-riddled.

She turned, twisting her snout from side to side, as if seeking something out. But she neither sniffed nor looked with her eyes; rather, as if sensing Kambunara, she began lurching in his direction. With a sickened heart, he understood what was happening. Moments later, as he was forced to defend himself against her clumsy yet heartbreakingly determined attack, and saw her rise yet again – and again, and again – he knew that nothing Ravana had done before or would do after this could be worse than this one act of sorcery. For what could possibly be worse than being pitted against your own beloved comrades and forced to fight them for your survival?

Across Lanka, vanars and bears found themselves faced with the same situation. As their rakshasa foes vanished, retreated, withdrew, they were replaced by their own fallen dead. It was not that this new enemy was particularly proficient or dangerous – their mangled condition and lurching, mindless movements made them easy enough to repel – rather that they could not be stopped and kept on coming and coming. For how could you kill something that was already dead? And there was also the fact that the armies of Rama had no stomach to fight their own kind, their kith and kin and warrior comrades. They fought to survive, but there was no heart in their fighting.

The battlefield was filled with lurching, mindless shadows battling improbably with Jambavan's bears and Angad's vanars. Lakshman turned away from this heart-sickening sight and faced Rama.

'My brother,' he said with a voice of steel. 'This time you will not let our followers be massacred. You will use the dev-astras and turn the tide of this war. I ask you this not to save myself or even you. I ask you this in the name of dharma.'

'But what good will it do to use them now?' Rama asked. 'Against our own dead?'

Lakshman made a sound of exasperation. 'This is a ploy of Ravana. After this round, he will send another wave of new foes against us. And he will keep sending more and more surprises and shocks until our great armies are whittled down to nothing and our spirit is broken.'

'We can withstand everything he throws at us,' Rama said. 'We can win this war honestly, without the use of maha-shakti.'

Lakshman shook his head. 'This war can never be won honestly, Rama. Can you not see that? How can it, when Ravana himself uses Asura maya against us?'

A rush of wind indicated the arrival of Hanuman. The vanar was still in the process of reducing himself as he landed – he was twice his usual size when he bowed to Rama with a look of some agitation. 'Rama, I fear Ravana has some new terror he plans to unleash upon us. Our forward armies are in no condition to withstand yet another sustained assault.'

Rama was shocked at Hanuman's condition. The vanar's body seemed to be one continuous open wound, the skin flayed as if it had been peeled off meticulously by some cruel interrogator. But the very agitation and energy of his friend reassured him; if Hanuman could be concerned about others, then he himself must surely be capable of continuing. 'Yes, my friend, we are aware of Ravana's latest sorcerous trick. He uses our own dead against us.'

'Nay, my lord, I speak not of that. I speak of the new attack that he is preparing to launch at us from the gates of Lanka.'

'New attack?' Lakshman stared at Hanuman. 'What have you seen?'

'When the winged creatures retreated, I flew after them, thinking to bring down as many as I could. I pursued them to the gates of the city, where I saw a great new host assembled, led by the rakshasa who bested me on my earlier trip to Lanka, Ravana's own son, the one named Indrajit. He was so named because of his once legendary defeat of the king of devas, Lord Indra himself. Do not take this new challenge lightly, Rama. He wields the weapons of the gods themselves, the legendary dev-astras. No living being can survive his assaults. On that day when I permitted him to ensnare me, if I had chosen to resist I cannot say for certain that I would have survived the encounter. And I can say with absolute certainty now that if he unleashes dev-astras at our forces, they will be slaughtered to the last vanar and bear.'

Both of them looked at Rama. He felt the intensity of their gaze like the heat of the noonday sun. He noted that Hanuman's wounds had already begun to heal and close: the vanar was possessed of the power to heal himself, of course, although that did not negate the agony he would have suffered when those wounds were inflicted. Vibhisena had spoken of Ravana's elder son with as much fearful awe as he had their brother Kumbhakarna. Hanuman was the only one who had actually faced and fought Indrajit. If he said the rakshasa was formidable, then he must be so.

'Very well,' Rama said quietly. 'I agree with you, Lakshman.

It is time to use the powers vested in me through the grace of the devas.'

Reaching within himself, he shut his eyes and called upon the maha-shakti that resided in him, waiting for this moment. In a flash of blinding blue light he was possessed of the Bow of Vishnu and the Arrow of Shiva.

He spoke a single mantra, taught to him and Lakshman by Brahmarishi Vishwamitra at Siddh-ashrama on a day some fourteen years ago. It felt like a past lifetime now. The instant he spoke the sloka, the arrow blazed with a fierce electric light that crackled like dried leaves snapping in a flash fire. He aimed the arrow directly overhead, bowing his head as he continued to focus his energies inwardly, drawing on the vast store of brahman shakti that infused his being, calling it and pouring it into the arrow. With a final sloka uttered, he loosed the arrow, setting the night ablaze with light, illuminating the sky and land for miles, then leagues, and then yojanas as it rose higher and higher. Finally the arrow reached the apogee of its flight and hung still, crackling and sparkling in the air with a light more intense than the sun. Then it vanished in a great flash, compelling anyone and everyone, including Rama himself, to blink but once.

When Rama opened his eyes again, the fogs of sorcerous darkness laid down by Ravana had been dispelled completely, and the land of Lanka was returned to its normal state once more. Across the island-kingdom, the resurrected dead, vanars and bears, collapsed lifelessly and were returned to their state of corpsehood, this time never to rise again. It was now late evening, for the day had passed in the course of the long fighting, and the sun was low on the western horizon, casting long shadows. But it was natural and the air of sorcery had been dispelled, and everyone breathed freely again, sighing with relief. For all knew at once that this was Rama's shakti at work.

Upon the hillock, Rama looked at Hanuman, whose body had almost completed its process of self-healing. As he raised his eyes to the vanar's face, he saw a deep gash upon Hanuman's cheek and forehead close and then smooth out until the skin appeared as if it had never been cut at all.

'Anjaneya,' he said. 'Expand yourself and carry us to the gates of Lanka, my friend. Let our forces be informed of our intentions and begin moving southwards as well. It is time to take this war to our enemy's gate and see if Ravana has the courage to end what he began back in the aranya of Panchvati.'

4

'They come,' Ravana said, his heads grinning and nodding with almost unanimous pleasure – only one exception on the extreme left-hand side of his rack appeared to be smacking its lips and drooling as if famished, staring down at the vast array of savouries that lined the enormous plinth before which its owner sat. The king of rakshasas was feeding himself, and perhaps that head had not received sufficient victuals as yet. Almost as if aware of this, he picked up a leg of some Lankan fowl, dripping with juices, and fed it to the hungry head, which wolfed down chunks of roasted flesh with ravenous appetite. Each of Ravana's six hands continued to eat and gesture and do various other things.

With one hand he gestured with a taloned finger and the image projected upon the far wall of the enormous chamber sharpened and grew in definition, becoming so clear that Mandodhari thought she could almost see the wounds on the giant vanar as he flew carrying the two mortal warriors on his shoulders. But then a diagonal slash on the vanar's neck seemed to fade, and she wondered if that was the result of the image's imperfection or Rama's sorcery. For she knew now that the Prince of Ayodhya was truly a master of sorcery on a par with her own husband, or how else would his army of monkeymen and bear beasts have been able to withstand the great military might of the rakshasa nation for this long?

The great hall of Ravana's new palace gleamed with polished

black surfaces, intricate sculptures, great hangings and works of art, vaulting façades, elaborate pillars, winding stairways, the whole a veritable cornucopia of architectural marvels. And to think this had all been raised in the course of a single night.

Mandodhari had still not recovered from the destruction of fourteen years of hard work by that wretched vanar spy, and would always miss the pristine alabastar Lanka that she herself had designed and raised while Ravana lay in the thrall of Rama's sorcerous brahman stone like a fly in amber.

But she could not deny that this newly renovated Lanka was beautiful too, albeit in a more hedonistic, more classical rakshasa style. That, after all, was Ravana's taste as opposed to her own. He preferred the ancient Asura ways in all things – including boudoir acts. That was why she had not permitted him into her bed for perhaps half a millennium, and no longer cared what he did and with whom in his palace of pleasures – which place, she had no doubt, he had resurrected as well, and decorated with even more sinful luxury and diabolic splendour.

She had finally reconciled her differences with Ravana, understanding late in their long marital accord that he was what he was, a destroyer of worlds and raper of civilisations. As long as she retained the dignity that befitted the queen of the realm and the stature of the mistress of Lanka, and he did not interfere in her governance of the people and their culture, she cared not whether he invaded the cities of the devas again and raped every devi in Swarga-lok. It was simply what he did, unpleasant and distasteful as it was, and she could not change it, so why should she waste her energy trying?

Besides, those he targeted usually merited their fate in some fashion. Take this upstart Rama Chandra, for instance, and his hypocritical rakshasi-murdering wife Sita. He had undoubtedly ravished their cousin Supanakha, encouraged his brother to partake of her womanly fruits as well, and then spurned her. When the whoring creature – for Mandodhari did not delude herself that Supanakha was an angel of virtue – had foolishly demanded that Rama, having bedded her, should now wed her, she had been mutilated and nearly murdered by the brothers. That was the rape and humiliation that had sparked off this whole war, after all, for even after the massacre of his forces at Mithila and numerous other provocations, Ravana had still retained enough self-will not to respond to Rama's devilish challenges. She had seen for herself how, after his resurrection with the aid of Supanakha, he had resolved to live a new, quieter life of consolidation and repair, culture and development, rather than conquest and ravage. But Rama, curse his mortal avarice, had not accepted that. Exiled after causing his own father's untimely demise, humiliating his clan-mother Kaikeyi, driving his own wet-nurse Manthara first to madness then to death, and having murdered rakshasas by the thousands in the aranya wildernesses in order to allow his mortal rishis and sages to ply their vile cult, performing forced conversions of the local tribal folk, he had hit upon this scheme to invade Lanka. She believed now that Ravana had been brilliantly manipulated by Rama, who had used his own wife as bait to lure Ravana to the forests of Panchvati, and once seduced by the mortal temptress, Ravana had been persuaded into bringing her back to Lanka with him, thinking he would be freeing her from Rama's yoke by doing so. And having engineered this whole thing himself, Rama then cried rape and kidnap and used these wanton lies to muster the support of the vanars of Kiskindha and the bears of the Himalyan cavelands.

And now his manipulations, schemes and sorcery had brought him to the gates of Lanka.

Her blood boiled as she watched the image projected on the far wall of the chamber, a vaulting fifty feet high and seventy feet wide. The vanar spy landed on the open field before the walls of Lanka, placing his mortal passengers gently on the ground. She squinted in disbelief and saw that the vanar's wounds were completely vanished now, as if they had been healed completely in his brief passage through the air. Surely that was sorcery of the highest order. She could not help but marvel at the mortal's command of Asura maya. How ingenious and devious, to parade about like a soldier of dharma and pristine virtue, while in fact using the blackest arts to accomplish his every desire. Finally, it seemed, Ravana had found a worthy opponent in this Rama Chandra.

Now she could hardly wait to see his bestial armies routed and Rama himself torn to shreds by Ravana. Or, the devi willing, by her own son Indrajit. For it was she this time who had suggested that their elder scion be sent out to destroy the invaders.

Ravana smiled around a mouthful of roast flesh at the back of Mandodhari's head. For once, his prissy wife was wholly supportive of his actions and decisions. He could read her innermost thoughts and was pleased at the reluctant but unrepentant espousal of his decisions, as well as her wholehearted antagonism towards Rama. Finally, he mused, he had everything he desired in the palm of his hand. A Lanka occupied solely by rakshasas, with no other Asura races to share the kingdom's past spoils or future victory; the mortal woman Sita in his possession; his arch-nemesis Rama at his gates, literally inviting his own death; and more maha-shakti at his disposal than he had ever been able to summon up, a veritable volcano of power waiting to be utilised as he deemed fit.

Why was it, he wondered idly, quaffing from three separate wine goblets at once, that things always seemed to achieve a perfect state of bliss just before the end?

Supanakha milled around the crowded square before the city gates, weaving expertly between the hooved nether limbs of the hordes of Lankan citizens and soldiers alike – there was little difference really, since every rakshasa was considered a soldier from birth, the only division being between those who were enlisted and provided armour and arms and sent out to fight, and those who were kept back to farm or harvest or store or serve or perform any one of the relatively lower-grade tasks in the country's social hierarchy, for the supreme varna of any rakshasa was that of warrior.

She had spent the past hours on the ramparts of the city, and then on the rooftops, watching as much of the progress of the war as she could glimpse or glean without actually venturing out upon the battlefields, stealing back into the palace from time to time to watch Ravana's constantly unspooling sorcerously projected images of various battles and fights.

But she had tired of those sorcerous projections, wherein everything seemed so immediate and real and yet was so false and ephemeral. Someone, a court wag and self-appointed prophet, had remarked idly in her ear that some day in the distant future people would watch such magical projections as entertainment. She had replied that they would all have to be possessed of brains like potatoes and a complete lack of life-force in order to sit idle and simply be content to watch life unfolding upon a giant screen instead of participating full-bloodedly in the business of life themselves. That had silenced the wag.

She watched as Indrajit issued a few last instructions to his generals and commanders, then stepped up to the cupola of his war chariot. Not a handsome man, like his younger brother, curse his untimely demise, Indrajit nevertheless possessed a magnificent personality at such times. He looked like the great warrior he was, formidable and indestructible, cruel and relentless. She licked her chops and promised herself that after this battle, she would be the first of Indrajit's legendary celebratory conquests – except, of course, that she would be the one conquering, not being conquered! She had learned a great deal of sexual art in Ravana's erstwhile palace of pleasures, and it would be delicious to pass it on to the warrior-prince of Lanka.

Well, cousin, are you prepared to go to war now?

She almost leaped out of her skin. Scanning the crowd around her without finding any trace of that familiar ten-headed form, she realised that Ravana was up to his old tricks again. Mindspeaking. She hated it when he did that, intruding into the private recesses of her thoughts.

But you do love intrusions, don't you, cousin dearest? Or let me rephrase that: you enjoy being penetrated, whether it's your mind or your—

'What is it?' she snarled, startling a group of diggaja rakshasas before her.

I come to invite you to join me in viewing the battle from a more comfortable place.

'I'm tired of watching your projections,' she grumbled. 'I want to see and hear and smell things first-hand.'

And so you shall. You can even join in the fray if you like. As I promised you would be able to.

She frowned, peering through the cluster of diggajas, who had moved away nervously after recognising the famous lust-mad cousin of their king. A commotion broke out suddenly, which she ignored. 'Indrajit is already in his chariot, ready to depart. Perhaps I should hop on with him and hitch a ride.'

He would run you through with his sword the instant you leaped up on that platform. He rides with no one, as you well know.

She sniffed. That was true. Indrajit fought alone, with no charioteer or archer, or even the usual protective circle of chariots that most commanders used to shield themselves in battle. 'Then how?'

Look up.

She looked up and saw Pushpak hovering overhead. Ravana's ten-headed visage leaned over the gleaming golden balustrade of the celestial vehicle and flashed multiple moustached and clean-shaven grins down at her.

*   *   *

As they hovered high above the southern plains of Lanka, the setting sun filling the sky with streaks of crimson and scarlet and the ominous deep orange shade of fresh heart's blood, Rama and Lakshman looked down and saw hordes of rakshasas milling about outside the looming stone ramparts and battlements of the capital city. The gates had been closed to them, Hanuman had reported before, and it appeared that they had remained closed.

What manner of king would bar his war-weary soldiers from returning to the safety of their own city? Was this how Ravana ruled his kingdom and ran his army? Surely it could not continue thus for long. No wonder he required such great mastery of Asura maya; only unnatural power could enable such a king to rule.

Rama looked down from his perch on Hanuman's shoulder and saw the last of his own forces arriving at a brisk pace, taking up position beside the other armies that had already arrived. The contingent of bears that had been with Kambunara in the valley were assembled here; Jambavan's far larger contingent would follow shortly, but by another route. All those who had been summoned had now arrived and were lined up in formation, maintaining the disciplined presentation that they knew Rama and Lakshman preferred, despite the terrible losses they had sustained and the grinding battles they had fought this seemingly endless day. Rama's heart ached as he estimated that perhaps three or four in ten had been lost already in the bitter fighting of the day, and virtually all those who remained fit enough to fight nevertheless sported some mark of injury or wound. That was further testimony to the morale of his warriors.

In case he needed further confirmation, as Hanuman descended with him and Lakshman, a great volley of cheers rose from the weary dust-and-blood-lined throats of his brave soldiers. The sentiments were familiar, the words oft repeated, but the enthusiasm displayed in their chanting was what roused him and moved him almost to tears. As Hanuman touched ground and bent down low enough for his two passengers to alight, the lusty chant reached a climax before dying down out of respect to their leader.

Rama exchanged a glance with Lakshman and saw that even his stout-hearted brother had a shine in his eyes. This time it was Rama who reached out and squeezed Lakshman's tautly muscled shoulder.

'You were right, Lakhan,' he said, resorting to the diminutive used by some of the vanar tribes, who found Lakshman's name impossible to pronounce. 'I owe it to these brave warriors to employ the dev-astras now. In fact, it is for their sake that I released that astra earlier. That missile did not merely dispel the sorceries of Ravana and undo the reanimation of our dead that his maya had achieved; it also infused each and every one of our soldiers with a share of our own brahman maha-shakti, creating for them an invisible kavach, a shield as it were, that will protect them the next time Ravana unleashes some new sorcery.'

Lakshman nodded thoughtfully. 'It will make them invulnerable?'

'Nay,' Rama corrected. 'It cannot guard them against honest weapons and natural violence. Those they must defend themselves against by using their own skills and strength. The astra only protects them from the use of other astras, shakti, or any kind of sorcery. Such as I am certain Ravana will deploy, for he seems desperate now and at his wits' end.'

Lakshman glanced in the direction of the capital city. The gates were still closed. 'I am not as certain of that as you are, Rama. I do not think him to be at his wits' end, but desperate, quite possibly. We have given him stiffer resistance than he expected.' He sighed. 'But he has also dealt us some telling blows.' He gestured at the forces assembled behind them on the flat southern plain. 'Look at how many we have lost. And this is only the second day of the war. I wonder if any of us will leave Lanka alive.'

'Perhaps not,' Rama said. 'But if we leave, we shall certainly not leave unvictorious.'

Both fell silent then as a great commotion broke out among the hordes milling about before the gates of the rakshasa capital. As they watched, the looming thirty-yard high wooden gates, each three yards thick and worked by a hundred rakshasas apiece, groaned open by degrees. They waited to see what would emerge.

5

Sita was barely in control of her senses, doubting everything she saw or heard or felt. Her wits reeled and her consciousness flickered like a guttering candle in a dancing breeze. Had Ravana truly come to fetch her from the ashoka grove, inviting her to come aboard his golden flying chariot, and brought her here? Why? Did he wish her to witness yet another of his demonstrations of sorcery and power? She had had quite enough of those . . . effects, for want of a better word. She wished only to be left alone, meditating quietly until Rama came and fetched her, releasing her from this unending tyranny. She wanted only that her ordeal should end, and end soon.

She sensed the familiar churning of her insides as Pushpak rose, carrying its occupants aloft, and clutched the sickeningly warm golden rod beside her seat for support. She hated herself for showing even that much weakness, but she had no wish either to fall or to lose the meagre contents of her stomach, that nutrition which she had reluctantly consumed only for the sake of the unborn lives she bore. She held on tightly until the vertiginous sensation passed, and only when she was certain that the vaahan had ceased its upward flight did she allow her eyes to slowly flutter open.

She saw Ravana standing at the prow of the vehicle, facing outwards like any general examining his troops. She saw that vile shape-shifting yaksi-rakshasi hybrid, Supanakha, crouched upon the balustrade beside her cousin, staring down as well.

She remembered that there was another gallery on the celestial vehicle where she dimly recalled having earlier glimpsed Mandodhari and various ministers of the Lankan court; but that was a lower section of Pushpak. On this uppermost gallery there were only the three of them. She grew aware that she was in the open air and a weak warm evening sun was lighting her face and upper body on the right side. In the distance she could see the horizon and the ocean, turned blood-red by the setting sun. The air smelled fragrant with the ripe, rich odours of the open countryside, and she wanted so badly to relish it, to savour the simple pleasure of being out in the clear air of Prithvi-maa once more, to have done with this endless nightmare, but she knew Ravana too well by now to believe that he had brought her out here for a soirée in the park. He had some devilish ulterior motive for taking her along on this trip, and she sensed with a sickening certainty that whatever it was he intended her to see, it lay below them at this very instant. She prepared herself as best as she could in her current state, and gripping the balustrade now with both hands, trembling slightly from weakness as well as trepidation, peered over the edge of sanity.

She was not prepared for the sight that met her eyes.

Rama.

Rama stood there below, far below, perhaps a few hundred yards distant, but it was still he, in the flesh, standing on a grassy barrow, with Lakshman beside him. Tears welled up at once, unbidden and undesired, and for once she did not suppress them as she had done with all her emotions in Ravana's presence. She let them flow, dripping one and then another upon the unflawed golden surface of Pushpak, where they did not linger or roll but were instantly absorbed by the metal skin of the celestial vehicle, disappearing into the fabric of the device itself. She fought to blink away their followers so she could see more clearly.

Rama and Lakshman stood before a great army of vanars and bears, so great that even from this height she could not see the end of the great host. Before them, on the great southern plains of Lanka, barely a mile separating them, were the hordes of Lanka, assembled before the city walls and gate in some measure of confusion, circling and re-circling, raising dust clouds in agitation, as if unsure of whether they were to retreat into the city or attack the sighted enemy. Within the walls of Lanka, just inside the great gates, were assembled what appeared to be all the rest of Lanka's populace, armed as well as unarmed, armoured as well as unattired. A great gleaming chariot was preparing to ride out through the gates even as she looked, and she thought she recognised the helmed head of Indrajit, Ravana's elder son. Behind him were several rakshasas in much smaller, less ostentatious chariots. Somehow she knew they were champions.

Her eyes found Rama once more, even though Pushpak had drifted slightly during this brief period, and they filled with tears again as she gazed adoringly upon the visage and form of her beloved after so long a separation. He seemed well enough, but so much leaner and thinner and paler. His dark skin, once almost bluish in hue, seemed to have faded to the colour of greenish wheatflour. She thought it must surely be the weakness of her vision and the dust of the field and the fading light of evening that deceived her. As she gazed at him, she saw several vanars and a bear or two approach and stand with him and Lakshman upon the mound as generals and lieutenants might stand with their king upon a battlefield. Of course, she knew none of them apart from the gallant Hanuman, whom she had recognised at once. She felt great sorrow at the fact that the forces and generals of Lanka were so much more familiar to her than were those of Rama. And once again she wished keenly that she had but her freedom and a sword, so that she might stand by Rama's side as well, like any of his war ministers, to do battle for his honour. For it was as much his honour he defended here as hers, for were they not one and the same? What was it he always said? *Where Sita begins, and Rama ends,*

I do not know, it is not possible to know. But where Sita ends, there Rama ends, this I know for certain.

I am here, my love. She wanted to scream the words. But the shame and humiliation of being in his enemy's chariot and a captive caused her to hold her tongue. And she could only watch as the great drama of war unfolded before her weeping eyes.

The gates of Lanka were barely open all the way when the war chariot flew out, its team heaving with all their might to get the great armoured vehicle moving upon its high wheels. Some rakshasas – either simply careless, or perhaps foolish enough to think they might aid their lord as he rode out – came into its path, and without so much as a warning shout Indrajit whipped his team and rode them down. Their bodies were churned and crushed beneath the spinning wheels, reinforced with metal and cruelly studded and spiked. The rest of the horde nearest to the gate reared back, issuing a disgruntled growl. Even the heavy lashes of the kumbhas upon their hides did not deter them from watching with baleful resentment as the Prince of Lanka rode out through their lines and on to the field of battle.

Indrajit rode his chariot to a suitable strategic position and then reined in the team. They chomped at the bit now, pulses racing, scenting the odours of the enemy and eager to continue, for they were blood-fed crossbreeds, weaned on the flesh of mortals and as vicious in battle as any rakshasa. Indrajit stood proudly arrogant in his chariot's well, gazing out at the army of invaders with an aspect that seemed openly contemptuous even at this distance.

Rama watched as a line of smaller, far less ornate chariots followed in Indrajit's wake, taking up suitably subordinate positions behind their leader. Following them in turn came a new host from Lanka, their armour still gleaming and unsullied by the dust of the field, their blades sharp and maces undented. They came, and kept coming, the new arrivals fanning out to form a wall from west to east that promised to match the length of the battlement wall of the city itself. He resisted the urge to catch his breath as the numbers continued to swell, until the army before them seemed almost an even match for his own host. And he would wager that there were still more rakshasas not yet assembled here: those oddly faced beasts that had emerged from the battlements only after the darkness fell were nowhere to be seen on this field.

His generals had assembled around him even as they awaited Lanka's next move. Now they were all silent, watching this great army arrayed before them. Suddenly their great advantage of numbers seemed substantially diminished. After taking into account their huge losses, they were now left with an army no more than twice as big as Lanka's own. And given the superior size, armour, strength and fighting knowledge of the Lankans, that was no advantage at all.

A flicker of gold in the air caught his attention again. He did not pay it much heed. He had already glimpsed Ravana's celestial vehicle hovering about overhead as it had done all day. He could see several faces gazing down from its galleries at the armies assembled on these plains, but he did not care. Let Ravana's spies examine him and his forces as much as they desired. There was no longer any call for subterfuge. This was open war and this the last battlefield in Lanka.

'The craven lurks in his chariot and will not even descend to the field of battle,' snarled Sugreeva with surprising vehemence. The king of vanars had been barely recognisable when he had approached Rama moments ago; the marks of battle were on his face and form, and yet he seemed renewed and invigorated rather than weakened. His age-bent crouch and pained expression had given way to a monarchical pride. Once again, like the first time Rama had laid eyes upon Sugreeva at Mount Rishimukha, he was reminded of his own father. This

Sugreeva put him in mind of what he thought Maharaja Dasaratha must have looked like on the field of one of his famous battles: proud, indomitable, unrelenting. He had already heard a brief account of Sugreeva's exploits in the battle of the canyon and marvelled at it. He felt a surge of pride that he was the cause, however unfortunately, of the vanar king's return to glory.

'If he will but descend to the ground and join swords with us, I will show him how kings should fight upon the field, instead of sending his minions out in hordes to do his killing for him.'

The King of Kiskindha added a few choice epithets to his outburst then snarled and spat furiously in the direction of Pushpak. For an instant all eyes in Rama's camp turned upwards towards the gleaming golden object in the dusky sky. Rama looked up as well, noting that there were two galleries on the vehicle: one a larger one which accommodated at least a couple of dozen rakshasas of varying breeds and kinds; and an upper gallery which was slightly smaller and held just two or three persons, one of whom was unmistakably Ravana, the other the treacherous Supanakha, and the third . . . the third . . .

Hanuman's paw gripped his arm. 'My lord!'

Rama started at the same moment, seeing what Hanuman and Lakshman and all the rest of them saw, but only the three of them recognised.

The third passenger in Pushpak was none other than Sita herself.

Indrajit raised his mailed fist and his herald at once lifted his long, elaborately carved bone trumpet. The call that issued forth was lowing and mournful, like a dirge. It silenced the chittering and growling in Rama's camp as well as the grumbling and resentful noises among the Lankan hordes. The kumbhas ceased their whipping and beating momentarily, for even the most recalcitrant rakshasa obeyed implicitly the call to battle. Ravana watched as the trumpeting was taken up and echoed by each of the hordes. In fact he had not yet given the order to issue the call of battle. The herald had been entrusted with the task of watching Ravana in Pushpak, waiting for the lord of rakshasas' signal. Instead Indrajit had given the command himself. Ravana knew that he could not rescind that order now without causing Indrajit to lose face: his son would be more likely to turn his chariot around and ride back into Lanka than brook being corrected by his father. Several of his heads sighed. If there was one rakshasa in Lanka he could not command by hook or by crook, it was his own son. On the other hand, he had been about to issue the order himself. And he had after all entrusted Indrajit with leading the army in this battle. So to all intents and purposes, Indrajit was the supreme commander today. Let the dog have his day.

He glanced back with two of his heads at Sita. She was clutching at the balustrade with both hands, trembling and tearful at the sight of Rama. He had glimpsed Rama and his cohorts staring up just now, when the ageing vanar had issued his futile challenge and spat rudely, and knew that both the paramours had seen one another and were profoundly moved.

That had been Ravana's intention in bringing her here today. It gave him pleasure to see her rend her heart, knowing that her beloved Rama was so close and yet so far. It would give him even greater pleasure to see her watching Rama die on that battlefield.

6

Rama had no time to dwell on Sita's presence above the battle-field. Pushpak remained aloft, several hundred yards high, its passengers watching from their safe remove like spectators at a feast-day celebration. The Lankan forces, rallying behind their several banners, began to march inexorably forward. Rama's generals looked to him for orders to march as well, but he indicated to them that they were to wait. He sensed the impatience of the vanars and the bears, eager now to strike openly at their foe after so much subterfuge and counter-subterfuge. All the scheming and battle strategy was well and good, but there came a time when warriors needed to face their enemy and match their armies' strengths to secure a decisive victory. Now was that time.

But the Lankan army halted when they were three hundred yards from Rama's lines. Orders were shouted by their generals, enforced by the kumbha sergeants and their vicious whips. After much grunting and grumbling and expelling of nasal fluids, the hordes reluctantly relaxed their arms and assumed a waiting stance.

'Do they desire a parley?' Angad asked scornfully beside Rama. 'Do not give them the satisfaction, Rama. We will fight them with our last breath!'

'It is not a parley they seek, son,' King Sugreeva replied, his voice sounding both stronger and wearier after his battles. 'They seek to call out our champions against their own, I warrant.'

And indeed that was what the rakshasas desired.

A moment later, a rakshasa from Indrajit's horde alighted from a chariot and strode forward to the centre of the battlefield, stopping midway between the two standing armies. He was a kumbharakshasa with the heightened stature and superior bulk of his kind, and bore a jet-black iron mace studded with vicious barbs and points. He flexed his muscles and roared a challenge. His demand was obvious: send someone out to fight. If you have someone worthy of fighting.

Almost every vanar and bear stepped forward, as well as every one of Rama's generals. Angad and Sugreeva were the most vociferous, along with the vanars Mainda and Dvivida. Rama quietened them all with a raised hand, showing them his open palm. When they were silent, he spoke, feeling the need to explain his choice even though his army would accept his decision without question.

'The Lankans are arrogant and overconfident. They challenge us in order to prove that they are superior and to demoralise us. It is necessary to show them decisively and quickly that we are more than their match in every way. The champion I pick must not only defeat the challenger but must crush him so convincingly that they should be left open-mouthed with awe. To this end, I request all you able and valiant warriors to stand aside and allow me to select the most powerfully endowed amongst you all.'

There was a moment's pause as his words were repeated in relay, reaching the farthermost vanar and bear, miles away. Then, with one voice, the entire assembled might of Rama's army replied without hesitation or second thoughts: '*Jai Sri Hanuman!*'

Rama nodded approvingly. 'Hanuman it is.'

Hanuman stepped forward with palms joined. Bowing first, he then prostrated himself on the dusty ground before Rama, touching his lord's feet, then Lakshman's as well. Both of them gave him the traditional ashirwaad. He rose to his feet again and strode out from their lines. As he walked, he chanted in his clear vanar voice: 'Siyavar Rama Chandra ki jai! Srimati Sita Maya ki jai!' *Praised be Rama Chandra, husband of Sita. Praised be Mother Sita, wife of Rama.*

Rama's forces echoed the words, keeping rhythm with Hanuman's steps as he walked to the no-man's-land between the armies where the Lankan champion waited. The rakshasas took up their own arcane chant as well, a kind of guttural howling with a ragged rhythm reinforced by the pounding of weapons and armoured fists against their helms and chest armour. Somewhere in that cacophonic noise was the word 'Dumraksa', which Rama took to be the name of the rakshasa challenger. It was only to be expected that the rakshasas would cheer the champion rather than their overlord.

The din raised by both armies was intense and fierce and was audible for yojanas around.

Hanuman stopped when he was within ten yards of his opponent. Rama noted that the vanar had chosen neither to expand his body nor to display his enormous powers in any fashion, and was pleased by his friend's wisdom. Hanuman had understood what he desired even without being told in so many words.

Sita watched from the railing of Pushpak as the Lankan champion roared and beat his mace upon the ground, gouging out great cavities in the earth. Then, raising the formidable weapon, the rakshasa bellowed one last time and charged the waiting vanar. She saw that Hanuman was unarmed and standing calmly, making no remonstrations nor calling out. The chanting of the armies had ceased and both sides watched with tense anticipation as their champions clashed.

Vertiginous and drained as she was, she did not understand why the vanar had not used his incredible powers. She had seen what he was capable of when he virtually destroyed Lanka single-handed, yet today he stood there like any ordinary vanar.

The rakshasa challenger charged at Hanuman with his mace raised. Swinging it with all his might, he brought it down at a diagonal angle aimed at the junction of Hanuman's head and left shoulder. It was a classic mace attack, designed to shatter armour and bone and crush the heart instantly. Any victim struck by such a blow would drop dead at once. She caught her breath, not because she doubted Hanuman's abilities, but because of the impassive manner with which the vanar stood there, moving neither back nor forward, nor responding in any way to the brutal attack. And because Hanuman was neither armoured nor protected in any way, bare-chested and naked except for the langot around his groin, seemingly vulnerable.

But at the last instant, Hanuman's left arm shot up, unerringly gripping the shaft of the downward-swinging mace. It was as if the rakshasa had struck an invisible force that did not resist or yield a fraction. The mace hung there in the air, gripped by both the champions. There was no struggle as such, for Hanuman simply stood there, left arm upraised, almost as if he was reaching up to pluck a fruit from a tree limb. The rakshasa, on the other hand, sweated and grunted and strained with effort until his eyes bulged enormously and his muscles popped and the tendons stood out in relief like a network of wires.

Both fighters stood like statues in a tableau. Like one of the enormous stone statues Sita recalled seeing in the Suryavansha palace at Ayodhya, depicting scenes featuring Rama's ancestors.

Then, slowly, the rakshasa's feet began to move.

Just a fraction at first, but the motion was unmistakable.

Then a little more, perhaps an inch. Then another inch.

He was sliding backwards, losing his grip.

Realising this, the rakshasa roared once, loudly, then pushed upwards with both his hands, his great back muscles now standing out in relief as he exerted all his considerable strength to attempt to push the vanar back, or tilt him off-balance at the very least.

Instead Hanuman raised his head, opened his mouth, and spoke a single phrase, loudly and clearly enough to be heard by both armies.

'Jai Siyaram,' he said.

And brought the mace down on the head of its owner with

a force so swift, so sudden, so powerful that the head of the weapon was driven through the crown of the rakshasa's skull, through his brain, through his spine, shattering each in succession, all the way down until it struck the ground itself and buried itself several feet down, together with the pulped remains that was all that was left of the Lankan challenger.

The stony silence that met the death of the Lankan champion was broken by a great roar of rage from the rakshasa hordes. Several rakshasas broke free of their lines and ran forward, unable to curb their anger. Some were lashed by kumbhas; others were methodically shot down by arrows from Indrajit's chariot. The acting commander of the Lankan army showed no hesitation in cutting down his own warriors; abjuring from wounding them in the legs, he aimed to kill, dropping a dozen-odd rakshasas dead in their tracks before the first of them could reach even halfway across the no-man's-land. Shouted orders by the kumbhas sent grumbling rakshasas out in pairs and trios to drag back the bodies of the insubordinates. After that, the rakshasa hordes settled for howling and roaring and otherwise spewing noxious fluids into the air, but none dared break their ranks.

Rama watched as Indrajit lowered his bow and gestured with a mailed fist. A flurry broke out behind him, and then a chariot rolled forward. Rakshasas scattered to make way for it, the charioteer giving no heed to whether or not he ran down his own countrymen, and the vehicle drove through to the no-man's-land. Then, without pausing, it swung around in a dusty arc and wheeled straight towards Hanuman.

*Cheeka*s of protest broke out in the vanar ranks, for Hanuman, despite his powers, was still unarmed. But the Lankan chariot came at the vanar without pause, its wheels trundling more silently than any chariot Rama had ever seen. In its cupola was a rakshasa with so much armour and cladding he could scarcely make out the creature's face. Only two ruby-red eyes glowed from within the helm, and a maw that might have been its mouth issued an unsettling banshee scream. From the manner in which even the front-line kumbhas stepped back hurriedly as the chariot rode past them, he understood that this new champion was greatly feared by Lankans as well. Someone in Indrajit's formation started a cheer that was reluctantly repeated by the rest of the Lankan army – or most of them at any rate, for the new challenger was clearly not loved by all of his people. The cry that rang out this time was 'Akampana!'

Hanuman stood impassively still as the chariot rolled towards him. The charioteer, a sneering fellow with a thin, reedy trunk like a poor imitation of an elephant's, whipped the broken-sur team with vicious glee, adding his own tinny voice to the Lankan cheer: 'Akampana! Akampana!'

The Lankan began firing arrows when he was a mere two hundred yards from the lone vanar. His aim was unerring despite the speed of the chariot. Rama saw an arrow strike Hanuman's right shoulder, the next his left shoulder, the third his chest, the fourth his abdomen . . . By the time the chariot came within striking distance, fourteen arrow shafts were stuck in the vanar's bare body, one in every major part of him, with three in his chest alone. Hanuman seemed to take no notice of these missiles and remained standing with the same impassive calm as the chariot bore down on him at the greatest speed its driver could muster from the frothing team.

Rama saw the leading broken-sur lower its segregated head to strike Hanuman, even as the vanar did the same with his own head, bending down and forward at the last instant. The animal and the vanar skulls impacted together with a sound like dried parchment crumpled in an angry fist, then the entire broken-sur team ploughed into Hanuman with the force of a wooden box striking a granite boulder. Flesh and bone were destroyed on impact and exploded into a shower of bloody rain that descended on the dusty plain as far away as the first lines of the nearest Lankan horde. The chariot followed, ploughing into the steadfast vanar even as it upended and flipped over. Hanuman's arms shot up, catching the overturning chariot, and he crumpled it with his bare hands until it folded and refolded into a splintered mess of metal debris. He threw the remains at the Lankan lines, to land just before the front ranks. The rakshasas scuttled backwards, tripping over their fellows behind, several collapsing like a heap of startled toddlers. The crumpled remains of the chariot crashed down and slid across the dusty ground, stopping inches from the popping eyes of a kumbha-rakshasa lieutenant too proud to step back out of its way. It resembled a child's plaything stepped on by an elephant's foot.

The charioteer had been mashed to pulp within his vehicle, Rama noted, but the Lankan within had leaped free even as the vehicle overturned, landing several yards to one side. As Hanuman straightened up after tossing the chariot aside, the rakshasa charged the vanar, swinging a metal mace with chains attached to its head and studded iron balls on the ends of the chains. He whipped it around with expert ease, till the balls were whirling blurs in the fading sunset light, and with the same banshee sound he had made earlier attacked Hanuman.

Making no attempt to bend or dodge the swinging apparatus, the vanar put his hand directly in the path of the blurring chains and balls. As if by magic, the entire thing wrapped itself around his bare fist, and yanking once, he pulled the mace towards him – along with the rakshasa holding it. The Lankan, thrown off his feet, flew straight into the vanar's other fist, which connected with his chest with a squelching impact. His banshee wail ceased at once, and he stared down at the vanar's arm, embedded so deeply in his chest that the fist attached to it had emerged from the rakshasa's back, clutching a dripping, still-pounding heart. Rama watched as Hanuman's fist squeezed the beating heart till it was the consistency of oatmeal porridge, then shoved the rakshasa away. The second challenger's corpse landed with a thud in the dust beside the crumpled remains of

the chariot in which he had ridden so proudly only moments
ago.

Rama had expected that Indrajit might lose patience after seeing
the fate of the two challengers, and simply roar and order the rest
of the army to charge his lines. But the rakshasa was evidently a
person well versed in battle etiquette and tradition. He displayed
an admirable restraint in the face of the enraged roars of his army,
and opted to send in another challenger against Hanuman – and
then another, and yet another. Staring across the distance that
divided them, Rama saw the son of Ravana gazing coldly at him
in a manner unlike that of any other rakshasa he had seen before
now, and he knew that he was facing an enemy who was a master
of the art of warcraft, a rakshasa whose prowess was comparable
only with that of his father, Ravana. Small wonder that Ravana
had chosen to let his scion command the army of Lanka while
he himself watched from the high vantage of Pushpak.

Angad and some of the other generals, unfamiliar with the
ancient war customs of the Aryas and rakshasas and other
warfaring races, grew impatient. After Hanuman had killed the
fourth challenger and while he was waiting for the fifth to ride
out on a trumpeting kumbha-sur, Angad asked impatiently, 'Is
he such a craven, this son of Ravana, that he dares not order
his army to charge us? He must know by now that Hanuman
can crush any opponent he sends against him. So why does he
waste time sending more fools to their death?'

Lakshman answered on Rama's behalf. 'He seeks to show
the world – both our armies, as well as the observers who watch
from a distance,' indicating the pushpak above and the high
ramparts of Lanka in the distance, 'that he is a fair and just
commander, hewing to the rules of war. So that when the history
of this war is written, it will record that Lanka fought fairly
and according to the code of warriors.'

'But that is a lie!' said the young vanar prince. 'What of the devilish sorceries employed earlier? What of the spies, the subterfuge, the use of killing stones and fog and other devices that are not lawful by the rules of warrior conduct?'

Lakshman and Rama exchanged an understanding glance with the vanar prince. 'Those he will probably blame on us, I suspect,' Lakshman said matter-of-factly. 'He might well spread the story that Rama the sorcerer was the one responsible for all the unnatural things that have happened up to now.'

'Rama the *sorcerer*?' Angad asked disbelievingly.

Lakshman nodded laconically. 'And being innocent of the true workings of the dark arts, most will believe his lies. We have heard from Hanuman, who heard it from my sister-in-law, about the elaborate web of deceit Ravana has already spun to justify his war against terror, even though he himself is the creator of that very terror.'

Angad swore in vanar phrases that Rama was almost glad he did not comprehend. As the vanar prince subsided, Rama added quietly, 'But I suspect there is another reason for all this charade of honourable warfare.'

'Aye,' King Sugreeva said, nodding with the wisdom of his age. 'I see it as well.'

Angad frowned. 'What is that, Rama?'

'He seeks also to show Hanuman's indestructibility, so that when he himself attacks our friend and defeats him in single combat, his own power will appear god-like, immeasurable. And then, when he leads his army against ours, their morale will be unassailable.'

Angad stared at Rama. 'But that . . . you mean he actually believes he will be able to kill Bajrangbali?'

Rama nodded grimly. 'Not just believes; he may well be capable of doing so in reality.'

Angad had no response to that statement.

7

The roll-call of challengers continued all through the night. After the first three or four encounters, the light faded completely, leaving both armies blanketed in darkness, with only the lights of Lanka itself visible. Indrajit ordered braziers to be set up in the no-man's-land, illuminating the front lines with garish highlights. Some more time-wasting formalities followed, and when the single-combat challenges eventually continued, things went on much as before, except that Hanuman now began to take a little more time before dispatching each new champion. The hordes, so belligerent and arrogant to start with, grew furious when they saw their first several champions dispatched with such nonchalant ease, but as the night went on, and the number of dead Lankan fighters mounted, they grew quieter and quieter, until by the time first light began to break on the horizon, they seemed stupefied. Rama saw several of them staring with glazed eyes at Hanuman as he swung a hefty four-footed rakshasa with tusks as long and curved as an elephant's round and round before releasing it. Such was the force of Hanuman's swinging that the rakshasa flew miles, arching high over the plains of southern Lanka before falling back to earth out of sight – probably in the ocean yojanas away.

At that, the rakshasas who had been staring glassily came alive, salivating and making curious low noises, their wet muzzles rising and falling in a manner Rama had not seen till now. Seeing their response, the kumbha sergeants came with whips flashing and lashed them bitterly, but even after lowering their snouts submissively they still continued gazing at the vanar standing alone and unconquered in the centre of the field.

'They have turned admirers,' Rama said. 'For when confronted by an opponent so powerful that one cannot hope to defeat him by any means, the mind of a warrior resorts to one of two choices: either to refuse to accept his superiority and risk one's life in a final suicidal assault; or to acknowledge his superiority and offer oneself in surrender to his greater power. The rakshasas of Lanka have begun to admire and respect our Anjaneya, it seems.'

'I wonder if Indrajit and his father knew this would happen when they decided to play this charade,' Lakshman said, smiling.

Rama glanced up at Pushpak. The celestial vehicle had been hovering in the same place for the entire night. Now, as the first rays of the sun caught the burnished surface of the vaahan, sending golden shards of splintered sunlight in all directions, creating a rainbow-like seven-hued refraction, he found his heart crying out at Sita's plight. How was she enduring this test of tests? To be so close to him, within sight, and yet unable to come to him. If she felt anything akin to what he himself felt, then her heart must be weeping blood. It took every ounce of his self-control not to raise his celestial weapons and use them to end this elaborate charade that Ravana had laid out, end this wretched war, and take his wife home. But thinking along these lines bred anger within his breast, the epic anger that he had restrained for so long through so many travails and struggles and disappointments. He shut his eyes tightly, breathing deeply to dispel the ghosts and demons that threatened to turn him once again into a killing machine. Once *that* Rama Chandra was unleashed, there could be no muzzling him.

Lakshman's gaze was on him when he reopened his eyes. 'Patience, bhai. It will not be long now. Let Ravana have his day. We will have ours.'

'Yes,' Rama said. 'Dharma will triumph in the end, as it

always does.' He paused. 'It is the long and painful waiting until that day arrives that tests the mettle of us mortals.'

The bouts of single combat ended suddenly.

First, shouts broke out on the ramparts of Lanka, followed by a great hullabaloo from the direction of the city. Shortly after, a rider came from the gates of Lanka with great haste. He rode up to Indrajit's chariot and delivered a message. After hearing what he had to say, Indrajit nodded and dismissed him, then called upon his herald. The herald was given instructions and sent out toward Rama's army. Taking great care to steer clear of the vanar champion standing alone in mid-field, the herald announced that he had a message for Rama's ears alone. With Rama's permission, he was brought to where the leaders of the invading army had assembled. Looking notably nervous, yet haughty, as heralds are wont to be, he spoke in a clear tenor, using classical Sanskrit highspeech that revealed him to be highly cultured and educated:

'It has come to my lord Indrajit's notice that some faction of your army has infiltrated the city of Lanka using devious means and undoubted sorcery. These demons in diguise are being repelled by our forces. My lord wishes you to know that while they shall not succeed in their devilish endeavour, he finds such treachery repugnant. It is an affront to the rules of warfare, and to any warrior with a sense of honour.'

To emphasise his meaning, the herald arched his thin stalk-like neck sideways and spat. At this, Angad and several of the other generals swore and surged forward. Rama raised his hand, halting them.

The herald eyed them carefully, then, seeing that they were not likely to attack, resumed his ornately decorative style of address: 'Under the circumstances, the single combat duel is called off and we withdraw our champions at once. It would be dishonourable for us to continue fighting a foe who indulges in such unlawful practices and insults the rules of warfare, shaming the very varna of kshatriyahood itself. My lord wishes you to be warned that he proposes to attack your lines and drive you back into the sea whence you came using your sorcerous aids. If you desire to leave this field alive, do so at once, desist in your campaign and retreat post-haste. If you are not gone within the hour-watch, you shall face the might of Lanka's hordes, and my lord has no doubt that when confronted with an honest battle, your devilish monsters so cleverly disguised will be routed and massacred to the last man. I bid you on his lordship's behalf farewell and call you to arms, to arms, to arms.'

With those final words, delivered in a proud, sneering nasal tone, the herald turned his back on Rama and rode towards his lines once more.

This time when Angad swore he was echoed by several other vanars. 'What did that pompous ass mean? Why did he keep referring to disguises? Who is disguised here?'

'Probably Jambavan and his forces.' Rama replied thoughtfully. 'Although if I understand his meaning in full, he implied that the Lankans now believe that all you vanars and bears are in fact mortals that I have somehow disguised as vanars and bears through sorcery.'

This time, even King Sugreeva swore. 'He will know the truth soon enough when he feels my talons ripping his vitals and my jaws upon his throat!'

'That he will, I have no doubt,' Rama said. 'But the herald's messages were merely words, and words can be woven cleverly into ingenious lies. That is why Indrajit uses a messenger, and why Ravana in turn uses Indrajit. They are merely a means to spread disinformation and conceal the truth. We must not be moved by them one whit. What is of import is the news that Jambavan and his bear army have successfully traversed the underground caverns and reached the city itself. We have forced Ravana's hand at last, and now we can put this charade behind us and finish the war we came here to wage.'

At his words, everyone subsided. King Sugreeva nodded sagely, showing that his newly acquired battle aggression had not entirely replaced his kingly wisdom and sense of justice. 'Aye, Rama, you speak truly. This is yet another clever subterfuge of the Dark Lord of Lanka to confuse and provoke us. See how he toys with us: first using sorcerous stones and the earth of Lanka itself, then sending hybrid creatures out of some hellish realm to attack us under cover of sorcerous darkness, and when he sees that his forces are losing the day, he pulls them back and changes tactics at once. But this time he will not cheat us of our goal. We are at the walls of Lanka, and our forces are already breaching their capital city. We must push through and secure the city now, and after that, there will be nothing left for Ravana to fight us for.'

'Except one thing,' Lakshman said, tight-jawed.

And he indicated Pushpak overhead, with Sita's tiny forlorn face visible even at this distance.

Sita had spent a wan and nerve-racking night, alleviated only by the sight of her beloved Rama and her brother-in-law Lakshman. Each time her champion – for he fought for her as much as for Rama, his people and the cause, she knew – vanquished another Lankan challenger, her heart leaped. Perhaps, she prayed, Ravana would see that Rama could not be defeated, just as his champion could not be, and would yield now. She knew this would not come to pass, but still she prayed. The sight of so much blood being spilled, even Lankan blood, even that of warriors, dismayed her. Perhaps it was the life growing within her – the *lives*, she corrected herself at once – or merely her weariness with so much war and violence. Either way, she wished now only to have done with all this, to have an end to this fighting. To go home.

When the ruckus broke out in the city, she understood at once what it meant.

From her vantage point, she could see the crowds running helter-skelter. They were heading for the tunnels, the subterranean network of corridors riddling the island that had either been created on the night of the sorcerous changes, or merely altered and expanded, she did not know which. From the commotion at the mouth of one of the tunnels visible from her position, it seemed that there was fighting going on there. Since Lanka had only one enemy, she knew that it could only be Rama's forces that had somehow infiltrated the tunnels and breached the city! Then victory was in sight at last!

She laughed, the first open-throated, guileless laugh she had enjoyed since . . . since that afternoon at Panchvati when she had chased after the golden deer and slipped and coloured herself with turmeric and Rama had found her that way, rolling in the grass, yellow-faced like a bride-to-be.

The slap took her by surprise. A backhanded blow upon her left cheek so resounding that it nearly caused her to lose her balance. She clutched at the railing, her head spinning, eyes unable to focus for a moment. She blinked away tears and stared into the snarling, fur-covered features and glowering yellow eyes of Supanakha.

'What do you have to laugh about now, Rama's—'

Whatever the rakshasi had been about to say next was cut off by a kick from Ravana's mighty foot. The shapeshifter was thrown clear across the width of Pushpak, a good ten yards or more, to land with a loud thump on the far railing and wall. She squealed with indignation and leaped towards her cousin, coming at him with the ferocious instinct of a cat rather than the lumbering power of a rakshasa. Perhaps that was what saved her life, for Ravana struck out at her with a careless blow, as if swatting aside a gnat rather than dealing with an enemy of any import, and her natural feline response brought her down on all four paws. She snarled and crouched in preparation for yet another leap.

'Enough!' thundered the rakshasa king. 'You've already given me reason to kill you, cousin. If you wish me to perform the execution right here and now, then it shall be so.'

Supanakha subsided, but not without a final glowering snarl. She licked at her haunches where they had struck the railing of Pushpak. Sita saw a red bruise rising there already, as well as another dark welt where Ravana's careless blow had landed. She felt sadness rather than satisfaction at seeing her abuser hurt thus; would this cycle of violence never end?

'How are you, my lady?' asked Ravana in a tone so gentle it almost made her forget who he was. But she had seen enough of his guile not to be fooled.

She ignored him studiously, staring out at the lightening sky. From below she heard the sounds of the Lankan army moving once more, and knew that battle was about to be joined. She had expected that the instant she had seen the commotion in the city and recognised it for what it was. Bravo, Rama. You forced their hand and compelled them to confront you at last in a fair fight. Now we shall see how the Lord of Lanka fares in a true battle.

Ravana paused, gazing down at her with all his heads in a manner that almost made her glance up. She resisted but was struck by the feeling, so overwhelming it must have some measure of truth, that he somehow knew her thoughts and was displeased by them in the extreme. Still she refused to look up at him and give him the satisfaction of a single word of conversation. As far as she was concerned he did not exist. It was the only way she could resist him now, for every gesture, every look, every word she granted would be twisted and misinterpreted to suit his own purpose. Only by acting as if he did not exist could she reject his advances totally.

After a moment of waiting, looming above her like an elephant with a raised foot, he turned and strode away, back to the front railing of Pushpak, where he stood once more, gazing out at the battlefield below while his heads continued their own bizarre battle of words and wits.

She stole a glance at Supanakha. The rakshasi sensed her gaze and glared back at her, but continued licking her wounds with no sign of aggression or threat. However much she might hate Sita, she hated Ravana more, and feared him too, and that was the only protection Sita could cling to for now.

She raised herself to her feet once more and took her place at the railing, determined to watch the battle to the finish, or for as long as her captor would permit her. She would pray for Rama's victory with her every breath now, until the war ended.

8

In the clear light of day they met this time, vanar and rakshasa and bear and two mortals, on the open field of battle, with no subterfuge or sorcery, shima or tactics, strategy or device. A straight-forward charge, army versus army, riding and racing headlong towards one another, meeting midway, clashing together with a noise so terrible that all the world seemed to stop still for a moment. Prithvi herself paused in her rotation around her own axis, as well as her revolution around the sun god's blinding orb, to wonder at the clash of two hosts so hellbent on one another's destruction.

Many wars have been fought since, and many were fought before.

But none akin to the war of Lanka.

Never before or since have such strange hosts through a chain of such extraordinary circumstances gathered on so mundanely idyllic a plain, marred only by the smoke-oozing cone of the newly reawakened volcano a few yojanas farther south. Never before had vanars gone to war in such numbers – and that too against rakshasas! Never before had rakshasas been confronted by an army on their own homeland. Never before had a war been fought for dharma by such misunderstood, maligned and mistreated ones as Rama, Lakshman and Sita – for in her own proud way she fought as valiantly as any other. Not every soldier wields a blade; not every battle is fought with violence; not all bloodshed is visible.

In the clear light of day, they clashed.

*   *   *

Like moths to the flame, rakshasas rushed towards Hanuman. Many of them were the same glazed-eyed observers that Rama had seen watching the vanar through the long night of combat, their aggression giving way to disbelief, then to fury, then to denial, then, finally, reluctantly, to awe and admiration. Many charged him without even swinging their blades or maces, merely rushing at him and allowing themselves to be mowed down, as if being killed by Hanuman was a consummation devoutly to be desired.

Those who attacked him did so with the silent, watchful stance of deer lashing at a tiger, purely out of reflex and instinct, yet knowing full well that the tiger would win and they fall. And so they fell. And falling spoke his name or mouthed it silently or simply held his image in their glazed eyes as they died. They had been killed by Hanuman.

Rama and Lakshman were out of arrows, and had to fight with their swords. Of course Rama possessed one last arrow, and that one alone was equivalent to all the arrows ever created since the beginning of time and until the end of days, but in staging this battle with apparent honesty and transparency, Ravana had brilliantly denied him the use of that celestial weapon. If Rama employed the Bow of Vishnu and the Arrow of Shiva now, he would be seen as resorting to unfair means, and confirmed as the treacherous invading sorcerer the Lankans believed him to be. He would not use it until and unless it was imperative to do so.

So he chose to fight like a mortal, like a kshatriya, like an Ayodhyan, like an Arya warrior, like a yodha. Like a man. And he did not stand apart from his army as Ravana did either; he waded into the thick of the combat, his sword flashing beside Lakshman's, both of them dispatching rakshasas by the tens and dozens with the methodical ferocity they had acquired over years – nay, decades – of fighting rakshasas. And as the battle progressed and the sun traversed the Lankan sky and the day grew long, the rakshasas of Lanka saw Rama and Lakshman fight and came to know them for the warriors they truly were. Came to know and fear them. Not because of the sorcery they thought they wielded, or the treachery which they believed was a part and parcel of mortal nature, but for their fighting skill and battlefield courage and sheer endurance, for these were all things that rakshasas understood well and admired greatly. Their awe and admiration for the two mortal yodhas grew steadily as the day wore on; and by the evening of that third day of the war in Lanka, word had spread across the blood-soaked field that Rama and his brother were truly great warriors, worthy of confronting and killing – or being killed by. For to a rakshasa, nothing was more honourable than being killed by a warrior of such stature and courage. In war, one could die of anything – a cut from a rusty weapon, an accidental nick by one's own comrade in the heat of battle, a pratfall, a clumsy move inefficiently parried, a convergence of serendipity and bad luck. But to be bested by a foe who was the greatest mortal warrior that ever lived – and this was the legend that grew around Rama on that third day of the war – was a death any rakshasa would willingly embrace.

But of course, they would fight bitterly for the privilege, not simply throw themselves down on his sword. These were not the glassy-eyed admirers of Hanuman who were so awestruck by the vanar's incredible power that they flocked like lemmings to his ocean. The rakshasas who thronged to Rama and Lakshman were the finest warriors on the Lankan field, the best of the best of their nation, seeking to pit their own skills against the best of the best of the mortal nations. A rakshasa was born, raised, lived and loved and trained with the omnipresent dream that some day he or she would face the hated mortals of Arya and do battle with them, helping rid the world of those terror-mongers who had plagued their kind for aeons. Once, their ancestors had battled mortals frequently. But most of the rakshasas in Lanka now had never seen a mortal before, let alone waged war against one. And so Rama and Lakshman were prized on that field, and every rakshasa worth their salt – and their nasal effusions – sought to fight them. And by the end of that day, judging by the piles upon piles of corpses around the two brothers, it almost seemed as if every rakshasa *did* fight them. The death count numbered in the scores.

And still they kept coming. And fighting. And dying.

The others fought bravely as well. King Sugreeva waved his tree and the waters of the horde parted to provide a bloody pathway down which he leaped and fought and slew the enemy. His son fought beside him and was amazed at first at his father's prowess, for this was the first truly great war he had ever seen his father fight. Angad matured and grew wiser in the course of that day, for every son listens to the tales of his father's great deeds with only one ear open and a sceptical mind, thinking always, 'Really? I'm sure I could do ten times better!' But it was only now, when he was pitted against the same odds on the same field, that he understood for the first time how great a warrior his father truly was. More importantly, he understood how great a king Sugreeva was. For the vanar lord could easily have stayed at a distance and watched and supervised the fighting from afar. But by risking his own life on the field, and staying from dawn to dusk and dawn to dusk yet again, and a third time, he proved himself to be more than just a king; he proved himself a comrade. The most valiant comrade at all. For though he was not the oldest on that field, he was certainly the only oldun with such authority and lineage, and his very presence, not to mention his prowess, was hugely inspiring to his army. He knew this, and fought the more valiantly for it, and his warriors fought the more valiantly for his sake, and died the more bitterly.

As Sugreeva earned his son's respect and admiration, so did each one of the heroes of Rama's army find their own place in the sun that fateful third day of the war. Not all survived it. Sometimes, as happens with war, the most unlikely ones fell, never to rise again, while the least expected ones survived, if not to fight another day, at least to look back on that day and speak of it to others for years afterwards. So it was that Mainda, the older, cynical champion of the Mandaras, outlived the battle, and Dvivida, the younger and more energetic, died, taking a spike from one rakshasa in his left armpit, and, in quick succession, six separate vital wounds from six other rakshasas, impaling him like a bug on a bramble bush. It made Mainda angrier than usual, and he killed all seven rakshasas in quick succession before going on to kill several sevens more. Mandara-devi would have been proud of them both.

Nala, the bridge-builder, fought like a bridge-destroyer. His natural ingenuity and keen visual acuity served him well, and he battled with a fervour that was as much intellectual as physical, using his talent for perspective and judgement of angles to leap and slash and cut and dodge, often killing his victims by tricking attackers to turn and thrust and kill their own comrades accidentally, while he leaped *cheeka*-ing out of the way. If there was a trophy for the fighter who killed the most enemies without actually resorting to violence himself, he would surely have won it.

Speaking of *cheeka*s, Sakra died on the field as valiantly as any warrior, although he killed not a single rakshasa. He was taking a message from one general to another, asking for reinforcements on the extreme left flank, and was killed by an axe-like bladed weapon flung by a frightened rakshasa at a cluster of bears who were taking a heavy toll on their enemy. Even as he died, he managed to pass on his message to a fellow angadiya, who scampered away to deliver it as Sakra breathed his last rattling breath. His brother would learn of his passing only a day later.

They all fought bravely and fiercely, vanars and rakshasas and bears and mortals. In the clear light of day, as the day waned and night came again, and by the honest darkness of night.

But some were more gifted than others.

From the very outset of the battle, Indrajit was a menace of sizeable proportions. Although a gifted sorcerer, he had clearly been ordered by his father not to employ magicks and Asura maya on the battlefield. In any case, he did not need to. For Indrajit, like his father, was possessed of abilities granted to him by the devas themselves, whom he had helped conquer once, and who served him even now, however reluctantly, as the ransom price they paid for their freedom and for his and Ravana's keeping their hordes away from the heavenly realms.

Every arrow he put to his bow and loosed was accompanied by a great onrush of wind and stormy rain and even thunder and lightning at times. The missile then loosed killed not one but a score of enemies. It was fortunate that he fought languidly, almost carelessly, as if aware that if he desired, he alone could decimate Rama's army, or the losses he piled up would have been tenfold or even hundredfold. As it was, his only goal seemed to be to face Rama, and so he only killed those who came in his way – be they rakshasas or vanars or bears, for Indrajit was of that breed of kings' sons who regarded all those of lower status than himself as being much alike. He ran over rakshasas fighting bravely for his own cause with the same careless impunity he displayed when killing a score of vanars or bears.

The hordes seeking out Rama and literally dying to face and fight the legendary mortal yodha hampered and impeded Indrajit for all of that day. There was also the small matter of his not wishing to slaughter several tens of thousands of his own forces in order to reach the enemy leader. Not that he cared a whit about killing that many of his own warriors; simply that it was not expedient to do so, and though he might be a psychopathic monster, he was not a *foolish* psychopathic monster and knew that a supreme commander did not massacre his own army.

After several unsuccessful attempts to make his way across the field to Rama's position, he finally saw that it would take the slaughter of a quarter of his own army to reach that position. At which point he settled for killing Rama's armies instead, which he did with dispassionate brutality, snuffing out the lives of scores of vanars and bears with his potent arrows, driven by the force of the gods of wind, storm, lightning, water, fire, air, and a score of others.

But as the day gave way to night, and the night wore on relentlessly, with no signs of the fighting abating, he grew impatient. And finally, as the armies fell back and rallied and charged again and then shifted again in one of those periodic adjustments that armies must make during battle, his opportunity arrived. A gap opened up between himself and Rama's position. And due to the falling back of the rakshasa hordes as well as a simultaneous movement of Rama's forces to the flanks and outwards, there was a clear pathway all the way.

Indrajit whipped up his team and rode his chariot with demonic fury straight at Rama.

Rama saw him coming and knew that he could not stall this fight or delay it any longer. But before he faced Indrajit, he wished to give a few vital orders to the generals, especially the ones on the flanks who were hard pressed by Lankan troops and needed reinforcements badly.

'Rama,' Lakshman said as he saw the great black chariot coming across the battlefield. It was still a mile away but approaching at a steady, relentless pace, slowed only by the piles of corpses and mangled metal and flesh and bone strewn across the ground. It would take several minutes more, but it *would* reach them.

'I see it,' Rama replied, then continued with the message he had been giving to the angadiya.

'Rama,' Lakshman said again, as Indrajit covered another hundred-odd yards.

Rama did not reply, but finished the message he had been giving, and only when the angadiya scampered away with a *cheeka* to warn his own warriors that he was coming through did he turn and join Lakshman, who was standing and staring at the oncoming chariot, his sword dripping blood.

'Use your weapons,' Lakshman said. 'Use them now.'

Still Rama did not answer.

Lakshman looked at him sideways, flicking the blood and gristle off his sword with a practised twitch of his wrist, an action he had repeated several hundred times that day alone. 'Rama, this is no time for arguments.'

'You are right, this is no time,' Rama replied. 'Let's concentrate on fighting this rakshasa.'

'Rama, this is no ordinary rakshasa,' Lakshman almost shouted. 'This is Indrajit, son of Ravana. He has the shakti of the devas themselves on his side. Remember what Hanuman told us? How he was able to capture him so easily? And what Vibhisena said? Indrajit cannot be defeated by mortal weapons alone! The devas gave him his powers and only the greater devas can destroy him. You must use the Bow of Vishnu and the Arrow of Shiva to counter the shakti of the other lesser devas that he uses. Do it now, Rama!'

Rama looked at his brother, unmindful of the chariot now bearing down upon them, only a few hundred yards distant and closing fast, or as fast as could be managed over that body-strewn field. 'I have already used them, remember?'

Lakshman stared at him, uncomprehending. 'But they are inexhaustible! You can surely use them again!'

'I can, Lakshman. But I used them before not as a weapon to kill, only as a means of uncloaking the sorcery that Ravana had cast over the whole of Lanka to conceal his own use of Asura maya. And for one other thing.'

Lakshman eyed the chariot, bouncing over bodies and living

soldiers alike in its haste to get to them. 'It would be nice if you told me what that one other thing is, Rama. I am in no state of mind to guess right now.'

'I used them to create a shield against Asura maya, my brother,' Rama said. 'That is why Ravana was forced to resort to honest warfare and called his son out to lead his armies against us here. Due to the maha-shakti of the Bow and the Arrow, I negated Ravana's Asura maya and shielded our own forces against its use. That is why we are in the process of winning this war today, and will win it decisively very shortly.'

Lakshman glanced around briefly. He did not seem convinced that they were winning anything that day, let alone the war, but he took in Rama's words with a frown. 'Even so, Rama, how does that prevent you from using the astras again? Employ them against Indrajit, destroy him, and we can go on and win the war.'

'That is the one thing I cannot do,' said his brother. 'For the moment I use them again, Ravana will be free to work his sorcery once more, and he will crush our soldiers with it before we can recover. I cannot sacrifice so many lives in order to save our own.'

'But you will sacrifice *our* lives in order to save theirs?' cried Lakshman in disbelief.

'If need be,' Rama replied.

And then the time for talk was past. For Indrajit's chariot was now within easy firing distance of their position.

9

Sita watched with bated breath as the black chariot reeled to a halt before Rama's position. Her heart yammered in her chest like a frenetic monkey as she watched Indrajit take up his bow and put an arrow to the cord. Why was Rama simply standing there? Why did Lakshman not do something? She saw the two brothers exchanging words and would have given anything in the world to hear what they said, but all she could do was see, and at such a time it was more frustrating than not seeing and not knowing. For at least then, she knew, she could not do anything. Watching from here, so close and yet so impossibly far, she felt as if she *could* do something, anything. But what?

What was it she had once heard a great sage say – or had it been her own father? Yes, it was Maharaja Janak of Vaideha who had said it. *The opposite of action is not inaction, it is waiting. They also serve the purpose of ka who only watch and wait.*

She watched and she waited now, as Indrajit raised his bow, took aim, and loosed a single shot at the two men standing a hundred yards away.

The arrow seemed to take for ever to reach its destination. At first she blamed her own debilitated condition for the seeming lapse of time, then she realised with a shock that it was not her alone: the arrow was indeed taking unnaturally long. For she could turn her head and see vanars and rakshasas fighting over there in real time, and look back and see the arrow still travelling slowly, sluggishly, like a pebble dropped into a jar of honey. And it was elongating and expanding as it went, growing in length as well as thickness and curving sinuously. She peered at it in disbelief, unable to comprehend the evidence of her eyes. What manner of arrow was that, to bend and wave and curve thus, and to move so slowly, like . . . like . . .

Like a snake across grass.

Then she saw it clearly.

It *was* a snake. Not just one now, but an entire mass of them, writhing and spitting and hissing as they flew through the air. And with each yard they travelled, at an impossibly slow pace, they multiplied in number, until by the time they had covered the hundred yards' distance between their source and their destination, there must have been several hundreds of them, slithering sinuously through the air like water snakes through a swamp.

She saw the morass of snakes strike Rama first, then, a moment later, Lakshman. Saw the snakes go through Rama, just like any arrow would, but winding and curving and slithering, as a snake did. She saw the fangs of scores of snakes bite into Rama's flesh, saw blood spurt, saw venom spray, saw flesh rend and the heads of the serpents pass into that flesh, that precious flesh, and delve deep within. She saw the tails of the serpents wriggling, their bodies buried deep inside the body of her beloved, the body of the father of her unborn children. She saw the same process repeated with Lakshman, saw both the men on whom her very life depended drop to their knees, then pitch face forward on the blood-and-gore-spattered grass of the mound, and lie still. The snakes that had entered their bodies writhed and wriggled and wrapped themselves around tightly, until every inch of their flesh was covered with the wriggling black and green and red and yellow creatures, and they appeared to be human no longer.

*   *   *

The word spread like wildfire, like lightning, for not only the vanars and bears but even the rakshasas of Lanka were aghast to hear of the news of Rama and Lakshman's deaths. Those rakshasas who admired them were aghast because they had longed for the honour of pitting themselves against those mortal champions in order to seek either the destruction of their lawful enemy or their own release from fleshly ties at the hands of such a venerated foe; those who genuinely hated them – and most rakshasas still hated them bitterly, blaming them for everything wrong in their nation and history – were aghast because now they would not have the pleasure of killing the two brothers themselves. The vanars were dumbstruck, the bears stricken. Not one soul on that field at that midnight hour between the third and fourth days of the war in Lanka was left unmoved by the news that Rama and Lakshman were no more. Not one heart was left untouched.

The fighting ceased at once. A truce was called, neither ordered by the commanders, nor voiced aloud, but simply enforced through the exchange of glances, the lowering of weapons and claws and talons, the lowering of eyes, the slumping of shoulders, and the walking away back in the direction of one's own lines. Slowly, with shuffling feet, like a crowd at a funeral procession, the rakshasas retreated to the Lankan side of the battlefield, the vanars and bears returned to the northern side. Even in the city, where the bear army of Jambavan had emerged from the cave tunnels to take charge of the centre of the capital, and was fighting in the streets for control of key sections of Lanka, the fighting ceased by mutual consent and both sides subsided.

On the mound where the two heroes had fallen, a ring was formed. By the time Angad and Sugreeva and Nala and Hanuman and all the other generals had made their way to the spot, the entire strength of Rama's armies was standing around, staring inwards with numb disbelief.

Hanuman bent low and sought to touch Rama's body, but the

serpents writhed and hissed violently and wrapped themselves even tighter around their victim. So completely were the two bodies covered by the sinuous creatures that not a hair on their heads or a tip of a fingernail was visible: it was as if a thousand snakes had knotted themselves around one another.

The vanar's lips parted in a snarl and he moved as if to tear the snakes off Rama's body, but Vibhisena, who had hurried to the spot as fast he could from his vantage point on a nearby overlooking hill, caught his arm and stopped him.

'No, my friend, this is the work of Takshak, the lord of snakes. Indrajit has called upon his potent power and used it against your master and his brother. You may tear out every last tail, but the heads will remain buried in their bodies, and if that happens you will never be able to remove them.'

'Then what are we to do?' Hanuman bellowed in anguish, his body expanding and contracting without his conscious knowledge, for he was sorely agitated and unable to comprehend what must be done. This was not a situation that he had ever thought would come to pass. He had no contingency ready to deal with Rama's death. The possibility had never even crossed his mind.

'There is nothing we can do,' said Vibhisena, after examining the bodies as closely as he could. 'I do not know of any mantra or astra that can counter the weapon of Takshak. The only one who might possess the power to counter it is Rama himself, who lies there bound inextricably and as one dead.'

'But are they truly dead?' asked Sugreeva gravely, tears running down his cheeks. For the question begged asking. 'Or are they only rendered unconscious by the venom of the serpents and bound by them?'

Vibhisena looked at the vanar king sadly. 'What difference does it make? We cannot remove the serpents, so they are as good as dead.'

'As good as is not the same as,' said a feeble voice. Vibhisena and Sugreeva turned to see the ancient vanar Plaksa being brought forward, supported by two muscular Jatarupas, his great-grandsons. 'If they are alive within that nest of snakes, then there may yet be a way to revive them.'

'How so, guru-dev?' asked Sugreeva.

'During the great war between the devas and the Asuras after the churning of the ocean of milk, the Asuras thwarted the devas by disappearing and returning again and again, for they were immortal, and although they could be killed, they possessed the ability to return to life from the netherworld. The devas, while immortal themselves, could not die at all, so they remained on the battlefield, suffering grievous wounds and unable to leave for even a moment, while the Asuras died and disappeared and then returned again, and other Asuras continued to wage war against the devas. Finally the devas were as ones dead, from countless wounds sustained over the course of the millennia-long war, and could barely continue fighting. At this time, Brihaspati, guru of the devas, brought vital medicinal herbs and tended to the devas, while chanting mantras all the while. In this fashion he revived them, healed every last one of their wounds, no matter how grievous, and restored them to their full fighting strength.'

Hanuman looked at the aged vanar and joined his hands together. Tears streamed down his snout. 'Mahadev, where might these miraculous herbs be found? Tell me, that I may go seek them out at once.'

The oldun sighed. 'Alas, if I but knew that, I would be the greatest healer in all the three worlds. All I know is that they grow only on the mountains Candra and Drona, which are to be found in the ocean of milk where the legendary amrit nectar was churned.'

'But that is a place of myth and lore,' Angad said, looking even more distressed. 'How may we find such a place?'

'Aye, mahadev,' Hanuman said passionately. 'But guide me to its location and I will bring back all the herbs you ask for. If I cannot recognise them, I shall uproot and bring back both the mountains you speak of, one upon each shoulder, that you may pick whichever and as many of the herbs as you deem necessary. But we cannot leave any stone unturned so long as there is hope of reviving my lords. I do not believe they can be slain when we are so close to victory.'

'Do not fear, my brave champion,' Sugreeva said with a look like fire in his vanar eyes. 'No matter what happens, I will see to it that the war is completed successfully, Lanka destroyed, and Sita rescued. This war is no longer Rama's alone; it is a war of dharma and we will see it through to the end.'

'I fear you may have to do so, my king,' said the wise oldun, his hands trembling regretfully as he contemplated the twin bundles of writhing serpents. 'For nobody has known the location of the ocean of milk or the mountains of herbs since the Satya-Yuga, and I do not know of anyone who can guide our brave Hanuman there. All the strength and power in the world is useless if one does not have knowledge, and I regret to admit that in the age in which we live, knowledge of such true things is fading. The devas alone know what will happen when the Kali-Yuga comes and the desire for knowledge itself departs from the world. But for now I can only say that I am not possessed of that knowledge, and I do not know of anyone who is.'

Hanuman stared at the face of the guru, then at his king, then at the rakshasa brahmin, in despair and disbelief. 'But without knowing the location, how can I—' He broke off, then tightened his jaw. 'No matter. I will go seek it out even if it takes me to the end of the Kali-Yuga itself. I will not return until I have found the mountains of herbs and brought them back here. As long as there remains a means of saving my lord, I will not rest.'

And with a fierce shout as intense as a battle cry, he flew up into the air and was gone.

'Hanuman!' cried Sugreeva. 'Wait—' But it was too late, the vanar had disappeared. The King of Kiskindha shook his head in anger and frustration. 'Where will he go? How will he find them? At least while he remains here he can aid us in the war against Lanka. For now more than ever it is imperative we press on and show the enemy that he may kill one or more of us, but in the end we *will* triumph against all odds, for ours is the just fight and the true cause.'

But nobody around him said a word, for all were silent and still shocked to the core by the sight of Rama and Lakshman lying bound head to toe by the snake arrows of Indrajit, their flesh inundated and poisoned by those wriggling creatures.

Sita cried out again.

'It is another of your tricks. Sorcery! Rama cannot be killed. He is a champion of dharma. You have used your Asura maya to create an illusion to deceive me, because you know that I will never accede to your demands. I am not fooled. Rama is still alive, and he will rise up again and resume his war and grind your faces into the ground.'

Ravana looked at her with several varying expressions of morose sympathy. None of his heads was grinning or even smiling, and that unnerved her more than if he had simply laughed aloud and mocked her. Instead he seemed to be genuinely sorrowful, and that disturbed her intensely. 'Your husband was a great warrior, princess,' he said quietly. 'But he is no more. Grieve for him as you will, I will not trouble you until you are done with your period of shok. After it is over, and you are ready to speak with me once more, I will come to you and we will discuss how best to continue.'

And he turned away and gestured. Pushpak, which had been hovering in mid-air for nigh on two nights and a day, began moving again, speeding towards the high vaulting ramparts of Mount Nikumbhila, from which point, she knew, it could enter the vast subterranean palace of Ravana. She did not understand how the palace could be in Lanka as well as in the mountain several yojanas away, but it was, and in any case, at a time like this it hardly mattered how Ravana deployed his sorcery.

But it *does* matter, she heard a part of her mind say vehemently. For this too is his sorcery at work. Just as he can create an illusion so immense – placing a palace in two locations at once – so it would be child's play for him to create the illusion of Rama and Lakshman struck down by snake arrows.

But the larger part of her mind hesitated. Over the course of the past two nights and a day, she had watched with her own eyes and seen Hanuman dispatch many rakshasa challengers. Then she had seen the battle joined and many more vanars and bears and rakshasas killed. Had all those deaths been illusions as well? If so, then why would Ravana have wasted so much time? He could simply have created this particular illusion the previous day, and pretended then and there that Indrajit had killed Rama. And what of Hanuman and the other vanars and bears gathered around the fallen two? What of the whole army collected there weeping visibly in distress? What of the hordes of rakshasas who had retreated like kicked dogs? If it were truly an illusion, then surely Ravana's forces would have continued their attack, pressing home the advantage of their enemy's shocked state to turn the tide and win the war. Why would they retreat and give Rama's forces time to grieve and recoup?

Most of all, she knew that Indrajit was indeed endowed by the devas, as was Ravana himself. And she knew that while much of Ravana's sorcery consisted of illusions, many were as real as anything born of mortal flesh and blood.

Still she could not let herself believe that Rama was dead. She simply could not. Not until—

'Prove it to me,' she said, struggling to keep her voice from revealing the turmoil of her heart. 'Prove to me that Rama is . . . that he is no longer alive. Let me go to him and place my hands upon his body and see for myself.'

Ravana turned back at the sound of her voice and

contemplated her with the same morose range of expressions. Pushpak continued to fly in the direction he had guided it, the wind of their progress gently ruffling the hair on several of his heads, except, of course, the two hairless ones.

Finally he said softly, his words sounding so sincere that she had to remind herself of his deviousness, 'I understand your need for closure. It is only right that a widow should have the opportunity to grieve over her husband's body one last time. Rama was a great warrior and deserves that much at least. However, I cannot permit you to go to him under these circumstances.'

There, she thought triumphantly, I have caught him out. He cannot let me examine Rama's body closely because he knows that I would then be able to see for myself that his 'death' is no more than an illusion! I was right to distrust him.

But even as this argument raced through her mind, Ravana added in the same subdued tone: 'What I can do instead is bring his corpse to you. I will arrange to have it brought within the day in order that you may grieve properly and accept the truth of his demise.'

And he turned away, leaving her dumbstruck, for even the strenuously objecting part of her mind could find no suitable retort to this simple statement of intent.

IO

It was nearing noon when Angad heard the sparrow. The only reason he noticed it at all was because the sound of its chirping was so unusual under the circumstances. Being a vanar, he was attuned to the natural rhythm of nature, and had observed the exodus of the birds when Ravana's sorcerous fog enveloped the island-kingdom. Since then he had not heard a single bird sound. Even the fact of the chirping might not have been unusual in itself, except that it was coming not from a tree or a grove – there were none within miles of this plain – but from the ground.

He looked up from the place where he was sitting, squatting really, along with the lakhs of other vanars and bears, near Rama and Lakshman's grotesquely snake-covered bodies. They had sat thus since the midnight hour when Indrajit's arrows had struck. After Hanuman's abrupt departure, the war council had conferred for long hours without finding any satisfactory solution. Finally, when they were approaching their wits' end and starting to surrender to despair, a missive had come from Jambavan, who still held the inner city, to say that he had elected to stay in position as it would be foolish to lose such a hard-won strategic advantage; besides which, it had been Rama himself who had ordered him to use the cave route to enter the city and hold it at all costs until the rest of the army breached the gates and entered as well, and he would not disobey that order now simply because Rama was not there to enforce it.

Nobody argued with this; it was the latter part of Jambavan's message that gave them pause for thought. Wait till sundown, said the bear king through the angadiya courier. If Rama is not revived by then, let us go ahead and complete the invasion of Lanka and honour his last wishes by fulfilling his dharma and rescuing Sita.

King Sugreeva had been arguing until then for an immediate continuation of hostilities. On hearing the bear king's message, he grew contemplative and conceded that waiting a day would not harm their cause much. Or if it would harm it, then so could acting at once. As the acting leader of their forces, along with Jambavan, he concluded that they would indeed wait until sundown, and if Rama and Lakshman were not revived by that hour, they would proceed with the war.

After that, it had been waiting, waiting and nothing but waiting.

The mood on the battlefield was one of grieving and heart-rending. Crowds of vanars and bears lined up and formed a procession to come forward in turn, view the snake-infested bodies, and then move on to allow others to take their turn. There was no formal grieving, as it had still not been confirmed that the Ayodhyans were truly dead, and Sugreeva would not have a single one speaking of them or acting as if they were so. So there was no weeping outright or beating of breasts or pulling out of hair, or cutting of bodies with claws and sharp blades as some of the tribes were wont to do at the funeral of a great vanar. Only the solemn queuing up and winding of lines as each and every one of the warriors, fit and wounded alike, came to see their fallen leader and offer a brief prayer.

As the sun rose and traversed the Lankan sky, the silence on the battlefield had grown thicker and denser, filling Angad's ears and brain until he thought he would scream with frustration. He could not bear to sit around here a moment longer, and yet he must. Hour after hour passed thus, and he began to admire the resolve and discipline of the Arya rishis who could spend years in meditation and spiritual contemplation. He occupied himself with great difficulty by thinking of Kiskindha and of his wife and the new life she was about to bear – or had borne already in his absence, for she had been close to her time, which was the only reason why she had not accompanied him on this campaign. He decided that if it were a boy they would name him Rama, and if a girl, Sita. Thus, with thoughts of home and family uppermost, he passed the several hours of waiting.

It was when the sun was approaching its zenith that he was slowly distracted from his reverie by the sound of the sparrow chirping. The very unexpectedness of the sound brought him out of his contemplation. He looked around, seeking its source, and to his surprise realised it was coming from the ground. He rose and walked around, seeking it out. Only yards away from where the brothers lay in their terrible living shroud, the ground was churned and ploughed up by a Lankan chariot that had crashed and overturned. At the place where the corner of the chariot's cupola had dug a furrow in the ground, he found the broken shell of an egg and the faint tracks of a little fledgling. A few feet away, beside the chariot's shattered wheel, he spied the tiny bird.

He knelt down gently, and moving with exaggerated caution scooped up the little newborn. It twittered and chirruped indignantly at first, its minuscule claws pricking his palms lightly, then subsided into a tiny ball of feathery warmth and lay there quietly.

'Hello, little one,' he whispered softly, still wistful from the hours spent thinking of his own impending fatherhood and the new life he would be raising on his return to Kiskindha. 'This is no place for you.'

He looked around. The endless lines were still moving past the mound, for all those who had already seen Rama and Lakshman once would queue up immediately to see them again in the wan hope that their situation might somehow have been resolved. But the only change that anyone could see was that the snakes seemed to grow more agitated when the sunlight began falling directly upon them, writhing and moving in frenetic patterns that were sickening to watch, and that once the sun had risen higher and grown stronger they had subsided by degrees, until now, a half hour-watch ago when Angad had last checked, they were almost as still as if dead themselves. He had actually reached close enough to touch the body of one particularly thick green snake the exact shade of a neem leaf, and only when it tightened its coiled grip was he satisfied that the wretched things were still alive.

Everyone assumed aloud that the snakes were susceptible to the harsh sunlight and as snakes were wont to do had grown sluggish and overheated by the constant exposure. Since snakes, being cold-blooded creatures, were also wont to die from prolonged exposure to direct sunlight, it was decided that everyone would ensure that no shade fell on the two bodies, in the faint, unconvincing hope that the snakes would wither in the heat and leave to go in search of cooling shade. Thus far that had not happened, and Angad secretly did not think that these sorcerous snakes shot like arrows from a bow would be affected by the sun as normal snakes were.

'But you would like the sun, wouldn't you, my little beauty?' he said softly to the fledgling in his palm, stroking its back with a finger. He carried it out of the shadow of the fallen chariot and into the sunlight.

The result was electrifying.

He stared in surprise as the little bird opened its wings and chirruped loudly. Loudly enough to attract the attention of all around. They looked up, staring in dazed puzzlement, their faces reflecting the stunned awareness of their loss, still unable to accept its reality. Angad stared down at the palm of his hand as the little sparrow grew visibly, expanding in size much the way that he had seen Hanuman do, but only to the extent that it became a full-grown sparrow. Even so, it was an astonishing transformation, accomplished almost in moments instead of the days it ought to have taken. And it had been precipitated simply by exposure to the sun. He could almost feel the warmth of Surya-deva enter the little body and fill it with energy. He recalled something Hanuman had told them on the journey, the tale of Rama's exploits in the dreaded Southwoods forest called Bhayanak-van, which Hanuman in turn had heard repeated by Rama's band of outlaw rebels in the wilderness of Janasthana during his years warring against the rakshasas there.

What was it Hanuman had said? In the Bhayanak-van fight against Tataka and her hybrids, the brahmarishi Vishwamitra had timed the confrontation to take place at noon, when the sun was at its highest and strongest. And the reason for this was because Rama was descended from the line of Suryavansha, the dynasty of Surya-deva himself, and derived much of his energy from that celestial orb.

It was almost noon now. And Angad was witnessing a just-born sparrow grow to full maturity with the aid of the sun god's light alone.

The sparrow twittered again, this time in the full-throated voice of an adult bird, and flew up into the air a few yards above the mound. All eyes turned to watch it instinctively. It hovered there, flapping its wings frantically, and Angad stared at it because he knew that sparrows, like most other birds, could not hover long in the same place. Certainly not as long as this one.

As he watched, the sparrow's wings beat faster, until they were a blur, seeming almost to stand still.

The sparrow split into two.

Now there were two sparrows, both full grown, both hovering. Both chirruped together, and instantly split into two apiece.

Now there were four.

They split into eight.

Then sixteen

Then . . . at this point, Angad lost the ability to count how many sparrows there were, for the splitting increased in speed, taking place so fast that it was as if sparrows were emerging from thin air – or from a beam of sunlight. In moments there were hundreds, then thousands, then tens of thousands, and finally a cloud the size of a small hill hung over the heads of the staring vanars and bears, and over the snake-infested bodies of Rama and Lakshman.

The sound made by those lakhs of sparrows was enormous, filling the air for miles around. Angad felt his father at his side, staring up in amazement. 'What are they doing? Where did they come from?' asked Sugreeva.

Finding himself momentarily unable to answer, Angad simply pointed.

The cloud of sparrows had resolved itself into a distinct shape, unmistakable even when seen from this angle. It was the shape of a gigantic eagle.

Plaksa came up slowly to Angad's left, aided by his great-grandsons. 'Garuda,' he said in a reverential voice. 'There can be no doubt about it. The lord of birds has himself descended from Swarga-lok.'

The enormous eagle-shaped mass of sparrows hovered a moment longer above the mound. Sensing what it intended to do, Angad broke out of his stupor and called out urgently to his lieutenants. They obeyed instantly, and the troops gathered around the mound responded with matching swiftness. In moments, everyone had moved back, clearing the mound.

The gigantic eagle, for that was what it was, Angad knew now for certain, dipped low, the point of its beak aimed at the prone form of Rama. Darting down, it plucked at a snake's tail and tugged at it sharply, yanking the snake free of Rama's body. It came loose with a sucking sound that was disturbing to hear, and with its head and body covered in bloody slime. Jerking its neck, the eagle gobbled down the snake as if it were no more than a worm. Then it pecked sharply at another snake, pulled it out and swallowed it down as well. It continued pulling out snakes and eating them with a seemingly bottomless appetite. Angad knew that this 'eagle' was in fact nothing more than a cloud of sparrows clustered closely together. How then could such small birds pluck out snakes almost as thick as a man's wrist and swallow them down one after another? It was that fact that convinced him that this was indeed Garuda himself, descended to earth.

'He is not permitted to come to our realm during this age, the Treta-Yuga,' explained Plaksa, as though he could read Angad's thoughts. 'Hence he chooses this form.'

'And he has come to save us,' Sugreeva exulted.

They watched as the great being consumed the last of the snakes binding Rama. The mortal yodha remained prone on the ground, his body covered with numerous lacerations resembling snake bites. For a brief moment of doubt, Angad feared that even the great bird lord's efforts had failed, that Rama was already dead and would remain so. But then he recalled something Plaksa had said earlier: If they are already dead, then why would Indrajit's arrow-snakes not leave the corpses? The only purpose the snakes serve is to keep them bound and helpless in a death-like state. For only by continually infusing their bodies with their toxic venom can they keep the sons of Dasaratha unconscious. The moment they stop biting them, the brahman shakti in their blood will rid their bodies of the toxins and they will revive.

Even as he watched, Garuda finished removing the last of the snakes from Lakshman's body as well.

Then the bird lord moved forward and extended his arms. They were bird claws, and yet they were also anthropomorphic hands, somewhat like the half-bird, half-man form of Rama's lately lamented associate Jatayu, whom Angad had seen on one or two occasions. Except that Garuda, the eagle lord of the heavenly realms, was much more beautiful, proud and fierce than Jatayu, the vulture lord of the hellish realms. Garuda touched his hands to Rama's forehead and leaned forward as if to kiss him. Angad distinctly saw the lord of birds draw something out of Rama's head, and watched as the thing, a greenish effusion like a wisp of jade-coloured liquid, passed out of Rama and into the sparrow cloud. Garuda repeated this with Lakshman, ridding both brothers of the toxins accumulated in their bodies.

Then Garuda moved back, the wind of his great wings compelling Angad and the others to move back as well.

After a long, anxious moment, Rama's eyes opened. A moment or two later he began to stir, first leaning on his elbow, then sitting up independently.

The cheer that rose from the assembled vanar and bear armies was enough to make the earth shake.

Soon after, Lakshman revived as well.

Both brothers sat up and stared at the remarkable being that hovered before them.

Rama joined his palms and spoke in a voice as calm and peaceful as if he had woken from a deep sleep, not a near-death state. 'You have brought our spirits back from the realm of Yama-dev who was transporting us to the afterlife. You have given us back our strength and rid our bodies of the last drop of venom. Who are you, great and shining one, and how may we repay you for this great boon of life you have given us?'

Out of the cloud of sparrows came a sound like a bird calling in the distance. It was the sweetest, most beautiful birdsong Angad had ever heard. In its tones he could hear something akin to language, yet far beyond the clumsy mechanism of words and their inefficient sounds. It was a pure, clear song that went directly to his soul and was understood perfectly in all its subtle nuances and numerous shades of meanings. Putting that lyrical song into crude speech would have made it sound something like this:

~*I am Garuda. I came here because you were entrapped by Ravana's son using the powers of the devas who were compelled to aid him in his war. Nothing on this realm could have saved*

*you. And your great and valiant follower, despite his enormous
strength and loyalty, could never have found the mountains of
herbs in the ocean of milk. Hence Lord Indra sent me here to
aid you.~*

'Indra-deva?' Lakshman asked. 'Why does he take an interest
in our lives?'

*~Recall who it was who felled you thus, and why he bears
his given name.~*

Indrajit. Literally, Defeater of Indra. So named for his victory
over the king of the realm of the devas. Of course Indra had
a vested stake in seeing Indrajit foiled. Angad smiled at the
irony and appropriateness of the deva's act.

*~And since he cannot come himself, for all the devas are
forbidden to directly use their powers to attack or defeat Ravana
and his forces in any fashion, he sent me here to revive you. It
was the only way.~*

Rama and Lakshman stood and joined their palms together
in perfect unison, bowing in tandem before the lord of all birdkind. 'We thank you, great one. Please assure Lord Indra on
our behalf that we shall do everything in our power to defeat
the rakshasa who once humiliated him and took his name as
a reminder of his victory.'

Garuda issued a sound that, had he been a mortal, would
have sounded like delighted laughter. *~You will indeed, Lord
Rama. We already know this. Farewell.~*

And with a flurry of wings, the cloud of birds blurred faster
and faster until in the gap between one blink of an eye and the
next, it simply blurred out of existence.

A single feather floated to the ground on the cool, refreshing
sea breeze that had suddenly begun to blow from the east.
Angad went and picked it up. It was a sparrow feather, tiny
and soft. He looked up at the clear, cloudless azure-blue sky.
The sun was directly overhead. The time was precisely noon.

11

Ravana received the news with equanimity.

'I see,' was all he said.

He sat upon his great throne and looked out impassively upon the crowd of ministers of war, generals, and other officers of Lanka's governance, several of his heads apparently sleeping or engaged in deep contemplation. *No, not contemplation*, Supanakha thought, *meditation*. But why is Ravana meditating at a time like this? And why is taking the news so calmly?

'My lord,' said one of the generals. 'I say to you, the leaders of the invading army, the mortals Rama Chandra and his brother Lakshman, have freed themselves of Indrajit's arrow-snakes and risen up once again. They appear to be unharmed and in perfect health. Even as we speak they are marshalling their troops and preparing to attack the capital.'

There was a pause during which everyone waited for Ravana to respond. The King of Lanka continued to gaze out into the distance with three of his heads, one appearing to be softly chanting some kind of sloka – or could it possibly be a *song*? Surely not! Supanakha resisted the urge to giggle. If she didn't know better, she would think that Ravana was growing senile at last!

Finally, one of his heads seemed to notice that everyone was staring at him. The head frowned and looked around. 'Yes, I heard you before. Rama and Lakshman are revived once again.

They are about to attack us. And you,' he indicated another general, 'said that the bear king and his forces are already in possession of the northern quarter and are preparing to fight their way out.' He nodded at yet another rakshasa, a war minister more renowned for his amassed wealth than his victories. 'And *you* said that the troops are on the verge of revolt, that there seems to be some rumour abroad that Rama's wife was unjustly abducted, and that I provoked this whole war and endangered the entire rakshasa race in doing so.'

The war minister paled and quickly made several obsequious gestures. 'Not in so many words, your majesty,' he said nervously.

'It is what you meant, if not what you said,' Ravana said imperiously. 'Let's stop beating about the bush now, shall we? We're in a sticky situation. The enemy is at the gates, their numbers are still greater than our own, and they have infiltrated our city. With the morale of our troops already faltering, we do not have much hope of turning this war around in our favour. And to make an already bad situation worse, it now appears that the whole thing might have been one great misunderstanding.'

'A misunderstanding?' asked one of the generals, a younger rakshasa sworn in quickly to replace his father, a veteran of the wars against the devas and a legendary warrior. The son was clearly not a patch on his illustrious forebear. He looked as if he had eaten something rotten for his morning meal. For that matter, almost everyone in the chamber looked wan and sickly, and the way they had blanched at Ravana's words made it clear that he had struck too close to the truth for their comfort.

'Yes, a misunderstanding,' Ravana replied. 'You know what I mean. These things happen. It's no use crying over it now, anyway. We will go on, of course. With the war, I mean. Send Indrajit out again, and don't fret, I've made arrangements for my brother to be awoken.'

'But sire,' said the minister for procreation. 'Your brother

Vibhisena has betrayed us and joined Rama's forces! In fact, we suspect it is his excellent knowledge of the city that gives these bear warriors the advantage.'

Ravana regarded the minister with two heads, one of which looked as if it was eyeing a crushed insect on the underside of a boot. 'I meant my other brother, minister. Now, if you will all leave me, I wish to undertake my afternoon meditation ritual. Do go ahead and make all the usual necessary arrangements to repel the invaders.'

Stunned silence greeted this extraordinary response.

After a pause, during which the heavy, anxious breathing of several generals could be clearly heard, Queen Mandodhari stepped forward. 'Is that all you have to say, my lord? We are facing the possibility of defeat against the greatest threat that has ever confronted rakshasa-kind, and you wish to undertake your afternoon meditation ritual?'

'Yes,' Ravana rumbled in a sonorous tone. 'One must keep up one's rituals regardless of all distractions.'

Mandodhari looked genuinely puzzled. 'Is that what you consider this situation to be? A distraction?'

'Yes, my dear,' Ravana said, yawning with two heads and making no attempt to conceal his boredom. 'A tedious, inane, irrelevant distraction.'

A chorus of anxious whispers spread like butterflies around the chamber. Mandodhari stepped closer to the vaulting dais, her silver anklets tinkling as she walked across the black marble floor. 'And why is that?'

Ravana looked down at her as if peeved that she actually expected an answer. 'Isn't it obvious?'

'If it was, I wouldn't be asking, would I?' She gestured at the roomful of anxious warlords. 'Pardon me, but I am not as well versed in the craft of war as these gentlemen. Pray do explain to me why this situation, which seems pressing and near disastrous to my guileless eyes, is such an irrelevance to you, my lord?'

Ravana sighed and shook two heads sleepily, then nodded wearily. 'Very well then. It is unfortunate that Indrajit's arrows were unsuccessful. But no doubt this is the result of more sorcery on Rama's part. As are the rumours among our troops and the confusion in their minds – all evidence of his continued sorcery. I have our royal wizards at work on this problem already and it will be redressed very shortly. As for the enemy advancing, well, I think you will all agree that my brother Kumbhakarna is more than sufficient to repel any and all comers – in fact, he's capable of destroying their entire army on his own, wouldn't you agree, my queen? And then there is still Indrajit and all you other great warriors to contend with. Not to mention the fact that I have yet to enter the fray and have not even fired a single arrow as of yet. That is why I require to undertake my afternoon meditation ritual, to prepare myself.'

'And will you?' Mandodhari asked.

Ravana regarded her for a moment. 'Will I what?'

'Fire a single arrow? Or more?'

He smiled then, with several of his heads at once. 'I began this war. I shall end it.'

He rose to his feet and said, in that manner which Supanakha found simultaneously arrogant and attractive: 'And I know only one way to end a war – by winning it. Does anybody here doubt that I shall emerge the victor in this conflict? If you do, then say so now. Otherwise, get the devil out of here and go and do your jobs, as I shall do mine. We have an enemy to destroy, and a war to win. Let's not waste time standing around here bickering like old women.'

At his words, the entire room erupted into activity. In moments everyone had exited hurriedly. Supanakha noted that several looked relieved and more confident than when they had entered, but the majority still seemed ill at ease and confused.

Mandodhari remained standing where she was, at the foot of the dais.

'I shall go and pray for you to be triumphant on the field today,' she said.

'Then you do believe I will triumph?' he asked quietly.

'Should I have reason to doubt it?' she asked in an even quieter tone.

'Have you ever known me to fail before?'

'I have never known you to act this way over a mortal woman.'

'This war is over a mortal man, not a woman. The woman is only a tool.'

'I see,' she said. 'Then why not return her now and resolve that issue?'

'All issues will be resolved soon. With the end of this war.'

'People are saying things.'

'It is what people do.'

'But this is different. They are saying you are acting oddly. Confused. Erratic. They say you are hardly seen in person. They say you are indulging in arcane sorceries that even the court wizards fear to speak about. They say omens are everywhere indicating the destruction of our country, our kingdom, our race. They say that Rama is not the evil villain he is made out to be, but a misunderstood hero who is the righteous one in this conflict. They say we are the villains to oppose him.'

Ravana shrugged. 'I said that this is a misunderstanding. But now it is a misunderstanding that can only be resolved by finishing this war. And I intend to finish it, one way or another. Let people say what they will. I can only do what I must. That is my dharma.'

'Your dharma?' She shook her head. 'They also say that Rama is a warrior of dharma, and that we are the ones fighting against dharma. They say that is why Indrajit's arrows did not kill him, because Lord Indra himself sent Garuda down to earth in the guise of a cloud of sparrows to resurrect Rama and Lakshman. And this is evidence that the devas, although bound by their ancient vows to you and compelled to serve you in your war, are in fact favourable to Rama and his forces and will subvert your every move to ensure your loss and his victory.'

He stepped down from the dais, taking his time, his impressive bulk dominating the chamber, a fitting figure for a room filled with magnificent statuary and art. He looked like the king he was. When he was on the same level as Mandodhari, he reached out slowly, gently even, and took her hands in his own. Even she looked surprised at this action. It was not a very Ravana-like gesture.

'You have told me all that the people say and the people think and the people believe. Now tell me what *you* believe.'

And he looked deep into her eyes, waiting for her answer.

The devil, Supanakha thought, curling her tail in the alcove in which she sat, he has truly changed, he has. Either that, or he is giving the most excellent performance of his life, and that is saying something, given that I am one of the finest actors of our time!

Mandodhari tried to shift her eyes away, caught off guard by the simple directness and gentleness of his query. But to ignore or avoid it would be as good as a reply in itself, and she was too intelligent to make that mistake. She forced herself to return Ravana's look levelly. Sighed deeply. And admitted the truth. 'I believe that you are my husband, and the master of Lanka. And that in all you do, you keep the welfare of this nation and race uppermost. Even if it serves your own purpose, it also serves the purpose of the rakshasa people. And that is why, however distasteful some of your acts may be to me personally, however much I disagree with your decisions and choices individually, as a whole I endorse you completely and support you with all my might and my strength. And I shall continue to do so until death parts us.'

He looked at her a moment longer, then bent down and kissed her. Supanakha craned her neck, trying to see which face he had used, but it was impossible to tell for sure from this angle. The first one on the right rack? Or was it the second

one on the left rack? Damn. If she had known he was going
to do that, she would have taken up a better spot.

Then it was over, and he was holding his wife in his arms,
so tenderly that Supanakha could scarcely believe this was the
same Ravana who enjoyed servicing several dozen females in
one night, and treated them all as if they were whores of the
lowliest class. And what was that bit about dharma? Ravana
and dharma? She scratched behind her ear with a half-extended
talon. Something odd was going on here, that much was certain.

'Continue believing and supporting me a little while longer
then, my queen,' he said softly. 'It is all I ask.'

After Mandodhari had left the chamber, Ravana glanced up at
the alcove where she reclined. 'You can come down now, my
cousin.'

She scowled, but descended quickly and lithely.

He looked at her contemplatively. 'I trust I did not hurt you
overmuch when I struck you in the chariot. But it was necessary to gain the mortal woman's trust and to make a point to
her.'

Was he really apologising to her? Impossible! Aloud she said
archly, 'Mandodhari was right, you *are* obsessed with that
woman.'

He gestured dismissively. 'It hardly matters now. Things are
coming to an end.'

'So I see.' She looked around as she stalked the floor slowly.
'I am trying to imagine Rama occupying this chamber as King
of Lanka.'

He chuckled. 'You will not succeed in provoking me today,
my dear. I am not that Ravana you could once rely on to tease
and arouse.'

She glanced up at him sharply. What did he mean by that?
'Who are you, then? Rama Chandra of Ayodhya?'

He laughed appreciatively. 'Nicely put. Now, enough banter.

I have a small chore for you. A little charade I wish you to enact.'

She swished her tail from side to side. 'Who do you wish me to play this time? You? I could do a better job than you're doing right now!'

He only managed a tiny humourless grin at that. 'Actually, I had in mind a role you're much better suited to play. I believe you've even played it successfully once before, and fooled none other than Rama himself, if only for a while.'

She pricked her ears up. Could he possibly mean . . . ?

'Yes, my dearest cousin. I wish you to take the guise of Sita for a little demonstration I have planned. This time, however, you needn't worry that you'll be found out. Because you'll only be seen from afar. And only for a brief while.'

12

They were ready to march on Lanka when Lakshman pointed
upwards at the sky. Rama glanced up, hoping to see Hanuman
returning, but it turned out to be Ravana's golden flying chariot
again. This time the Lord of Lanka had altered the vehicle –
or commanded it to alter itself, more likely – to display only a
single level. And from what Rama could make out at this distance,
there were only a handful of people riding in it. He watched
as it came closer, much closer than it had before, and descended
low enough that he could see the figures riding within as clearly
as he could see Angad and Sugreeva on the field ahead, super-
vising the formation of ranks for the advance.

There were only two persons in Pushpak. Ravana himself.
And Sita.

Rama and Lakshman exchanged a glance. Rama knew what
Lakshman meant by that look: What is that devil up to now?
He wondered the same thing, but didn't waste time speculating.
He had a feeling he would find out soon enough.

When Ravana's voice rang out, he had been expecting it for
several moments. It was the only reason for the rakshasa to
halt the flying chariot at such a place, directly before Rama
and hovering over the middle of the field, perfectly placed to
be visible to all Rama's forces as well as to Lanka's troops by
the walls of the capital city. The voice was a booming baritone, amplified somehow through Ravana's sorcery, for once
again the tide had turned and a new chapter had begun in the

annals of the war: anything was possible next, from sorcery to treachery.

'Rama Chandra of Ayodhya,' said the voice that so many had feared for so long. 'You have committed genocide against the Asura races at Mithila, you have slaughtered innocent rakshasas and other Asuras on countless occasions, you have ravished and tortured and mutilated my cousin Supanakha, and killed her brothers, you have conspired with Sugreeva the Usurper and on his behalf murdered his brother Vali, the rightful vanar king of Kiskindha. Your crimes are countless, your offences beyond measure, and now, by invading Lanka and attacking my people without rightful provocation or cause, you have proved yet again that you are a tyrant with an infinite capacity for cruelty. You are an enemy of dharma, and so it is only fitting that you be judged by the laws of dharma itself.'

Nala, who was the nearest to the brothers, looked up angrily and shouted, 'How dare he! Rama, you must stop him from speaking more lies and deceit. Cut him down with your celestial astras.'

Several hundred other voices echoed Nala's sentiments, shouting angry threats and retorts at the vaahan hovering above them.

Rama replied steadily, 'If I attack him now, it will be perceived that I did not wish him to relate my alleged crimes and sought to shut him up. I must let him continue to the very end. After that, I shall take action if necessary.' He called out to his people, his voice carried across the field by instant word of mouth, '*Let him speak!*'

Lakshman nodded. 'The more lies he speaks, the more he strengthens our cause.'

'Wisely said, my brother,' Rama said.

But Ravana did more than speak next.

Instead, he turned and grasped Sita by the shoulders. At that, both Rama and Lakshman lost their composure. To see Ravana so much as touch Rama's wife, to see her wriggling in his grip, and his muscular arms grasping her forcefully with power enough to crush her to death in an instant, was more than either one could bear. This was beyond lies and insults; this was an affront to the dignity of Sita and a mortal threat to her.

At once, Rama spoke the sloka of incantation and the Bow of Vishnu appeared in his grasp, glowing blue even in the bright light of afternoon.

'This is the reason why you came to Lanka, is it not?' Ravana's voice boomed. 'To recover this mortal harlot of yours to whom you would not even give the status of wife. This woman who seduced me and persuaded me to help her flee your tyranny by bringing her to Lanka where she would be safe from your wicked treatment. And now I find that in fact she is in league with you, and has been all along. That both of you devised this ingenious plan to dupe me, exploiting my sense of dharma and fair play. In fact, she is your mate in the commission of wrongdoing. Your partner in evil. It has taken me far too long to understand this and to recognise her for what she truly is. But now I know. And knowing her true evil nature, I will not let her survive to dupe other unsuspecting males and provoke other needless wars. Too many have died already. You have rejected my previous efforts to make peace and consistently thwarted every attempt to parley. Now I ask you one final time, before all your forces as well as mine, do you agree to yield here and now, and return home across the ocean with your army?'

Lakshman clenched his sword tightly enough that his fist turned white. Had it been any other metal but steel, it would probably have bent. As it was, the imprint of his fingers would certainly be embedded permanently in the grip of the weapon. 'It is a trick, Rama. Do not listen to him or answer. Fire your arrow now. Destroy him!'

'I cannot,' Rama said softly but fiercely, even as his heart agreed with Lakshman. Shouting as loud as he could, he replied: 'If you wish this war to end here and now, rakshasa, then you have but to release Sita. Hand her over to me this instant, and I promise you I will return with my forces, never to come back to this land again. *But first take your hands off my wife and face me like a man, you craven!*'

Ravana's grin was visible even at this distance, as was his hand on Sita's neck. His wrist alone was thrice as thick as her slender throat. Lakshman shook the sword in a wordless threat, and at that the rakshasa grinned even more broadly, all his faces showing their teeth together. 'So you refuse yet again. As I expected. Then you leave me no choice. I trust that by doing what I do next, I will show you that your threats and abuses and terror tactics will not move me one whit. For I am the descendant of Pulastya himself, and we are honourable soldiers of dharma. It is in the name of dharma that I commit this execution of a known enemy of the Lankan state.'

And without further ado, he raised a dagger in another fist and, holding Sita's head backwards in a grip so firm that Rama could see the imprint of the rakshasa's fingers on her pale neck, he slit her throat from side to side, allowing her life-blood to gush out in a torrent, staining the railing of Pushpak, and splashing below on to the field of battle, on to the shocked ranks of the vanars of Kiskindha.

Lakshman howled his anguish and leaped forward as if he would attempt to spring up on to the flying vehicle. And indeed, as he bounded across the fifty-odd yards to the spot where Sita's blood had been spilt, he seemed capable of leaping twenty yards high. For both of their maha-shaktis had been activated once more and Rama could feel the power coursing through his veins. He could not stem it this time any more than he could stop himself from loosing the Arrow of Shiva.

'Sita!' he cried. And released the cord of the bow.

The arrow shot forward in a blaze of blue light, racing towards Pushpak where Ravana stood, holding Sita's lifeless body like a rag doll. It sped over Lakshman's head even as he roared and leaped high in the air. But in a blur of movement faster than anything Rama had seen before, the celestial vehicle vanished from sight. The last thing he saw was Ravana's ten heads grinning malevolently at him. But even in that moment of ultimate tragedy, he would recall that one of those ten heads, just one, was neither grinning nor smiling, merely gazing at him with a sincere, almost sorrowful expression. Perhaps it was the preternatural clarity of vision resulting from the maha-shakti awakened within his blood, or the intense stress of the moment, but he would carry that final image with him to the end of his life: and the conviction that that single face, bearing an expression so starkly different from the nine others, was the true face of Ravana.

The arrow passed through empty air, and, not finding a target, halted. It hung there a moment, then vanished as well, reappearing instantly in Rama's hand.

Lakshman's leap carried him through the same space a fraction of an instant later. His sword sliced through empty air as well, finding no opponent. He fell back to ground, landing easily on his feet, and looked around, seeking out his enemy. Finding none, he howled his anger and frustration.

'To Lanka,' he roared at the top of his voice, his words amplified by the power of his shakti, resounding across the battlefield.

As one, the ranks of vanars and bears responded with anger and outrage no less than Lakshman's. 'TO LANKA!'

The armies of Rama charged forward.

Sita heard the roars of Rama's armies and heard the reverberation of their charge. She felt a secret thrill ripple through her body: Rama's forces were attacking! That could mean only one thing. That Rama and Lakshman were alive and leading their armies in a final assault on Lanka.

Her joy was short-lived. A towering shadow loomed across the grassy ground of her exotic prison.

She turned to see Ravana standing beside her. He was uncharacteristically silent and subdued, his faces for once revealing almost nothing of their inner processes. It was the first time she had seen him so subdued, and it frightened her more than any display of machismo or power. Still, she would not show him any emotion.

'My husband's armies are attacking,' she said to him proudly. 'It will not be long now before he comes and frees me, and deals with you.'

He sighed. 'It grieves me to disagree with you at a time like this, my lady Sita. But I am afraid your husband will not be going anywhere now, or ever again. I intrude upon your privacy only to carry out my promise. As I said I would, I have brought you proof of Rama's demise. I urge you yet again to accept his death now and make a mutually beneficial pact with me. I will leave you with this evidence and return shortly to have your final answer. This is the last time I will parley with you. The next time I come here, if you are still unwilling to co-operate, I will do as I must. Perhaps even as my son did to your husband.'

And with those words, he laid down an object he had been carrying, turned, and left the ashoka grove.

She scarcely dared to walk the five or six steps to the spot where he had placed the object. And when she had covered that distance, seemingly miles to her heightened consciousness, she could barely work up the courage to uncover the cloth that concealed the item.

When she did, her entire being froze with shock.

Rama's severed head lay there, staring up at her blindly, his skin turned deep blue and his face covered with numerous snake bites.

*   *   *

Rama was lost in the fog of brahman. It had been fourteen years since the last time he had surrendered himself to the power of the maha-shakti. Then, Brahmarishi Vishwamitra had been there to leash him and help him control himself. Now there was nobody with the power to control or restrict him, only the blinding blue fury that burned his every cell, set his brain ablaze and turned him into a remorseless fighting machine. He was barely aware of his actions, sensing only that he was killing a great number of the enemy, slaying them by the dozen, the score, then the hundred, and still the numbers mounted steadily . . . None could face him, none could survive. He loosed the Arrow of Shiva repeatedly, using it to kill entire companies of rakshasas at once, to blast holes in the walls of Lanka, to smash through the gates of the city, to swat hundreds of rakshasas from the ramparts like ants off a platform.

Then he grew aware that he was within Lanka, and killing more rakshasas, destroying houses, bringing down entire structures with a single loosing of the arrow. He employed his sword now, for it was not seemly to use the arrow for such trivial destructions as killing rakshasas. He could slay countless numbers with his blade alone, flashing, swirling, circling, swinging, flying, leaping, severing, hacking, cutting, slicing . . .

He came to his senses once, briefly, in a scene of such carnage and destruction that he was shocked to the core. It took him a painful moment to realise that he had been responsible for this devastation. All around him his followers were battling the enemy. He saw Nala and his company fighting a rakshasa in a chariot surrounded by a force of albino rakshasas with long curved spears for weapons. He saw Sugreeva battling a rakshasa wielding a mace, using the same spear shaft as his weapon. He saw Angad pitted against a trio of female rakshasas who screamed like banshees and sent their young scurrying to nip and claw at Angad from behind, but Angad's angadiyas, now no longer needed to pass on messages, for the time for talking was long past, fought the little rakshasas, meeting them at their own height and matching their ferocity.

He saw houses burning and citizens screaming, children being flung from rooftops by desperate parents, falling to the ground to land injured but still alive while their parents died consumed by flames. He saw sights so terrible he wondered why men fought wars and whether any cause was worthy of such carnage and horror, whether dharma itself was sufficient justification for such violence. He felt the war lust swell up inside himself again, and fought to control it. But then he remembered his last glimpse of Sita's face, that look of utter surprise as Ravana cut her throat, as if she had expected him to treat her roughly, rudely, even violently, but nothing as drastic as this, nothing as final as death.

And he submitted to the call of his fury again, hating himself for doing so, but hating even more the one who had driven him to this pass.

Ravana.

He would slaughter every last rakshasa in Lanka until he found and fought the king of rakshasas. Where was Ravana?

13

Sugreeva saw Rama resume fighting and almost turned away. It was excruciating to watch the mortal fight in this state: not only because of the sheer brutal efficiency with which he slew the enemy, giving them virtually no chance of reprisal or defence, but because of the anguish that drove him. He felt some of that anguish too, for he knew what it was like to have one's wife taken by force and forced to submit to an enemy, though in his case that wife had been married first to the same enemy, his brother Vali, and so in a sense was only returning to her first husband. Whereas Rama had lost Sita first to the most dreaded foe of all living races, Ravana, and now to that final enemy of all creatures, the lord of death. From whose cold embrace she could never be returned.

Sugreeva fought on with anguish as well, but in his case it was tempered with experience, age and wisdom. He grew slowly aware that while their forces had entered Lanka and were in occupancy of the capital city, the rakshasas were still fighting back with great vehemence. This war was approaching an end very fast, but it was far from won yet.

He had just dispatched a particularly troublesome opponent, a burly mace-wielding rakshasa, and had cracked his tree in doing so, when he heard the noise and felt the thunder.

At first he thought it was the killing stones once again, Ravana's sorcery at work. But what would be the good of using it here? Did the Lord of Lanka intend to kill his own people as well as the enemy? For how could mindless sorcery distinguish friend from foe?

Then the afternoon sky darkened.

And he looked up to see a shape looming high above the city spires. So high above, in fact, that he thought at first that the rakshasa was floating in the air. For the creature's head was so far above the ground that he could not even see it clearly. All he could see was a body so enormous it towered upwards endlessly, tapering as it went higher, until its upper body and arms and head were lost against the brilliant blue afternoon sky.

Then the rakshasas all around began crying out triumphantly, 'Kumbhakarna! Kumbhakarna!' And he knew that this was the other brother that Vibhisena had warned them about.

Angad gazed up in horror as the looming form towered above them all, rakshasa and vanar and bear alike. From the exultant shouts of the rakshasas all around, he knew who this mighty being must be, but even so he could not comprehend the evidence of his senses. Could anything be so enormous, so powerful? And a rakshasa at that? To see a mortal enemy this huge was almost enough to cause him to freeze into permanent immobility. For how could he fight such a mountain of a being? How could anyone fight this creature?

He watched with naked horror as the giant rakshasa stopped and looked down, examining the scene before him. Very faintly he could make out a gargantuan head peering down, tilting one way, then the other. Then the rakshasa seemed to reach a decision, and with a roar that vibrated through Angad's very bones, he raised one impossibly large foot and brought it down upon a mass of vanars swarming through the city gates.

The giant foot came down upon the closely crowding vanars like Angad's own foot might come down upon a bunch of grapes. A thousand vanar lives were squashed instantly, along with a few dozen rakshasas. Twisting his foot this way, then that, the giant raised it again and grunted with approval at the result. Then he put the foot down and used the other one to step on a party of bears battling a rakshasa in a chariot. This time Kumbhakarna attempted to avoid injuring his own kind, and almost succeeded. But the edge of his heel touched the back of the chariot a brief, glancing blow. That was enough to send the chariot flying end over end, throwing its occupant, apparently a rakshasa general of some importance, so far up in the air that he must surely have been flung all the way to the ocean, like that opponent Hanuman had swung and thrown on the battle-field that—

Hanuman!

He alone could tackle this impossible mountain of a rakshasa. Where was he? Still searching for the mountains of herbs? If only there was some way to let him know they had need of him, that Rama and Lakshman had already been revived and it was he they required now, for without him this monster would surely destroy them all, even if he killed half of his own forces in the process.

But several hour-watches later, as the sun was setting again, there was still no sign of Hanuman. The situation was growing desperate now. Most of their troops had concealed themselves within the ruins and remains of Lankan structures, often only yards away from their rakshasa enemies. For the moment, this seemed to be working. Kumbhakarna was roaring and calling out in anger, his bellows filling the sky and his breath so great that the stench of it wafted down to where Angad stood in the foyer of what was once a grand mansion of some rich rakshasa. The giant's breath stank of rotting meat and wine on an epic scale.

Angad looked at his father and at Rama. Rama, who had been a whirling dervish of violence until King Sugreeva had called to him to desist as they needed to speak. At first Angad had thought Rama would strike down the vanar leader without a second thought, but then he saw recognition cloud Rama's bright blue eyes – those eerie eyes that would haunt Angad's dreams for ever – and he lowered his dripping sword. Once Rama had subsided, Lakshman followed suit at once.

'Use your weapon, Rama,' Lakshman advised. 'But be careful not to draw his attention, or he will attack our friends as well. And they will not all be able to move out of his way quickly enough to avoid being crushed.'

Sugreeva agreed. 'For all his bulk, the giant is fast.'

Rama nodded slowly. 'I must draw him out somewhere in the open, away from you all. Perhaps if I race out into the field and attract his attention, taunting him and forcing him to follow . . .'

Angad frowned. 'But if you do that, you will be exposed and unable to conceal yourself.'

Rama shrugged. 'It is the only way.'

Sugreeva shook his head. 'No, Rama. I have seen something of your powers. The maha-shakti you possess, as well as the astras, they give you great power to kill and destroy, but they do not protect you personally against blows or weaponry. If the giant crushes you beneath his foot, you will be killed. It may be more difficult to destroy you or Lakshman than any of us, but you are not completely invulnerable.'

Lakshman glanced at Rama. 'Then let me go. I will draw him out and you shoot him with the Arrow of Shiva from the safety of a hiding place here in the ruins.'

Rama shook his head. 'We will both go. Two can dance better than one, and he will not know which of us to chase.'

'He will know soon enough the instant you fire the arrow at him.'

'Once I fire the arrow, nothing else will matter.'

Vibhisena cleared his throat. Mostly a silent observer, and grown pale at the sight of his countrymen slaughtered and his city devastated, the rakshasa nevertheless continued to offer his advice whenever needed or asked for. He offered it now. 'It may not be that simple, Rama. My brother Kumbhakarna was granted the gift of indestructibility by Lord Brahma himself. It is another matter that he fumbled the boon and was cleverly given the gift of narcolepsy as well, compelling him to sleep for half a year at a stretch. I do not believe either the Bow of Vishnu or the Arrow of Shiva, or indeed any other celestial weapon, will harm him.'

Rama and Lakshman both stared at Vibhisena. 'Are you certain of this?' Rama asked, looking vexed.

'Absolutely,' Vibhisena answered. 'Your astras and your maha-shakti will be no match for him. To the best of my knowledge, Kumbhakarna cannot be destroyed.'

Before anyone else could speak, a great crashing sound came from somewhere nearby, perhaps only a mile away. A vanar came leaping in, eyes goggling with fear. 'The giant is attacking again.'

They came out of the ruined mansion to see Kumbhakarna, his patience worn thin by now, stamping on houses at random, uncaring whether they were occupied by friends or foe. Each time he brought his foot down, a house was razed to the ground, with all its occupants crushed to fragments like the rubble of the structure itself, sending up a puff of dust several hundred yards high. Puffs of dust were visible all across the city as Kumbhakarna continued his rampage with a vengeance.

'He is slightly irritated now,' Vibhisena said. 'He has poor eyesight and the failing light is making it harder for him to see.'

Angad stared at the giant pounding lives and buildings into rubble like a child squashing sand mounds on a beach.

Rama called on the Bow of Vishnu and set the arrow to it.

Lakshman turned to him. 'What are you doing, bhai? You heard Vibhisena. Even dev-astras will not destroy the giant.'

'We must do something,' Rama said grimly. 'Those are our people dying there. I cannot stand by and let him continue killing our troops unhindered.'

Lakshman gripped Rama's arm firmly, preventing him from drawing back the bowstring. 'Rama, listen to reason.'

Rama stared at his brother with an intensity Angad had never seen on his face before. 'The time for reason is long past, Lakshman. It is only time for the madness of war now. Leave my hand and let me shoot.'

Lakshman's hand remained on Rama's arm, his eyes returning Rama's intensity with a fire of his own. Angad felt sick to the stomach at the prospect of the brothers fighting one another, after all they had been through together and endured.

'My lords!'

The voice of Kambunara turned all heads. The bear was waving at them from the end of the street, from behind a partly destroyed wall that hid him from the gaze of the giant on the far side of the city. 'I have found Jambavan. Come quickly, he wishes to have words with you at once.'

With a sense of great relief, Angad saw Lakshman release Rama's arm. Rama lowered the bow and it vanished at once, along with the arrow. They hurried over to where the bear stood, taking care not to be seen by the rampaging giant. The air was filled with dust from the many places Kumbhakarna had already destroyed.

'Come, my lords,' Kambunara said, 'I will take you to Jambavan. He is in a part of the city directly in the giant's path, so we must be careful. I know a way that will keep us from his sights, but it is infested with the enemy.'

'Wait,' Angad said, as the bear turned to lead them down the street. 'Why did Jambavan not come here with you? Wouldn't that be easier than taking us all to him?'

Kambunara regarded him sadly, swiping with the back of his paw at the light coating of dust on his snout, and sniffing. 'He is dying, young vanar. That is why he cannot come himself. He is dying and wishes to share his last thoughts with Rama before he goes to meet his ancestors in the last cave.'

* * *

The sound of the giant's work was deafeningly loud in the quarter of the city where Jambavan lay. The bear lord was leaning back on a slab of stone that appeared to have once been part of a roof, or the floor of a higher level in some structure that was now destroyed. It was difficult to tell which one, for virtually every building in this street had been crushed either partly or wholly by the rampaging giant. Dust was everywhere, as well as the stench of the giant's effusions, and Angad winced as he passed a house where several bears had evidently taken refuge. The structure was completely demolished, the debris stained pink with the blood of the unfortunate bears. He glanced up at the shadow of Kumbhakarna, cast in sharp relief against the setting sun, and prayed that he was not given such a death. When and if he went, he wished to do so fighting hand to hand to the bitter end.

Jambavan had fought to the bitter end as well, judging from the numerous wounds and arrows on the bear's body. Angad counted over two dozen arrows before he gave up, and the sword and blade wounds were at least double that number. He thought it incredible that the bear lord was still alive and breathing.

'Rama,' Jambavan said with genuine warmth and pleasure. 'My son, my eyes have thirsted for the sight of your handsome face. And yours, my son Lakshman.'

'My friend,' Rama said sombrely. 'What can I do to make you more comfortable?'

Jambavan managed a grin, revealing bloody teeth with more than one gap between them. 'You can get me a basket full of river fish, so fresh they're still jumping out of the basket to escape!'

Everyone grinned at that. 'Apart from that?' Rama asked, taking the bear's paw in his hand.

'Apart from that, he says.' Jambavan chuckled, then turned his head, coughed, and spat out a gob of blood. 'I'd settle for honey then, but you won't find that either, not in this hellhole of a city. Rakshasas hate sweet foods almost as much as they love mortal flesh. Roasted, mind you, with a seasoning of their traditional spices.'

Angad saw Kambunara shoot Jambavan a stern glance.

Jambavan sighed. 'But I'm rambling as usual. It's hard for an old bear to change his fur at this age, my friends. But I shall try to come to the point more directly. I see that you have a situation here.'

'That we do,' Rama acknowledged. 'Vibhisena has just told us that even my bow and arrow cannot bring down the giant, yet I wish to try. What other choice do we have?'

'Choice?' The bear king coughed and spat again. 'There is always a choice. But you will not need to resort to desperate measures. Hanuman will deal with that jumping jackass out there. No, don't fret about him – not unless he chooses to stomp on this very house right now! Now that would be a nice turn-up, wouldn't it?' He laughed his rumbling bear laugh, grimaced sharply in acute pain, then subsided at once. 'But that isn't what I wished to say to you either. The reason I called you here was to say that you must forgive Sita.'

Rama stared at him silently.

Jambavan leaned closer, putting his blood-smirched snout almost on top of Rama's own nose, and repeated himself more loudly. 'I said, you must forgive—'

'There is nothing to forgive,' Rama said, frowning.

Jambavan sighed. 'There is always something to forgive, between lovers. But in this case, you are right. There is nothing to forgive – except what you imagine! Either way, forgive her. Love her unconditionally, and be glad you have her back. It is a treasure devoutly to be desired and few ever possess it, or, having lost it, regain it again.'

Angad had no idea what that meant, but even he could not fail to miss the obvious. 'My lord Jambavan,' he said, 'pardon my interrupting, but perhaps you have not heard yet . . . Our lady Sita . . . she was . . .'

'She is alive and well,' Jambavan said quietly, his small dark eyes twinkling at Angad. 'She is kept in a cave that is not a cave deep within the mountain below the Temple of Shiva. What is the mountain called, brother Vibhisena?'

'Nikumbhila,' said the stunned rakshasa. 'But when you say she is alive, how—' Then he stopped short. 'More sorcery?'

Jambavan shook his head. 'No. The execution was real. Except the victim was not Sita. It was a shapeshifting yaksi-rakshasi crossbreed named . . .' He waved a paw with three arrows sticking out of it. 'I can never recall names.'

'Supanakha,' Lakshman said at once. 'Of course!'

From outside came a great crashing and splintering, but this one sounded farther away. In confirmation, one of Angad's vanars called out, 'The giant has moved away! It is safe to go out now.' Angad made a be-quiet gesture at the vanar, but the rest of the group paid the cry no heed. He looked at Rama's face. There was such an utter absence of emotion visible on it, it put him in mind of the demonic fighting machine he had seen earlier. He swallowed nervously. Rama's anger was a rakshasa to be dreaded in its own right.

'You know this for a certainty, how?' Rama asked in a voice so completely without inflection or tone that the absence itself suggested an emotional level too great to express.

Jambavan shrugged. 'We are the ancient ones, we know more than we are supposed to. Just as I know that Hanuman will return and take care of your giant pain in the foot out there. But you must remember what I said to you, Rama. *Trust her!* No matter what turmoil rages in your mind, believe her. She loves only you, and you alone. Never doubt that for even an instant.'

Rama was silent for a moment, then abruptly he hugged the bear king fiercely. Jambavan hugged him back, but his eyes had glazed over, and Angad could see that the great being's strength was failing fast now that he had finished speaking what he had desired to say.

'Enough, enough,' coughed the bear. 'If you wish to push my arrows inside my wounds, at least add some new ones!'

Rama let go of him at once. Jambavan laughed. 'I was only jesting,' he said. Then fell into a coughing fit. 'Only . . . jest . . .' He could not finish.

From outside, a great din resounded. A cloud of dust puffed into the ruins in which they were clustered, obscuring their vision for several moments. When the fog had cleared, Jambavan's eyes were shut and he was no longer breathing.

Rama cried out and hugged the bear again, tears spilling from his eyes. But barely had he begun weeping than a noise like boulders mashing against each other sounded from outside the ruined house.

'*Rama*,' came a great voice from everywhere at once.

Rama rose to his feet. 'I know that voice.'

He looked at the bear king once again and then bent and kissed Jambavan affectionately on his furred brow. 'I will return, my friend.' And he went outside, followed by the rest of them.

14

Rama came outside the house to find a giant face staring down at him. His followers reared back at once, exclaiming. But he stood his ground. For he had recognised the voice of Hanuman the instant the vanar had spoken. He glanced around briefly, making sure that Kumbhakarna was not in the vicinity – but the lookout had spoken truly, and the giant was visible in the distance, several miles away, wreaking havoc in another section of the city. Until he noticed Hanuman's presence here, they would be safe for a brief while.

Then he gazed up at the mile-high figure of his beloved friend and champion. He was not surprised to see the vanar in this expanded form, but what did surprise him were the two objects Hanuman bore upon his shoulders: two enormous mounds of earth, each several hundred yards high. Rama had no doubt that where they had stood originally, before Hanuman uprooted them, they would have been far higher, veritable mountains each. He could see the roots of trees and bushes and dark soil on the underside of each one, testifying to the strength which must have been required to uproot them from their original resting place. Yet Hanuman bore them on his shoulders as easily as skins of water.

'Rama,' said the vanar, smiling at the sight of his favourite mortal. 'Forgive my inability to greet you and Lakshmanji appropriately. As you can see, I am somewhat burdened.'

Sugreeva swore a vanar phrase. 'How on earth . . . ? Are those truly what I think they are?'

'The mountains Candra and Drona,' said Hanuman. 'With the herbs of revival that Plaksa spoke of. I could not make out the herbs themselves and had already wasted enough time in the search, so I simply brought both the mountains here. You may take what we require and I shall return the mountains to their original resting place later.'

'But how did you accomplish this, my friend? And why are you not surprised to see myself and Lakshman already revived? I suspect that you have learned much even while away.'

'That I have,' rumbled the vanar. 'For Jambavan has been my guide as before, speaking to me in my mind and showing me the secret way between worlds. That is how I flew from this mortal realm to the heavenly worlds, and found the ocean of milk where these mountains rested. That is also how I learned of your happy revival at the behest of Garuda, lord of birds.' He paused. 'But I will have to relate my adventures later, Rama. For right now I believe there is yet another rakshasa who wishes to challenge me.'

And he bent his knees and leaped upwards, flying like an arrow straight up. A fraction of an instant later, rushing through the space Hanuman had just vacated, came the giant Kumbhakarna. The rakshasa raged with fury at having missed his opponent, then looked down and saw Rama and his companions. At once he roared and stamped down angrily. Rama leaped back, but he knew already he would not be fast enough. The giant's foot rose and fell with the speed of a hammer striking an anvil. The ruined street went suddenly dark as all light was blocked out, and Rama cried out at the thought of all his followers crushed together.

But when the sole of the giant's stinking foot was merely a foot or two from crushing Rama's head, it stopped suddenly, then rose once again – and kept on rising!

As the foot grew smaller, Rama saw that Hanuman had leaped down again just in time, grasped the giant rakshasa and was lifting him back into the sky. Because Hanuman was still carrying both mountains, he had had no choice but to use his feet to pick up Kumbhakarna. The rakshasa's face reflected his shock at encountering someone as large as himself – for Hanuman had expanded himself further in those few moments when he had flown upwards and returned, making himself the size of the rakshasa. And he was continuing to grow.

'Rama,' Hanuman shouted in a booming voice as he rose into the sky. 'I will place the mountains outside the gates of Lanka, to avoid crushing any of our warriors. You must send Plaksa there at once to find the herbs of revival. I will deal with this beggar in the meanwhile.'

And he flew up and then at an angle, and was lost behind the slanting debris of a demolished house. Rama turned at once to his companions. 'Angad, you are entrusted with this task. Find Plaksa and take him at once to the mountains. Once he finds the herbs, bring them here right away. I will stand guard in this spot to ensure that no Lankan forces attack this house.'

Angad stared at him, puzzled. 'But Rama, you and Lakshman are already revived. Why do you still require the herbs?'

Lakshman clapped the vanar on the back, hard, admonishing him playfully. 'For our good friend Jambavan, young prince. Now, less talk and more walk! Go! Do as you are told!'

Angad went.

The giant struggled to break free of Hanuman's grip, but the vanar kept his feet tightly clenched together. Flying with two mountains upon his shoulders while carrying aloft a giant rakshasa of epic proportions was not exactly the easiest thing he had ever done, but he knew that if he dropped any one of the three, he would certainly kill a goodly number of his own comrades; even the fact that he would demolish half of Lanka at the same time was not enough to balance out that cost. So he focused his energies on flying straight and true and keeping himself as well as his three burdens aloft. He passed ruined areas crushed by the giant's rampage, and noted that the corpses of rakshasas as well as vanars and bears lay in the wreckage. What arrogance! To slay one's own warriors along with the enemy! What use was a weapon so large that one could not control it or direct it accurately?

Then he was past the city and over open country. Still he continued. For he knew that once he set this giant fool down, he would need all the room he could spare. He wondered if he ought to take Kumbhakarna back to the mainland, where there was little chance of running out of space, but he did not think he could maintain his threefold burden that far. He looked down at the part of the island they were flying over now: it was the central section of rolling hills and ghats and valleys. Would this do? But only a short run would take the rakshasa back to Lanka, and that was something he could not chance.

Finally he hit upon the only practical option.

He flew out over the ocean. Kumbhakarna roared his indignation as the rolling hills of Lanka fell behind them and pristine blue water appeared below. He intensified his struggles until Hanuman knew that he could not hold on much longer. The realisation had finally penetrated the rakshasa's dense skull that he stood to lose less by falling than by allowing himself to be carried farther away. He seemed to hate the water, judging by the way he struggled frantically.

'Or, judging by the way you stink,' Hanuman said aloud, 'maybe you fear bathing more than death!'

He was perhaps a hundred yojanas out at sea when he felt his grip on the giant's shoulders giving way at last. He looked around. Nothing but open ocean was visible for as far as he could see in every direction. 'This is as good a place as any,' he mused aloud. He rose as high as he could before releasing his grip abruptly and letting the giant fall, howling, to land in the sea with a splash great enough to raise a small tidal wave for yojanas around. 'Go ahead and start your bath, I'll join you in a minute,' he said cheerfully as he turned back towards Lanka. 'Oh, and don't forget to wash behind your ears!'

He flew back to Lanka at a much faster speed. By the time he reached the battlefield outside the gates of the city, he was pleased to see Angad and Plaksa already there, waiting. He set both mountains down on the centre of the field, joined his palms in a respectful namaskaram to the vanar guru, and said, 'Forgive me for my haste, mahadev, but I have a rakshasa who needs my attention urgently. I pray you find the herbs you need quickly and that they are as efficacious as they're believed to be.'

'Bless you, Maruti Anjaneya,' said the ancient vanar. 'You have done what no being in the mortal plane has ever done before. Later, you must tell me how you accomplished this extraordinary task, that I may record it for posterity.'

'I shall do so most happily, guru-dev,' Hanuman said. 'Now, I take my leave.' And without further formality, he shot upwards, feeling his body surge with the freedom of being released from the three enormous weights he had carried before, and zoomed back to the spot where he had left Kumbhakarna.

The giant was waiting for his return, compelled by his warrior's pride. The ocean here was deep, but not deep enough to submerge the rakshasa completely. As Hanuman approached, he saw Kumbhakarna's head and shoulders, and the upper part of his torso up to the lowest of his ribs, visible above the surface. The titan roared as he saw Hanuman approaching in the sky. He shook his fists and opened his jaws, bellowing a challenge.

Hanuman responded by flying straight at him, and crashing into the giant's chest at a speed so great that the air around them both boomed with a resounding thunder loud enough to ripple the ocean waters and be heard all the way back in Lanka.

Angad heard the booming crack of sound and knew that it was caused by Hanuman. The vanar had joined battle with

Kumbhakarna then. He clenched his fist, silently wishing his comrade strength and honour in the fight. Then he returned his attention to helping find the herbs that Plaksa was seeking. The ancient vanar had said that while the herbs were miraculous in their efficacy, if the subject had been dead more than a certain time they were of no use. For beyond a certain period of time the brain, lacking the air carried to it by the pumping of blood through the body, began to perish and rot. And once the brain rotted, reviving the body was pointless. So they had only a limited amount of time to find the herbs. According to the ageing guru, that meant doing so before the sun set completely.

Angad glanced over his shoulder at the western horizon. From the top of the mountain he could see the sun already at the end of its journey, the rim of its circle touching the horizon line. In only moments it would descend below that line and the time to save Jambavan would be past. How cruel it would be for Hanuman to have travelled all the way to Swarga-lok and brought back these two legendary mountains of myth, and then to lose Jambavan because they could not find the right herbs in time. No. He would not let that happen.

He searched desperately in the fading light.

Rama climbed the last few yards to the top of the ruined structure. After making sure that the delicately poised slab of roof was not likely to collapse under his weight, he straightened up and looked around. From here he could see across most of Lanka, as well as the entire clearing below. The streets here were packed with vanars and bears. King Sugreeva and the other leaders had assembled as many of their forces as possible within this section of the city. Rama's words would be conveyed to the rest through the usual system.

'My friends,' he called out. 'I have the best news of all. Sita is alive and well, but she is still Ravana's captive. What we saw earlier was yet another deception of the Lord of Lanka.'

Cheers rose raggedly from the weary army. He held up his hand. 'But hear me out. For time is short and we are in enemy territory. Jambavan the bear lord lies stricken. Yet Hanuman has brought back the two mountains of magical herbs from the land of the devas, and the vanar Plaksa, aided by Angad and Nala, is searching for the herbs of revival. We have every confidence that they will find them and resurrect the lord of bears successfully within the hour. But we cannot stand by and wait. Hanuman has removed the giant Kumbhakarna from Lanka, leaving us free to battle the rakshasas on our own terms. Now is not the time to grieve for lost comrades or generals, nor to lick our wounds and rest, nor even to cease our struggles. Now is the time that will test our mettle to the utmost. It is time to crush the rakshasa menace once and for all, to free the lady Sita, and rid this land of the evil of Ravana and his sorcerous tricks for ever. And so I ask you, one and all, to join me in one last effort to claim Lanka and drive our enemies to the sea. Push them back until they have nowhere to go but water and fire.' He pointed to the southernmost tip of the island, where the volcano rose smouldering beside the ocean. 'All the way to the last yard of lava-scorched land. For only then can our war be over and dharma triumph. Give me this one last time your courage, your strength, and your warrior's skills. In return, I will give you the victory of dharma over a-dharma!'

The roar that greeted the end of this speech filled the city of Lanka for miles around, echoing the booming thunder of Hanuman's flight moments earlier.

Rama spoke the sloka of summoning and the Bow of Vishnu and Arrow of Shiva appeared in his hand.

Raising the bow, he aimed an arrow directly at the most distant quarter of the city, the innermost sanctum of Ravana and the only area that his forces had not yet breached. He loosed the arrow, and watched it fly blazing through the evening sky.

It landed in the inner city with a resounding clap of sound. A blinding white light exploded outwards in concentric circles, travelling back towards Rama. He shielded his eyes from the flash, and still felt the light searing the very core of his vision. When he opened his eyes again, one large section of the triple walls surrounding the inner circle lay in ruins. He pointed in that direction, and gave the order to charge. With a roar of fury, his army surged forward.

15

Lanka was burning. Yet again.

Ravana looked out from the veranda and saw the flames engulfing the mansions of his ministers, generals, nobles and the richest merchants of the land. If Hanuman's rampage had destroyed the poorer sections of the city-state, then Rama's arrows were ravaging the richer sections, completing the work of demolition.

He saw Lankan citizens crowding the gates of his palace, begging for sanctuary against the invading troops of Rama. They were all fat merchants and the spoilt, soft, rich rakshasas he had cultivated for their shrewd trading and wealth-creation. They were of no use now. He needed warriors.

'Open the gates and let them in,' he told the captain of his palace guard, Narantaka, a kumbha who was the bastard son of Kumbhakarna himself, which made him Ravana's nephew. Or was he Ravana's own bastard? Hmm. Sometimes it was hard to be sure, after so many dalliances and impregnations. In one sense, of course, all of Lanka was his extended family.

'And after they're in, close the gates and then kill them all.'

'Sire?' said Narantaka, staring at Ravana.

'That group there,' Ravana gestured casually, 'knows where most of Lanka's wealth is concealed, here as well as in foreign lands. In the event that they're captured alive, they won't hesi-tate to share that knowledge, or even some of their wealth, to save their perfumed lives. Dead, their knowledge goes to the netherworld with them. I want them all killed, down to the last rakshasa, rakshasi and child.'

Narantaka looked at him briefly with a look that reminded Ravana so strongly of the face on the extreme end of his left rack that he felt certain that this was his bastard, not Kumbhakarna's. The captain saluted silently and marched away to carry out his orders.

By the time Ravana emerged from the palace a little while after sunset, the courtyard was littered with corpses. He gestured to Narantaka, who stood smartly before a company of palace guards, awaiting his next orders. 'Leave a couple of kumbhas to burn the bodies,' he said. 'The rest of you follow me.'

'My lord,' Narantaka replied. 'What of your family and the palace staff? Should we not remain here to guard them in the event of an intrusion by the enemy?'

Ravana glanced at him. 'They can look out for themselves. Besides, your company has the last fresh troops in Lanka. If you stay here, the enemy *will* attack. That's why I need you to ride out with me, to stop them before they do.'

The captain looked as if he wished to say something further, but then he saluted and gave the necessary orders. Ravana climbed aboard his chariot, took up the reins and rode out without waiting to see if Narantaka and his troops followed. The streets of Lanka's richest quarters were a shambles, destroyed by Rama's arrows – or, to be accurate, his arrow, for he was using the Arrow of Shiva over and over – and not a house remained untouched. And these were the structures freshly raised by the sorcery of a few nights ago, during Ravana's reconstruction of the city. It was hard to believe, looking at it now. It looked like a city that had been under siege for years, not days. That was what dev-astras did, accomplishing in hours what would take days to achieve through ordinary muscle power and siege machines.

And to think that two mortals leading an army of vanars and bears had done it all.

He allowed himself the luxury of laughter, his amusement growing as he passed ever-increasing sights of destruction and distress. The greater the devastation, the more intense his amusement, the louder his laughter, and the faster he sped his chariot.

Laughing loudly enough to be heard over the din of battle and destruction, Ravana, Lord of Lanka, drove his chariot at manic speed through the devastated streets of his ruined city.

Hanuman was grappling with Kumbhakarna underwater. The vanar was gripping the rakshasa around the waist, with his head pressed against the giant's belly, and was attempting to wrap his hands him around in order to pick him up, invert him, and bring him down head-first on to his thigh. But Kumbhakarna was no stranger to wrestling tactics, and had immediately grasped Hanuman's neck and pinned it in a vice-like grip. Now he was using his other elbow to pound on Hanuman's upper back. Each blow was powerful enough to raze mountains, and every time the giant's elbow splashed down it threw up an explosion of water hundreds of yards high. Hanuman could actually *feel* the blows, which was an indication of how strong Kumbhakarna was. And the giant's grip on his neck was tightening inexorably, choking off the last breath he had in his lungs.

He opened his eyes and saw dark water everywhere. The sun had set during the first moments of their clash, and here, almost a mile under the surface, the ocean was a deep midnight blue. He saw sea creatures swimming in the depths, no doubt wondering at these two enormous newcomers who had descended into their world and were causing such a maelstrom. Among the creatures of the deep he recognised the pale ones with the jagged teeth and the large fins. There were several of them quite close by, and he could see their dead black eyes glinting even in this dim light as they watched the struggle of the titans with dispassionate interest, no doubt waiting in the hope that one or both of them would be left to provide fodder for their evening meal. For several hundred evening meals, in fact, considering the size of them.

Hanuman knew these creatures well – they were the tigers and lions of the oceanic depths, the prime predators of this world – and the sight of their gliding bodies gave him an idea. He had to do something quickly, for he could not breathe now, and the giant's relentless grip was forcing the last air out of his lungs, bubbling slowly out his pursed lips to rise lazily towards the distant surface. The elbow hammering down on his back was starting to hurt as well; the giant seemed to be testing the strength of the individual links in his spinal cord. If this continued much longer, he would soon have a choice between dying by drowning, or from a broken back. He had to do something fairly quickly.

His right cheek was pressed against the right side of the giant's bulging belly. A great deal of Kumbhakarna's bulk was fat, although like many an extremely obese person, the rakshasa possessed powerful muscles beneath those rolls. After all, even a fat person needed the strength to carry his own weight!

He turned his head very slightly, feeling the pressure on his neck increase exponentially, and opened his mouth, ignoring the disgusting fetid odour coming from the rakshasa's unwashed skin – when had he last bathed anyway? In the Satya-Yuga? Then, bracing himself for the undoubtedly wretched taste, he bit deep and hard into the roll of fat on the giant's midriff. At once the skin and flesh parted, and the horrible stench and flavour of raw meat filled his mouth. He almost gagged, choking, and at once swallowed a great gout of ocean water. Which of course went down the wrong way, into his lungs, and that in turn made him start to cough.

At the same time a small burst of blood spewed out of the gaping wound, billowing out and unravelling in ribbons on the ocean tides, carried in two separate directions at once. One ribbon of blood passed directly through the throng of dead eyes flicking their tails desultorily. As the blood reached them, they convulsed suddenly, as if stricken by fits, and started to wag their tails furiously, swimming this way, then that. Meanwhile, Kumbhakarna, belatedly realising that he had been injured somehow, ceased his elbow-pounding and reached down to feel the spot at his waist where Hanuman had bitten him. Hanuman, choking on ocean water as well as the disgusting fatty flesh and blood he still had in his mouth, wriggled fiercely, and with an effort broke free of the giant's grip.

Just as the first of the finned predators reached him. He saw the first one, an enormous white beast with a mouth full of more teeth than he had thought it possible for any mortal creature to possess, approaching with ferocious speed, just as a cheetah covers ground incredibly swiftly when in pursuit of her prey, and lunge directly at his face. No doubt to get at the mouthful of bloody flesh he still had between his teeth. He spat the mouthful straight at the sea predator, hitting it on the tip of its snout. It swerved upwards instantly, snatching the flesh and chomping down on it so hard, the morsel was divided neatly into three pieces. At once the other predators, following close behind, lunged for the two remaining pieces, and began to fight over them in a frenzy. Several more of the creatures swam past the frenzied group and made for the source of the bleeding – the wound in Kumbhakarna's waist. Hanuman moved back out of the way, a lashing fin slapping him hard on his shoulder and a mouthful of jagged teeth missing his fingers by a whisker, and kicked hard, launching himself upwards and away from both the rakshasa and the frenzied pack of sea predators.

He broke the surface coughing and gasping, spitting out flecks of bloody flesh and emptying his lungs of the salty water he had swallowed. Several fish were regurgitated as well, swimming away in panic the instant they splashed back into their natural habitat. 'Sorry, little ones,' he muttered, then coughed one last time and looked around.

Kumbhakarna was only a few yards away, but too pre-occupied to notice him. The giant was thrashing around madly, no doubt feeling the deadly bites of the undersea predators in his already wounded belly, and not liking the idea of becoming an evening repast for the denizens of this watery world. He reached down into the water with both hands, and Hanuman saw his fists re-emerge clutching two of the white predators in one hand and a third big one in the other. The creatures thrashed furiously, and one managed to squirm and bite Kumbhakarna deeply in the tender space between his taloned thumb and fore-claw. The rakshasa howled in pain and smacked the creature down hard on the surface of the ocean, not realising in his fury that slamming water creatures into water might not be the best way to injure them. He flung both fists as far as he could, and Hanuman saw the predators go flying miles away, thrashing in the air as they went, their fangs flashing even in the darkness. He didn't wait to see where they landed, but instead took in a great deep breath and then quickly dived underwater and launched himself at the giant again before Kumbhakarna could spot him coming.

This time he went low, much lower than the rakshasa's waist. He saw several dozen more predators, fins twisting wildly, rushing for the source of the blood they scented, and dived below them. The ocean was darker here, difficult to see through, although he could glimpse as well as feel any number of shoals of fish and those odd gelid creatures with the numerous tenta-cles floating about him. He had estimated the distance well, and was prepared when his shoulder slammed into the giant's ankles. He grasped the two hairy rakshasa feet at once, and yanked hard with all his strength.

Kumbhakarna roared – Hanuman could feel the reverbera-tion of the sound all the way down here, rippling through the water, as well as through the giant's body itself – and lost his balance completely.

That was the chance Hanuman had been waiting for. As the rakshasa toppled over, he pulled Kumbhakarna's feet upwards. They rose easily, without much resistance except for the water itself, for Kumbhakarna had nothing to hold on to. When he had the rakshasa's feet at his own waist level, Hanuman shoved them upwards with all his might; then, when Kumbhakarna was fully inverted and thrashing about desperately, he pushed downwards, literally shoving the rakshasa's head down towards the bottom of the ocean.

But while the rakshasa was no genius, he was no pushover either. He used the momentum of Hanuman's downwards shove to propel himself faster, braced his hands on the ocean floor, and somersaulted. Hanuman sensed this rather than saw it, for their struggle had raised such clouds of mud and dirt from the ocean floor that the water was a swirling fog through which he could barely see a thing. Also, he had to surface again to breathe, and when he did so, he saw Kumbhakarna's feet emerge from the ocean several hundreds of yards away and then topple back, and then, moments later, the giant's head and torso came out of the water. Kumbhakarna vomited out a great mouthful of ocean water, plant life, and even one of the squishy tentacled things. He gasped in several deep breaths, rubbing the salt water from his eyes, which had turned red. He had accumulated a great deal of undersea weed upon his bald pate, which almost resembled a wig of sorts, the kind that Hanuman had seen some of the richer classes of Lankans wearing during his first visit to the island.

'Shall we dance?' Hanuman asked him with a cocky grin.

Kumbhakarna bellowed again, and charged at him.

This time, when Indrajit appeared, Rama did not waste time on parleys and heralds and warnings. All the formalities of war were done with. This was a fight to the last now. He had granted Indrajit the luxury of firing upon Lakshman and himself once, and had experienced first-hand what his lethal arrows could achieve. He had no intention of allowing the rakshasa a second opportunity.

The instant the black chariot turned the corner and rode

down the avenue, Rama took aim. The Arrow of Shiva could assume any form suitable to a missile, depending on the user's desire. Rama had only to imagine it to be barbed, and it would be; hollowed with a rounded point, in order to pass through flesh and bone more smoothly, and it would be so.

This time he called upon the celestial arrow to alter itself into the shape of a snake.

Not any ordinary snake either. He called upon Takshak himself, lord of snakes, the serpent that coiled eternally around the neck of Lord Shiva the Destroyer.

For this was Shiva's arrow after all. And Takshak was Shiva's servant to command.

As he drew the bow's cord back to its maximum, Lakshman, standing beside him, whispered into his ear. 'In the name of our father Dasaratha. If his sons Rama and Lakshmana are righteous soldiers of truth, unbeaten in valour, then may these weapons of Shiva and Vishnu bring about the destruction of this unrighteous rakshasa.'

Rama loosed the arrow directly at Indrajit, aiming for the slender crack between the top of the rakshasa's armoured breastplate and the bottom rim of his helm.

The chariot thundered down the avenue directly at him. The arrow sped towards its target.

16

Hanuman lost track of the passage of time. All he knew was that he and the rakshasa giant had been fighting for hours, and that both had succeeded in injuring the other several times in different ways. The rakshasa had proved unusually adaptable, learning to use their situation to his advantage. Hanuman had swallowed enough ocean water to fill a small inland sea, and every bone in his body felt as if it had been pounded by Indra's hammer on the anvil of the gods like a sword's blade.

They faced each other in the dark waters, eyeing one another silently. Bellowing and shouting took too much effort, and they had spent the last hour-watch or two wrestling and hammering and lashing out in relative silence, only the splashing of water and the thud of fists on flesh and the slapping of palms against bodies providing accompaniment. Now the rakshasa glared at him balefully, that part of his pale skin visible above the surface blotched with bruises and rents and cuts. Hanuman knew those cuts must hurt dreadfully when washed by the salt water, because his own certainly did. But the giant looked as if he could take far worse and still continue fighting. He looked, in fact, as if he could keep this up all night for a thousand more nights – or even a century. If the legends about him were true, as Vibhisena had claimed, then once awakened and challenged to a fight he could go on indefinitely, or until he won. Hanuman assumed he had never been defeated yet, for who on this mortal realm could fight and defeat a giant of this stature?

The question was, could he?

We are evenly matched, Hanuman told himself. That is the worrying thing. He can fight on like this for ever. And I cannot take for ever. The war must be won soon, and Sita regained. Even now, Rama may require me back in Lanka to press home the last phase of the war. I must finish this combat and put this foe down once and for all. Kumbhakarna cannot be allowed to return to Lanka alive, for then he can single-handedly destroy our entire force in mere moments.

And yet, the more he thought about it, the more he felt that the only way to kill Kumbhakarna was in fact to bring him back to Lanka. But the trick was to do so without allowing him to go on another rampage of destruction which would endanger Hanuman's comrades. It was an enormous gamble, and one he hesitated to take, but no other solution offered itself.

He wished Jambavan were here now, so he could ask him for advice. The bear lord's guidance had proved invaluable in his quest for the mountains of herbs, and he knew their bond was far greater and older than any other he had experienced, with the sole exception of his bond with Rama. If Jambavan were here . . .

I am here. Ask me what you will, my friend.

Hanuman's heart leaped. 'My lord,' he said aloud without realising he was doing so, 'you are revived then! Plaksa was able to find the herbs and adminster them in time?'

The rakshasa stared at him in befuddlement. 'Hrrggh?' he grunted, confused and suspicious at this odd question, which he thought was posed to him.

'Oh shut up,' Hanuman said to him. 'Can't a vanar even speak to his friend for a moment?'

Angad found the herbs; Plaksa adminstered them in the nick of time, just as the sun fell below the horizon line. I am well now, and wholly healed. Ask me your question.

Hanuman told him his plan, this time speaking in his mental voice. Kumbhakarna continued to eye him suspiciously, taking cautious steps to one side, foolishly thinking that because

Hanuman was distracted, he would not notice the rakshasa trying to approach him from an angle.

It is a bold plan, but a good one. Do it. Do it quickly, but make sure you do not falter. Remember who you are and what you fight for, and let nothing stand in your way.

With your blessings, I shall, Hanuman said silently.

Then he turned and began striding back towards Lanka, deliberately walking slowly enough for Kumbhakarna to follow. He could have risen out of the cold ocean water and flown easily back to the island-kingdom, but the giant could not fly, and the whole point was to draw him back to Lanka.

For several moments he thought that the giant had seen through his plan and would not follow. But then again, what else could the rakshasa do? Stay out here in the ocean? He had already spent more time in water than he had probably spent bathing in his entire millennia-long existence! And with that wound in his side and the sharp fangs of the ocean predators still pricking him from time to time, he could hardly find this a very pleasant place.

At last Hanuman heard the enormous sloshing sound of Kumbhakarna starting to stride through the water as well, following in his wake.

He led his quarry back to Lanka.

Ravana howled in rage and anguish. He felt the pain of Indrajit's wound in his own throat, as if the Arrow of Shiva had passed through his flesh and severed his neck, decapitating him. He felt the blood gush out of the open wound, the heart still pumping in disbelief, the arms, those arms that had once wounded devas and held a sword to the throat of mighty Indra himself, jerking spasmodically and dropping their weapons, the head rolling in the dirt and mud of the city avenue, its open eyes staring blindly, filling with debris and grit even as the pupils dilated one final time, expanding until they were staring into oblivion.

He whipped his team so hard, the lashes not only drew blood, but gouged strips of flesh as well. The horses, for he used only the finest prime Kambhoja stallions, shrieked in pain and galloped even faster, risking breaking their legs and toppling the whole chariot. He did not care. He wished only to reach the spot where Indrajit had fallen and to avenge his death. For the pain he felt was a father's pain, and it was genuine. This was one of those rare occasions when the Lord of Lanka was not acting or performing for effect; he was being himself.

It was an angry, anguished father that turned the corner on two wheels and started down the avenue at a pace that should have been too swift for even Rama to retaliate. But Rama was ready and waiting. And though Ravana's bow was drawn and ready to fire, Rama's bow was quicker, his arrow swifter, his aim deadlier. And his quiet rage was more potent than Ravana's howling fury.

The two arrows met in mid-air, and Rama's missile shattered Ravana's in half, splitting it perfectly through the middle of the shaft before speeding on to its target, seeking to bury itself deep in Ravana's neck and do unto the father as it had done unto the son.

But this was not to be the moment of Ravana's death. For even as the Arrow of Shiva sped towards him with unerring accuracy, the lead horse of Ravana's team did indeed stumble over a helmet lying in its path. By chance, or perhaps by serendipity, it happened to be the helm of Indrajit himself, separated from that rakshasa's skull when his decapitated head struck the ground and rolled aside. The horse's foot stepped on the curve of the helm, and its shin shattered. The horse fell, whinnying with agony, and with it fell the team, and with the team, the chariot. And as the chariot tilted, preparatory to overturning, as chariots are wont to do when their horses fall at such high speeds, Ravana's body shifted in the air, and where his neck had been a fraction of a moment earlier, his shoulder now presented itself. The arrow struck the fleshy muscle of his right shoulder and passed through it. This was not a snake-arrow, simply a pointed one, and as the

Arrow of Shiva always did once it had struck its target, it vanished at once, returning instantly to Rama's hand only a moment after he had fired it, ready to be used again.

The chariot overturned in a spectacular somersault, flinging both cupola and rider yards across the broad avenue. Ravana came crashing down with the debris of the chariot, landing in an ignominious prostrate position – right at Rama's feet. The rest of the team, screaming with pain as their bodies were broken and mangled with the force of the fall, thudded sickeningly on the hard ground, their lives crushed into silence on impact. The chariot and its wheels and rigging, shattered into pieces, fell on all sides.

Ravana stared up at Rama.

The Arrow of Shiva was pointed directly at his throat. The Lord of Lanka reached for his sword, but he had lost it in the headlong crash, along with his bow. He curled his fingers to issue a sorcerous gesture, but the look in Rama's eyes told him that his foe would unleash the arrow before he could even start to conjure anything. He lay there for a long, breathless moment, as warriors of both sides ceased fighting and turned to gaze in wonder and disbelief at this extraordinary sight. What twist of fate had brought Ravana thus to Rama's feet, weaponless and disadvantaged? Nobody knew, but it had happened somehow, and with a single arrow Rama could end Ravana's life.

'Rama!' cried Lakshman by his side, his own eyes glowing with the blue light of brahman shakti. 'Now!'

Rama loosed the arrow.

Hanuman paused when he was in sight of Lanka. He had taken a circuitous route, careful not to come within sight of the island-nation too soon, for Kumbhakarna might well have charged straight at his homeland then, eager to continue his earlier rampage. Now he was where he desired to be, and could still hear the rakshasa sloshing behind him. He had deliberately let the giant fall behind, hoping thus to anger and provoke him further.

Already, he knew that the long, cold walk through chest-deep water had irritated the titan no end. Several times Kumbhakarna had bellowed a wordless challenge to him, its meaning crystal clear despite its lack of coherent language: Stop and fight me, you craven. Stop running away from me!

He had simply grinned and continued.

Now he moved more quickly, heading straight towards the part of Lanka to which he had wished to bring the rakshasa. Reaching the edge of the land, he climbed ashore, pausing briefly to shake the water from his fur as best he could. He twitched his tail several times, then caught it in his hands and wrung it out gently. Looking back over his shoulder, he saw Kumbhakarna approaching, his pale face mottled with bruises as well as apoplectic anger. He took advantage of his posture to stick out his tongue as well as point his rear at the approaching rakshasa. Kumbhakarna roared with rage and began to run as fast as he could, causing the ocean to surge violently for miles around. Waves splashed over the foothills on this side of Lanka, submerging the land for several hundred yards. Fortunately, Hanuman knew, they were miles if not yojanas away from the city of Lanka itself, where his comrades were.

He waited until Kumbhakarna was close enough to reach out and grab him, then, at the last possible moment, he rose up into the air, floating just out of reach. The rakshasa roared and clambered on to the land, trying to leap up to grab the vanar.

Hanuman moved back a few hundred yards, leading the rakshasa on. He did this for several miles, until they were at the place where he wished to bring the giant. Then he turned and flew a little way further, before descending to the ground.

At the sight of his opponent earthbound again and within reach, Kumbhakarna lurched forward, grunting with frustration. Hanuman turned and raced up the steep slope, continuing to taunt and mock the giant all the way. The rakshasa grew more incensed with each new gesture and action, and tried to run faster. By the time they reached the top, he was out of breath, but as eager to fight as ever.

That was when Hanuman turned and faced him.

On the rim of the smouldering volcano.

Rama's arrow struck the elaborately carved headpiece that covered all ten of the rakshasa's heads and was attached to the back of his breastplate in an ingenious design, breaking the whole thing loose. The gold-plated metal carving clattered to the ground, smoking where the Arrow of Shiva had passed through it.

The arrow reappeared in Rama's hand again.

Lakshman, about to cry out in exultation, stared at the prone Ravana.

The rakshasa king was unharmed.

Ravana himself felt the top of his central head, then another head, then yet another, deducing that he had not been harmed. He seemed as stunned as Lakshman.

'Rama?' asked his brother. 'Why did you not . . . ?'

'One does not kill a foe who is unarmed and prostrated before oneself on the field of battle, Lakshman,' Rama said. 'It would be dishonourable to kill Ravana thus.'

Lakshman stared at him, eyes goggling. 'But—' he began to say, then stopped. His features were conflicted, his expression agonised. But finally he said in a choked voice, 'Why should we show him any honour when *he* fights without honour?'

'Because we are Dasaratha's sons. Shishyas of Brahmarishi Vashishta and Vishwamitra. Children of Kausalya and Sumitra. Kings in waiting of Ayodhya, mightiest of Arya nations. Because we are kshatriyas, bound by the code of the warrior. Because we are followers of dharma.'

Lakshman had no answer. He turned back to glare at the prone Ravana, still lying on the ground of the avenue. 'What do you intend to do then?'

Rama lowered his bow slowly. 'Ravana, you have committed grievous crimes too many to count. Your sins are legendary, your transgressions too great to be adjudged easily. You have carried out violence against me and my loved ones, whether directly or through your minions, such as Manthara and my stepmother Kaikeyi, the yaksi Tataka and her hybrids, the demoness Supanakha and her brothers and their thousands of followers, the hordes of Lanka and the hordes you sent to Mithila . . . too much for my weary heart to recall or recount. You have robbed me of years of my life, of my wife and of my peace of mind; you have slain my friends and their loved ones. Yet here on this field of battle, I fight as my father's son, my mother's pride, the student of my gurus, an Arya kshatriya, and a warrior of dharma. By my own code of honour, I cannot kill you under these circumstances. Therefore, I entreat you, rise now and go back to your dwelling, and return again at sunrise on the morrow to the fields outside the city, and at that time I shall finish what you began, and end this war as well as your life. Go now, before I change my mind and dishonour myself and all who respect me.'

Deathly silence lay across the avenue. Elsewhere in the city, crumbling slabs and bricks fell from ruined structures, wounded and dying rakshasas and vanars and bears groaned and begged for oblivion, fires crackled, and the shouts and screams of warriors still fighting continued unabated.

But every one of the few hundred soldiers of both sides who were within sight of Rama and Ravana stared with numb minds and silent, open mouths.

They watched with incredulity as the king of rakshasas rose to his feet, looked up at Rama with his ten heads, performed three perfect namaskarams with his six hands and without a word turned and walked back up the avenue the way he had come.

17

In the hour before dawn on the night immediately before the fifth and final day of the war of Lanka, Mandodhari came in search of her husband.

The halls of the great palace were empty, the chambers of pleasure and of dining and other fleshly indulgences all desolate and devoid of any pleasure-seekers. The vaulting walls and ceilings, richly festooned with the finest examples of Lankan art and sculpture and crafts, threw back the hollow sounds of her footfalls with the ghostly echoes of a museum at night. Even the palace guards were not at their posts. The hordes of sycophants and harem-whores who usually stayed close by their master had fled, either to hide in the labyrinths below Mount Nikumbhila, or to surrender themselves to the mercy of Lord Rama, who was already a legend among the Lankans. The tale of his sparing Ravana was the only thing anyone could speak of; it was said also that the invaders' soldiers would not harm a hair of any rakshasa who voluntarily laid down arms and submitted meekly to Rama's lordship.

Lanka was a lost cause, she knew that beyond doubt. What she wished to know was whether Ravana was lost as well.

The great doors of the throne chamber were ajar. She stepped through without challenge. Never before had she known Ravana to be so bereft of self-worth that he would leave his doors ajar, his guard-posts unmanned, his palace devoid of sycophants. Never had she imagined she would see such a day.

And yet the day had come, and here was Ravana, seated on his enormous throne, in the chamber that dwarfed even him, that seemed as large as kingship itself, as ornate and intricately decorated as the politics of governance, as vulgarly ostentatious as the price of luxury, as black and polished and obsidian as the onyx eyes of the worm Ouroboros that twined around itself, swallowing its own tail, repeating the circle of life, karma and rebirth eternally.

She stopped before the throne and waited for some sign of greeting or acknowledgement from him. But he remained seated in that same stance, legs sprawled akimbo, heads leaning back against the specially carved cushioned backrest, multiple pairs of eyes staring up into space, several hands clutching several goblets of wine.

Had she not known better, she could have mistaken him for any drunk rakshasa noblemen, one of those rich sods who drained away their inheritance and their life in endless nights of wine-steeped self-indulgence and self-pity, mingled sometimes with the companion vices of debauchery and gambling.

But this was Ravana, her husband, victor of a thousand wars, champion of countless combats, destroyer of worlds, conqueror of realms, lord of the armies of the hell realms, master of the wealth of Kubera, treasurer to the devas, father of her sons. He did not give in to despair, depression or alcoholic stupor.

And yet here he sat, alone and abandoned by all, desolate in his own gaudy chamber.

'My lord,' she said to him. 'Is Lanka lost?'

He barely stirred. But two of his heads lost their glazed obliviousness and lowered their eyes to look upon her. 'Need you ask?'

'Then why do you not still fight? Why do you not rally our armies? Why do you not unleash your powerful sorcery and repel the invaders? Why do you sit here all night drinking wine and brooding alone?'

He took a sip of wine. 'The fight is lost. Our armies are

routed. My sorcery is impotent. But the wine is still good. Would you care for some?'

She stared at him until he looked away. 'Is that your only response? To give up?'

He sighed and put down several of the wine goblets. Two of them teetered on the edge of the surface he set them down upon and fell, clattering, to the floor. The sound of metal on marble was loud and the echoes reverberated through the empty halls and corridors. 'What would you wish me to do? Shall I read out the roll-call of dead champions, generals, sorcerers and illustrious warriors?' Without waiting for a response from her, he held up two of his hands in a manner that suggested he was unrolling a scroll, and pretended to read sonorously: 'Mahaparsva, Mahodara, Virupaksa, Dhumraksa, Akampana, Prahasta, Yupaksa, Viradha, Kabandha, Narantaka, Devantaka, Trisiras, Kumbhakarna, Indrajit, Malavya, Vidhujjivha, Malyavan, Atikaya, Kumbha, Nikumbha, Prajangha, Sonitaksa, Makaraksa, Vajradanta, Matali . . .' He smiled a malevolent smile with one face. 'Some of those are your sons by me, others are mine by other wives. Shall I go on? The list is long and we could spend the rest of the night poring over the names.'

'Enough!'

Rama tossed aside the imaginary scroll. 'All our champions are dead, our generals as well; even our sorcerers have been cut down, and we are bereft of all our sons, legitimate as well as bastards. The city is overrun and in chaos and ruin, my last supporters have fled or surrendered, and only hours ago, Rama himself had an arrow to my head.' His moustached lips twitched in a wry smile. 'My heads. My sorcery was rendered impotent the instant I killed Supanakha, for she bore in her second belly the secret that revived me and was responsible for all the shakti I possessed. I could perhaps conjure up more by sacrificing some of Vibhisena's brahmins, but I seem to have exhausted my supply and the few that might have eluded me have gone over to the enemy, along with the rest of the deserters.'

'Why did you kill Supanakha?' she asked. 'If killing her cost you such a heavy price?'

He shrugged. 'Shall I spend days explaining everything that led up to that moment from thousands of years ago? Or shall I just cry off with the standard response of monarchs when asked uncomfortable questions regarding unsavoury methods employed in a past administration, namely, "It had to be done, and someone had to do it"?' He spread his hands. 'Nothing I say now will convince you, my queen. Why waste time even discussing it?'

'Because I cannot desert you and Lanka, nor do I wish to die in a war over your lust for an ugly and morally decrepit mortal woman,' she replied coldly.

He looked at her with five heads, a sixth joining the others a moment later. 'Is that what you think this war was all about? My lust?'

'What else could it be? I do not see anything else being fought over. No continents conquered or invaded, no power struggles, no wealth amassed or lost, no kingships acquired . . . What else is this war about if not Sita, the wife of Rama?'

He shook his head, rising slowly to his feet. Coming down the stairs of the dais a step at a time, he stopped at the lowest one and looked at her steadfastly. 'This war is not about any woman, and never was. This war has been waged for ever. It is the eternal war, the mother of all wars. It is not merely about me, or Rama, or our differences. In another time, he and I were friends and much beloved of each other; in another time, we may be so again. We shall be so. Yet in this age, and this place, we are at war. And neither of us, if pressed hard, can answer honestly and truly why. For the reason goes to the very soul of iti-haas itself. And as you know, the word for history means simply, "that is what happened". There is no logic, no rationale, no justification, no moral side to choose, no right or wrong, no good or evil, or even shades of grey . . . There is merely an event, a relationship, a war or the end of war. Some day, perhaps, you will be shown why this particular war happened, and why it ended as it did, why it had to end as it did. But now, today, I cannot explain it to you in any terms you can understand. Or I can do so, but to do so I would require a scribe of prodigious talents and profligacy, and some six or seven volumes, consuming several thousands of scroll-pages.' He pretended to glance around. 'And I do not see any scribes at hand at this moment, nor do I think I can keep Rama waiting that long. For it is approaching the hour when I am designated to meet him on the field for our final encounter and it would not be seemly for me to be late to my own death.'

She caught one of his arms. 'Then you knew all this would transpire? That you would be defeated, that Lanka would fall, and that you would go to face Rama thus, helpless and bereft of your army, your sorcerous powers, your . . .' she gestured, '*everything*?'

He looked down at her with a variety of expressions displaying affection, gentleness, tenderness, even something approaching love, if it could be called that. 'If I tell you I did, will it make your heart easier?'

'Tell me the *truth*!' she cried. 'For once!'

He smiled sadly with all his heads at once. 'The truth is too great a burden. I must bear it alone to my grave.' He kissed her gently on the forehead and walked past her.

She turned, tears streaming down her face. 'You owe it to me,' she shouted. 'I am your *wife*!'

He looked back at her. 'No,' he said. 'You are now my widow.'

And he left her standing alone in that desolate palace of unspeakable luxury and finery, and went to meet his end.

Rama surveyed the field. All the survivors of his armies had assembled here again, and it was a telling sight, for now at a glance he could see how many had been lost. Perhaps four out of ten of the original number who had assembled on the shores of the mainland weeks ago remained now. At least another three of the remaining six of those ten were wounded to varying degrees, several grievously. And not one of that number was without some injury or wound. All were exhausted and near collapse, including himself. For even with the shakti of brahmin in his veins, he was still mortal. And mortal flesh had its limits.

But it was still an army, and it was still his to command, and it was a victorious army.

A cry went up, and he saw the thread of dust in the distance, raised by the approach of a single chariot. A few thousand of Lanka's troops stood on the field as well, their heads hanging in shame, their bodies mutilated, battered, and in several cases mortally injured. They had not formally surrendered to him, but they might as well have, for they had ceased fighting hours ago, after the last of their leaders had been slain. All night the war had raged on, and he himself had killed more than he could easily count, and each one of his generals and lieutenants had been injured in their combat with Ravana's greatest warriors. But they had triumphed in the end. And the four precious herbs from the mountains that Hanuman had brought back, the mrtyasanjivani, visalyakarni, sauvarnakarni, and samdhani, had been wonderfully efficacious in reviving those seriously injured. Already, Sugreeva, Angad, Nila, Sarabha, Gandhamadana, Jambavan, Susena, Vegadarsi, Mainda, Dvivida, Nala, Jyotimukha, Panasa, and many others, all slain in various combats, had been revived, healed, or wholly resurrected. Only those who had been torn to pieces physically were beyond the power of the herbs to heal, which number included a great many loved ones, including little Sakra, the tribe-goddess Mandara-devi, and even the aged guru Plaksa, who had been killed by a falling roof while attempting to heal the bear Kambunara. In the ultimate irony, Plaksa had left instructions with his great-grandsons that in the event of his demise he was not to be revived at any cost. He had already passed on the knowledge of how to select and use the herbs, and wished to be allowed to go to his well-deserved next life in peace. Rama had ordered that his wishes should be adhered to.

Now, Rama watched as the chariot approached up the length of the field, and stopped several hundred yards away. He was prepared for subterfuge, for sorcery, for deception and deviousness. After all, this was still Ravana, and he expected the Lord of Lanka, like any ferocious aggressor, to be more dangerous in defeat than he had ever been before.

18

When the voice of Ravana spoke within Rama's mind, he was not surprised. He had been anticipating some kind of mind game. The only unexpected thing was the softness of Ravana's tone. It sounded almost . . . gentle.

Are you pleased, Rama?

He answered by speaking quietly, preferring to use natural speech rather than respond to Ravana's magicks. 'I am ready.'

But you must be filled with joy and relief. You finally have me at your disposal, the war is won, and you will soon regain Sita. You have achieved a great victory, one that will be remembered and celebrated for millennia. In some future age, you will be worshipped as a deva descended to earth in mortal avatar for your accomplishments and deeds in this life.

'I am a warrior performing his duties. It was ever my task to work diligently to achieve my goal, regardless of the fruits of success. I do not desire to be worshipped as a deva, nor am I one.'

Are you quite sure of that?

Rama frowned. 'What do you mean? If you seek to dupe me somehow, you will not succeed, rakshasa.'

Succeed? I have already failed! Do you wish to hear me say it? I have failed, Rama. I have lost to you. Lost everything. My kingdom, my army, my wealth, my power . . . and now I am about to lose my life. I have nothing to gain now by lying to you. This is perhaps the only time that Ravana has nothing to say but the truth.

Rama was nonplussed by this admission. Of all the things he had been expecting, this was not one. Still, he could not be wholly convinced that the rakshasa was not employing some device so clever it seemed entirely naïve. He could not believe that it was in Ravana's nature to admit defeat, and to admit it so openly, honestly and graciously.

But what do you really know about my nature, Rama? Like everyone else, all you know of me is based on my behaviour, my words and my deeds.

'That is how all men are judged by their fellows, on the basis of their words and their deeds.'

But which words and which deeds, and at what time?

Rama shook his head. 'I do not follow your meaning.'

If a son sees his father steeped in wine all hours of the day, indulging himself in fleshly pleasures with three hundred and fifty wives, while he neglects his mother painfully, grows too corpulent even to lift a sword, let alone wield it, how would that son judge that father? Why, he would think him to be a mere debauch! Whereas that same debauch, only a decade or so earlier, might have been one of the greatest warrior kings that ever lived, leading a vast host against great odds, and winning unwinnable wars against the most terrible warring demon races that ever existed. If we are to judge people by their deeds and their words, then we must also weigh which deeds and which words, and at what time.

'Do not refer to my father. He has nothing to do with this.'

But of course he does. Why do you think he was named Dasaratha: He Who Fights in Ten Directions? He spent his life fighting me and my minions, and now his son is about to become legendary for his defeat of a certain villain named Ravana, who happens to have ten heads.

'Names and numbers, they mean nothing to me.'

Much more than names and numbers, my young god-in-the-

making. *There is the matter of Vishnu, who is destined to have ten avatars, the Dasavataras as they are called. Of whom seven have already been born and passed by.*

Rama frowned again. He knew of only six avatars of Lord Vishnu. Who was the seventh that Ravana was referring to?

Every hero must have a villain to destroy, in order to prove himself a hero. But not every villain needs a hero in order to prove himself a villain.

'What does that mean, rakshasa?' Rama asked bluntly. He could not understand what Ravana intended with this debate – or lecture, really. But he did not wish to deny his enemy the right to parley, if that was what this unusual exchange was to be called.

That I existed long before you, Rama Chandra, came into this world in this form, and I will exist again, and again and again, long after you take your samadhi and depart this mortal coil.

'If I have to be born again a thousand times to rid the world of your menace, I shall.'

A thousand times is too many. Thrice more would be sufficient.

'Enough talking now. Come down from your chariot and face me on the field of battle.'

So you prefer violence to civilised conversation then? And they call me a villain.

'You were given several opportunities to talk civilly, rakshasa, and you chose to eschew them for violence. You have left me no choice but to speak in the only language you seem to understand.'

I am sure that kings and leaders of great nations will justify their wars and invasions of foreign lands in much the same terms in future ages. That does not make those wars and invasions any less evil. But perhaps you are right. The time has come at last to end this particular conflict. Already it drags on past my endurance. You do not know how long I have awaited this day, this hour.

'Then come and reap the harvest of your actions.' And Rama raised his bow and drew the arrow.

Ravana stepped down from his chariot. The Lord of Lanka was clad in the traditional garments of civilised Arya everywhere – for Arya meant literally 'noble', and was not a race or creed but a way of life – a pristine white dhoti around his lower limbs and a white ang-vastra draped loosely around his upper body, the end of the strip of cloth wrapped around his lowermost right forearm. He wore no crown on any of his heads, and every one of his foreheads had been anointed with the red ochre that signified that he had performed his acamana ritual that morning and offered suitable prayers. Rama had received reports that the king of rakshasas had been spotted entering the Shiva mandir earlier, although he still could not fathom how he had travelled there from the palace in the inner quarter of the city without being seen by Rama's troops, who were everywhere now. It did not matter any more; they were now at the end of all deceptions and subterfuge. Whatever sorcery Ravana had planned, Rama would counter it with his dev-astras and his will. He would not let the rakshasa leave the field alive this time.

When Ravana was perhaps fifty yards away, he stopped and faced Rama. The rakshasa carried a throwing javelin covered with gold plate and carved in exquisite detail: the filigree working was visible even at this distance, catching the light of the rising sun. It was an unusually ostentatious weapon to bring to such a vital encounter. Rama had expected something more deadly or exotic. But then, perhaps Ravana thought to confuse and deflect his attention with such an object, while his real attack would come from a wholly different direction. He remained alert for any and every possibility. Hanuman was already overhead, hovering in mid-air, arms crossed across his chest as he watched the contest sternly, ready to intervene on Rama's behalf at any time that he saw deception on Ravana's part. Lakshman, Angad, Sugreeva, Nala, Jambavan . . . his supporters were stationed at strategic points, ready to face an attack from the most unexpected quarter, be it from below the ground, from the ocean, even out of the sky. They had become veterans now of the wiles and ways of rakshasa warfare. They were masters of this field.

One last thing, Ravana's voice said in his mind.

'I am done with speaking, rakshasa. Raise your weapon and strike if you will. Or I will strike at you first, it does not matter to me either way. But cease your speaking and act.'

You may strike at me any time you wish. But I shall say this one thing anyway. After I am gone, care well for the twins. For they are my legacy to the world, and my parting gift to you.

Twins? Legacy? Gift? Rama found himself growing angry and impatient with the rakshasa's riddles. 'I do not know what you speak of, Lanka-naresh. But I will hear no more. Now, raise your weapon and fight.'

And with those words, Rama pulled back his arrow and prepared to fire upon Ravana.

Ravana nodded. All his ten heads dipped and rose in unison. Then he hefted the ornately worked gold spear in one hand, raised it, pulled back his arm, and flung the weapon hard towards Rama.

Rama stood his ground, allowing the spear to fly straight at him. He had promised himself that he would let Ravana have first strike – and even first blood, if it so transpired – so that when he fired upon the rakshasa, no one could question his right to do so.

He knew he could move and dodge the spear should it threaten to impale him in some vital organ. But because of the miracle herbs, even that would not be needed. And he would rather endure even a mortal wound manfully than step aside and dance for Ravana. So he braced himself, fully expecting the spear to pierce him fatally, prepared for the impact and the pain.

Every pair of eyes in both the assembled armies watched the spear as it flew through the air towards Rama.

Then, when it was merely yards away, it fell like a dead weight, piercing the ground almost half a yard short of his left foot, which he had placed forward in his usual archer's stance.

He was shocked as well as suspicious. Surely Ravana could not have missed? The master of war himself? No, there was something deliberate in this near miss. Of that he was certain. But he would not waste time trying to fathom it. He would act before the rakshasa's plan, whatever it might be, could take effect.

With a sloka on his lips, he loosed the Arrow of Shiva.

The missile flew across the field, blazing with blue flames clearly visible in the morning light.

And struck one of Ravana's heads, the one on the extreme left side. The head was decapitated and fell with a dull thud to the ground, rolling several yards away. The arrow returned to Rama's bow. Without hesitating, he fired it again, decapitating another head, this time the one on the extreme right hand of Ravana's rack. He saw the blood spurt and the head lopped off, falling beyond the rakshasa. He fired again. And yet again. Nine times in all.

Until only one head remained.

Rama paused, staring at the lord of rakshasas. Why was Ravana simply standing there, doing nothing? Why did he not retaliate to Rama's attacks? Surely he had other weapons, other devices? Why was he not acting, using them, deploying sorcery?

Because you shot so swiftly, he told himself, stilling the uneasy voice in his head. You shot so swiftly that he had no time to retaliate.

But now Ravana did have time, as Rama paused and wondered at his inaction.

And as he watched, the rakshasa raised his six hands, flexing his powerful muscles, and gestured, as if unleashing a sorcerous spell.

At once, Rama loosed the arrow a tenth time.

And decapitated Ravana's last head.

For a long moment, the King of Lanka stood there on the field, headless, blood pouring from ten separate wounds, the white bone that fixed each head to his unusual spine visible in some of the cavities.

Then, slowly, almost majestically, with an illusion of dignity and grace, the dark lord's body pitched forward and fell on the mud of the field. It lay there, still and lifeless, to all appearances dead.

Rama lowered his bow and stared at the fallen body of his enemy. It could not possibly be that easy. Surely Ravana had engineered some deception here, some sleight of hand or Asura maya.

It occurred to him that perhaps the rakshasa had used a shapeshifter in his place, instead of appearing himself. That seemed unlikely, since this combat was now a matter of honour, but who knew how low Ravana would sink?

Unconvinced, he called out to Lakshman and Nala to check the body and confirm that Ravana was dead.

They did so. Lakshman bent down, examined the body closely, then rose and nodded. 'He is dead, Rama.'

Even then Rama was not satisfied. 'Call someone who can identify him.'

'I will identify him,' said a rakshasi, stepping forward. Rama had noticed her earlier, standing to one side along with several other rakshasis, but had assumed they were widows seeking the corpses of their fallen husbands among the dead, or perhaps even one of the many delegations that had been approaching him to beg for mercy for themselves and their surviving relatives. Now, as she removed her veil, he saw that she was clearly a woman of some distinction.

Vibhisena started forward from his place among Rama's supporters. 'Mandodhari,' he called. The rakshasi paid no heed to his call, but as he approached, she permitted him to walk alongside her. Together they went to where Ravana's body lay and bent down over it.

As the rakshasi began to sob and weep uncontrollably, embracing the mutilated body of the dead rakshasa, Rama grew certain at last that the impossible had indeed been achieved. He had killed Ravana. The nemesis of the three worlds was dead at last.

ATI SAMAPTAM

LORD OF LIGHT

After the death of Ravana, Lanka's survivors hailed Rama as he entered the city in a triumphant victory procession, and a delegation of nobles and ministers approached him to beg that he assume kingship of their nation.

He refused flatly, and at first was inclined to leave it to the Lankans to select and install their own king. But when they insisted that he choose for them, he said simply, 'At a time like this, you require an honest, righteous ruler. I know only one such rakshasa. Ravana's brother Vibhisena.'

Mandodhari was inconsolable at Ravana's death, but after her initial breakdown on the field she regained her wits and her composure, and met Rama with an aspect of unrelenting accusation. 'My husband did not fight you,' she said in a tone the more galling for being so quiet and controlled. 'He permitted you to slay him. It was an act no less than murder.'

'My lady,' Rama replied patiently, 'if he allowed me to slay him, then surely it ought to be called suicide.'

But she would not listen to further argument, and turned her face away with the final, chilling words, 'May your wife come to know how it feels to be separated from her husband thus. Ravana was a being of many faults but he was also a great king, a great leader of men, and his name will live longer than yours. There may be many Ramas; there will only be one Ravana.'

He did not respond. She had the right to speak her heart.

Besides, widows were entitled to say whatever they wished. He focused instead on the wearying task of settling in the new council of governance under Vibhisena, and undergoing a brief formal ceremony during which he wished aloud that the conflict between rakshasas and mortals would end this day for all time.

'When the rakshasa race itself is on the brink of dying out,' one sardonic minister replied, 'where is the question of further conflict? You have weeded out the worst of us, Rama, but in doing so you have also ensured our extinction. Perhaps not today, or even in a year, or a hundred years, but some day in the distant future there shall be a new Lanka which recalls nothing of its rakshasa past, and is occupied entirely by mortals. This much you have achieved at least: you have rid this mortal plane of the last vestiges of the Asura races. Surely you will be remembered and celebrated throughout history for your acts.'

Rama sensed and heard the cynicism in the rakshasa's words but did not argue the point. When one has won the war, one should not stoop to petty squabbles. Besides, there was no untruth in what the fellow said. Some day, he thought, looking down from the balustrade of Pushpak, which he had commandeered, there would truly be a new Lanka, a Lanka of peace and prosperity, and this jewel of an island-kingdom would be populated with people as beautiful as the land itself, dark and comely and pure of heart and soul. If only they did not allow the poison of the violence that had been committed here in the past to resurface.

He had Hanuman extinguish the volcano, which was already dying after the vanar had wrestled the giant Kumbhakarna into its maw. The enormous bulk of the titan had consumed the rest of the volcano's fire, and it took very little effort – only a few giant fistfuls of water and dry sand – to snuff it out completely. Reshaping it with his bare hands, Hanuman turned it into yet another mountain, the highest now on the Lankan landscape.

With Ravana's sorcery gone, the Lankans would have to rebuild their city the hard, old-fashioned way. Perhaps that was for the best. For they would be occupied with productive work and would have no energy or time to spare for unfruitful thoughts of revenge or retaliation. As he observed the people straggling through the ruins of their once great city-state, Rama did not sense any great animosity or hostility, only the sullen relief of a defeated populace.

Sita was seated beside him now, on the cushioned seat of Pushpak, resting her weary body. He had been shocked to find her so depleted and pale and thin. But she was alive, and still in her senses, and had sustained no major injuries. They had much to speak of, but there would be time for that later, once they were safely back in their rightful place.

Right now, all he desired was to return home. For the exile was finally over, his demons slain – literally – and Sita regained. He had nothing else to hold him here, or anywhere else. And there was an entire nation waiting to receive him, and welcome him back. He had already sent Hanuman ahead as his emmissary to inform his family that he was returning, and as he watched Sita resting languidly, neither wholly awake nor asleep, he waited for the vanar's return.

Lakshman came up beside him, glancing at his sister-in-law. 'How is she? Angad and Nala have laid out a repast for us on the lower level. Will she join us there to feast?'

Rama put his arm around his brother, hugging him warmly. 'Nay, my brother. She needs rest now more than food. Perhaps later, when she has been able to recover a little, she will feel her appetite return. Right now, she is still absorbing the shock that her ordeal is finally over.'

Lakshman gestured to Rama to come over to the far side of Pushpak. Rama went with him.

Lakshman turned and said softly, too softly to be heard by Sita, 'Rama, there is a rumour among the vanars and the bears . . .'

Rama had heard several hundred rumours in the past day, most concerning Ravana and how the dark lord was not truly dead but concealed somewhere, biding his time to return, even if it took ten thousand years. He put his arm over his brother's shoulder. 'Lakshman, if we believe every rumour, we will be imagining Ravanas leaping out of our own shadow every minute.'

Lakshman shook his head. 'This one is not about Ravana. It is about Sita.'

Rama looked at him curiously. 'What about Sita?'

Lakshman looked around uncomfortably, then glanced back at Rama. 'The question that is being asked is this: how do we know that the Sita we saw killed earlier was not the real Sita, and that this one is not the shapeshifter Supanakha?'

Rama removed his arm from Lakshman's shoulder. 'How can you even tolerate such an ugly lie?'

Lakshman sighed. 'Rama, do not take offence. Consider for a moment. After all the deceptions of Ravana, is it not possible?'

'No.' Rama's voice was without anger, but it was firm.

'But Rama, how can you know for sure? After all, it was only because Jambavan told us that the first Sita was actually Supanakha with her appearance altered that we knew that bhabhi was still alive. Had Jambavan not told us, we would be thinking today that this woman was Supanakha, would we not?'

'No,' Rama said again. 'You might, others might, but not I. I know that this is Sita, my wife, and your sister-in-law, Lakshman.'

Lakshman inhaled deeply, then released another breath. He looked around in frustration. 'There is a simple way to prove it.'

'I will not hear of it.'

'Rama, if not for yourself . . .'

'I am her husband, I am satisfied, I do not need to satisfy anyone else.'

Lakshman looked at him thoughtfully. 'You are also the King of Ayodhya now, or will be in a short while. You owe a duty to the people. You recall the vow of kingship: to put dharma before self, to put the law of the land before one's own welfare or gain.'

'You do not need to remind me of my vows. I know them well. And this matter has no bearing on them.'

'But it does, Rama. The law says that a woman who has been away from her husband and has lived in another man's house for more than one night must prove her chastity or be assumed to have committed the crime of adultery. That is the law, as I need not remind you.'

'Yes, of course,' Rama began, 'but—' Then he stopped. And thought through the implications of Lakshman's words. He saw that Lakshman was indeed correct: while the law was not meant to cover wives abducted by rakshasa kings and spirited away by force to distant lands, Sita's case did indeed fall under its purview. 'Even so,' he conceded reluctantly, 'it is the husband's prerogative in such a case to choose to accept his wife back or reject her, regardless of whether or not she has . . .' He could not bring himself to utter the offensive phrases, and to his relief Lakshman nodded hurriedly, as embarrassed as he was. 'And as her husband, I believe completely that she was neither touched by Ravana nor did she once yield to his embraces . . .' There. He had said as much as he was willing to say. 'I accept her back unconditionally as my lawful wife.'

'Yes, yes, yes, Rama, and I support you wholeheartedly, and would do the same if I were in your position, Devi forbid,' Lakshman said softly. 'But you are no ordinary citizen, nor is she an ordinary woman. You are the King and Queen of Ayodhya, and the minute we reach home, you will assume your crowns and your kingship and queenship. And kingship demands a far higher standard of morality and law, and dharma.'

'Then what would you have me do, Lakshman?' Rama said, now starting to lose his patience at last. 'Would you have me test her to be certain of her identity? And even if I ascertain that she is who I believe her to be, there would still be aspersions cast on her purity, according to you. So what would you have me do? Ask her to take the agni test to prove herself?'

Lakshman stared at him wide-eyed. 'Bhai.'

Rama realised the implications of what he had said.

'But it is perfect. By taking the agni test, she will prove both things simultaneously: that she is indeed Sita, and not a shapeshifter in human form; and that she is pure and unsullied by any other man's touch.'

Rama shook his head. 'No, no, no. I will not subject my wife to such a test. It is inhuman and irrational, and offensive to her as well as to me.'

'But your wife is the queen of the civilised world now, Rama.'

'No,' he said again. 'I will hear no further argument on this matter. Sita will not undergo the agni test.'

'Sita will indeed undertake the agni test.'

They both turned to find Sita standing a mere yard away. She still looked wan and pale, but in her eyes was a glimmer of something they both recognised: her steely will.

'Sita,' Rama said anxiously. 'You ought to be—'

'I am exhausted and bruised and starved,' she said, 'but not dead. I will do this, Rama. I will undertake the agni test.'

'You do not need to, my love,' he said gently. 'People will always find some new rumour to gossip about. We have been through so much, together and apart; we will endure this as well.'

'And we will survive it as well,' she said. 'I do not doubt that, nor do I doubt your resoluteness, my love. But I am not doing this for you, nor am I doing it for myself, nor am I doing it to silence those who start such rumours, nor even those who repeat them and thereby give them credence.'

Although she did not look at Lakshman as she said this, her brother-in-law flushed hotly and glanced away.

She continued calmly, 'I do this for Ayodhya.'

'For Ayodhya?' Rama echoed.

'Yes. The kingdom has waited fourteen years for the rightful king and queen to return. There must be no shadow of doubt, no whisper of rumour, not even the tiniest spot of a stain to mar the perfection of that moment. Your road to the sunwood throne must be unquestioned and unchallenged by anyone, for I know that by Ayodhyan law, even the king and queen are subject to the same laws of dharma as their citizens, and none are above it. If we do not undertake this test, Rama, anyone at any time can raise this question again. Let me undertake this agni pariksha now and stamp out the rumour for ever more.'

Rama was silent when she finished. He looked at Lakshman, who was flushed with embarrassment, but nodded silently, agreeing.

'Very well then,' Rama said. 'Let us leap this final hurdle and return home.'

They held the test on the mainland, travelling there by Pushpak, which Vibhisena showed them how to manipulate until it was enlarged into a great vessel of many score levels, enough to bear the entire vanar and bear armies. The celestial vehicle flew as easily and smoothly with this enormous load as it did when only two or three passengers rode it. And despite the swiftness of its movement, none aboard felt any discomfort or unease. Although the vanars and bears *cheeka*-ed and howled at the sight of mountains and valleys and plains, and then wide-open ocean water, rolling beneath them at the speed of the wind.

They reached the mainland two hour-watches before sunset. With so many hands to work, it took little time to assemble the required dried branches and sticks and lay them out upon the sandy beach for a length of some ten yards as demanded by law. Then Lakshman set about the task of lighting the fire and speaking the appropriate slokas over it, taking care not to make a single slip, for then he would be required to start all over again.

When all was in readiness, he turned and nodded to Rama. Rama looked at Sita. 'Are you sure?'

She smiled at him with the same wan smile she had worn since he had found her in the cave beneath the city. At least she did not weep in his arms and shake uncontrollably as she had done at that first reunion. He was proud of how dignified and self-possessed she looked.

He walked with her to the start of the long walkway, already blazing with foot-high flames. He kissed her once, then left her.

Sita did not resent the test. She understood how doubt could creep into the mind of any person and take root. She could also understand the external perception that most would have of her situation: a defenceless woman, captured and kept prisoner for weeks by the most powerful demon lord, arch-enemy of her husband. It would be hard for some people to believe that she had not been raped, ravished, violated in some fashion or other. They would wonder how she could have resisted so long. And she could hardly expect them to believe the truth: that Ravana had in fact never approached her with force or a lustful gaze. The closest he had come was in badgering her, hectoring, taunting, seeking to break down her mental defences. But to the end, all he had done was threaten her verbally, not abuse her physically. It had perplexed her all this while; now she was left wondering if perhaps he had never intended to do anything to her at all. If perhaps it had been his intention all along merely to use her as bait to bring Rama and his armies to Lanka. But why would he wilfully cause his own destruction?

She set aside these and all other questions and prepared herself for the pariksha.

The test was simple enough. The fire was real, the threat to mortal flesh and life and limb agonisingly real as well. Only the mantras that Lakshman had spoken over the fire, and which she was now required to repeat the companion verses to, could keep her from being consumed alive. No Asura or rakshasa could hope to speak the same mantras and survive; Agni, the deva of fire, would know and destroy them at once. And of course, if there was any trace of impurity in her – if, for instance, she had indeed committed any transgression against Agni, for the marital vows were always sanctified by the holy fire, whether she had done so willingly or unwillingly – she would be burned alive. It was an ancient, cruel test for women who had been violated against their will, but it was also a test devised by women themselves, to prove their purity under circumstances where doubt arose.

She stepped on to the flaming logs, the verses already on her lips, and measured her footsteps by the rhythm of the Sanskrit slokas.

Before she knew it, she was stepping on to warm sand once again, and a great cheer rose from the watching assemblage of vanars and bears.

Rama came and hugged her. 'My love, my love,' was all he said.

She smiled and looked back at the long fire walk. Had she truly stepped through that without feeling a thing? Apparently she had. And she had not a burn nor so much as a stain to show for it. Even her garments were untouched.

Lakshman came and bowed before her, touching her feet. 'Bhabhiji, forgive me if I offended you in any way. I desired only to set all doubts at rest.'

'Lakshman,' she said, and felt tears springing to her eyes, 'you have no need to apologise. I know that in all you do, you wish only the best for Rama and me.'

She looked at her husband and her brother-in-law, then at the masses of shouting and leaping and dancing vanars and bears. 'I think a celebration is in order now. I can see that everyone needs it.'

Rama nodded. 'But ours will have to wait until we return home.'

He gestured at Hanuman, who had arrived shortly before they left Lanka with the news that Ayodhya was awaiting them with great eagerness.

*　　*　　*

Pushpak flew swiftly across the land, reduced now to merely one level as only the three Ayodhyans and Hanuman were aboard it. Rama had taken leave of King Sugreeva and Jambavan and all the others back on the shore of the mainland itself, with promises to visit soon and stay in touch, and when he had parted from them, he felt almost as he had felt when parting from his family in Ayodhya that fateful day fourteen years ago.

Pushpak moved at a tremendous pace. At this rate, Hanuman had told them, they would be in Ayodhya before sunset. And indeed, the speed was so great, Rama had nothing to compare it to any longer, except perhaps Hanuman himself!

He almost wished he could make it go slower, to savour the moment, the luxury of being with Sita again, of looking upon her heart-shaped face, that slender throat, those eyes he could lose himself in for hours. He looked down at the endless forests blurring past underneath and wished that they could return to that simple cottage in Panchvati, could play in the high grass and rub turmeric on one another's faces and laugh and kiss and spend all day in the dappled sunlight falling through the leaves, and perhaps later, when they were done with affection, they could go down to the river and slake their thirst and then dive into the cool, perfect water, and enter that beautiful, silent world. And afterwards, as the forest dimmed and the sunlight faded, and the birds filled the sky with their deafening cacophony, they could sit by a fireplace and eat a simple meal before retiring for the night to straw pallets on a mud floor swept by Sita herself with a thrash-broom and sterilised by Lakshman with cow urine, and then made fragrant by rose blossoms strewn in the corners.

But he knew wistfully that such a thing could never come to pass. Tonight he would sleep on velvet cushions and silken sheets would cover his body. So be it. As long as he had Sita by his side, nothing else would matter. And Lakshman would have Urmila again. For Rama had not forgotten that these past fourteen years, his brother had been separated from his bride.

Fourteen years. And now it seemed to have flowed past like the river rushing by below Pushpak. Had it really been that long?

Then he realised that the river was the Sarayu, and that the wooden arch speeding by below was Mithila Bridge. And that they were on Kosala land now. There was the raj-marg winding its way steadily alongside the river, bordered on the south by the pressing darkness of the forest. Except that there was no Bhayanak-van any longer, no dreaded Southwoods, no Asuras lurking in those dark wildernesses. And that was his doing; he had rid the world of all demons, including his own.

And then he saw the lights, and heard the faint chanting.

Ayodhya was glowing. She had put on her best face for him once more, as she had done on the night he had returned from Mithila with his new bride, he and his three brothers, and his father and mother, and the other queens. But this time there were people on the raj-marg as well, holding up oil lanterns blazing in endless perfect rows. On the riverbanks. On the walls. On the city streets, which he could glimpse now. On the rooftops. And at the balconies of a thousand homes.

Ayodhya was burning with happiness.

For Rama. For her long-lost liege, returning home at last.

He could see the palace now, so familiar it brought an ache to his heart and a tear to his eye. He could see the troops lined up on the avenue, their weapons gleaming in the light of the mashaals, their uniforms immaculate, and he could hear their voices now, raised in perfect harmony, singing the raag Deepavali. It filled his heart and his ears and enveloped him with warmth and love and affection. He looked down at Sita and saw her face lit up with the glow of the lights below as well as from an inner flame that he knew was the first sign of thawing of the icy terror that had imprisoned her all this while. She would be well now. She would return to life. And he would care for her better than he cared for himself. For she was Ayodhya, and he loved her. And he was with her now, he was home, and he would stay for ever. Nothing would ever separate them again.

He looked down with her, their hands clasped, their throats choked with emotion, Lakshman and Hanuman behind them, all four of them silenced by the grandeur of the scene, the rich tableau laid out before them, an entire city – nay, an entire nation – turned out to greet them and welcome them back. And Pushpak dipped, slowing at last, coming to a perfect halt then descending smoothly, silently, to bring them to the level of the ground before the palace entrance. And Rama saw his mother, ageing and white-haired, and Brahmarishi Vashishta, looking much the same as ever but with perhaps a few more lines on his ancient face, and Bharat, and Shatrugana, and was that Nakhudi? And that stately old man in a general's uniform, could it be Bejoo? So many faces, so many memories, so many loved ones and sights and sounds and things, all swirling together in a miasma of light and song and beauty.

He gave Sita his hand to hold for support and helped her out of Pushpak. Together they stepped out on to the soil of his native land. At last, finally, they were home.

GLOSSARY

This 21st-century retelling of The Ramayana *freely uses words and phrases from Sanskrit as well as other ethnic Indian languages. Many of these have widely varying meanings depending on the context in which they're used – and even depending on whether they were used in times ancient, medieval or present-day. This glossary explains their meanings according to their contextual usage in this book rather than their strict dictionary definitions. AKB.*

aagya: permission.

aangan: entrance; courtyard.

aaram: rest.

aarti: prayer ceremony.

aatma: spirit; soul.

aatma-hatya: suicide.

acamana: ritual offering of water to Surya the sun-god at sunrise and sunset.

a-dharma: the opposite of dharma; unrighteous; an action or belief that is against the natural laws.

agar: black gummy stuff of which joss sticks are made.

agarbatti: incense prayer sticks made of agar; joss sticks.

agni: fire; fire-god.

agnihotra: fire-sacrifice; offering to the fire-god agni. Originally, in Vedic times, this meant an animal-sacrifice. Later, as the Vedic faith evolved into vegetarian-favouring Hinduism, it became any ritual fire-offering. The origin of the current-day Hindu practice of anointing a fire with ghee (clarified butter) and other ritual offerings.

ahinsa: the opposite of violence; pacifism.

Aja-putra: literally, son of Aja, in which Aja was the previous Suryavansha king of Ayodhya; it was common to refer to Aryas as 'son of (father's name)'; e.g. Rama would be addressed as 'Dasaratha-putra'.

akasa-chamber: from the word

'akasa' meaning sky. A room with the ceiling open to the sky, used for relaxation.

akhada: wrestling square.

akshohini: a division of the army with representation from the four main forces – battle elephants, chariots with archers, armoured cavalry, and infantry.

amar: eternal.

amrit: nectar of the devas; the elixir of eternal life, one of many divine wonders produced by the churning of the oceans in ancient pre-Vedic times. The central cause of the original hostility between the devas and the Asuras, in which the Asuras sought the amrit in order to gain immortality like the devas but the devas refused them the amrit.

an-anga: bodiless.

anarth ashram: orphanage.

anashya: indestructible.

an-atmaa: soulless.

angadiya: a messenger of Prince Angad; loosely, a courier.

angoor: grape.

ang-vastra: length of cloth covering upper body – similar to the upper folds of a Roman toga; any bodily garment.

anjan: kohl; kajal.

apsara: any of countless beautiful danseuses in the celestial court of lord Indra, king of the devas.

aranya: wilderness.

arghya: the traditional washing of the feet, used to ceremonially welcome a visitor, literally by washing the dust of the road off his feet.

artha: meaning, purpose, motive.

Taken together, artha, karma and dharma form the trifold foundation of Vedic philosophy.

Arya: literally, noble or pure. Commonly mispelled and mispronounced as 'Aryan'. A group of ancient Indian warrior tribes believed to have flourished for several millennia in the period before Christ. Controversially thought by some historians to have been descended from Teutonics who migrated to the Indian sub-continent and later returned – although current Indian historical scholars reject this view and maintain that the Aryas were completely indigenous to the region. Recent archaeological evidence seems to confirm that the Aryas migrated *from* India to Europe, rather than the other way around. Both views have their staunch supporters.

asana: a yogic posture, or series of postures similar to the kathas of martial arts – which are historically believed to have originated from South-Central India and have the same progenesis as yoga.

ashirwaad: blessings.

Ashok: a boy's given name.

ashoka: Indian fir or *masth* tree.

ashubh: inauspicious.

ashwamedha: the horse ceremony. A declaration of supremacy issued by a king, tantamount to challenging one's neighbouring kingdoms to submit to one's superior strength.

astra: weapon.

Asura: anti-god: literally, a-Sura or anti-Sura, where Sura meant the clan of the gods and anyone who stood against them was referred to as an a-Sura. Loosely used to describe any demonic creature or evil being.

atee-sundar: very beautiful. Well done or well said.

ati-samaptam: The end of a tale or recital; epilogue.

atma-brahman: soul force; one's given or acquired spiritual energy.

atman: soul; spirit.

avatar: incarnation.

Awadhi: Ayodhyan commonspeak; the local language, a dialect of Hindi.

awamas: the moon's least visible phase.

awamas ki raat: moonless night.

Ayodhya: the capital city of Kosala.

Ayodhya-naresh: master of Ayodhya. King.

ayushmaanbhav: long life; generally used as a greeting from an elder to a younger, as in 'live long'.

baalu: bear (see also rksa).

badmash: rascal, scoundrel, mischievous one.

bagh: big cat, interchangeably used for lion, tiger and most other related species of large, predatory cat.

bagheera: panther or leopard.

baithak-sthan: rest-area; lounge.

balak: boy.

balidaan: sacrifice.

balu: colloquial term for bear.

bandara: monkey; any simian species.

barkha: rainstorm.

ber: a variety of wild Indian berry, yellowish-reddish outside, white inside, very juicy and sweetish.

bete: child.

beti: daughter.

bhaang: an intoxicating concoction made by mixing the leaf of the poppy plant with hand-churned buttermilk. Typically consumed at Holi celebrations by adult Hindus. Also smoked in hookahs or traditional bongs as pot.

bhaangra: robust and vigorous north Indian (punjabi) folk dance.

bhabhi: brother's wife or close friend's wife.

bhade bhaiya: older brother.

bhagyavan: blessed one; fortunate woman.

bhai: brother.

bhajan: a devotional chant.

bhakti: devotion.

bharat-varsha: the original name for India; literally, *land of bharata* after the ancient Arya king Bharata.

bhashan: lecture.

bhayanak: frightening, terrifying.

bhes-bhav: physical appearance.

bhindi: ladyfinger, okra.

bhojanshalya: dining hall.

bhor: extreme; as in *bhor suvah*: extreme (early) morning.

bhung: useless; negated.

bindi: a blood-red circular dot worn by Hindu women on their foreheads to indicate their married status. Now worn in a variety of colours and shapes as a fashion accessory.

brahmachari: see brahmacharya.

brahmacharya: a boy or man who

devotes the first 25 years of his life to prayer, celibacy, and the study of the Vedic sciences under the tutelage of a brahmin guru.

brahman: the substance of which all matter is created. Literally, the stuff of existence.

brahmarishi: an enlightened holy man who has attained the highest level of grace; literally, a rishi or holy man, whom Brahma, creator of all things, has blessed.

brahmin: the priestly caste. Highest in order.

broken-sur: 'sur' meaning 'head', 'broken-sur' literally means 'broken-head'. A mutant cross-breed used in Lanka as a beast of conveyance and burden.

buddhi: intellect; mind; intelligence.

chacha: uncle; father's younger brother.

chaddar: sheet.

Chaitra: the month of spring; roughly corresponds to the latter half of March and first half of April.

charas: opium.

chaturta: cleverness.

chaukat: a square. Most Indian houses were designed as a square, with an entrance on one wall and the house occupying the other three walls. In the centre was an open chaukat where visitors (or intruders) could be seen from any room in the house.

chaupat: an ancient Indian war strategy dice game, universally acknowledged to be the original inspiration for chess, played on a flat piece of cloth or board by rolling bone-dice to decide moves, involving pieces representing the four akshohini of the Arya army – elephants, chariot, foot-soldiers, knights.

chillum: toke; a smoking-pipe used to inhale charas (opium).

chini kulang: a variety of bird.

chital: a variety of spotted deer found in the forests of the Himalayan foothills, considered the most beautiful of all deer.

choli: breast-cloth; a garment used to cover a woman's upper body.

chotti: pigtail.

chowkidari: the act of guarding a person or place like a sentry or chowkidar.

chudail: banshee; female ghost; witch.

chunna: lime-powder or a mixture of lime-powder and water; used to whitewash outer or inner walls; also eaten in edible form in paan or mixed directly with tobacco.

chunnri: a strip of cloth used by a woman to cover her breasts and cleavage, also used to cover the head before elders or during prayer.

chupp-a-chuppi: hide and seek.

crore: one hundred hundred thousand; one hundred lakhs; ten million.

daiimaa: brood-mother, clan-mother, wet nurse, governess. A woman serving first as midwife to the expecting mother, then later as wet-nurse, governess and au pair.

dakshina/guru-dakshina: ritual payment by a kshatriya to a brahmin on demand.

daku: dacoit; highway bandit; jungle thief.

danav: a species of Asura.

darbha: a variety of thick grass.

darshan: the Hindu act of gazing reverentially upon the face of a divine idol, an essential part of worship; literally, *viewing*.

dasya: slave; servant.

Deepavali: the predominant Indian Hindu festival, the festival of lights. Also known as Diwali.

desh: land; country; nation.

deva: god. Several Indian devas have their equivalents in Greek and Norse mythology.

dev-astra: weapon of the devas; divine weapon.

dev-daasi/devdasi: prostitute.

devi: goddess.

dhanush-baan: bow and arrows.

dharma: sacred duty. A morally binding code of behaviour. The cornerstone of the Vedic faith.

dharam-patni: wife; literally, 'partner in dharma'.

dharamshala: a traditional resthouse on Indian roads in times past, where travellers could partake of free shelter and simple nourishment. Literally, 'shelter of dharma'.

dhobi: washerman (of clothes).

dhol: drum.

dollee: palanquin; travelling chair.

dosa: a flat crisp rice-pancake, a staple of South Indian cuisine.

dhoti: a white cotton lower garment, worn usually by Indian men.

diggaja: a breed of rakshasas.

diya: clay oil lamp.

drishti: vision; view; sight.

dumroo: a small x-shaped drum with sounding tassels. Dumroo-wallah, or He who Plays The Dumroo, refers to Lord Shiva the Destroyer, who plays the dumroo to make all of us monkeys (mortals) dance to his rhythm.

gaddha: donkey.

gaddhi: seat; literally, a cushion.

gaja-gamini: elephant-footed.

gandharva: forest nymph; when malevolent, also a species of Asura.

ganga-jal: sacred Ganges water.

ganja: charas; opium.

garuda: eagle, after the mythic giant magical eagle Garuda, the first-of-his-name, a major demi-god believed to be the creator and patron deity of all birdkind.

gauthan: village; any rural settlement.

gayaka: singer.

Gayatri: a woman's given name; also the most potent mantra of Hindus, recited before beginning any venture, or even at the start of one's day to ensure strength and success.

ghaas-phuss: grass and straw.

gharial: a sub-species of reptilian predator unique to the Indian subcontinent, similar to crocodiles and alligators in body but with a sword-shaped mouth.

ghat: literally, low-lying hill. Burning ghat usually refers to the places in which Hindu bodies are traditionally cremated.

gobi: common term for cauliflower as well as cabbage.

gotra: sub-caste.

govinda: goatherd.

gulmohur: a species of Asian tree

that produces beautiful red flowers in winter.

guru/guruji: a teacher, generally associated with a sage. The 'ji' is a sign of respect; it literally means 'sir', and can be added after any male name or title: eg, Ramaji.

guru-dakshina: see dakshina.

guru-dev: guru who is as a god, or deva; divine teacher.

gurukul: a guru's hermitage for scholars; a forest ashram school where students resided, maintaining the ashram and its grounds while being taught through lectures in the open air.

gurung: a variety of bird.

hai: ave; hail; woe. An exclamation.

halwai: maker of sweets.

hatya: murder.

havan: sacrificial offering.

hawaldar: constable.

himsa: violence, bodily harm.

Holi: a major Indian festival and feast day, celebrated to mark the end of winter and the first day of spring, the last rest day before the start of the harvest season; celebrated with the throwing of coloured powders and coloured waters symbolising the colours of spring, and the eating of sweetmeats (mithai) and the drinking of bhaang.

Ikshwaku: the original kshatriya ancestral clan from which the Suryavansha line sprang. After the founder, Ikshwaaku.

imli ka butta: tamarind.

Indra: god of thunder and war. Equivalent to the Norse god Thor or the Greek god Ares.

indra-dhanush: literally, Indra's bow; a rainbow.

ishta: religious offering.

iti-haas: Sanskrit for literally, 'This happened'. The Indian word for history.

jadugar: magician.

jagganath: relentless and unstoppable Hindu god of war; another name for Ganesha; juggernaut.

Jai: boy's given name; hail.

Jai Mata Ki: Praise be to the Mother-Goddess.

Jai Shree: Praise be to Sri (or Shree), Divine Creator.

jaise aagya: as you wish; your wish is my command.

jal murghi: a variety of Indian bird; literally, water-fowl.

jal-bartan: vessel for drinking water.

jaldi: quickly; in haste.

jalebi: Indian sweet, made by pouring dough into a tureen of boiling oil in spiralling shapes, removed, then drenched in sugar-syrup.

jamun: a common variety of Indian berry-like fruit, purplish-black, deliciously sour.

janayu: ceremony marking the coming of age, usually of a brahmin male. Also known as thread ceremony.

japmala: a beaded prayer chain used for rote (jap) recitations.

Jat: a proud, violently inclined, North Indian clan.

jatayu: vulture, after Jatayu, the first-of-its-name, the giant hybrid man-vulture, second only to Garuda in its leadership of birdkind.

jhadi-buti: literally, herbs and roots; herbal medicines.

jhadoo: Indian broom.

jhilli: a variety of Indian bird.

ji: yes (respectfully).

johar ka roti: a flat roasted pancake made from barley-flour.

johari: jeweller.

ka: the self, or rather, that immeasurable part of the self which is eternal, cannot be slain, wounded, harmed, or ended; it is that aspect of brahman within us that connects us to the universe at large and enables the commission of karma.

kaand: a section of a story; literally, a natural joint on a long stick of sugarcane or bamboo, used to mark off a count.

kabbadi: a game played by children and adults alike. India's official national sport.

kachua: tortoise.

kaho: speak.

kai-kai: harsh cawing sound.

kairee: a raw green mango, used to make pickle.

kajal: kohl.

kala: black.

kala jaadu: black magic.

kala kendra: art council.

kalakaar: artist.

kalarappa: ancient South Indian art of man-to-man combat, universally acknowledged to be the progenitor of Far Eastern martial arts – learned by visiting Chinese delegates and later adapted and evolved into the modern martial arts.

kalash: a brass or golden pot of a specific design, filled with rice and anointed ritually, tipped over by a new bride to bring prosperity into the house during her home-coming ceremony. A symbol of the good fortune brought by a new wife to her husband's home.

Kali: the goddess of vengeance. An avatar of the universal devi.

Kali-Yuga: the Age of Kali, prophesied to be the last and worst age of human civilisation.

Kama: god of love. The equivalent of the Greek Eros or sometimes Cupid.

kamasutra: the science of love.

karma: deeds.

karmic: pertaining to one's karma.

karya: deeds.

kasturi: deer-musk.

katha: story.

kathputhli: puppet.

kavach: shield.

kavee: poet.

kavya: poem.

kesar: saffron, extremely valuable then and now as an essential spice used in Indian cooking; traditionally given as a gift by kings to one another; worth several times more than its weight in gold.

khaas: special; unique.

khatiya: cot; bed.

khazana: treasure-trove; treasury.

kheer payasam: a sweet rice-milk preparation.

khottey-sikkey: counterfeit coin/s.

khukhri: a kind of North Indian machete, favoured by the hilly gurkha tribes.

kintu: but; however.

kinkara: a tribe of rakshasas and celestial beings.

kiran: ray (usually of light); a girl or boy's given name.

koel/koyal: Indian song-bird.

Kosala: a North-Central Indian kingdom believed to have flourished for several millennia before the start of the Christian era.

koyal: Indian song-bird.

krita: the first age.

krodh: wrath.

kshatriya: warrior caste. The highest of four castes in ancient India, the armed defenders of the tribe, skilled in martial combat and governance. Kings were always chosen from this caste. Later, with the Hindu shift towards pacifism and non-violence, the brahmin or priestly caste became predominant, with kshatriyas shifting into the second-highest position in contemporary India.

kul-nari: schoolgirl; *kul* being Sanskrit for school, *nari* meaning girl/woman.

kumbha-rakshasa: dominant species of demons, lording over their fellow rakshasas as well as other Asura species because of their considerable size and strength; named after Kumbhakarna, the mammoth giant brother of Ravana, who grew to mountainous proportions owing to an ancient curse that condemned him to absorb the physical mass of any living thing he killed or ate. Unlike Kumbhakarna, the kumbhas (for short) do not grow larger with each kill or meal.

kumkum: red powder.

kundalee: horoscope.

kurta: an upper garment with a round neck, full sleeves. Like a shirt but slipped over the head like a t-shirt.

kusa or kusalavya: a lush variety of grass found in Northern and North-Central India, long-bladed and thick.

lakh: a hundred thousand.

langot: loin-cloth.

lingam: a simple unadorned representation of Lord Shiva, usually made of roughly carved black stone, shaped like an upward moulded pillar of stone with a blunt head that is traditionally anointed. Typically regarded by some Western scholars as a phallic object; a controversial view which has been repeatedly disproven by Indian scholars and study of ancient Vedic texts.

lohit: iron.

lota: a small metal pot with a handle, used to carry water.

lungi: a common lower-body garment; a sheet of cloth wrapped around the waist once or more times and tucked in or knotted, extending to the ankles; unisexual but more often worn by men.

maa: mother.

maang: the centre point of the hairline on a person's forehead.

madhuvan: literally, honey-garden; a garden where honey was culled for the purpose of making honey-wine.

magarmach: Indian river crocodile.

maha: great. As in maha-mantra, maha-raja, maha-bharata, maha-guru, maha-dev, etc.

mahadev: great one.

mahal: palace; mansion; manse.

maharuk: a variety of Indian tree.

maha-mantra: supreme mantra or verse, such as the maha-mantra Gayatri. A potent catechism to ward off evil and ensure the success of one's efforts.

mahish-asura: a crossbreed of buffalo and rakshasa.

mahout: elephant-handler.

mahseer: a variety of Indian fish.

mahua: a variety of Indian tree.

malai: cream.

manai: a variety of Indian tree with heavy creepers.

manch: literally, platform or dais; also, a gathering of elders or leaders of a community.

mandala: a purified circle.

mandap: a ceremonial dais on which prayer rituals and other ceremonies are conducted.

mandir: temple.

mangalsutra: a black thread necklace worn by a married woman as proof of her marital status.

mann: mind.

mantra: an invocation to the devas.

mantri: minister.

marg: road.

marg-darshak: guide, mentor, guru.

marg-saathi: fellow-traveller; companion on the road.

martya: human; all things pertaining to humankind.

mashaal: torch.

masthi: mischief.

matka: earthen pot.

maya: illusion.

mayini: witch, demoness.

melas: country fairs, carnivals.

mithai: traditional Indian sweetmeats.

mithaigalli: sweetmeat lane; a part of the market where the halwais (mithai-makers) line up their stalls.

mithun: Indian bison; a species of local buffalo.

mochee: cobbler.

mogra: a strongly scented white flower that blooms very briefly; worn by Indian women in their hair.

moksh: salvation.

mudra: gesture, especially during a dance performance; a symbolic action.

muhurat: an auspicious date to initiate an important undertaking. Even today in India, all important activities – marriages, coronations, the start of a new venture – are always scheduled on a day and time found suitable according to the panchang (Hindu almanac) or muhurat calendar.

mujra: a sensual dance.

naachwaali: dancing-girl or courtesan.

naashta: breakfast; also, an early evening refreshment (equivalent of the British 'tea').

naga: any species of snake; a species of Asura.

nagin: female cobra.

namak: salt.

namaskar/namaskaram: greetings. Usually said while joining one's palms together and bowing the head forward slightly. A mark of respect.

namaskara: see namaskar.

nanga: naked.

Narak: Hell.

naresh: lord, master. A royal title used to address a maharaja, the equivalent of 'your highness'.

natya: dance.

nautanki: song-and-dance melo-drama, a cheap street play.

navami: an infant's naming day.

neem: an Indian tree whose leaves and bark are noted for their proven, highly efficacious medic-inal properties.

nidra: an exalted, transcendental meditative state, a kind of yogic sleep.

odhini: woman's garment used specifically to cover the head, similar to pallo.

Om: the trisyllabic universal invo-cation believed to purify the soul and attune it to the infinite brahman.

Om Hari Swaha: Praise be to the Creator, Amen.

Om Namay: Praise be the Name of . . .

paan: the leaf of the betelnut plant, in which could be wrapped a variety of edible savouries, espe-cially pieces of supari and chewing tobacco.

pagdee: turban; headpiece; headdress.

pahadi: a hill dweller or mountain man. Often used colloquially to connote a rude, ill-educated and ill-mannered person.

paisa: in the singular, a penny, the smallest individual unit of coinage, then and now. In the generic, money.

palai: sandy ground. Also pilai, or pillai.

palas: a variety of Indian flowering tree.

palkhi: see *dollee*.

pallo: the top fold of a woman's sari, used to conceal the breasts and cleavage of the wearer.

panchayat: a village committee usually of five (panch) persons.

parantu: but; however.

pari: angel; fairy.

parikrama: a ritual demonstrating one's devotion to a given deity, often consisting of walking several (hundred) times around a temple as well as the performance of related rituals and prayers.

pariksha: a test or examination.

Patal: the lowermost level of Narak, the lowest plane attainable in exis-tence.

patang: kite.

payal: a delicately carved chain of tiny bells, usually of silver, worn as an anklet by women.

peda: a common, highly popular Indian sweet made of milk and sugar.

peepal: a species of tree with hanging roots and vines.

phanas: jackfruit.

phera: ritual circling of a sacred fire.

phool mala: flower-garland.

pisaca; a species of Asura.

pitashree: revered father.

pitchkarees: water-spouts; portable

hand-pumps used by children in play.

pooja: prayer.

pradhan-mantri: prime minister.

Prajapati: Creator; The One Who Made All Living Things; also used as a term for butterflies, which are believed to represent the spirit of the Creator.

pranaam: a high form of namaste or greeting.

pranayam: a yogic method of breathing that enables biofeedback and control of the senses.

prarthana: intense, devout prayer.

prasadam: food blessed by the devas in the course of prayer; a sacramental offering.

prashna-uttar: question-answer.

pravachan: monologue or lecture, usually by a guru or mentor; to be imbibed in rapt silence.

prayaschitt: penance.

Prithvi: Earth.

pulastya: a descendant of Maharishi Pulastya, one of the Prajapati or mind-born sons of Brahma through whose procreative efforts the mortal realm was populated. He is believed to have received the Vishnu Purana and communicated it to Parasara, who made it known to mortals. He was father of Visravas, who in turn fathered Kuvera and Ravana, and was regarded as the forebear of the rakshasa race.

pundit: priest; master of religious ceremonies.

purana: an ancient treatise or narrative; literally, old, ancient.

purnima: full moon; full moon night.

purohit: see pundit.

pushpak: a flying vehicle described in ancient Indian texts, anti-gravitational devices whose technological basis was said to be once known but is now forgotten; also 'chariots of the gods'.

putra: son.

raag: a scale in Indian classical music, consisting of a certain blend of notes in a related confluence, designed to produce a specific effect on the environment. E.g. Raag Bhairav was said to be capable of inducing rain, Raag Deepak to cause oil lamps to light.

raat ki rani: colloquial name for a common Indian flower that blooms only at night; literally, 'queen of the night'.

rabadi: a popular Indian dessert of thickened sweetened milk, over-boiled until the water drains and only thick layers of cream remain.

raja: king; liege; clan-chieftain.

raje: a more affectionate form of 'raja'. The 'e' suffix to a name ending in a vowel indicates intimacy and warmth.

raj-gaddhi: throne; seat of the king.

rajkumar: prince.

rajkumari: princess.

raj-marg: king's way; royally protected highway or road.

rajya sabha: king's council of ministers, a meeting of the same.

raj-yoga: an advanced form of yoga, the ancient art of self-actualisation.

rakshak: protector.

rakshasa: a variety of Asura; roughly

equivalent to the Western devil or demon. Singular/male: rakshas or rakshasa. Singular/feminine: rakshasi. Plural/both: rakshasas.

rang: colour; usually, coloured powder.

rang-birangi: colourful.

rangoli: the traditional Indian art of creating elaborate patterns on floors, usually at the entrances of domiciles, by carefully sprinkling coloured powder.

ras: juice.

rasbhurries: a very sweet, sticky and juicy wild berry; literally, 'juice-filled'.

rath/s: chariot/s.

rawa: a type of flour.

rishi: sadhu.

rishimuni: holy man.

rksa: black mountain bear.

rudraksh: red beads, considered sacred by Hindus.

rudraksh maala: a Hindu rosary or prayer-bead necklace strung with rudraksh beads.

rupaiya: rupee. The main unit of currency in India even today.

sabha: committee; parliament.

sadhu: literally, 'most holy' or 'most auspicious'; also used to denote a penitent hermit; holy man.

sadhuni: a female sadhu or woman whose life is dedicated to prayer and worship.

saivite/shaivite: worshipper of Lord Shiva.

sakshi: a woman's close female friend.

sala: a variety of Indian tree.

samabhavimudra: celestial meditative stance.

samadhi: memorial.

samasya: problem, situation.

samay chakra: the chariot wheel of Time, turning relentlessly as god rides across the universe. A cornerstone of Hindu belief.

samjhe: 'understood?'

sammelan: a friendly gathering; a meeting.

sandesh: message.

sandhyavandana: evening oblation; ritual offering of water and prayer to the sun at sunset; see also acamana.

Sanskriti: Arya culture and tradition.

sanyas: renunciation from the world; the process by which one gives up all one's worldly possessions, attachments and relationships, taking sanyas, and becoming a 'sanyasi'.

saprem: supreme.

Satya-Yuga: Age of Truth.

sautan: husband's second wife; one's rival for a husband's affections.

savdhaan: caution.

seema: borderline; boundary.

sena: army.

senapati: commander of armed forces, a general.

sesa: rabbit.

shaasan: a type of low-lying couch with a backrest or armrest.

shagun: a variety of Indian tree; an auspicious event or occurrence.

shakti: strength, power, force. Used to describe divine power of a god, as in Kali-shakti or Goddess Kali's power.

shakti-shaali: possessed of great strength.

shama: forgiveness. Colloquially, 'excuse me'.

Shani: god of weapons and destruction. Equivalent to the Roman god Saturn.

Shanivar: Day of Shani; now marked as Saturday because Shani is believed to correspond to Saturn; but probably a quite different day in the ancient Vedic calendar.

shantam: quiet, calm, serene; literally, 'be at peace'.

shanti: colloquialisation of shantam.

shastra: a science; an area of study.

shatru: enemy.

shikhaar: the hunt.

shikhsa: education; learning.

shishya/s: student/s of a guru.

shok: grief.

shraap: curse; terrible invocation.

Shravan: a month in the Hindu calendar; usually the month of the rains; also, a boy's given name.

siddh: successful; blessed.

silbutta: grinding stone and board; pestle and mortar.

sindhoor: a blood-red powder used in marital rituals. Traditionally applied by a husband on his wife's hairline (maang) to indicate her status as a married woman. Hence, unmarried women and widows are not permitted to wear sindhoor. Although a bindi (dot) is now used as a modern equivalent and worn universally as a fashion accessory.

siphai: soldier; guard.

sitaphal: a variety of Indian fruit with sweet milky pods.

sloka: sacred verse.

smriti: hidden; secret.

soma: wine made from the soma plant; a popular wine in ancient India.

som-daru: a kind of wine.

sona: gold.

spasa: spy, informant.

stree-hatya: murder of a woman.

sudra: the lowest caste, usually relegated to cleaning, hunting, tanning and other undesirable activities. The lowest in order.

suhaag raat: wedding night.

supari: betelnut.

Suryavansha: the Solar Dynasty, a line of kings that ruled over Kosala; literally, the clan of the sun-god, Surya.

su-swagatam: welcome; the traditional ritual greeting offered to a visitor.

sutaar: carpenter.

swagatam: greetings, welcome.

swaha: a term used to denote the auspicious and successful completion of a sloka or recitation; corresponds to 'Amen'.

swami: master; lord; naresh.

Swarga-lok/a: Heaven.

swayamvara: a ceremonial rite during which a woman of marriageable age was permitted to select a suitable husband. Eligible men wishing to apply would line up to be inspected by the bride-to-be. On finding a suitable mate, she would indicate her choice by placing the garland around his neck.

taal: rhythm; beat.

tabla: an Indian percussion instrument, a kind of drum sounded by striking the heel of the palm and the tips of the fingers.

tamasha: a show; performance; common street play.

tandav: the frenzied sexually charged celestial dance of Shiva the Destroyer by which he generates enough shakti to destroy the entire universe that Brahma the Creator may recreate it once again.

tanpura: an Indian stringed musical instrument.

tandoor: an Indian barbecue.

tann: body.

tantrik: a worshipper of physical energy and sensual arts.

tapasvi: one who endures penance, usually with an aim to acquiring spiritual prowess.

tapasya: penance.

teko: prostrate one's head, touching the forehead to the ground as a demonstration of devotion and obeisance.

thakur: lord; landowner.

thali: a round metal platter used for eating meals or for storing prayer items. The Indian equivalent of the Western 'dinner plate'.

thrashbroom: a broom with harsh bristles, used for beating rugs and mattresses.

three worlds: Swarga-lok, Prithvi, Narak. Literally, Heaven, Earth, Hell.

tikka: ritual marking on forehead.

tilak: ash or colour anointment on one's forehead, indicating that one has performed one's ritual prayers and sacrifices and is blessed with divine grace to perform one's duties.

tirth yatra: pilgrimage.

Treta-Yuga: Age of Reason.

trimurti: the holy Hindu trinity of Brahma, Vishnu and Shiva, respectively the Creator, Preserver and Destroyer.

trishul: trident.

tulsi: a variety of Indian plant known for its efficacious medicinal properties and regarded as a symbol of a happy and secure household; always grown in the courtyard of a house and prayed to daily by the woman of the house; also, a woman's given name.

upanisad: an ancient sacred Indian text.

ur: primordial. Before all others.

uraga: a species of Asura.

vaid: physician trained in the art of Ayur-vaidya, the ancient Indian study of herbal medicine and healing.

vaisya: the trading or commercial caste. Third in order.

vajra: lightning bolt.

valakam: welcome.

valmik: termite, white ant.

van: forest, jungle. Pronounced to rhyme with 'one'.

vanar: bandara; simian; any monkey species, but most commonly used to denote apes, especially the intelligent anthropomorphic talking apes of this saga.

vanash: a variety of Indian tree.

varna: caste; literally, occupational level or group.

varsha: rain; a woman's given name.

Veda: the sacred writings of the ancient Arya sages, comprising meditations, prayers, observations and scientific treatises on every conceivable human area of interest; the basis of Indian culture.

vetaal: a species of Asura; somewhat similar to the Western concept of 'vampire' but not usually synonymous.

vidya: knowledge.

vidyadhari: a scholar or student.

vinaashe: destruction; death.

wagh-rakshasa: a crossbreed of tiger and rakshasa.

yagna: religious fire-ritual.

yaksa: a breed of Asura believed to have possessed shape-shifting abilities.

yaksi: a female yaksa; a species of Asura capable of shape-shifting; closely corresponding to (but not identical to) the Western concept of Elves.

Yama: Yama-raj, lord of death and king of the underworld; literally Death personified as a large powerfully built dark-skinned man with woolly hair, who rides a black buffalo and carries a bag of souls.

yash: fame; adoration; admiration.

yodha: great warrior, champion.

yoganidra: the supreme state of transcendence while meditating, usually indicated by the eyes being partly open yet seeing only the apparent nothingness of brahman; a divine near-sleep-like state.

yojana: a measurement of distance in ancient India, believed to have been equivalent to around nine miles.

yoni: female sexual organ; the 'yang' of 'yin and yang'.

yuga: age; historical period.